THE KING'S DAUGHTER

Book Cover Design
+2348147445821
Esther S
Designer Pro247

Book Formatting
hDigitals Design Studio

Dedication

To my Heavenly Father,
JEHOVAH AVINU

For you Dad,
".......for as a prince hast thou power with GOD and with men and hast
prevailed"
Genesis 32:28b

Acknowledgement

My praise, thanks, glory to GOD The FATHER, GOD the Son - JESUS, GOD the HOLY SPIRIT - The Three in ONE, I am forever grateful.

To my family, love always and thank you for your help.

To Olubunmi Adeleye & Bukunola Oladunjoye, thank you so much for your help and encouragement.

To Sis Oyin Sowemimo, thank you for the time taken to read and edit carefully and meticulously, I am very grateful.

To all those who encouraged me in one way or the other, thank you.

To you the reader, thank you.

Prologue

They were walking up the hill towards the house, their strides quicker than usual and awkward as they had their hands full, carrying all sorts of things. The boy's strides were longer, he made good use of his long legs, walked faster and he had less to carry. His companion on the other hand though skinner, tried to walk as fast as she could but could not catch up with him and this made her furious. She thought of all ploys to deter him from his mission to get to the house before her but could think of none. Her arms were aching from what she was carrying and he refused to help her with her wares.

It was all her fault, she had plucked fruits from almost every tree and plants they went past; agbalumo, igba, ebelebo, tangerine, awin, avocado, then disaster struck as she climbed the guava tree. She should have known when Omoniyi refused to climb with her, she thought it was because she had gathered too many fruits and he did not want to carry any more. She soon realised why, when she climbed the guava tree. She sat on a branch to enjoy the view, shouted to Omoniyi the landmarks she could see when suddenly she screamed, lost her grip on the branch and fell.

She landed on the ground with a thud, thankfully the branch was not far from the ground. She escaped with a few bruises but yelled again, scratched, quickly unbuttoned her shirt, hopped up and down, threw her shirt on the floor and marched on it until the white shirt blended with the colour of the terracotta ground.

Omoniyi watched with amusement as she jumped up and down and wondered what traditional dance she was attempting to do on her shirt. He walked closer and smiled. Yes, his few experience with ants on the guava tree had taught him not to jump on the tree without a survey of the branches for any sight of an ant or its army. He hoped she had learnt her lesson. He picked up the few things he had gathered from their walk around the farm and headed towards the direction of their home, he was tired and hungry.

When she did not get any help from Omoniyi but rather he picked up his things and started walking away, she quickly picked all the 'treasures' she had gathered from their walk, placed them on her shirt, tied it and ran after him, calling him to wait for her, he didn't, he just went straight ahead of her.

At the top of the hill, they walked towards the garden in their home which was an enclosure of evenly cultivated shrubs and in the middle was a flat array of green grass, a tree and a flower bed in the middle. This was unlike the orchard where they had been coming from, which had long rows of trees, spaced out on hundreds of acres of farm land bearing different fruits which were tempting and desirous to eat.

In their secret part of the garden Omoniyi dropped the tins, bottle tops, some other metal objects they had picked up from the garage and sat on the grass. His countenance was not a happy one and the look he gave his companion was a fiery glare. However, she was calm, knelt down, untied her shirt and placed on the ground all the fruits she had plucked from the orchard and some other items. She knew he was annoyed as she had started to wind him up with her words, which were sharp as an adder's bite; painful but true.

She had unleashed her tongue at him, when he refused to help her after she fell from the tree. She narrated a catalogue of other 'events', some she exaggerated on the facts but the bottom line was, he was unhelpful, arrogant, unkind, selfish and useless. She struck out each bite, like that of an adder's tongue, then she finished off with the one thing Omoniyi will never joke with, his claim to the throne. She told him he was unfit to be a king if he could not help just one tiny little helpless girl; what a useless, good for nothing heir he was. He became furious, demanded an apology, got none and an argument ensued.

"I am king you have to obey me."
"Until one is crowned king one does not boast of what he is not."
"I am a prince but I will be king one day and then you will bow to me."
"Until then! I am equally a princess and I will not belittle myself. I also have the right to rule this kingdom."

Omoniyi watched as she picked up her earth stained shirt, dusted it, tied it round her waist, hands on her narrow hips, rolled her eyes like the moon rotating over the earth and stood there shaking her legs poised for a fight. He remembered the dance she did earlier on the shirt when the army of ant launched an attack on her. He laughed uncontrollably, fell on the ground, clattered the tins and planks they had gathered to make an armour tank which will carry their toy soldiers to battle and to her annoyance scattered the pile of fruits she had just picked from the orchard. She re-launched her attack, a viper attack.

"It shows from your behaviour that you still have a lot to learn, how can a so-called king be rolling on the floor, laughing like a mad man. Where is your dignity? Where is your self-respect? King my foot! You are just a mere child, a commoner for that matter."

Omoniyi recoiled from his position on the floor, he hated being called a commoner, he was a prince, that was what his mother told him. Furious, he grabbed the first thing he could find and hurled it at her. He missed her face as she shielded it with her hands. How he wished the object had hit her and scarred that beautiful face for life.

He was still mad at her, he furiously picked up another object to throw at her again, to inflict her with the pain he felt from her spiteful words. He really hated her at that moment. There she stood, her hands still covering her face, giving no sign of any emotion. Was she angry, mad or even sad? He moved closer to pull her hands away from her face, when suddenly, he saw the crimson flow, roll down from her hand onto the once white shirt that was now a mixture of earth and blood. He was filled with anguish and remorse. Had he done that to her? All the emotions that surged through him earlier vanished as he gently removed her hands from her face.

"I ... I...."

"What is going on here? What are you two doing standing so close to each other, do you want me to call Olori for the two of you? Omoniyi you should be .... Ha aaaaaa! What is this? Kilo sele? What did you do to your sister, yeeeee e gba' mi ooooooooo!"

This page has been left intentionally blank

Contents

This page has been left intentionally blank

CHAPTER ONE

O moniyi sat beside the window sill, reminiscing over the turn of events that happened between him and his sister over twelve years ago. How he wished he could turn back what happened, then, life would have been more bearable for him. However, he had lived for so long without her, without her taunting voice, sharp but wise tongue and her love. He loved that girl, no matter what anyone said, she was the love of his life, the one he saw in his dreams every night and the one he longed for, Monisola Oluwafiadekemi.

He tried to catch a glimpse of her as she stepped out of the car but the bodyguard blocked his view. He wanted to run downstairs, grab her and never let her go but his mother had sternly warned him to make himself scarce from the family reunion and only to appear at dinner time. How was he to survive before then without seeing her?

Monisola took her time getting dressed for dinner, her home coming dinner. She was still full from the lunch she had, which had not yet fully digested and she wasn't interested in the dinner or whatever they had planned. Her mind was only on one person.

She knew she was more than thirty minutes late but she wanted to make sure everyone was seated when she joined them and most especially for him to be seated. As she walked down the stairs she thought of the last time she had seen him, hurting and yet being so brave not to cry. Her father had said as a leader in the making, the one thing one must never do, was to show one's emotions in public, no matter what. Her lips had been trembling but she had bit them until they drew blood just like the one Omoniyi had drawn from her hand when he threw an object at her.

Thank GOD she had shielded her face with her hand from being struck. She still had the mark on her hand and was probably the main reason why she could not forget that day or even him and the decision that had been made. Her father had decided that it was untoward to have two aspiring heirs in the same kingdom, fighting for the same throne, coupled with the fact that they were from different mothers, the Olori and Iyawo. It was too risky and in order to pacify everyone, Monisola had to go. She was the victim yet the one that bore the brunt and was sent on 'exile'. Now she had returned and she was to meet face to face with her number one contender, Omoniyi.

She braced herself for the duel. With her head held high and her back straight, she walked towards the dining room. The dining room as she remembered was the one place she dreaded to enter especially when her father had visitors. It was always a time for her to display her newly acquired knowledge of a game, skill, book, fact or anything for Kabiyesi to show off his daughter and later Omoniyi when he arrived on the scene.

As soon as she walked in there was a hush in the room, she stood still and glanced at everyone in the room; her father, mother, Ayaba her step-mother, her half-sisters; Morenike with her husband Kayode, her younger half-sister Morolake with her husband Taiwo, then her eyes met that of her contender. She masked her emotion, raised an eyebrow and then went to sit.

The conversation in the room continued but she did not participate and neither did he. They looked at each other, trying to read each other's mind. She taunted him with her eyes but instead of being timid he equally teased her with his. The boy had become a man.

After dinner, while others chatted about the latest events and news, they both slipped out to the garden which had been a playground as well as a duel arena for them when they were young. A lot had happened then but now they just stared at each other, words unspoken, hearts beating and pulses racing inwardly but on the outside, all is masked.

"You've grown more beautiful."
She looked at him shocked. Of all the times she had thought of this reunion those were not the words she had rehearsed in her mind or expected to hear. She looked at him wondering what had happened to him all these years.
"You've also grown."
He waited, surely she hasn't lost her sharp tongue. Please GOD, not that, that was one of the reasons he loved her.
"At least your body is now proportionate to the size of your head."
He couldn't help it, he laughed without any reservation, not even when

she gave him one of her appalling looks. He grabbed her and pulled her to him, hugging her as if he would never let go again. At first she was tensed, as she was not used to such open show of affection and surely he must be familiar with protocol. She was still trying to get her brain and mouth to vent out a painful remark but her body refused such atrocity, rather she indulged in the warmth and pleasure engulfing her. It was so long since any one dear to her had hugged her. She missed this.

"I missed you." she whispered.
"It's been hell living without you all these years. I'm so sorry for what I did that day."
Still held in his hands, beaming with smiles, she looked up and saw tears in his eyes. For goodness sake who mentored this man, he was soft, too soft, both in and out.
"Don't tell me you still torture yourself with that childish stunts you pulled, it was a mistake and moreover I provoked you and I should be glad that it wasn't my face that got hurt."

His fingers ran over the exact lines of the scar on her hand, the thin lines of amassed skin on her perfectly smooth light skin coloured hand, he kissed it and muttered, "I'm so sorry."
His lips set a shrill of fire on her body. She snatched her hands away and wondered what had come over her. Why was she feeling this way with him, it was an abomination, this was her brother, her father's heir apparent, the one to replace him any day any time.
She turned to go but he held her firmly, that she could not pull out of his hands. The boy had grown indeed.

"I don't want you running away from me, I'm your ....."

He couldn't even acknowledge her as his sister, he must be feeling the same way she felt. She snatched her hands away from him and ran all the way to her room. She had to keep away from him, in fact she was going to make sure that their paths never crossed again.

She ignored him for days but each day was torture for her as she longed to hear his voice, see his face and be wrapped in his arms. Why was she still feeling this way, definitely something is wrong with her that she could feel this way about him as she had not felt like that about anyone else before, except Ray. Ezekiel Raymond Chukwuemeka Ezuruonye III as he likes to call himself, was one guy who was turning her head in. She had practically ran away from him and she still is and hopefully he will finally get the message that she wasn't interested. However, the problem was that Raymond never took no for an answer, he is adamant, strong headed and unbearably difficult.

She laughed as she remembered the first time she met him at a party. She wasn't keen on parties but her very good and close friend Chichi had begged her to come to her party and how could she refuse her true friend's request. Looking back now she wished she had. It took Raymond one second to lay his eyes on her, there and then decided he wanted her as his wife. Monisola had never heard anything so absurd, the effrontery of the guy. She tried to avoid him for most part of the night but he was in her face throughout and eventually she had to leave. She thought she had gotten rid of him until she found him at her door step with roses and very apologetic. She allowed him in, they talked but the fact remained the same, he wasn't joking as he still wanted to marry her. They argued, disagreed, made up but he wasn't deterred, he wanted to marry her. Very unlike her she gave him a catalogue of her background as she still had interest in the royal stool of her father's kingdom, he was even happier that his children will have royalty in their blood. She asked for time with the intention that he would forget her and move on but he called her every single day. She got so frustrated that she called her friend Chichi who was also fed up as he pestered her to talk to her friend.

In the end Monisola decided to go on a date with him for just one day, hoping to use every trick in her book to get rid of him. What a shock and surprise she got when he took her to Paris for the day. He was so different from the pestering ogre he was that she thought she was dreaming. He opened doors for her, pulled the chair out for her to sit, made sure everything was perfect the way she wanted it, held her hands and did everything a lover would do. He wanted to buy her an engagement ring she refused and he was okay with it. Monisola felt she should have asked if he could stop pestering her with his proposal but she was enjoying the attention he was giving her that she did not. For a week he treated her like the princess she really was but when at the end of the week she suggested they dated but not to be seen in public together, he returned to his monstrous mood again.

Eventually he agreed to her conditions but couldn't help it when she insisted they could not hold hands or show any affection while in the midst of friends least of all in public, he flipped and they called the whole thing off. She didn't see him for a whole week and what peace of mind she had but soon realised it couldn't last forever when Chichi called to let her know he was back in town. Immediately every nerve of her body was on edge, then she knew she couldn't continue with him so she decided to call a truce. What did Raymond do? He tried to be nice and sweet as he had been in Paris but when she finally realised what his intentions were, she fled from him. She was so glad for the opportunity to come home and forget her pest.

She moved away from the window as she shuddered at her many encounters with Raymond. In a way she loved him but could never, ever marry him because in so many things they were incompatible. He was loud, she was quiet and reserved. Raymond did not understand or know the meaning of wait or patience, everything had to be now according to his dictionary, diary and schedule. She could hide and mask her emotions and no one would know if anything bothered her but Raymond would not let a fly pass by. He had to tell you how it flew, the colour and the audacity it had, to fly past a princess and a prince-to- be without greeting them. She would lose her sanity if they were to be married and worst of all, if she was in pain or smothered by any worries, Raymond would never know because once he asked if she was alright and she affirmed in the positive, that was it, he wouldn't bother to think to ask or probe further. For her that was dangerous as she had been brought up to hide her inner most feelings even from the ones that are close to her.

She walked out of the house and strolled towards the garden; she needed the fresh air to clear the thoughts of Raymond from her mind. She was deep in her thoughts that she didn't notice that Omoniyi had been watching her from the window of his study. Since he could not concentrate on his work, he left the room, walked towards the garden, after all, he needed some fresh air too.

"Why have you been avoiding me?"

She jumped and almost fell over; he quickly grabbed her arm to steady her.

"I'm sorry I didn't hear you come."

"I'm sorry I didn't mean to scare you."

"Why are we so apologetic with everything?"

"I don't know. Maybe you've not forgiven me for what I did."

"Omoniyi, that was when I was a young girl, I've left all those childish behaviour behind me, I am now grown up."

"And you seem to grow more beautiful each time I see you."

"We've only seen each other once since I arrived so I couldn't have grown into anything."

He told her he had seen pictures of her sent to his sisters and father during the past years and he couldn't help but notice the ever-growing beauty.

"Why didn't you come home all these years?"

"To do what? There can only be one heir to the throne and moreover what stopped you from visiting when you came to England?"

"My mother warned me not to as she did not want anything bringing back the past."

"What did she mean by that?"

"Well the last time we were together we caused a whole lot of contentions between our mothers and father did not like it."

"No matter what, we were just children and meant no harm and nobody asked what provoked you, otherwise they would have known who to blame."

"I can assure you father knew what a sharp razor you have for a tongue and I guess his decision to send you abroad for the sake of peace. I've never seen your mother so angry before, she was livid with wrath. For months I dread coming near her, now I know where you get your temper from, like mother, like daughter."

"You know as one who is to ascend the throne sooner than later you should learn to keep your comment to yourself, I believe the word is being tactful and not be biased as you cannot take side with any party, your judgement must be impartial."

"I am not judging anyone, all I said is like mother ..."

"Why not like father like daughter? I can't really say like father like son because you don't take after him especially his hardness, you are so soft and level headed I guess that's why I love ...."

She covered her mouth in horror and realisation of what she had just said. Was she going mad? She turned to leave but he held her and turned her towards him.

"I love you too, always have and always will."

"You cannot love me I am your sister."

"I love you as my sister and I can love you as a man loves a woman, in fact I do."

He bent to kiss her and that was when she realised that both of them must be insane and if there was any decency still left, one of them should flee. She decided to be the heroine and she ran until she was in the safety of her mother's room.

Omoniyi could not sleep that night, he should slap himself for openly declaring his love to Monisola. However, he smiled, after keeping it for so long from her, he was glad he did. What he was unsure of now, is, what next? He ran after her when she fled from him, but discovered she wasn't in her room. He also went to his sisters' rooms with the pretence of wanting to chat only to find out she wasn't there. He did not know how much time she was here for but he hoped to spend every minute with her and hopefully gain her to his side. He sighed and drooped heavily on the bed, he knew Kabiyesi would never agree to his demands, there was too much at stake, too much left untold and too much to lose. He loved his father but he knew that love could never be compared to what he felt for Monisola Oluwamuiremiwa Oluwafiadekemi Omolabake Adewunmi. He would shed his last name for her if a leopard could shed his spots. He had to start planning and fast if he was ever to claim her as his.

———

THE VERY NEXT day he surprised both mother and daughter as he was the first to knock at their apartment door.

"My Prince, good morning. Have the maidens not gone to the river to fetch your bathing water, let me get my 'osuka', I will quickly run to fetch it."

Omoniyi laughed, he could see where Monisola got her sense of humour from.

"My mother and queen, good morning, we both know that even if the maidens fail to get my bath water, the mere sight of you with a bucket would bring the whole palace including the king at your beck and call."

They both laughed. He did not want to waste any more time so he went straight to the point.

"Is my sister awake, I have not seen her for three days and I have a feeling that she has not totally forgiven me for what I did years ago and ..."

"What rubbish, of course she has forgiven you, abi why should she harbour such malignant thoughts in her bosom against you my Prince. Monisola! Monisola!"

If only she knew how close those words were creating a sensation in him, Olori would not have mentioned Monisola's bosom.

Monisola had been sleeping but the shout of her name especially coming from her mother, made her jump out of bed. What did she want? It was only nine in the morning; couldn't she have some peace and quiet? She refused to answer but slowly walked up to where her thunderous yell came from. Did no one teach her about decorum, a whole queen shouting on top of her voice!

When she got to the living room she was rubbing her eyes which were sore as a result of not being able to sleep since the first crack of dawn when the stupid noisy cockerel started croaking like a frog instead of crowing or was it the frog that was croaking at the same time as the cockerel? Well she wasn't interested, she just wanted to sleep without seeing Raymond chasing her in her dreams and begging her to marry him.

"Mother you called."

"Good morning Princess Monisola."

Her eyes popped open when she saw Omoniyi starring at her in her skimpy night wear. Thank God she had draped her robe over it though it was just above knee length. This was not good, not with their declaration of love for one another. Oh GOD please help me.

Her mother must have misinterpreted the horror on her face when she shouted again.

"So, it is true! I thought my prince was pulling my legs when he said it. How could you Monisola, how could you?"

Monisola tried to pinch her arm to assure herself she was not dreaming otherwise why would a prince, heir apparent be so dumb to tell her mother what happened between them last night.

"Mother what are you talking about?"

"Talking about bi it bawo? How could you claim to be a GOD-fearing person and be harbouring hate for your brother?"

Now, who was mad? Her mother or the dumb prince?

"Mother I still don't understand what you are saying"

Omoniyi secretly laughed and enjoyed the pun of words going on between mother and daughter. No, he had been wrong, it was not like mother like daughter, this daughter was far more intelligent than her mother and was cunningly trying to deduce what had been said and what was assumed. Didn't Morenike say she studied International Relations, smart girl, you would do your father proud. Okay time to break this juggling of words.

"I asked Olori Tinuola to intervene in this ongoing feud between the two of us as I have only seen you the first night you came back and you have been avoiding me since then."

Liar! She told him with her eyes.

I dare you to tell her what happened last night he replied the facial message.

"Oh!"

"Oh what, is it not true? Why don't you just forgive him, I'm sure you know he is sorry."

She looked at him and almost laughed when she saw the way his eyes looked like a whimpering puppy. She was going to get him, tit for tat. Without any emotion or trace of her thought she said, "I forgive you; Prince Omoniyi I no longer harbour any wicked thoughts against you" looking at him but her eyes telling him otherwise.

He stretched out his hands as a peace offering, she took it and held it limping.

"Is that how you forgive? Give your brother a hug and tell him you love him."

Good gracious where did her father get this scattered wit of a woman for his wife, couldn't she see beyond the charade the two of them were playing? Hug him! Tell him you love him! What had started this in the first place?

Omoniyi drew her to him, hugged her and planted a kiss on her forehead. With barely a whisper and gritting teeth she said, "I'll get you for this."

"I will be eagerly waiting for a proper kiss" he stated in a very low volume matching hers.

"Can I invite my princess for breakfast in my office" he merely added the office for her mother's sake.

"Of course, but not today, I need to catch up on my beauty sleep."

"What nonsense! She will be with you within a matter of half an hour my prince."

As soon as he left, Monisola turned to her mother, this time with a bit of irritation. "Mother I am sure I do not have to remind you that I am no longer a child and I can decide where, when and what I want to do."

"Busola! Mary! Where are you girls, do I have to shout before I am heard? Monisola the girls will escort you to your room and help you get prepared."

"For what, Mother?"

"Your breakfast with Prince Omoniyi of course, you never can tell the good that will come out of it."

"Like what? Give me half of the kingdom, I am not interested."

"Of course not, I meant you might find one of his friends attractive and good enough for marriage. After all you are not getting any younger, though I must say you grow more beautiful each passing day, I must start...."

Monisola did not wait for her mother to finish her conversation as she hurried in quick steps to her own apartment.

"I'm glad you joined me though I was thinking of somewhere more private but I gave your mother my word."

She ignored him and joined him in the back seat of his automobile which was the latest model of Mercedes, sleek and classy, unlike her father's ubiquitous limousine which attracted undue attention. His fingers tapped some meaningless rhythm on her arm and rested on her hand, she tried to pull out of his hold but he held it firmly under his grip. Her mind flashed back to their conversation last night, the hug this morning; definitely things were not going well. She must find a way of breaking away from him before someone got hurt.

His timing could not have been better as she picked up her cell phone and saw Raymond's number; she wasn't in the mood for this. She was tempted to switch off her phone but then thought better of it, maybe it was just the distraction she needed from Omoniyi.

"Hi Raymond." She felt Omoniyi's hand loosen his grip from her hand, good!

"I'm fine and you."

"I miss you too." No, I don't, I'm enjoying my peace of mind, all thanks to your absence.

"I'm not sure yet but I'll let you know; I've got to go."

She dropped the phone on her lap, closed her eyes and smiled.

"So, who is Raymond?"

"A friend."

"What kind of friend?"

"How do you mean?"

"Boy-friend, lover?"

She kept silent, thinking which of the choices he gave would be used as an ammunition against him.

"My ex."

"What happened?"

"None of your business."

"You are my business!" Omoniyi stated and tightened his grip on her hand.

As the car sped along the only road that led from the palace to Ifedolapo town, she remembered how she had often thought and dreamt of that road ever since she was taken as a child from home. She remembered the security post at the entrance of the palace which had been a hut with one or two guards but now had been replaced with twenty-four-hour police monitoring check point.

The various huts and sheds along the way had been replaced by a wider road, further down was a stop point with a petrol filling station, a shopping mart with toilet facilities and new amenities. She wondered what happened to Iya Gbenro's shed which had a small palm wine joint and a vulcanizer beside it. Things had definitely changed.

The traffic got a bit busy as they approached the junction into town. She noticed the town still had some of its old buildings, monumental statues and also some new designs. She hardly saw anyone carrying their wares on their heads for sale. Rather there were small structures like kiosks-built side by side and used by the traders in displaying their various wares from biscuits, gala, sweets, to Robb ointment, Panadol, bulbs, CDs, DVDs. They also had insecticide to kill pests such as cockroaches, flies and of course mosquitoes; she wondered if they had one to wade off Raymond. She remembered one of the manual spray pumps they sprayed across the room every evening before they went to bed. She got into trouble several times when she sprayed it on Omoniyi, Foluke, the dogs or anything that annoyed her. Also, there were road signs almost everywhere, something that was a rarity in the past. It seems people now relied on the road signs than going to the women - Iya oni boli, Iya elepa', Iya olosan, who were permanently stationed beside the cross road where they sold their wares. These women were often asked by visitors for directions to anywhere in the town and sometimes some of the villagers also engaged them in conversations to hear the latest gossips around.

Omoniyi's office was one of the new buildings featuring the latest architectural design which was beside the old colonial styled offices occupied by the town council and local government. His office was just like stepping into another time zone and finding yourself in New York, London or Tokyo. As she walked into the building it was top class style and design right from reception to the board room. She was impressed. She sat in the reception lounge of his private office while he walked in talking to his PA.

".... And did you let them know we've been waiting for the past one week. You know we cannot afford any further delays as we have clients waiting on us and we don't do business with time wasters. In fact, I have no business with them, get Andy and tell him his suppliers have failed and I want my money back. Meanwhile get Raj on the phone, tell him we need ten thousand by mid- day tomorrow. I want ....."
He stopped and walked back to the reception lounge and looked at her, "Aren't you coming in?"
"I don't know, what do you want me to do?"
"Come on, you are not a stranger here, you are part of this. Musa meet my sister Monisola, Moni this is Musa my friend and.......well let's say PA. Don't be fooled by the title there is more to him than that. He has a business degree from the States with lots of experience but I just dragged him here to use his skills and he is going back next month or have you moved it again?"

"Sir I'll let you know." Musa replied without a glance at Monisola.
Omoniyi smiled at his PA and friend who had insisted he was coming for just six months and he had spent about one and a half

years. Together, they had completed major projects Omoniyi knew he couldn't have done on his own as they were both passionate and tenacious about their work. He wondered who will replace him when he decides to go. He glanced at Monisola, nay he needed her for the bedroom not the board room.

Omoniyi chaired the meeting, he was apt and ended ten minutes earlier than usual. In previous meetings he spends fifteen out of the thirty minutes scheduled for the weekly meeting and on this occasion, he knew he had better things to do. Monisola was waiting for him. Actually, she wasn't, she sat quietly observing the meeting and very unlike her, staring at Musa his PA with a perturbed look.

"Now I can give you a hundred percent of my time and attention" he turned to her which caught her by surprise as she had been staring at Musa.

"Oh! I thought you had more important business to attend to."

"You are the most important person to me and my priority, top on my list."

"If father calls you now and demands for your presence at home what will you tell him?"

"I have a very, very urgent matter to attend to." he stated with a wry smile.

"We both know that is not true." Monisola smiled for the first time since she stepped into his office.

"Who cares!"

Monisola looked at him, she knew definitely Omoniyi had changed and he wasn't one to play childish games with, she only wished there was something she could do.

He saw that look on her face again. "Are you falling for my PA?"

"I beg your pardon?"

"I noticed you were staring at him during the meeting and you have the same look on your face now."

She took a deep breath, "I don't usually do or say this as I give everyone a benefit of doubt but I don't like your PA. There's something about him that I can't lay my finger on but I just do not trust him."

Omoniyi was shocked, he knew his sister was blunt and did not mince words but to come outright and say that of his friend, using her own words was being biased and he was not going to tolerate that. He was about to tell her he was thoroughly ashamed of her when Musa came in and almost immediately he saw a reaction on Monisola's face and body despite the fact that she had her back to the door and could no way see who had just come in. He decided to hold his tongue.

"What is it Musa? I made it clear I wasn't to be disturbed." Omoniyi barked out at him.

"Yes, but I got hold of Andy and he said he would deliver in two days' time and was very apologetic."

"I don't give a toss if he is. I do not want or like his method of doing business. He is unreliable, unprofessional and I wonder why I agreed to do business with him. Get Raj on the phone and tell him ...."

"I already spoke to him and the shipments are on the way"

"Good. Why then are you still mentioning Andy! Anyway, make sure Raj has all the necessary details of the location for delivery, I do not want this project to be delayed any more. I intend to finish and pass inspection before the deadline. Do I make myself expressly clear?"

"Yes boss."

"Drop the boss bit, I am still your friend, I just hate time wasters like Andy. Who introduced him anyway?"

"I did sir" Musa answered hesitantly.

"Hmm! That's all for now" Omoniyi stated, still wondering about Monisola's reaction towards Musa. Maybe it was just a fragment of her imagination, at least everything had been going well with their business relations and he had no cause for alarm. Musa interrupted his thoughts which made him not the least suspicious but clearly irritable.

"Where will you be when I want to contact you?"

"I believe I have a cell phone and you have the number."

"Yes, just in case..."

"I do NOT want to be disturbed" he yelled at him and Musa left immediately.

The rest of the day was spent with Monisola in his out of town apartment and he enjoyed every moment of it. They did a lot of catch up and despite the distance and years spent apart they found they had similar likes and dislikes.

They teased and made fun of each other and when she told him about Ray which at first had been a slip of tongue, that made him tensed but as she continued he couldn't help but laugh.

"The guy must be hopelessly in love with you."

"Hopeless or mad, I don't care. All I want is peace."

"What if he is the one chosen to marry you?" he asked her seriously.

"Are you hard of hearing, I said it is either he drives me mad or we end up hurting one another. We are not compatible, we are like cheese and chalk, epo' and omi, oil and water, we don't match."

"Are we compatible?" Omoniyi asked subtly.

She looked away from him. She had been enjoying every moment until now.

"Niyi, please don't go there."

"Why not?"

"Are you insane? We are siblings, it is an abomination!"

"You are not ..."

He was interrupted by his phone ringing.

"Yes!" he shouted as he answered the call.

"I told you I did not want to be disturbed. I don't care, look Musa you are disrupting a very important meeting and I hate it when people cannot follow simple orders and you know me. I DON'T want to know if Andy is your friend or father's brother, I do not want his business, tell him to take it somewhere else.

Is that a threat? If that is it I'll see you tomorrow then. What! Are you serious? Ok give my secretary your keys. I'll see you at the club."

He threw the phone down and wiped his face with both hands hoping the conversation he just had was a dream and he needed to wake up from it.

"Omoniyi, is everything okay?"

He turned to Monisola, for a minute he had forgotten his sweetheart was there, he tried to smile but the look on her face told him she wasn't fooled.

"Musa just quit on me!"

Instead of relief, Monisola's face was more troubled. What was it with Musa and his sister?

"Moni, is there something I should know about Musa that you are not telling me?"

"Honestly Omoniyi, I am sure today is the first time I've met him but I just… there's something about him that just gives me the creeps. I don't understand it and I don't like the way things have turned out, please be careful about him. Don't be alone with him. Please for the love we share as blood brother and sister just leave him and let him go."

He looked at her, she was a bit shaken, he walked to her and held her in his arms to assure her everything was going to be okay. Was it, or was he fooling himself about their close ties?

CHAPTER TWO

If only he had listened to Monisola things would not have turned the way they did.

Within a week of Musa's quitting his job, he ordered assassins to kill Omoniyi his business partner who refused to sign the deal he had made with Andy which unknown to Omoniyi, was for drugs and firearms deal and not the shipment of materials for their building project. The police apprehended the culprits who confessed they had been hired by the victim's business partner. Musa was apprehended at the airport trying to flee the country with a fake passport.

Omoniyi was shot several times, lost a lot of blood and according to the doctors it was a miracle he did not die immediately.

"I'm sorry, all I have to say is we've tried all we can and what we do now is just hope for the best. He is responding to treatment but he has lost a lot of blood and would need a donor." The doctor informed Kabiyesi and the others in the hospital room where Omoniyi had been admitted.

There was silence in the room but Monisola was the one to break it as nobody seemed to realise it was a matter of life and death and time was of essence.

"I'm sure that won't be difficult, my father or Ayaba Adekemi would be a suitable donor."

Again, there was a deafening silence from both her father and Omoniyi's mother. Monisola didn't want any time to be wasted as it seemed his life was at stake so she asked the doctor to go ahead and start the process.

The result of the blood tests came and Monisola understood the reason behind the silence from both parents that had been tested. However, the question was whose lineage did Omoniyi come from? As this wasn't the time and place for such questioning she asked the doctor to find a donor within two hours and if none could be found she would get in touch with her contacts who would be able to provide one in less than twenty-four hours.

A donor was found, blood transfusion was made and the prayer of the family was that Omoniyi would come out of this ordeal intact. He came out of coma but all was not well.

Monisola held his hands as the doctors gave him the news, it was devastating but there was hope. Some fragments of the bullets had been lodged in the spine, which were removed but there were other complications with the blood transfusion coupled with the possibility he could never walk again.

"Omoniyi you cannot give up just like that, you have to be strong, father and your mother are relying on you to pull through."

"Father and mother, I can understand but what about me, how do I continue like this, depending on others before I do simple tasks for the rest of my life, it was better if...."

She quickly covered his mouth to silence whatever pronouncement he was about to make on himself.

"Omoniyi, I will not allow you to think or utter such profanity. I am grateful you are alive and the doctors have given their verdict but the matter is in the hands of GOD who can do the impossible. Please don't give up, I can't bear you being like this, I beg of you brother, please be strong for the sake of your family, your people, your kingdom."

"Do you honestly think the people would want a lame man for their king?"

This time she lost her cool and calm poise and spoke angrily.

"I don't know what I have to do, to get it into that thick skull of yours, you are not lame, you are at the moment physically challenged and by GOD's grace and with the right treatment you will get better. If I hear you talk yourself down again I am going to come down heavily on you, do I make myself clear?"

He watched her without any emotion and turned to look outside the window. He should be out there taking her out to see the world and all around them but he was stuck in this position, which could be for life, he regretted ignoring Monisola's apprehension about Musa.

"What happened to Musa?"

"All I care is about you getting better."

He lurched forward and grabbed her hands, "I said what happened to Musa?" he shouted at her in an angry tone.

"I don't think you should concern yourself with that ingrate, he has been apprehended by the police and he is also wanted by the FBI who would be dealing with him as soon as the Nigerian government is through with him."

"FBI?"

"I contacted my sources and my premonitions about him were ....."

"I regret not listening to you."

"Omoniyi we can't afford to live on regrets, life goes on but please do one thing for me, please stay alive."

They both looked at each other knowing that life was what they could hold on to at this very moment.

Omoniyi was getting better, the doctors were thinking of discharging him and Monisola was thinking of making a quick dash to England for a week and rush back but 'something' kept holding her back. She was walking towards his room when she overheard a conversation between him and the doctor.

"Do I make myself clear, I mean no one is to be told."

"I know it's my responsibility to keep patient's confidentiality but they are your family, they need to know, more so if you ...you...."

Monisola decided it was time to make her appearance known.

"More so what? What is this conversation about?" she walked in confidently, her gaze on the doctor hoping he will tell her more. Omoniyi's stern face made it difficult for the doctor to speak and he excused himself and left the two of them alone.

"Omoniyi, please tell me what is going on, I'm your sister, talk to me."

He looked at her, blurted out with so much hatred, "You are not my sister for GOD's sake."

Monisola flinched not at what he said but the way he said it. She had never seen him so angry and filled with such hatred before not even when he struck out at her when they were young. She silently prayed and hoped she would get to the bottom of the cause of his outburst. He had expected her to be shocked or bombard him with question but then he wasn't surprised, he was talking to her royal highness, princess cool cucumber.

"Omoniyi, you will always be my brother no matter what."

"Even though we are not blood related."

Again, she gave no sign of shock or surprise. She definitely knew something.

"Well now that I am dying, you have an unhindered access to the throne, I'm sure that's what you always wanted."

This time he was shocked as she gave him a full brunt of her mouth.

"Your royal highness Prince Phillip Omoniyi Adewunmi, heir to the Adewunmi throne, if you still harbour in your heart the idea that I am contesting for our father's royal throne then I do implore that you dislodge the idea from your head as I have no such intention. I no longer live under that illusion. I am older and wiser. Moreover, I am more willing to spend the rest of my life working with people who need help and are out there than indulging in royal affairs that ......"

"But we both know that royal affairs involves helping people, your people, your kingdom."

"I have not finished and don't you dare interrupt me."

He pulled her towards him with all the strength he had and was about to kiss her but she pulled back.

"Omoniyi 'ewo leyi, eje ati omi ara kan na ni wa, it's an abomination, we are siblings."

"I am not your brother!"

"You are and will always be, no DNA test or paper can dispute that, you are my father's son, his heir apparent, we share the same name and come from the same loins."

"Honestly I am telling you, you are not my sister."

"I know we are not blood related, I cannot question that, the only thing I know is that Omoniyi I love you as my brother."

"Do you love me more than that?"

She did not respond.

"I suppose now that I am lame and cannot bring myself to do my manly duties you reject what we both feel and know is true."

The sting of her hand on his check caught him unawares.

They both looked at each other, one pair of eyes flashing like lightning and the other laughing.

"Gosh, I wish I could taste all that fire buried inside of you and ravish you."

She was about to slap him again but he held her and pinned her to him.

"I want you; I want you Monisola even on my death bed I can't help it."

"You are not going to die Omoniyi, there is hope. GOD is willing and able to make you better, listen to me, we will get the best ..."

"Even all the money your father has can't make me better, I am cursed just like my father."

"Omoniyi, you will always be an Adewunmi, no matter what."

"How did you know, who told you, father?"

She shook her head.

"My mother?"

"No one told me, the blood test ... Omoniyi, let's forget about the past, what we have to do now is get you the best treatment and soon you will be back home in your ...."

"Would you have married me?"

"I would have stopped tormenting myself if I knew what you and father were trying to hide."

"I don't understand."

"Father lifted my exile ban some years back and asked me to come home, I refused."

"What? When? Why?"

"I refused because I knew I was in love with you and if I saw you and one thing led to another my father will kill me. Honestly, I thought I was a wretch having such feelings for my own blood brother and imagine if I came and lured you into what we shouldn't do, definitely it would be an abomination and wreck your position as prince royal so I just stayed away giving all sort of excuses."

"What made you come this time?"

"I heard you were involved with someone so I knew definitely our paths will not come to that."

"I've always loved you Monisola, right from day one."

"Hm! Are you sure about that? Have you forgotten all the battles we had before we were caught that day when you struck out at me?"

"There are so many things I regret Monisola, so many."

"Ssh! Life is not about regrets, it's about living, hoping and loving."

"I want to love you."

"But you do, we are..."

"Please don't call me your brother, I want to be your lover and don't you slap me again."

She moved away, not that she was afraid of slapping him again but she was afraid of what he was asking.

"Even if we .... if we...."

"You don't see me as a man."

"Omoniyi, please stop interrupting me, I hate it. I want to but I can't. It's nothing to do with your challenges now, you are still a man body and soul...."

"Thanks."

"Don't interrupt, bushman."

"Yes, Princess Cool Cucumber."

"What? Is that another name you've added to your name list for me?"

"You still remember?"

"I forgot to bring my memoirs with the list of names, 'Tirin gbeku' Orun` bi oke Langodo, Ese bi ese eshinshin." (Translation: A Skinny girl with a long neck like Langodo hills. Legs like those of a fly).

He started to laugh and then began to choke, she quickly brought him water but he only took a few sips before he started smiling again.

"Gosh, Monisola I don't believe you, you are one heck of a girl, I must tell CDB ..."

"CDB? E wo tuni yen? What is that again."

"My very, very good friend, I told him all about you, the guy can't wait to meet you, he's heard so much about you."

"So, you've been divulging our secrets and escapade to another."

"Only to CDB, he's one ...."

"Let's talk about us, have you told father how you feel, about me."

He didn't even bother to respond.

"He's the only one I'm afraid of, it would break his heart because he sees you as his son. Omoniyi, please get better and then we would take it from there."

"What do you mean?"

"When you get better I will confront father with my feelings for you, in that way, your position is not jeopardised because I know it will hurt him and I will be able to figure out what to say or do."

"That's if he doesn't kill you first, no thank you, brave princess I'll do the talking."

"No! You must never approach father on that matter, it will break his heart."

"It won't be the first."

"You told him about us?" she asked in disbelief.

"No! I'm not that stupid, it was about a girl I once knew."

"What happened?" she asked when he offered no further explanation.

"Forget it, it didn't work out."

"I'm sorry."

"For what? It wasn't your fault. In fact, I was getting over you ..."

"I ...I... should never have come."

"Who knows, maybe you would have been Mrs Ray by now."

"Omoniyi do you hate me that much!" She laughed.

"Honestly I want to see this guy that causes your pulse to race each time his name is mentioned."

"I can assure you, my pulse and in fact my whole body race because I want to get away from him as far as possible. Honestly the guy presses the wrong buttons and I just want to blow up and explode."

"Would you explode for me?"

She looked at him, there was a mixture of emotions in her heart, especially one that she did not want to think of.

"I don't know how."

"What do you mean you don't know how, you just said Ray..."

"Ray makes me mad with anger not what you are thinking."

"Anger? Don't tell me you ...you... gosh! Why won't the guy pester you, you are a beautiful woman, surely you don't need anyone to tell you that and you know what we guys want when it comes to Omo to lewa, ti o fi ewa Oluwa han, a beautiful girl like you."

"Is that what you do, chasing innocent girls all around."

"Innocent? Who? Those girls out there, Na lie, none of them are 'inno' not even a cent."

"Not every girl is like that, I'm sure you might have come across some before."

"Well one and going by what you've just told me two. How do you do it? What of your boyfriend, did he not want you, se oju e' fo ni, is he blind?"

"Omoniyi you are rotten, when did you become like this, you used to be so timid about girls."

"Not after I met you and your sharp tongue, honestly apart from B, no girl and I mean no girl fit do any shakara, mo ma la mole ni."

She gasped and let go of his hands.

"What! You think say you go get am?"

"Get what?" she asked wondering what he was talking about.

He looked away. Why did he still have this stigma of inherited blood disease from his biological father even though Kabiyesi had spent years and money to see him cured.

"Omoniyi, talk to me."

"Don't mind me, I'm just joking. How come no man has ever touched you?" he quickly changed the subject.

"Can we talk about something else please."

"No, I'm interested, how did you resist the temptations? Did our tutors give you a different lesson I did not get?"

She laughed, "What are you talking about Omoniyi? What lessons are you talking about?"

"Don't tell me you didn't receive lessons from Old owl?"

"Old owl?"

"That old man, what's his name again, Ba, Ba, the name escapes me now."

"Barinde."

"Yes! Barinde. You have a computer brain to remember all these names."

"You might remember if you learnt it in the first place."

"Your sharp razor tongue hasn't been tamed. How? When there's no man to tame it. Honestly if I had known I would have tried to resist all those girls that were tempting me. It's all Larinde's fault"

"Barinde! What has he got to do with that?"

"Well I asked him how one can resist the wiles of temptation, he said I should read the bible. Well I did, Solomon the wisest couldn't, he had a thousand. Samson the strongest was caught on Delilah's laps and ..."

"Omoniyi, do not blaspheme."

"Don't interrupt bush girl, ok but I tried, I did try but you need sheer will power. What's your secret?

"I don't have a secret I only obeyed what father made me promise."

"What? He asked curiously.

"I took an oath."

"I don't like the sound of this."

"It's not what you think, I gave my word, I did not swear or do anything I just gave my word."

"And you are still holding to that?"

She nodded.

"What are you made of, steel? I wonder who the man will be to break you."

"I thought we were eloping."

"Not with these legs, yes I'll get better but I don't want that experience again, I had it with B."

"B, who is she?"

"No one, just a girl I met a while ago, she was younger than she looked, one thing led to another and then I discovered I was her first," he shook his head and shuddered.

"I want to find you a real man before I die, one that is worthy of you."

"Omoniyi, you are not going to die but live to declare GOD's glory in the land of the living."

"I can also declare GOD's glory in heaven because when I make it there, believe me, it is to the glory of the LORD."

"Have you asked JESUS into your life, to be your LORD and saviour?"

"I have but keep going back, honestly if I could go back and change some things about my past, mistakes, decisions, I will. Oh GOD help me!"

"Let's pray." She held his hands and said, "Father we come before you, humbly bow before your throne of grace that we may obtain mercy and find grace in times of our need. My brother Omoniyi and I ask for forgiveness of our sins from our youth and up till this moment and even after. Lord JESUS, please forgive us, cleanse us from all iniquities, purge us and make us whole, pour your Holy Spirit upon us afresh and give us life eternal with you in JESUS name. Amen."

Monisola opened her eyes but with his eyes still closed, Omoniyi continued from where she stopped.

"Lord I know I have been bad and done things I shouldn't have done, please forgive me, I wish I could ... I should have known better but all these are excuses. I'm really sorry Lord for all I've done, my way of living, some good and some bad. I have two requests no three. Before I die, I want to see B again, I want to say how sorry I am. Lord if possible, I want to see my sister, Monisola get married to a good man, one that deserves her. I can't think right now I would have made suggestions but you know who is right for her and one more thing I want to spend eternity with you. Please bring me to your kingdom, that's what matters most. Thank you Father GOD, thank you Lord JESUS, thank you Holy Spirit, I love you."

Both siblings conversed, reminisced about the past and by the time Monisola left, she was happy, a bit relieved though still burdened. She quickly prayed, Lord please let him be here tomorrow alive and well.

She did not go back to the hospital until two days later as she had to run errands for her mother and also check her work emails as she had some urgent matters to deal with.

"Hi there kid sister, where have you been, you missed" Omoniyi asked as soon as she walked into his private room in the hospital.

"Kid sister indeed. Olori had a million errands for me to see to, honestly one day, I'm going to ..."

"You dare not do anything to that lovely woman, she's a mother indeed to everyone."

"Everyone but me, she treats me like her sister not a daughter."

"How can she, when Kabiyesi treats you like his favourite, 'Monisola this, Monisola that, Monisola is a fine example of how a woman's commitment...,' he goes on and on, honestly everyone including Morenike and Morolake mimics him every time but of course not to his face"

"I'm not his favourite he just sees me as a right-hand man or whatever, we rarely see eye to eye"

"Eye`meji ki je asa, two lions cannot rule at the same time, one will eventually step down for the other"

"So, you are ready to take over" Monisola asked eagerly.

He ignored her, "GOD answers prayers. I've had one prayer answered from that night we prayed. B was here"

"When? How did she get here so soon"?

"Her spirit was here, I felt it"

Monisola was a bit worried, she moved closer and looked into his eyes but he gave nothing away.

"She died a while ago, I hope I meet her when I get to heaven, at least I have a friend there, I'm worried about you, who is going to take care of you?"

"I thought we were eloping?" she teased him.

"Oh, shut up, I reject that in Jesus name, abomination"

"Are you okay Omoniyi, I've only left you for a few days and you are already hallucinating."

"Kai! I no fit insult your father because I dey throw stone for my own backyard, your mouth like 'halli'. I am serious, I want you to get married as soon as possible."

"Except you are willing to marry me I don't see how soon that can be."

"Are you doubting GOD's power? He can do the impossible."

"Are you rejecting me, GOD can give you a change of heart."

"I am your brother never ever forget that."

"But..."

"No more buts. I am and will only be your brother and nothing more. You will soon meet someone who will fulfil that need that I ...... CDB was here too and my..."

"Was his spirit here too?"

He seemed to be in a world of his own for a moment and then he slapped her hand, "You are so cheeky. He was here flesh and blood with a gift from B."

"Oh, so he is an angel!"

"Ma fun e' lese to ba gbe enu re dake" (O shout up before I give you a good beating)

"Ma binu, Sorry but you are not making sense"

"Oh! So I am talking rubbish now or going senile."

"No, you are scaring me, Omoniyi please don't leave me."

"I have to, I can't be around forever and moreover you've managed without me all these years."

"Omoniyi please I don't want to go through a separation again."

"I'm not leaving ... yes I am, look here you've got to be strong, strong for the others. I can't have you all fall apart when I'm gone, Monisola Obinrin alagbara bi okunrin meta."

"I don't want to be strong; I've always done that all my life, I can't" she began to sob.

"Look here", he gently placed his hands on her face, "You have to pull yourself together, you are now the beacon in the family, you've been prepared for this for a long time; now began to walk the work. Be there for father, he is strong but every man has his moment of weakness. My mother! Sweet Mother! Love so pure! She sacrificed a lot, a lot for me, take care of her, just like you take care of your own mother. I love you all."

They hugged and after a while they talked.

"Have you spoken to father?"

"No, I don't want him to know."

"You have to otherwise I'll tell him; I can't carry the responsibility alone and your mother will never forgive me."

"Ok I'll tell father but not my mother, it will bring back more memories, my father died of the same disease, we thought I was cured from it but I guess it's hereditary."

"Are you sure, you can always have a second opinion."

"Let me be Monisola, get one of the nurses for me please."

By the time she got back to the room he was asleep and looked peaceful. She moved closer and could see him breathing steadily, thank GOD. He was scaring her with all his talks. She made him more comfortable, rearranged his things in the cubicle separating his underwear and vests. She was folding one of his shirts when she saw a small toy car, something a little boy would take around with him. She wondered where that came from. None of her nephews or nieces had been here so she wasn't sure where this came from. She folded the shirt and placed the toy car on it. She knew her brother liked his things kept exactly where he wanted it, so she tried to make everything easier for him. Maybe she should ask one of his assistants to be here and help him with his things until he returned home. Yes, she'll tell father tomorrow.

She was sitting staring into space when she heard a knock, thinking it was one of the nurses, she asked the person to come in, she was shocked when she saw her father.

"Good evening father."

"Good evening Oluwamuiremiwa."

She acknowledged the signal her father gave her that something serious was going on.

They sat in silence and soon the doctor came in, he spoke with her father but in low tones she could hardly hear. What were they talking about? She tried to eaves drop but she could hardly hear a thing. She sat back, closed her eyes for a minute and she was soon fast asleep.

He was looking at her and saw her in a different light. She is a remarkable girl, well a woman now, how times fly and you never know but take things for granted. Well there was no going back now, he was going to enjoy what they had now - life. He could no longer think about her the way he used to and to him that was a sign from GOD that she belonged to another. He only wished he could know who so that he could tell him to take care of his one true love, sister and friend. Monisola woke up to find Omoniyi smiling at her, she quickly rubbed her eyes and hoped she wasn't seeing things.

"What are you afraid of, every one of us will die one day, so what's your problem."

"Please don't talk about death Omoniyi you are scaring me."

"I don't mean to but it is going to happen."

"Please, stop it."

"Ok but remember when it happens there is nothing to be afraid of, just hold on to GOD and let Him comfort you. I love you Monisola, never forget that and I want you to live life to the full; don't let anything stop you, get married, have children, as many as you want and love, love the man you say yes to."

"We could have our own child if you..., we..."

"I bind that spirit in JESUS name, Monisola don't make me send the deliverance team on you."

"But you said ....."

"Forget what I said, listen to what I am saying and get that evil thought out of your spirit, soul and body in Jesus name."

Monisola tried to keep calm but she couldn't, she did not want to believe what she was hearing, it wasn't what he said but the message behind it.

Her father and Ayaba Adekemi came in and as they were talking, tears welled in his mother's eyes. Monisola still did not want to read the message behind it. She needed fresh air so she left them and went for a walk. She ran and it was only when her feet started hurting, that she realised she did not have her running shoes on. She went back to her car and drove off.

Back in her apartment she had a bath and soaked herself in oils and herbs, her body absorbed the stimulating effect as well as eased the pain but not the one brooding in her heart. Lord I can't deal with this pain, please Lord help me, I can't go through this again.

By the time she got back to the hospital, Omoniyi was sleeping so she went through her emails, replied, deleted and left some unread. She started working on her next project hoping everything would have worked out with Omoniyi getting better and helping her with it though looking at it, some might involve travelling. She was writing reports into the night and only got up when she needed to use the toilet or when the nurse came in to check on Omoniyi.

"You need some sleep you know," Omoniyi stated when he woke up.

"Hi handsome prince, I was just thinking of giving you a kiss to wake you up."

"I don't need your kiss any more, I'm looking forward to the one I receive when I get home."

"Has the doctor discharged you? No one told me anything."

"Stop listening to your head, Monisola, listen to your heart."

"I'll start packing your things."

"Monisola, I don't think I want you here, please go back to the house."

"But you just said you were coming home."

"Monisola ma da mi pada, je kin ma lo si ile ogo tin duro demi ati Oluwa mi. I have to go to my heavenly home."

"And if I refuse?" She took a deep breath, nodded her head and then shook it again.

"You are a wicked girl." he said with laughter.

"I know." she replied with a wink.

The next few days she spent between her apartment and the hospital. During the day she slept or did a few things but at night she was with Omoniyi, sitting beside him reading the bible, praying or arranging his things the way he liked them.

"You will make a good wife someday."

"Yes, I know, when you come out and we ..."

"I hope he realises what a gem you are and treats you well."

"You've always treated me well."

"Don't fight with him, don't try to order him around as you do your subjects; he is the man of the house, don't ignore him like you do the rest of us and do your own thing, involve him in all you do, learn to trust and love again, never give in to fear."

"I'll start packing our stuff."

"If you pack my stuff, I don't need them where I am going but if you pack your stuff I don't know where you are going because I am not going there. I've been there but my Lord and Master paid with His blood to get me out of there, so, no going back there for me. If you want to go there, good bye we will never see again."

"It's hard to let go Omoniyi."

"Let me go, please."

She cried, he offered comfort but she refused. They did not talk any more, she slept in the day time and he slept throughout the night as he was getting weaker and weaker. Soon the family began to come in, each hoping to cling to the last memory of him. Omoniyi being who he is asked them to leave him in peace and hold on to the memories they had shared. Ayaba Adekemi did not leave his side and after the first night he sent her home as she was encroaching on his space.

Monisola came in when he slept and arranged his things for him. She brought change of clothes, swapped the CDs of the audio bible on the player, rearranged the room and brought in some of his pictures from home. She left early in the morning before he woke up and left a note promising to be back later.

She came the third night hoping to do her usual routine without disturbing him but as soon as she walked in, he made the effort of sitting up and tried to talk to her.

"Omoniyi, you should be sleeping, I'm so sorry I disturbed you, I just wanted ..."

"To sneak in and out, like you've done for two nights. By the way thank you for restoring order into this room, I like the way you've brightened it up and made it look more comfortable."

"It's my pleasure, I'd love to do more if you let me."

"No thank you, I'm just fine. What have you been up to?"

"I have this project I'm working on and it's so exciting, I can't wait to show you."

"Let's see then."

They talked about it and he gave her the names of people to contact.

"Of course, you will take the lead as soon as you are discharged."

"Monisola, I told you ..."

"It would be great to have you on board and I'll learn a few things from you."

"Monisola, I drove my mother away and I will not hesitate to do the same to you."

"I am your wife you cannot do that."

He moved to press the button and she quickly apologised.

"I will not tolerate any nonsense."

"Yes, I'm sorry" she started to sob.

"Come here, I didn't mean to scare you but you are driving me crazy with your sinful talk. I'm born again now you know, I'm heavenly bound."

She started to sob again.

"Monisola I would bundle you out myself if you don't stop your crying, haba! I'm not even dead and you are crying, do you want to speed things up."

There and then she decided she wasn't going to cry.

"That's better, now where were we?"

"We were planning to elope and get married."

"Marry you, I will dash you to that my brother Ray or what's his name."

"At least you got the name right and I know that's on purpose to torment me."

"I will not only torment you, I will make sure I conduct the wedding ceremony."

"You are looking for trouble Omoniyi."

"Why do you always call my full name, wetin do Niyi?"

"Niyi is like calling a headless chicken but Omoniyi is calling the full name with meaning and interpretation and we can call our son's name Omoniyi"

"Too late, another already bears the name. B had a boy; he was here the other day."

"The yellow toy sport car."

"How did you know?"

"It's in the pocket of your favourite shirt."

"Hm! Keep both for him, one day he would come for it."

"Why don't we bring him up as our son."

"He is your nephew and you are his aunt"

"Omoniyi..."

"Wo ma yo mi lenu, sora re`."

"What do you want to eat?"

"Now you are talking, what about frog's eye and rabbit tail."

"Yuk! Omoniyi!"

"What! Have you forgotten you ate it before?"

"I did not! I only pretended I did so that you would eat it", Monisola looked away feeling guilty.

"Ah! Monisola! You are a wicked girl, you better repent. I wonder what your children would get up to especially the girls."

"They would be brought up as ladies and ..."

"Not if your father has anything to do with it."

"I don't think father has the zest for military training for his children anymore. Look at how Morenike and Morolake were brought up, I never had pink dresses, in my time I wore khaki trouser and white shirts."

"Monisola!!!"

"Honestly, try and remember."

"I guess he was trying to make up for the son he did not have."

"Thank GOD you came along, life took a different turn for me."

"How?"

"I had a partner in crime and also one I could put the blame on."

"What on earth are you talking about?" Omoniyi asked perplexed.

She swallowed hard and looked away.

"Monisola you better confess your sins now."

"Okay, remember when the fire broke out on the farm on one of our camping trips with father?"

He looked at her in horror.

"Don't look at me like that, I didn't know it was going to spread; it was meant to catch the bush animals that had escaped and I was trying to catch them and forgot the fire...."

"Your father said it was you but I never believed it, Monisola how could you!"

"I had to lie, I was afraid father would beat me and also ashamed that I could not catch ordinary bush meat."

"Oh! So, what were you trying to catch? An antelope! All by yourself with a match stick. Honestly I felt sorry for you when father whacked your bum and I had to lie that it was me. My goodness! Any more revelations?"

She told him more and when she saw the way his mouth was opened in disbelief, she asked why.

"Do you know the one thing that has been going on in my mind over and over again all these years and had left me baffled? Why would a father send his daughter on exile and give an outsider claim to his throne?"

Monisola laughed. "First you are not an outsider and my father knows me and the kind of person he had trained me to be and I guess he saw you as a better prospect for the throne so he chose you."

"I don't understand."

"With all the mischief I had been doing to get his attention and with you on the scene, father did not want to take chances with me so off I went to be trained as a little princess, while you got his attention and the throne. At first I hated you but then I guess with my hormonal changes and teenage crush on you, I couldn't help but fall in love with you. I used to dream about coming back as a beautiful princess and you begging me to marry you and of course I said no. I should write a book on those silly fantasies"

"Monisola, I'm sorry if ..."

"Oh, shut up, I don't need your stupid sympathy."

"Do you know you are so rude."

"Pot calling kettle black."

"I'm the most humble, easy going person you've ever met"

"Yeah right! Only if I don't press the right button otherwise you are flaming with fire."

"Ah! I salute you; you do know how to press the right buttons and I do have a fit of rage. I am sorry for your husband."

"Do you think I will ever find someone?"

"Why not, you are beautiful, intelligent..."

"I don't mean that, will I meet someone like you, know him like I know you, love him as much as I love you?"

"Yes, you would find someone far better than me because I would not be able to give you that which you deserve, my princess."

"If only you heed to what I say and I could be carrying our ....."

"And have him or her cursed for life, no thank you."

Monisola sighed deeply and wanted to give in to the anguish in her soul but one look from Omoniyi and the last warning to throw her out made her compose herself.

"Do you want me to bring you anything from home?"

"No, I have everything I need here though I'll like some home cooked meals, these hospital meals are beginning to bore me."

"Okay, I'll go to the market and cook."

"Let someone else do that, I need you here."

"But you said..."

"Do you want to deny your brother the pleasure and comfort of your presence? Honestly you do not know how much you've done for me these past days. Your strength to go on is what is keeping me alive and I dare to hang on to whatever time I have left. You are that one person in my life that I respect for her courage and selfless attitude. You are a strong woman Monisola, sometimes I wish you were a man and I would have easily passed the baton on to you."

"Omoniyi you better take another good look at me and see me for who I really am. I am not strong, in fact that is one of my weakest characters, I fall apart at the slightest wind of adversity but only camouflage my countenance and hold on to GOD. Honestly if I did not have or know GOD as I have come to I would have been locked up years ago. I can't handle the slightest pain or cry from a child or person suffering, it tears me apart. I only summon courage and strength from GOD and ask to be a source of strength for the person I'm helping. I've seen so many things, mostly negative in life that I question GOD and ask why but then who am I, I just get on with my work and do the best that I can do."

"Therein lies your strength. The ability and courage to go on in spite of what the situation is, I wish I was as determined as you, I would have faced and conquered many battles, no matter the consequences."

"Let's not dwell in regrets, I wish I could take you out and get some fresh air or watch the sun set."

"I'll rather see it rise, it's the promise of a new day."

"Ok, but I can't promise I would be wide awake to do that."

"Ole, lazy bone, what time of the day do you get up?"

"I don't have a specific time; I get up when I want to."

"Ka re` Omoba, ma jaiye ori e`."

"It's nothing to do with that, I work late into the morning after I leave here and sometimes my mother doesn't let me sleep when she wants to talk."

"What about? What is so urgent that can't wait? Oh! I see, planning for you to take over when I'm gone."

"What do you mean? Seriously Omoniyi I've told you I'm not interested in the throne."

"What is so important then?"

"She ... she wants me to get married."

"Ah! I see. I guess you are eager to play along since I am not man enough for you."

"What? Omoniyi seriously you need to make up your mind about us, one minute I'm your sister the next...."

"Eh! It's enough! I know what I said, it's just that I am human and .... anyway, when is the wedding?"

"Which wedding?"

"The one you and your mother are planning."

"She is not planning a wedding"

"You just said she was."

"She is planning for me to get pregnant." Monisola quickly looked away.

"I don't understand."

"I made the mistake of telling mother I wasn't interested in the throne before I came and when all these events started unfolding she asked me what my plans was. I told her go back to my job and life but she said it was impossible as father would want me to take over, at least until an heir is produced and that I had better start charting my way to freedom. At first, I didn't understand but when she painted the picture, things became clearer. If I get pregnant father will have no choice but to let me go, heir or no heir but then how do I get pregnant when I gave him my word or better still when I haven't found true love. Honestly Omoniyi I'm seriously planning to run away."

"Do that when I am gone, until then you are not leaving my presence."

"Please be serious."

"I am. After I'm gone you can sort yourself out, until then I am your main priority after GOD of course. Let the lion and lioness sort out their problems"

"It's not fair on mother, I'm the only one she has."

"Well, all it takes is for her to have a rendezvous with Kabiyesi and with much prayer, I tell you that heir will come."

"What about your son, surely he is the solution to all these."

"Leave my son out of these, he is not an Adewunmi."

"Of course, he is, his father is!"

"Monisola if you try to ... any way I know CDB would not disappoint me, he gave me his word."

"Meaning?"

"My son is not to be involved in all these royal mess but to live a total free life."

"You were not bound so ..."

"If I were not, I would have summoned enough courage to tell your father about my feelings for you and probably we would have been married with seven children."

She hit him with the magazine on his laps and kissed her teeth. "Stupid man, seven indeed, what do you take me for?"

"A very fertile baby producing factory."

"GOD help the woman you marry."

"Too late for that."

"You never... okay I'm sorry. What should I do about my mother's suggestion?"

"That is your problem, my own request is that you stay with me till I'm called and I mean stay. I'll tell someone to bring your things tomorrow."

"Omoniyi, you can't keep me here..... I mean I would like to go out for ..."

"With what you and your mother are planning, I'm not taking any chances and moreover this is a safer haven for you to be far from all the palaver going on at home and have a fresh mind to think. I won't pester you to get married or fornicate I just want you by my side. I need you."

The last statement was made with urgency and plea.

"Why me?"

"I love you and for the life of me I can't think of anyone else who would not drive me mad and kill me before my time."

"You know you need to be more patient with people, it's a character a king requires at all time."

"I know, I'll pray for you and father not to be in lack when exercising it over your subjects. People are difficult Monisola, they are stiff necked and sometimes I want to bang some heads together or cut it off all together."

"Thank GOD we are not in the olden days era, heads would just be rolling."

"I'll try and fix them back when I come to my senses and ask GOD for forgiveness."

"Forgiveness! After you've committed murder, GOD deliver us. I would have run away longest time."

"You, I will tie to my side or my bed and all you will do is just to have babies every nine months."

They laughed and then shook their heads.

"Thank GOD for new eras and enlightenment."

"Thank GOD for GOD."

"I've got to go; I'll see you tomorrow."

"I mean it Monisola, I need you here and you need to be here."

"What would I tell my mother?"

"That Prince Omoniyi wants you here, what else?"

"And your mother? I don't want trouble."

"She can visit and learn a thing or two from you about being strong."

"I'm not."

"You are and are going to be. You need to pull yourself and everyone together in one piece, no falling pieces; no matter what people say or suggest or wag with their tongue, just stay put, no shaking."

"Eh! I've told you; I can't take any more of this."

"Then I have to train you, if that is the last thing I do."

True to his words Omoniyi did not let her out of his sight, even when he slept and she went for a walk and came back, he complained.

"I only went for a walk around here, it's not like I went to town or somewhere else."

"I told you not to leave my presence." he whispered muttering all the strength in him to sit up.

She rushed to his side to help him but he held her hands firmly, sat up and asked her to pump up the pillows.

"Why don't we go out tomorrow, I'm sure the fresh air would do you good."

"No thank you, I'm not leaving this room."

"But I can't stay here every day, I need to go out."

"I can assure you; you are not going to spend the rest of your life here as I would soon be going"

It was this kind of talk that made her want to leave and run away.

"Omoniyi I can't cope with the way you talk; it's driving me crazy."

"What do you want me to do, sweet talk you and tell you everything is going to be okay, is that what you want to hear?"

She refused to answer him and turned her back to him, trying to fight back the tears.

"You can leave, I'll ask one of the guards to stay with me."

She quickly turned to him, shook her head, held his hands and kissed it.

"Too late I've made my decision, you are banished from my presence."

She looked at him not believing her ears but when she saw the thin line of smile she let go of his hands and baited her eyelids.

"Moju moju fo ju gbagi, you can bait those eyelids for all I care, you would do as you are told young woman."

"Yes, my lord, I will try and obey you and stay put provided you ......"

"Don't you dare say anything that would make me spank you, you are not too old for me to put you across my knees....."

"I would wrestle you to the floor man or no man." She quickly replied.

"Ah! Monisola."

"Don't doubt me, Heidi didn't train me for nothing you know."

"So, she has turned you into a guerrilla fighter or what are you trying to say."

"I only act in self-defence."

"Self-defence indeed, you better be careful otherwise one blow or kick to your beautiful face you go get contour; no wonder Heidi's face get different angles, na all the kicks and blow she done receive from her students."

"Omoniyi! GOD forgive you and your mouth."

"Amen in Jesus name."

The next day when Omoniyi did not get up as he usually did, her heart began to beat faster than usual. She quickly got up, felt his pulse, he was still alive but very cold. She quickly pressed the alarm and ran to get the doctor.

It was later when their father came did she leave him and it was only to go to the bathroom and back again. When she came back to the room, there were about three doctors in the room and when the third one introduced himself as the Chief Consultant of the hospital, Monisola's mind was already racing and all she wanted to do, was run out of the room but remembered she had promised to stay till the very end. She held his hands and began to pray and read the twenty third Psalms to him. The next few days were not so good and in fact Omoniyi had grown worse and had to breathe with the help of the ventilator with a nurse constantly by his side. Close family came and went but she stayed. Her mother begged her to come home but she refused and was left alone.

That night she dreamt Omoniyi was waving and saying goodbye to her, smiling and telling her not to cry but be strong for the family. She woke up scared and rushed into his room. The look on his face told her, her dream had lied. He was in a sitting position with a nasal mask on which he removed as soon as he saw her.

"My instruction was never to leave until I go, is that too much to ask." The anger in his voice surprised her and she almost answered in like manner but restrained herself.

"Omoniyi you gave us quite a fright, I only went into the adjourning room as directed by the Chief Consultant as he was bent on throwing me out of the hospital if I did not get a decent sleep and ...." She looked at her watch, "that was just two hours ago, your royal highness, anything else?"

He frowned and waved her away. She moved closer, gave him a peck and whispered, "Stop scaring me, I will only delay your going if you continue."

He slept most of the time until the morning he woke up, asked for his favourite meal, wore his favourite ole` ntele afa` and listened to his favourite music. By mid-day he asked for his mother and father to join him for his meal at three o'clock which they did. He hardly ate but he encouraged them to eat theirs as they still had a long journey ahead of them. They talked, reminiscence about old times, laughed and shed a few tears. At exactly five fifty-five he asked if his mother could go home and bring him some papers he had forgotten to sign, they were urgent and must be sent to his business partners the next day. He also gave her the keys to the safe in his private study. Ayaba Adekemi refused and asked if Monisola could go instead, she was about to take the keys from her but one look from Omoniyi made her step back. Reluctantly Ayaba left and promised to be back.

He and the man whom he had grown to love and call father talked in low tones, father shaking his head and holding his head high. Finally, he turned to Monisola and beckoned for her to move closer, he took her hands which were shaking and held it firmly, it was so firm that she felt a surge of power overcome her which she could not understand but soon did as he spoke.

"Oluwamuiremiwa Monisola Fiadekemi, a woman of great strength, a woman full of GOD's power and a woman for such a time as this. I am passing the baton to you, it's a greater responsibility but I know that Almighty Jehovah who has seen our father and I through will also see you through and the generation after.

Oluwa a di e mu, oni subu, to ba subu Oluwa yio gbe' o dide, o si duro. Omobirin bi Deborah, bi Esteri Aya ba, mo ni fe re, ore mi, aburo mi, a o pade lese JESU."

He smiled, laid back on the pillows, still smiling and suddenly she felt his grip loosen and then he went.

MONISOLA WAS WORKING like an automated machine, she took charge over all arrangements to be made and she had everything under her control.

She arranged for Ayaba Adekemi's elder sister from America to be with her and also for her father, his best friend and confidante from childhood, who travelled all the way from Australia. She warned her mother to keep her distance from the two grieving parents and also stopped all her talks about eloping with one of her distant cousins. When her sisters started to wag their tongue and told her to her face that they hoped she was satisfied as she had accomplished her mission of coming home to kill their brother so that she could be next to the throne, she simply replied that they had the opportunity to do likewise, kill her and ascend the throne though she wondered who of the two will carry out all the responsibilities. From then on things went smoothly as they were no objections to everything she did or said and soon the final day came.

In the morning she didn't want to get up from the bed, she wished she could just lie there but she knew people were depending on her. As part of tradition, both parents were forbidden to attend the funeral so she also forbade her mother not to. There were so many people she had not seen for years that came, they offered their condolence and in some cases she had to offer her shoulder for some to cry on. During the church service as the tributes were being said she wondered what Omoniyi would have thought of all these, probably said something funny, she was about to smile but restrained herself as people would think otherwise. When it was her turn to speak, she walked to the pulpit and read the poem she and Omoniyi had composed when they were children, titled 'My Best Friend'.

Omoniyi:
My best friend is my sister Moni
I like her because she makes me laugh
I like her because I have someone to play with
Even though she is a girl she plays with me and do things boys would do

Sometimes I don't like her because she makes me cry and Father has said as a big brother I should not.

I love my sister I love my friend.

Monisola:

I do not have a best friend but I have a brother who is my best friend

His name is Omoniyi and I like him a lot

I like him because he is my friend and he plays with me

I like him because he takes the blame for the naughty things I do

I like him because when I climb trees and do things boys do, he does not scold me but tells me to be careful

I like Omoniyi and when I grow up I want to be his princess because I know he loves me and will take good care of me.

After reading the poem she used the opportunity to thank everyone who came, for those who intended but could not make it and she wished everyone present a safe journey home.

The place of rest was a private land and only a selected few were invited. Monisola stood with her sisters and their husbands and children and they all bade farewell to Omoniyi. Others also paid their tributes. When the rain started, everyone went back to the house but she stayed. She waited in the rain as the diggers covered, sealed, erected a stone and then they left. She stayed. What was she waiting for? She waited again. Maybe Omoniyi would get up and ask if they had all gone and it was time to come out as he was tired of playing the silly hide and seek games. They had done it several times when they were young, they would both hide from their friends for hours and when they left, both of them would come out of their hiding place, be it from the trees, under the shrubs and sometimes they ran away from the soldier ants that had gathered forces and were out to get them. She waited and waited but he did not call out her name or jump behind her and cover her face with his hands and made her scream with fear. She waited until her brother in-law came to get her. She went with Kayode and when she turned to look back to see if he was there, she saw someone standing by the grave, she couldn't see who it was but she knew that he was a man, a very tall man.

At the palace, a quiet reception was held, people were talking in low tones, consoling themselves with memories of Omoniyi. She had nothing to do so she went out to sit in the garden. The garden which had been their duel ground, playground and meeting place was void of any emotion or atmosphere. It did not offer her the solace she so desperately wanted and the comfort she longed for. GOD where are You in all these, I can't take any more, please help me, she screamed inside.

"Excuse me Miss Adewunmi."

She turned to see who it was, maybe some friend wanting to offer their condolence. She didn't recognise the face but she stood up to greet him.

"Thank you for coming I..."

"I'm so sorry to disturb you but I wanted to see you before I left."

"Are you leaving already?"

"I can't stay, I have to go."

"Thank you for coming Mr ...?"

"Daniel, Omoniyi and I ...., I'm sorry I have to go."

"Please stay" it was a whisper but he could hear the cry in it.

"I... I.."

She stepped back and let him go.

A few weeks later Monisola was on the plane going back to England when she got another bombshell that tore her heart apart. Raymond was married. Back in her house she put everything in order, changed and drove to her office to check out where her next assignment was, she had been away for too long. Her personal assistant Valerie was glad to see her, sad about what happened and offered her condolences. Valerie hugged her and for the first time Monisola felt a twinge in her body as if the frozen part of her body were beginning to thaw and the ice was breaking but she knew the ice in her heart was still frozen and it would take more than a hammer to break it down.

Her office was filled with flowers and sympathy cards, the air had a strong fragrance and she felt she was going to choke. She asked Valerie to send the flowers to people at the nearest hospital, retain the cards and send out thank you notes to everyone. She went out of the office to get some coffee but the coffee tasted like water as her body was under the siege of caffeine; it had been the only thing she could take into her body as she could not eat. She knew it was only a matter of time before her body gave in to exhaustion and acute fatigue as she had only had two hours of sleep each night since Omoniyi died that day.

Omoniyi! Omoniyi! GOD why! Her heart cried as she was driving home later in the evening and as she did not want to cause another fatality or heartache in the family, she put on the radio hoping her mind would focus on whatever was being said. Her mind failed to engage with what the presenter was saying so she changed the station; music, yes music would do her good.

"When you have a question that no one can answer
What do you do?
You just stand

When you have a problem that no one can solve
What do you do?
You just stand

When the pain in your heart cuts a hole in your soul
What do you do?
You just stand

You stand and face the Maker of your life
And tell Him JESUS I just don't understand
But right now, all I'm gonna do is just stand

I stand because I know You are with me,
I stand because I know You will never leave me
I stand because You have the answer to my needs

Staaaaaand
Yes, I will stand
I won't look back but I will stand"

THAT NIGHT SHE couldn't sleep, she turned and tossed, sat, stood, she was restless. She was tempted to make another cup of coffee but she dare not otherwise she will be moving closer to the borderline of insomnia. Every time she closed her eyes to sleep she kept seeing him, he was there right in her dreams and many times she told him to leave her alone. Her phone rang, she refused to pick it because she knew it was him.

"Monisola, please pick up the phone, I need to speak with you, I can't do it over the phone, I'm in England and I must see you." His voice spoke over her answering machine but she refused to pick up the phone or speak to him.

"GOD please tell him to leave me alone, I don't want to ever see him or hear his voice again and tell him he should stop disturbing my sleep, I need to sleep."

Her doorbell rang and immediately she got scared. Who would be visiting her at this time of the night and why? Her answering machine gave her the answer she sought, it was Chichi. Chichi! Did she promise to call her or visit and she had forgotten? Lately a lot of things had been skipping her mind. She got up and went downstairs to open the door.

"Chic!" she used her endearing word to call her, "It's so late to come all the way here. Did I forget to do something I promised......"? She stopped as soon as she saw Raymond standing behind her. She left the door opened and went upstairs to her room.

There was a knock on her door she ignored it and when it came again, she stated in a clear and firm tone, "Raymond please leave me alone."

"It's me Monic."

Monisola breathed a sigh of relief when she heard her friend use her nickname which had stuck as a result of the one she called her, Chic. "Come in."

Chichi came in, she was looking drowsy, yawning and she was wearing her pyjamas underneath her coat. Monisola patted her side of the bed for her to sit.

"I can't stay, I want to go home and sleep; Mano is waiting for me downstairs."

"And the visitor you brought to my house?"

"Monisola, I can't help with that, he's being pestering me for a week and I won't be held responsible for throttling his neck, please hear him out, the worst he can do is tell you to be his second wife and if you agree, good for you."

Chichi and her boyfriend Mano finally left, she left the door opened for Raymond to leave, instead he moved towards the door, pulled her in and closed it.

"We need to talk."

"We do not need to ... please go to your wife, I want to sleep."

"I am not going anywhere until you hear me out."

"Ok two minutes."

"First of all, I'm sorry for the loss of your brother, please accept my deepest sympathy and may his soul rest in perfect peace. Secondly I want to apologise for not being there for you, it was circumstances beyond my control, please forgive me."

"Thank you, apologies accepted, congratulations on your wedding and I pray for a fruitful marriage, please leave."

"Monisola I am deeply sorry; I regret doing this to you...it was...."

"Raymond I have accepted your apologies and everything; please leave me alone in peace, I just want to be left alone."

He moved closer to hug her; she ran from him.

"Raymond, I want you to leave this minute if you don't, I would call the police, only to make you leave because I do not want to be committed to prison for your murder so please leave."

"It's not that bad Monisola I just want to explain."

"Explain what!" she screamed. "That you jilted me or that you got married when you told me you will wait for me. Two weeks was all I asked for Raymond. Two weeks! You couldn't wait, you got married. Do you know what, you don't owe me any explanation just go."

"When you asked for two weeks I told you it was too long that I needed you to be there with me in the village but you didn't listen."

"Listen! Raymond you wanted me to listen to you when I had just lost my brother? My family was going through a difficult time and you want me to listen to you talk about marriage, what was I supposed to tell my father? I was getting married and visiting my in-laws! Please Raymond don't belittle my trust in your intelligence."

"You were not there at the village so you didn't know the pressure I was under."

"Oh! So, one of your town's men came up to you, held a knife to your throat, demanded you marry and you had no choice but to obey and marry the first village damsel thrown at you."

"Adanna and I have known each other since childhood and it was common knowledge that we were to be married."

"And yet you came to me asking me to marry you, are you a fool or what? Raymond please leave me alone I've had enough of you, I don't want to ever see you again, please."

She was sobbing now.

He came nearer she stepped back.

"Why are you running away from me?"

"Have you forgotten that you are married?"

"So?"

"Simply put, you belong to another and I don't want GOD's wrath to fall on me because He has joined you together."

"It's you I love."

This time she lost it, she just screamed, "LEAVE ME ALONE RAYMOND, PLEASEEEEEE leave me alone."

When he left she cried and cried, she cried because he would never know she loved him, yes she loved him. Even when he was behaving like a pest and winding her up with his proposal of marriage, she loved him and was only waiting to break the ties with Omoniyi before she said 'I will' to him. It was all over now, Omoniyi gone, Raymond gone, she was all alone, all alone.

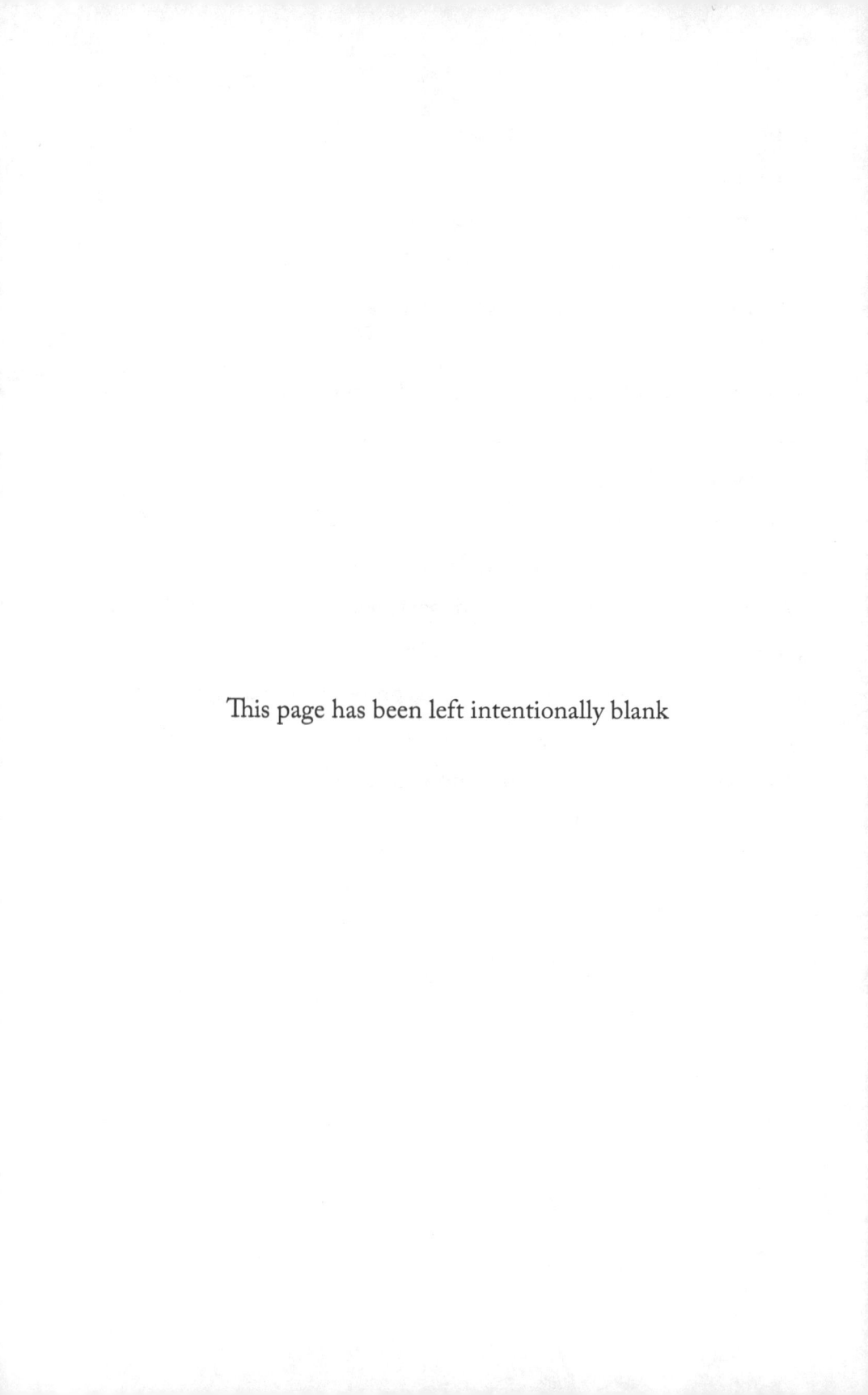

This page has been left intentionally blank

CHAPTER THREE

She knew life would not return to normal for her again with Omoniyi gone and Raymond out of her life. She still could not bring her mind to accept the word 'd-e-a-d'; so, she consoled herself that Omoniyi was gone and his last words to her was that they will meet at the feet of Master Jesus and that she looked forward to. As for Raymond he was out of her life for good.

With one gone and the other out of her life, she knew she was living an extraordinary life as it was just the grace of GOD seeing her through all these. She remembered the song she heard on the radio about standing, yes that was all she was going to do, just stand. She had asked GOD countless times the questions on her mind, even voiced them out but she did not hear anything from him. She guessed her hatred for Raymond was the reason why she couldn't hear from GOD. She told GOD to mind other affairs of her life but that of Raymond was a closed case, as she was both the judge and jury for that case. Of course, GOD was the overall Judge and had told her to hand the case to Him; but she was unwilling as she preferred holding on to the hatred she had for Raymond rather than exposing her love for him. How could she love him when he betrayed her love? Monisola! You let Raymond break your heart. How could you, a woman of substance and calibre fall for a commoner and he broke your heart?

Monisola looked into the mirror and laughed. Who was she fooling? Who was a commoner? Are not all men equal before GOD? So, who was she to judge and who was she punishing if she did not let go, definitely not Raymond but herself. Raymond was enjoying his life as she heard a baby was on the way, so why couldn't she let go and live her own life. The more she held on to the bitterness, anger, hatred and all, the more Raymond would keep on enjoying his life, having more children and more wives if he wanted. In future if their paths should meet he would tell his children that she was the woman he wanted to marry and the children would be glad he didn't as she would look like an old, haggard, hard face and embittered, raggedy woman. The picture was so clear that she quickly snapped out of it and rejected it.

"GOD I'm willing to forgive Raymond, please help me."

She woke up the next morning, jumped out of bed and decided it was a beautiful day. It looked and felt beautiful even though the sky looked grey and bleak but it was the day the Lord GOD had made and she was going to rejoice and be glad in Him, the maker of the day and the day in itself.

She had her shower, sang while getting ready and made sure all the clothes she wore, even her accessories were all coloured no single trace of black. Omoniyi told the family that he did not want them to mourn for him for long and all the family had stopped wearing black clothing weeks after the burial but she still did. She continued because she was mourning not just for Omoniyi but also the love she lost. Looking at it now, it was silly because really, you cannot mourn love. GOD is love, HE is alive, so she is going to live her life, throw herself into her work, work and work tirelessly.

When she got to work her enthusiasm died right there. Her team had been called again to look into project areas that had not been completed, they were to start work on them, complete them and commence on new projects. The deadline for the proposal for new projects was in spring and the teams would be out on their project fields before the end of next year. The news did not go well with her as she did not want to go out of the country, she wanted to stay in England; she just wanted some peace and quiet. Her feelings right now, was that she wanted to be alone and on her own as she was not emotionally prepared to deal with people.

Valerie was excited about all the work and opportunities of seeing new places and meeting new people. However she was disappointed when Monisola told her that due to the length of the engagement of the particular field work, the areas assigned, coupled with financial constraint, only the lead people would be going on these field trips and though she would have loved Valerie to come with her as they both work well together, it was likely she would opt out from this period and assignment.

Monisola had a meeting with the two main project leads who understood her point and reasons but one of them asked her to give it another thought in a couple of months as she still had time on her side. Monisola went to her office knowing she had made up her mind and was surprised when Mark followed her into her office.

"Moni, I think what Sheila was trying to say is that you give it a couple of months to go through the process of healing of your loss and maybe a change of scene is what you really need to complete the healing. I know it is not as easy as said but it's a step, especially when you have to reach out to others to comfort, console and love. It's like they are sucking what you have left but therein lies your strength because you've been through what they have been through or more than they have gone through and you will be able to reach out to them. Can you please give it another thought?" he patted her on the shoulder and left.

Monisola sighed deeply, she never heard Mark speak in such soft tone and reflective manner before. As head of the operations team he was always barking out orders and was a go-getter. Hearing from him now was seeing another side of him she had never see before and she was touched. However, she had made her decision, she was not going out this year or next; she was staying home to rest and reflect.

"Moni, I have a Daniel on the line who would like to speak to you."

Monisola came out of her thoughts and looked at Valerie. "I'm sorry I didn't quite catch that."

Valerie looked at her, took a deep breath, wondering if her boss would ever be the same person she was before she went on holidays.

"Daniel would like to speak to you."

When Monisola gave her a blank look, she shook her head; she knew Monisola had not yet recovered from the tragic death of her brother. She exhaled, opened her mouth again, "I said....."

"I heard what you said but who is he?" Monisola replied with a blank expression.

"A man that wants to speak with you."

Monisola rolled her eyes at Valerie and told her to take a message.

"Moni ....." she attempted to appeal to her but one look at her again told her it was a closed case.

"Valerie please take a message" Monisola firmly asserted.

———————

THAT EVENING MONISOLA called Chichi and while they were doing their catch-up gist she asked for Raymond's number.

"Why are you asking for his number?"

"I'll like to call him."

"Don't be silly, I mean why ask for it when you have it stored on your phone."

"I deleted him."

"Him or it?"

"Chic please give me his number." Monisola pleaded.

"On one condition."

"What? I only asked for his number I didn't say I was going to call him", Monisola stated, trying to put up a facade.

"As if! Anyway, my condition is, don't come crying to me that you gave in to him because I know you will."

"He's married for crying out loud."

"So! That didn't stop you from loving him" Chichi replied in a smug tone.

Monisola gasped and whispered, "How did you know?"

"Goodness! Do you want me to count the number of years we've known each other and have been friends? Even though you don't acknowledge me as a best friend but I do know you Monisola Adewunmi and yes you are my best friend."

"How did you know?" Monisola asked again as she knew she never mentioned anything to her best friend.

"At first I didn't."

"I never gave you the impression I did or said anything."

"Monisola I know you; I've been one of the few privileged human beings to come close to your royal highness and I can tell when things are not just right, you know they do not add up."

"Such as?" Monisola asked wryly.

"The sudden need to go to Nigeria and escape from Raymond. I have never seen you run away from any human being. Even when faced with the most dangerous criminals, you face them squarely, so why the need to run away from Raymond just because he asked you to marry him even though he was a pest, I couldn't figure it out. Knowing you, you would have called his bluff and moved on but no you didn't and when I started putting two and two together it finally made sense."

"What two and two?"

"You refused to see him after the wedding and wouldn't even talk to me then ...."

"I'm over him now."

"Good for you. So why call him now?"

"That is why I don't want you as my best friend; you are so inquisitive."

"Why the need to call him?" Chichi asked again.

"I want him totally out of my system and I don't want to make the same mistake twice"

"What mistake? When did you make the first one?"

"See what I mean Miss Inquisitive. When are you and Mano going to get married?"

"Monic ..... Raymond's number is ..."

"I said when are you and Mano getting married?"

"Hold on."

There was silence from the other line, then Monisola heard quick footsteps, heavy breathing, opening and closing of doors

"Chichi what's happening?"

"Hello Monisola."

"I'm here where are you?"

"In my house."

"Of course, I called your phone so you should be home but why can't you speak?"

"I can, am I not speaking to you?"

"Who is there with you?"

"What mistake did you make?" Chichi ignored her question, wondering who was more inquisitive of the two of them.

"Don't ignore my question, who is there with you, is Raymond ..."

"Mano."

"Isn't he going home? It's getting late."

There was silence.

"It's okay if you don't want to talk."

"Actually, I do want to talk, I've been waiting for you to call me."

"Chic you don't have to wait for me to call. You know I'm always here, all you have to do is call."

"I did call, sometimes you didn't pick the phone and when you did I could sense you didn't want to talk so I .. I ..."

"Okay I'm here now or do you want me to come over?"

"No!"

Monisola heard the sharpness of her voice and sensed something was wrong. "Chic I'm going to drop the phone and drive straight to your house just make sure you open the door."

"Please, no, I'm okay, I......" she started crying.

"It's alright Chiamaka, please don't cry, please"

Chichi laughed and wiped her tears, "I should be the one consoling you not the other way round."

"I'm okay, please tell me what is going on, is it Mano?"

Chichi nodded her head and whispered "Yes"

"Has he done something to hurt you?"

"No! No! I'm okay. We are okay, we are ....."

"You are ......" Monisola continued, helping her friend to trace her thoughts after a bout of silence from her.

"Sleeping together."

At first what she said didn't register but after a few seconds it finally did.

"You've slept with him as in ...."

"We did it" Chichi's voice wrenched out.

"Why?"

"Why? What do you mean why, isn't it obvious why?"

"No! The last time we spoke you said you were going to wait until he asked you to marry him and it will be after you got married."

"Well he didn't ask me so I asked him."

"You asked him to marry you and then slept with him. What has gotten into you?" Monisola asked, looking at the clock, calculating how fast she could drive to Chichi's house and back as she could tell something was definitely not right.

"I'm sorry for falling below your standard Miss righteous and royal majesty."

"Hey! I am not condemning you neither am I condoning what you did, I just want to know what happened between our last conversation about this and now."

"A lot." Chichi whispered.

Monisola sighed, indeed a lot had happened.

"Why did you do it, sorry it's none of my business but you said you were going to wait?" she cupped her forehead with her hand and wished she could just turn back the clock on some of the events that had happened these few months.

Chichi laughed, "I guess it's the disease that runs through the Ezironye's lineage, we can't wait."

"Leave Raymond out of this, it's you we are talking about."

"Well I blame him, partly."

"Raymond couldn't have forced you to sleep with Mano."

"Gosh! I thought you were over him and you are quick to jump to his defence."

"I'm getting to that point; I must have that number but let's get to the bottom of this."

"Okay" Chichi agreed as she knew her best friend would figure a way out of this present predicament as she herself couldn't figure a way out.

"Did you do it once or you are still into it?"

Silence. Maybe Monisola was not wearing her professional counselling hat today as she expected a more logical attempt to solve the problem at hand.

"Ok forget I said that, very stupid of me, what do you want to do? What if you get pregnant?"

"I'm not that stupid, I'm on the pill and moreover I've tried to stop Monisola but I can't, I've just lost my sanity, sense of moral and all."

"I'm sure it's not that bad."

"Do you want to try it?"

This time it was Monisola's turn to be silent.

"Good! So, you better forget about Raymond's number because only GOD knows what is going to happen when you two meet."

"We are not going to see each other; I'm only going to talk with him. Moreover, he is married and there is no way I am crossing that line, adultery is not my portion in Jesus name."

"Fornication is my portion and if Jesus comes I am doomed" Chichi laughed huskily and Monisola could hear the despair in her voice.

"I think you better stop whatever is going on between the two of you, it's really cutting at your heart."

"And my soul and before you know it, I will be so wrapped up in it that I won't ... I won't know......"

Chichi cried and cried.

"I can't take this I'm coming over." Monisola scrunched her face, got up and looked for her car keys

"Please don't you will only make it worse."

"I'm not coming to shame you I'm only..."

"Please don't. Mano would not like it."

"What?"

"Ever since we ...we ... he's become so possessive, I can't be alone with another man, otherwise I'm seducing him. I can't call my friends or family they would interfere, honestly I don't know what to do."

"Leave him." Monisola stated firmly.

"What? After all these years and what I've done, I can't."

"Would you rather you lost just your virginity to him or lose your life?"

"What?" Chichi was shocked. She wondered which angle Monisola was evaluating her ideas from. Loose her life!

"I am going to be frank with you, I have seen a lot of cases like Mano, where the guy does not trust the girl because she made the biggest mistake of throwing up her legs for him to come in before a proper commitment of marriage and he thinks that is what she's going to do to every Tom, Dick and Harry she meets. He follows her about because the one thing he cannot do is to trust her. He is forever thinking if she did it with him then she can do it with anyone and GOD help her if he catches her looking at another man, she is as good as dead as he will kill because of lust and jealousy. Chiamaka I beg you call this thing off before it destroys both of you; GOD is willing to forgive you if you are willing to repent."

"What if he offers marriage?"

Monisola took a deep breath because she was sure Chichi already knew the answer to her own question.

"Has Mano asked you to marry him?"

"No, he doesn't even want to hear about it."

Monisola could not sleep that night, why on earth did Chichi get herself into this mess. To the ordinary eyes it wasn't a big deal, everyone sleeps around these days but she knew Chichi wasn't someone like that. Her friend is the kind of person whose heart was fully committed to GOD and His ways right from their secondary school days. Monisola often made fun of her and told her she'll end up in a convent. Something must have gone wrong somewhere but she wasn't sure where.

The next couple of weeks were busy for Monisola as she still had a lot of work to do from the time she had been away from the office. Usually she would have completed all her outstanding tasks, queries, research etc, the first week she returned but this time she was taking her time because her mental alertness was not as apt as it was and she needed time to recover. If only she could stop thinking about him. She didn't know it was this hard otherwise she wouldn't have allowed herself to fall in love with him in the first place. It was nothing compared to the love she felt for Omoniyi but then Omoniyi was her brother in every aspect of the word, Raymond was like a lover. Please GOD don't let me ever fall in love again, I don't want to go through this again. She laughed at herself and she was sure GOD was laughing with her because they both knew HE would not answer that prayer especially since it seemed HE was getting her prepared for something, something and not someone because she refused to think along that line.

She knew she had been putting off the inclination but she could no longer, so that afternoon she called his direct line in the office.

"Good afternoon, this is Ezekiel Ezironye speaking, how can I help?" Good she needed his help.

"Good aft....."

"Monisola!" he sucked his breath

"I ... Yes!" How did he know it was her?

"Can I call you back, please?"

"Okay .... I only..." The line went dead, well GOD you won't say I did not try, I obeyed oh! Even if it was late obedience. She wondered what she meant by late obedience. Jesus please help me, she pleaded.

Her phone rang and she slowly picked it up.

"Hi! Sorry I didn't want to use the office line and I also didn't want to be disturbed, how are you?"

How are you from Raymond and also sorry in the same sentence, GOD is working wonders.

"I'm good! And you and your wi.... family?"

"Adanna is good and would soon put to bed."

"By GOD's grace and she will deliver safely in Jesus name."

"Amen" he affirmed and waited for her to speak.

"I wanted to say I'm sorry for the way I treated you the last time. It was uncalled for; I should have been more courteous no matter what our differences were. I should have been more cordial, receptive. I just want you to know that I've forgiven you and I hope you will forgive me also."

There was an awkward silence between them.

"You are a true royal breed, you always maintain your grace and dignity no matter what and I know I deserved the treatment you accorded me, royalty or not you are also human and yes I forgive you."

"Thank you, I do appreciate that, I have to go now, I have a lot on my desk, my regards to your wi..."

"Monisola have you truly forgiven me?" Raymond interrupted her.

"Are you doubting my credibility?" Monisola asked, already regretting her decision to make things right between them.

"Monisola have you really forgiven me, honestly if I could turn back the clock, I would have waited and will still choose you, I still love you Monisola." Raymond said the last statement with a softness in his voice that Monisola had never heard before. However, it was too late and she not want to hear it.

"Raymond I've got to go."

"I need to hear you say it Monisola", his tone was getting forceful.

"Raymond I've forgiven you."

"Say it"

"Raymond, I've forgiven you and I'm trying to forget you."

"Say it!" he shouted. Not only was his voice forceful but it also had a richness of arrogance to it.

"Never! I will never say it." she stated adamantly.

"Then you will carry it in your bosom for the rest of your life."

"I hate you." Monisola whispered.

She heard him laugh and she ended the call.

"I love you Raymond but you will never hear it from me, that I promise you and I will not carry you or your love in my heart ever again."

She closed her eyes and tried hard not to cry. She had cried enough for Raymond and she was letting go.

Her mobile phone signalled a message received, she picked it.

"Monisola I know you love me and I will always do too."

She deleted the message and the number. She was even more determined she was getting over Raymond at all cost.

Life was getting better, she was sleeping and eating well, even thinking logically with minimal distractions but she still felt a prod in her heart. GOD what do you want from me. You asked me to forgive Raymond, I have, I've even called him twice after that, what again?

Few days later she knew the reason for the tug at her heart when her father called to let her know that he was in town. She welcomed him, asked after every one back home and after a few minutes said she had to go. The next day he called her several times but she refused to pick his calls and on the third day he came to her office to take her out for lunch. She refused. Before he left, he politely asked her to join him for dinner at one of her favourite restaurants he always took her to whenever he was in town, she agreed without any enthusiasm.

She met him at the restaurant and they went straight to the dining area to eat. He tried to make light conversation but she only answered in monosyllables. Eventually he asked her to join him in his country house but she made her excuses.

"Oluwamuiremiwa that's an order, I have tolerated enough of your silliness." Kabiyesi barked at her.

The driver drove them to the country house, which was a small but well decorated stately home and maintained by a resident housekeeper. Under normal circumstances Monisola would have been happy to be there but even the beauty of the surrounding did nothing to calm the rage that was brewing on the inside of her. Her silliness, tolerate? Who did he think he was?

Her father had a couple of things to do so he asked her to wait in his study and by the time he finally came down she was past caring if he was the king of the whole isles, she was livid with anger.

"Monisola Oluwamuiremiwa Oluwafiadekemi Omolabake Omo Adewunmi obirin to re wa, obirin bi okunrin meta....." her father started eulogising her.

"Please go straight to the point sir."

Her father sighed, he knew he had stepped on the toes of this little giant of his and he would have to brave himself to take all the arrows she shoots at him and hoped none would pierce his heart because no matter what, she is his daughter and he loves her.

"Your mother and I are very sorry that we have not come to see you since your brother passed on, even Ayaba Adekemi has been asking after you and enquiring about your wellbeing, your sisters...."

"Sir, I have asked you to go straight to the point." Monisola looked straight into her father's eyes with no emotion whatsoever.

Oluwa sanu mi, owo' re ni mo wa bayi o. GOD please help me with this my daughter, Kabiyesi prayed silently.

"Why have you not come home or even called?"

"I have a lot of work to do and I did speak to Olori and Ayaba."

"Ok, that is good; we all miss you especially since he passed on but....."

"I will be leaving at five past the hour sir."

Her father looked at the clock, he had precisely five minutes to talk or even less than that as she had said the word leave in five minutes and not give him five minutes. Well, she learnt all these from him and what he had sown he was now reaping. GOD why didn't this child come as a boy, I wouldn't be having this kind of conversation with a boy, we will just shake hands and that's it but with this one, GOD help him.

"Monisola why are you angry with me?" her father attempted to appease his daughter.

"I am not angry; I am raving mad at you." Monisola spiteful said in anger and rage.

Her father shuddered at the venomous words that came out of her mouth as well at the impact of its depth and intention. Oluwa gba mi o! GOD help me.

"What did I do?" her father asked innocently wondering if there was more to this matter that he was not aware of.

"You know exactly what you did; the right question you or rather I should be asking is why did you do it?"

Her father sighed deeply, he had to cross this river now or he would risk losing the love and respect from his daughter.

"I was protecting you, our heritage and inheritance, our interest to secure the throne", her father reached out for her but she moved away.

"Remember I asked you before and this time I want you to tell me the truth; which is more important to you, family or throne?"

This was not a yes or no answer, it went deeper. To affirm that it was family she would probe again and to deny the throne was to deny himself and what he stood for.

"Monisola it is not as easy as you think, the world is changing and thank GOD you are no more a child but a beautiful woman with wisdom so you have to apply wisdom...."

"Why did you hide Omoniyi's paternity from me?"

"It was for your own good", he replied firmly.

"How?" Monisola asked and took another step away from him.

He was not going to lose his daughter because of his past actions, so he moved closer.

"You can only assume the throne if there was no male heir. When Omoniyi came I decided to give you the opportunity I never had, to live your own life, free from all the dos and don'ts that comes with the title, I wanted my little flower to blossom in her own right."

"Even if you knew that Omoniyi and I loved each other?"

"That is why I made you take that oath. It was for your own good as a son will forever be a son nothing can change that, not even a DNA test"

"Who was Omoniyi's father?"

"Monisola, Omoniyi is my son no matter whose seed planted him in his mother's womb. I thought I could give him the life he never had the chance to live, the opportunity to be who.....better and greater than his biological father could give him. I tried Monisola ......what I did, I did because I wanted the best for you, best for Omoniyi........"

She looked at her father, GOD had indeed saved him from her wrath this night, for she was going to disown him but then how can one disown one's father. A father will always be your father as you carry his DNA, how much more GOD the owner of life Himself.

She ran to his open arms and they both cried.

"I am so sorry my daughter, I never meant to harm you, I only had your interest at heart."

"I understand now but it was painful."

"As much as Raymond?"

She went numb, how did her father know.

"I know little girl; I know, that's why I'm your father."

She smiled, now she was over Raymond for good. But there was still one more thing; she could feel it in her heart. O GOD what next!

CHAPTER FOUR

Things were getting to normal though she preferred the grace period GOD was giving her. She had learnt in her walk with the LORD over the years that there were different times and seasons in her life, sometimes HE carried her, and sometimes HE made her walk. There were seasons of grace where everything she asked for were granted, even unspoken words and there were times where HE seemed afar off and she stood alone. Most times her disobedience was the cause of the separation, sometimes it was trials and sometimes HE was teaching her how to soar on HIS wings, learn to be calm, be still and allow HIM to do what HE wants to do.

Such was the time now, she knew GOD was up to something but she just didn't know what and it was no use stretching her neck to see how or where or when, all she had to do was to stay calm and be still.

Everyone around her were getting ready for Christmas and were in the frenzy mood but she withdrew from all the activities in church, at work and she told her mother she wasn't coming home.

"Who are you spending Christmas with?" her mother asked

"No one."

"You want to spend Christmas all alone?"

"I've done it several times this won't be the first."

"Why don't you come home then and be around family."

"I'm sure you will all enjoy it without me."

"It won't be the same without Omoniyi, he made it so special for everyone even the workers, I can't think how this year will be."

"Just enjoy it and thank GOD for it."

"So, when are you coming home my daughter?"

"Olori I told you I am not; I need time to sort myself out."

"Are you still pining for him?" her mother landed with one of her questions that always threw her off balance.

"Who?" She asked with caution.

"The young man your father told me about, why didn't you tell me? I'm your mother but I am always the last to know anything about you."

"I didn't tell anyone about Raymond and I don't know how Kabiyesi knew."

"You know your father will always find out, so you have to be extraordinary careful."

"Are you hiding something from him?" Monisola asked as she heard the emphasis her mother placed on the word extraordinary. Her mother evaded her question and asked her routine question every time they spoke over the phone.

"Monisola, when are you going to give me grandchildren?"

"Shouldn't I get married first? Mother I am not ready for a relationship now; until GOD sort me out or I allow HIM, nothing is going to happen."

"I am praying for you."

"Thank you Ma."

"I love you my daughter."

"I love you too Mother."

She was finally completing most of her tasks at work and was hoping she would meet all her deadlines so she won't have to take any work home. Her plans were to rest and have time to herself, to pray, reflect and plan towards the New Year. She was still staring at the paperwork in front of her when Valerie popped into her office looking worried. Monisola groaned inwardly, what was it again.

"It's him again", Valerie said in an uptight manner.

"Him?"

"Daniel."

"Daniel?"

"Yes, the same Daniel that has been calling you forever and you refuse to pick or return his calls."

"I don't know any Daniel, what is his surname?"

"I don't know and he said you wouldn't know as he only introduced himself on first name basis."

"Valerie, please take a message."

Valerie came into the office, slammed the door and moved closer to her desk. Monisola heard the door slam, watched her move and was anticipating what she was about to do and what action she should take. However, the tone of her voice stopped her.

"Monisola, I have been taking messages from this guy and I am not about to take one more until you speak to him. He has called all the times I've told him to call, I've made up all excuses that I can for you;

I have even lied and asked for forgiveness every time. I am about to tell him you've gone to the moon and would be back next week, please don't make me do that or else I won't be able to look at him again."

"Has he been here?" Monisola asked bewildered.

"Back and forth ever since you returned from your trip to Nigeria."

Monisola looked at her, she knew Valerie sometimes did exaggerate a little bit and could give different versions of the same story and she wondered which version she was hearing now.

"Ok! Ok! We met for coffee once and we spoke about you."

"Me? Whatever for? When? Why?"

"Well he seemed like a nice guy when I first spoke to him and finally seeing him proved it. You need to ...."

"Hold on a minute, where exactly is this conversation leading to, I hope you are not trying to hook me up with this guy."

"He is not just a guy, he is Daniel, he knew your brother..."

"How do you expect me to believe that when my brother is not here to prove it?" she was getting upset now and her voice was shaking.

"Moni, please I didn't mean to upset you but you have to meet Daniel, I can't keep the charade anymore and once you get to know him for who he is, things will work out."

Monisola took a deep breath and tried to exhale slowly, she hoped she wasn't hearing what Valerie was saying and the context in which it was said. She had worked with Valerie for a while now and despite the 'friendship' between them she had tried to maintain a strict working relationship and she sincerely hoped she had not overstepped her boundary.

"Valerie please tell Mr Daniel to call me in exactly half an hour's time on my direct line and I would speak with him and I'll like to see you immediately after."

Valerie saw and noticed the change on Monisola's face and tone, boy was she in trouble, she had overstepped her boundary big time.

"Good afternoon" a male voice greeted Monisola as soon as she picked the call.

"Good afternoon Mr Daniel, how can I help you?"

"I've been trying to get in touch with you after the funeral and I just wanted to apologise for my abruptness on that day. I am so sorry I couldn't wait to talk with you that day, it was so emotional and I....."

"I'm sorry I don't understand, but who are you?" Monisola didn't want this conversation with an unknown face or identity to continue.

"I'm Daniel we met right after the funeral of your brother Omoniyi, you wanted to talk but I couldn't stay, I had to go"

"I'm sorry but I still don't remember but thank you for calling. I have to go now......" she wanted to end the call now.

"Monisola, please can I see you" his plea was soft but firm at the same time.

Monisola did not know what to make of the situation Valerie had roped her in but she decided she was going to change her PA there and then.

"Mr Daniel ..."

"Please call me Daniel, I need to see you and from what I've heard from Valerie you need to see me so we can talk ...."

"I don't want to see you and I will prefer you never call my office again; I do not have time for whatever you are proposing and as such it is best you forget whatever you've heard and ....."

"I will be in England later this week, I will see you on Thursday and then we can talk."

"I said I don't want to see you." Monisola shouted at him.

"I need to see you, I am still in shock and can't get over Omoniyi's dea...., I need to talk to someone about the loss of my brother and dearest friend; please Monisola just give me a bit of your time and I would never trouble you again."

Valerie had arranged the restaurant where they would meet and Monisola strictly told her it was a business meeting and she would be back within an hour. She was almost at the venue when she remembered she did not ask for his photograph or anything to recognise him with and they had agreed to meet at the foyer of the hotel where he was staying. Goodness what was she thinking of, that he would have a rose or bunch of flowers to identify himself; she was going to find someone to replace Valerie otherwise she will do something she did not want to do.

As she walked towards the foyer she quickly looked around to see if she would recognise anyone but didn't until she saw a figure get up from one of the seats and was walking towards her. For a second her heart literally stopped beating. It was him! It was the same figure she saw standing by the grave when Kayode came to lead her away from the resting place into the house, she didn't see who it was but she knew that he was a man, a very tall man. As he moved closer, she recognised it was the same man she had begged to stay with her when she was restless and had gone into the garden to seek solace and comfort, now the pieces of the puzzle were falling into place.

They stood facing each other for a while neither of them said anything but just looked.

He looked lean and his face had the strain of restlessness in him.

She looked lean and her face looked like everything around her was calm but her eyes told him otherwise.

"Thank you for coming."

"I remember you now."

"I'm sorry I couldn't wait that day I was very distraught."

"I understand."

"I know we've booked lunch but I don't want to eat, do you want to come up to my room...." he saw the look on her face. Of course, Princess Monisola would do no such thing. "I apologise Princess Monisola, how stupid of me, we'll go to the restaurant and I'll watch you eat."

She smiled for the first time and seemed to relax, "Actually I'm not hungry, can we take a walk?"

"Sure, if you don't mind leading, I hardly know anywhere."

"Where are you from, I mean where do you live?"

"I move around but my home base is in Chicago, shall we?"

"Aren't you going to get a coat?"

"A coat?" he asked absent minded.

"It's cold out there even if it's not as cold as Chicago but I'm sure you won't want to catch a cold, please get your coat, hat, gloves and scarf, I'll wait here for you."

"Yes, your royal highness."

"I'm Monisola Adewunmi."

"I'm Daniel Benjamin, I'm grateful to meet you at last."

It was meant to be a brief walk and talk but they had been talking for well over an hour and had almost walked the length and breadth of Hyde park.

"Can we sit down please?" Monisola asked.

"I'm sorry I forgot my manners, please forgive me."

"It's not your fault I should have worn my trainers or some sensible shoes. I thought I was only going to spend half an hour."

He smiled and for the first time she noticed his shiny white teeth in contrast to his black velvet skin; his face was quite handsome.

"Do you want to leave now?" his voice broke her journey of thought about his physique. She felt shy and stupid at the same time especially when she remembered she had refused to speak to him.

"Honestly no, I wish I could stay but I have to get back to work, can I see you again?"

He shook his head.

"I'm sorry, I don't mean to impose myself on you." Monisola was cross with herself for asking such questions. Decorum! Her brain screamed.

"It would be an honour your highness but I would be leaving tomorrow morning" he stated with a hint of disappointment.

"Was it a business meeting you came for?"

"Yes, but that ended three days ago, I was hoping to spend the rest of my time with you to talk."

"I'm so sorry honestly I didn't remember who Daniel was and I thought Valerie was making things up."

"Valerie, how could I ever thank that lovely, patient and kind young lady, I do owe her for putting up with my desperation."

"Were you that desperate?"

"Yes, I was trying to be very chivalrous by not storming into your office and demanding your attention. Honestly you don't know how much I appreciate this; I can now get on with life and thank GOD for the memories I have of him."

"I'm glad to be of help."

There was an awkward moment and silence between them.

"Can I be of help?"

She looked at him and wondered what he meant by that.

"Can I help you the same way you have helped me, I'll try if I know how but you have to let go."

"I don't understand you."

For the first time ever, he broke his own work ethics and code of conduct, he held her hands and looked into her eyes, "I want to help you if you will allow me, to go through your grieving and healing process through GOD's grace, mercy and love."

She did not have a clue of what he was saying.

"Monisola I know you are still grieving for your brother and only if you allow GOD to take the pain and hurt, then you can receive love, joy and peace in that area just as you have been here for me today, please Oluwamuiremiwa let me help you."

"How do you know my name?"

"I know more about you than you know about me, you have always been the topic of discussion between Omoniyi and I, he never stopped talking about you."

Now she was scared. "I have to go."

He let go of her hands and they walked back to his hotel where she got a taxi back to work.

Christmas day came and went, Monisola was thankful for the time she spent by herself as it seemed she had become a total stranger and did not know who she was again. She searched her soul, to question herself and all around her. She remembered that song about standing and turning to her Maker and asking HIM all about life's questions and sorrow. She took that step she had been afraid to take and asked GOD why Omoniyi had to die, had she stayed and not gone home would he still be alive? Why? Why? Why? When she did not hear anything but was so overwhelmed she began to cry, she cried and cried. A few days after, she was washing her mug when her telephone rang, it was Daniel, she didn't want to answer it but she had to, to thank him for the gifts he sent to her for Christmas though she wondered how he got to know her address.

"Hi Mr Daniel."

"Good afternoon Princess Monisola."

"Good evening sir."

"Why the sir?"

"If you keep calling me princess, I will be formal with you, Monisola will do just fine."

"Yes, your royal highness."

"Thank you for the gifts."

"Do you like them?"

"Does it matter?"

"Well I'll like to give you what you like not just anything."

"I don't want anything from you."

"Why?"

"I don't really know you and I haven't done anything to deserve the gifts."

He laughed if only she knew.

"GOD gave His only begotten son because He loved us whether we deserved Him or not, I give people I love gifts especially those that are precious to me and as Omoniyi's sister you are precious to me."

This was what she had been thinking about after she met him, she didn't want a tie with him because of Omoniyi or anything, she just wants to be left alone.

"I don't think I want you giving me gifts and I don't want us together because of the past."

"I don't understand you?"

"My meeting you is because of Omoniyi, he ... he is in the past and I know I will see him in eternity but for now I just want to be alone."

"I see."

"Please don't misunderstand me I...."

"I understand you very well, I won't bother you again, good bye."

That was easy she thought as she put the phone down, she liked it that way but she wondered why the tug in her own heart.

This page has been left intentionally blank

CHAPTER FIVE

Monisola put all her effort into her work and by Spring she knew she had covered all grounds and was ready to plough into more but she restrained herself for two reasons. First, she did not want to start on any new project and secondly she was still finding and discovering herself.

She was looking into the little, little things in life that could make a difference. A smile, a thank you, a request with a please and meaning it, a compliment, all which she did before but now with a difference. Taking time to talk to people and finding out how they really were and not the casual 'hello' and 'how are you' pattern.

She was more inclined to the elderly, her neighbours, people in the community, her parents, family, people in church. She had begun to pray and ask GOD to open her eyes to the area where HE wanted her to function as she had heard her team leader in her church group talked about GOD's calling into ministry and gifts of the Holy Spirit. The calling wasn't necessary to preach or be a pastor but that unique gift that GOD has given to everyone to function in the body of Christ and world at large. She had been reading and meditating on the book of first Corinthians in the bible and chapter twelve had been one of great emphasis to her. She knew definitively she wasn't called to be an apostle, prophet, teacher, evangelist, thank GOD for that; not that there was anything wrong with them but she just didn't see herself in those roles. What then was her calling or gifting? She took time to pray and asked GOD to show her, when HE did not answer immediately she gave it a rest and knew GOD was up to something again. Please LORD don't let it be another lesson, heart or soul wrenching exercise, I can't take any more. I'm still recovering from the last one we did and I don't want to struggle with you anymore I just want you to have your way.

As soon as she completed her team induction classes in church, she was posted to the usher's team and she hated it. She just did not have it in her to stand and direct people to their seats and then remain standing throughout the service. Although she encountered some difficult members of the congregation, she was able to use a bit of diplomacy to resolve whatever the issues were.

After two weeks she knew this wasn't her area of calling or whatever terminology it was, and she wanted out. She made the mistake of telling the leader of the ushers' team, who concluded that it was GOD testing her ability to be humble and serve others. She didn't have a problem with serving others and of course as a human being she still had an element of pride in her but she just didn't want to be an usher! She was meant to be in the team for three months and honestly could not see herself surviving the three months without a hitch with the team leader. She decided to boycott going to service all together. And what was her excuse? She was busy at work when she practically had nothing to do. On one of the Sundays she decided to call Raymond and they got talking and when the conversation started to lead her astray she ended it. Indeed, an idle mind was the devil's workshop. She prayed and asked GOD to forgive her and went back to church.

The ushers' leader thought it was time to teach her how to humble herself before GOD and man. Well, she had no problem with GOD, as she either humbled herself or HE would do it Himself, and as for man, she had no problem with some of them too. Neither did she have a problem when she was posted to the overflow section which was not within the main auditorium but a separate hall with a mixture of nursing mothers, toddlers, people with wheelchair for easy access and perpetual latecomers.

The first thing she noted at the first pandemonium service was a mixture of noise, cries, argument and battle for space. There were some people who wanted to sit in the main hall and in the front row but came late to church when it was a quarter of a minute to saying the grace and ending the service. When such people were directed to the overflow, they came in grumbling and were hard faced. She decided to do something about the situation, she thought of making the hall more spacious and dividing the area into various sections. She asked for help from some of her team members, some of the male ushers in the main auditorium who looked hefty and fit for the job, as well as those perpetual latecomers and they were to arrange everything the night before the next service. They all came but most of the males complained and murmured about missing the football match on TV. After everything was set, Monisola surprised them with a buffet and drinks which had been prepared by some of the ladies. The guys roared with Hallelujahs and soon settled down to eat and watched the games as well as having a bit of time socialising. Ifeanyi who was her team leader in the training class, came to her shaking his head in disbelief and looking around at the transformation.

"Monisola you are one heck of a girl; how did you get all these arranged"

"It's easy, I just practised what you taught me." Monisola beamed with delight as she looked around her, pleased with the outcome.

"When did I teach you all these, I can assure you that ushering, networking and hall decoration were not part of my class notes." She laughed, "O yes they are - the gifts of the Holy Spirit, the ministry of helps, encouraging and all, the Holy Spirit just helped me see who was the best fit for each task and all I had to do was ask; though I haven't figured out what to do with the latecomers."

"What latecomers?" Toyin, Ifeanyi's wife asked as she joined them in the conversation.

"Some of the guys here and others who come after the grace has been said", her husband laughed.

His wife looked at him, mumbled and turned to Monisola, "The same thing our team leader here was taught."

Monisola looked from husband to wife and was at a loss of what innuendo she had just missed.

"Okay! Okay! I confess, I was a perpetual latecomer before I was delivered."

Monisola could not believe her ears and had to blink twice. Impeccable, easy going Ifeanyi! Impossible!

"What do you suggest then?" she asked.

"I can't think of anything now, maybe later." He walked away knowing his impeccable image had been tarnished in the eyes of his students. Well no one is perfect he consoled himself.

"What about a small desk over there to sell the tapes of the messages they've missed and some books especially those on punctuality?" one of the ladies suggested.

Someone laughed and stated that wouldn't get him up early from his bed on a Sunday morning as it was his day of rest, as he worked six days a week.

"I'm sure we would think of something to do."

The next day it was a moment of surprise each time someone came in, the transformation caught them unawares. The section for women with babies was at the far corner with a room for them to breast feed and also change dirty nappies; it also had a television screen for them to watch the service. Next to that was the toddler section which had a play mat and some toys and books which had been donated by mothers whose children had outgrown them.

The wheelchair section was nearer the exit and this made it easy for users to access the building where they could just stay in their chair or join the congregation, the choice was theirs. The late comers were directed either to the middle or the back seats which reduced any disruption during service. At the end of the service the ushers stood at the three exits directing people out of the hall which also reduced the traffic and tension at the end of service.

"Yes! We did it" the six ushers came together to thank GOD and congratulate each other.

"Wow, what a delight to end service without feeling the drain out of you but actually feel refreshed"

"I might stay in this team if this is how service will be every Sunday" Monisola quickly counted herself out of that thought. No way!

At work while her colleagues and teams were submitting proposal for their project fields, she occupied herself with research and what she termed home run, simply put she wasn't venturing out of her locality. Sheila ignored her completely and Mark was disappointed, but there was nothing he could do she had made her mind up. She thought of projects she could research on just in case she was called upon last minute but her mind was not in it so she shelved it for another time. The next Sunday she made friends with a young man, a visitor to the church who came in a wheelchair. He was struggling to get in so she ran to his aid, helped him and made sure he was comfortable. She left him to attend to one of the toddlers who was learning the skills of getting one's attention and making one run at her beck and call. She had told Sarah who was just eighteen months not to move near the radiators but each time Monisola moved away she would quickly go there and stick one of the toys there.

"Sarah, has anyone ever told you about the law of jurisdiction? In lay man's language it means I hold the authority around this section and the number one rule is do not come here, stay in your toddler's section and stop putting toys in the radiator. Didn't anyone inform you of the rules?"

The little girl shook her head looking bewildered as if she understood.

"Alright then I'll pardon you just this once but not again otherwise I advise you to get a lawyer."

"Don't worry Sarah I'll be your legal representative."

Monisola turned to see who overheard her conversation with the little girl; it was the guy in the wheelchair whom she had helped.

"I didn't mean any of the things I said", Monisola apologised profusely.

"I know but I wonder who I will represent, the little girl or the very sweet and beautiful lady."

Monisola was thankful someone called for her attention as she was embarrassed by the comment, she asked to be excused and went to see what was required. After the service while everyone was going out of the hall, she noticed the young man was still sitting in his wheelchair and did not make any attempt to move, she walked towards him and as soon as he saw her he smiled.

"Did you enjoy the service sir"

"Yes, I did especially in the likelihood of a job offer from Sarah or yourself, Miss....?"

"I'm Monisola."

"Monisola, what a beautiful and unusual name; my name is Andrew, I'm pleased to meet you", he offered her a handshake.

She took it smiling but when she heard the next sentence the smile disappeared and she withdrew her hands.

"Has anyone told you, you look so beautiful and sexy", when he saw her reaction, he laughed, "Come on don't tell me that is not one of the compliments you've been dying to hear, honestly we need to meet up and let me show you how good a man I can be as this wheelchair is no barrier to what actions I can perform in bed."

Monisola was shocked that she opened her mouth and could not say a word. However, she quickly recovered and gave him a short future snap of his life if he ever opened his oral cavity to utter such profane words in the house of GOD or ever dared to voice any of his filthy imagination to her again. She would make sure that not only does he remain in the wheelchair for the rest of his life but his mouth would be tied to it.

"I hope my brother has not been giving you any trouble."

Monisola turned to see another version of Andrew standing right behind her.

She couldn't say a word at first because she was so upset but she shook her head.

"Please I do apologise on his behalf he can be nasty at times but he really does not mean any harm."

Monisola looked at Andrew, yeah right, harmless boy my foot, he knew exactly what he was saying and meant them.

"It's all right I have to go, please excuse me."

"See you next Sunday, sexy legs."

She heard his brother telling him to behave and Monisola knew she had trouble in her hands. GOD I told you I didn't want to be an usher; see the troublemaker I have to deal with now."

She had completely forgotten about Andrew all through the week until Saturday night when she was planning what to wear to church. Firstly, she hated the so-called uniformity within the ushers' team. She didn't want to dress like every other person and definitely did not want to wear the different colour combination every Sunday, what happened to jeans and a white shirt and trainers. She knew she was kidding herself about the likelihood of disregarding the uniformity dress code but she was getting fed up with it. Secondly no matter what she wore her designer tailored made clothes fitted her perfectly as most of them were her work clothes and since she had to dress professionally from

Monday to Friday, she wanted to dress down Saturday to Sunday if she had her way. Going back to Andrew, she wished she had a long skirt, baggy shirt and tied her head and ears with a scarf; she groaned and went to iron something suitable.

Andrew came late and he almost distracted the service but since she was not serving in the area she looked away and concentrated on her section and duties. After the service he came to her.

"Are you still mad at me?" he asked as he moved towards her.

"No."

"Why have you been avoiding me and looking so serious throughout the service, your countenance alone was about to crack the walls."

Monisola asked GOD for help before she gave him another tongue-lashing comment. When she didn't say anything, he laughed.

"Cat got your tongue or you ran out of sermons? Monisola please say something and make my day and I'll have something to make me laugh for the rest of the week until next Sunday."

She turned to him and for the first time felt sorry for him.

"Please don't feel sorry for me I hate it when people do that."

"I'm sorry, it's just that ...what about your friends and family?"

"I don't have friends, they all deserted me after the accidents and well my brother has a lot on his plate and can't possible add me to his list."

They got talking and he told Monisola about how he ended up in a wheelchair as a result of an accident which was not a fault of his but he happened to be a passenger in a car which got hit by a truck, the setback he's had and thoughts of facing a bleak future.

"I don't understand."

"I don't have anyone to take care of me; in fact, I don't want anybody,

I just want to be on my own."

"You do need help and what about your brother, can't he help?"

"He's more concerned about his wedding and I don't blame him especially when he had to delay it after the accident. I'm at my wits end, I live with my brother, he will be getting married soon, I don't want to live with them but I have no one to help me."

Monisola sighed, maybe this was her home run project but then she remembered the comments he made about her and that was an area of concern for her.

"Don't worry I won't bother you again, I know everyone has their own problem, I don't want to be a burden to anyone but I just feel I should talk to someone; I guess I saw a friendly face in you and you are a very ……"

She shot him a piercing look he laughed and continued, "…. a very lovely sweet sister that can take a guy's mind off his worries and make him laugh and please don't try to stop being yourself because of the comments I make, I just say them to make myself happy and you are beautiful and ... you know what I mean."

Monisola took a deep breath and smiled but then changed her smile into a frown. She decided there and then she would help him though she didn't know how and she hoped GOD would show her how.

"Do you have a phone I could call you on?"

"Phone, Sexy M wants to call me; coming to church wasn't a bad idea after all."

"Is that why you come to church, to chat girls up?"

"What I come to church to do is none of your business; everyone has their own agenda, myself inclusive so mind your business."

She almost changed her mind again; he did have a sharp tongue and she hoped he could tame it at least while she was around him.

"I would like to do something to help if you don't mind but you have to promise me not to call me..."

"Sexy M, I don't care if you want to help me or not I will call you what you are, beautiful, sexy, pretty, sweetie, enchanting, want to hear more?"

"Honestly no, can I just have your number."

"Why do you want my number?"

She was getting fed up now, she was offering help and yet he was being smug, she got up to go.

He didn't stop her; she walked a few yards before she turned and walked back to him.

"You are making it difficult for me to help you."

"If help does not come from you, GOD will send another help and I will wait."

Monisola smiled, now she knew the kind of person she was dealing with.

"Okay I am willing to help on one condition."

"Your condition or GOD's condition Sexy M?"

"GOD's condition is for me to help you and I also have my condition, which is watch your mouth boy or I deal with you."

"I like that but then why should I, it's a free country and I have the right to express myself, Sexy M."

"I'm warning you."

"I'm quivering."

They laughed and they talked more.

Monday morning, she was already in the office by seven o'clock and by the time Valerie came in at nine she had a list of telephone numbers to call, places to visit and stuff to do, she was very excited and ready to get to work.

"You seem so excited", Valerie said as she came in to Monisola's office, looking at her and wondering if the old Monisola was back.

Monisola laughed, yes she was, but since the Daniel episode she had kept business, strictly business until now, well this was a home run for her, all she wanted her to do was a few calls to some of their clients and problem solved.

She also met Andrew's brother, Peter, during the week and things were sorted. She was eager to see Andrew on Sunday, surprise him and hopefully he would be too dumbfounded to speak but she doubted that, she would have to wait to find out.

On Saturday night, she was getting ready for church the next day and preparing for the week ahead when she received a call from her father, her mother had been admitted to the hospital and he wanted her to come and see her as it was urgent. Her fears grew worse when he said she was in Switzerland. Monisola knew her mother only went to Zurich when she wanted a break from everyone. GOD please whatever it takes don't let anything happen to my mother, please just let her live. She quickly sent messages to Mark and Valerie, telling them she had a family emergency to attend to. She asked Peter and Ifeanyi to continue with the surprise for Andrew and lastly for some reasons unknown to her she sent a message to Daniel that she just received an urgent message regarding her mother and she just wanted him to know. That was dumb she said to herself but still sent it anyway. Early Sunday morning she was already on her way to the airport to board a flight to Zurich, she prayed all the way, asking GOD to be with her on this journey and to return safely with good news. When she got to Zurich she quickly boarded a train to take her straight to the hospital and as she walked into the hospital she remembered the last time she was in one and what the outcome was. Please GOD, help me, I don't want another member of my family to die, please heal my mother.

She was directed by a nurse to where her mother was. One word she would ever live to remember Heidi for was Krankenschwester; if she refused to do anything one mention of *Krankenschwester* was enough to get her attention as she had a fear of them ever since she got an injection from a nurse, it was a very painful experience. Each step she took towards the room seemed to weigh her down. What was she going to find out when she entered the room, another life ebbing away? Her mother was still young and she was her closest family. She realised the longer she dragged her feet the longer the delay in finding out what was going on.

Her mother was in the room alright but not on the bed which seemed as if no one had laid on it, she was standing by the window starring into space. She walked towards her and it was only when she touched her mother's arm did she realise someone was in the room.

"Mother" Monisola called softly, trying to keep a steady hold.

She turned to look at Monisola and sighed heavily.

GOD please I'm begging, please. Monisola silently prayed again.

"Mother are you alright?"

"I'm fine", her mother answered, making an attempt to smile.

"What happened?"

"Ni bo ni mo ti fe bere bayi, where do I want to start from?"

"The beginning would do."

Their conversation was interrupted when a nurse came in; she smiled when she saw Monisola. She asked her mother if she was her sister, she shook her head smiled and introduced Monisola as her daughter. She blinked twice and said they could easily pass for sisters.

There were no concerns from the series of tests done so her mother was discharged and as soon as they left the hospital she told Monisola she didn't want to go home.

"Why?" Monisola asked baffled at her mother's request.

"I want to go somewhere I can think", her mother clasped her head in hands and shook it.

"Mother if I heard correctly, the nurse said you should take it easy and not stress yourself, we should go home straight away and have you in bed resting"

"Rest? Monisola ina jo mi oni ki ma rest, I'm on fire how can I rest?" Her mother started to cry and without any delay Monisola bundled her into a cab and headed straight home. On hindsight she wished she had tried to be patient with her mother and probed further because as soon as they got to the house, fire indeed was burning.

Her father was there in the house and so was another young man.

She looked from her mother to her father and then to the young man, she dread what the explanation was going to be, but thank GOD, no one was dying though she wasn't sure if her father was not about to send someone to an early grave with the look on his face.

"I have been waiting for twelve hours, start talking."

"Father I think Mother needs to rest, the nurse said ....."

"I can see you are part of the conspiracy; I should have known, like mother like daughter."

Monisola stepped back, her father was blaming her for something she did not even know about. GOD thank you for keeping my mother alive, do I handle this matter or should I let go and You have your way, because I'm getting irritated now, Monisola silently prayed.

She left her carry case in the living room and went to the bathroom; she washed her face and sat on the edge of the bath. What was going on with her family, it had been one thing after the other recently, maybe she should just leave them to sort out their problems themselves and live her life. She shrugged, her mother needed her this moment and she would stand by her or should she, judging by what she saw downstairs, her mother was the guilty party but then who knew the story behind it, she might have had no choice hence the consequence of what she did.

Monisola went back to the living room, everyone was seated miles apart and no one was talking, at least she did not miss any part of the conversation yet.

"Would anyone like tea or coffee?"

No one answered. She went into the kitchen, made herself coffee and took it to the room.

"Mother I think you should start talking" Monisola decided to break the silence in the room.

"Does anyone have a recorder; I want everything recorded and documented." her father stated categorically.

No one answered him and his statement made her mother defiant and she began to speak.

"I never intended for this to happen but it has happened and to be sincere I am happy how this has turned out, though not all will agree with me. It happened right after you were born" she turned to Monisola who for the life of her could not understand.

"In fact, before then", her mother continued. "I was the wife of Zachariah Omoloba the heir apparent and a successful Engineer and as such I was to be pampered, well cared for and lavished with gifts. I wasn't brought up that way; I was the daughter of a hardworking farmer who was brought up with the ethos of working for a living and believed in the saying that the idle mind was the devil's workshop. For a while, I allowed all the attention, lavishing and pampering, eventually I got bored and wanted something to keep me busy. Thank GOD I got pregnant and I was looking forward to the joy of motherhood. As soon as Monisola arrived, apart from the first few weeks I did not have my daughter to myself; it was either Iya Oba your grandmother was there or some relatives or nursing maids. The only time I practically spent with you were when I was breast feeding you or if I got the chance to change a nappy or bathe you. I know to some women I may sound ungrateful but please tell me what the joy of motherhood is, if you cannot nurture the child you carried in your womb for good nine months.

I tried to get pregnant again but didn't and I was told not to worry. However, that soon changed when your grandfather died, my husband became Oba and of course the future had to be secured so a male heir had to be produced though you also had the equal opportunity to rule after your father. I guess my husband soon became engaged more in the affairs of his people as should be expected of an Oba and with all the new development going on, the issue of an heir rested a bit.

However, things took a different turn after I still couldn't get pregnant and by and by my husband married a second wife, Omoniyi then came on the scene but I took everything in my strides. It was painful but who was I to complain. I occupied myself with different things, home affairs, women affairs, children wellbeing and all. However, when Kabiyesi decided that Monisola was to be taken away to live in another country and brought up by a total stranger I was distraught; in fact, I went mad. My daughter was the victim and yet she was the one being punished. I was left with Ayaba and her two daughters both of whom I cared for as my own, including Omoniyi. I had no choice and as a mother I couldn't help but care for them. Soon after the birth of Morolake I decided I wanted to study and find something to do and I came here to Switzerland; England naturally was my first choice as my daughter was there but your father did not allow me as he did not want me to disrupt my daughter's life, in what way I do not know but I obeyed his command. He paid me a surprise visit during my first year and one thing led to another and it wasn't until two months after he had left, did I realise I was pregnant. My first instinct was to call him and let him know but a voice told me why should I, do I want this one to be taken from me as well. I didn't think of that statement at that time but during my holiday I wanted to spend time with Monisola my own daughter and your father refused. In fact, I wasn't allowed to see you, I was right at the gate of the house but Heidi said Zachariah left strict instructions for Monisola's lifestyle not to be disrupted. I thought it was a joke, I called Kabiyesi and he confirmed it and he also warned me. There and then I decided this child I was carrying was my own and I would nurse and nurture him alone.

Things were going on well with Toluwanimi and I, motherhood was what I had expected it to be though my heart longed to tell Monisola of her baby brother but I couldn't. When he was seven years old Kabiyesi suddenly remembered he had an Olori and he wanted me to come back. Yes, I had been home for a few weeks when Toluwanimi was three or so but I knew I couldn't risk taking him home so I was desperate and began to look for a way out. Monisola was in a boarding school then, Heidi was no longer required and I think she wanted to move closer home so I offered her a proposition to take care of Toluwanimi for me until I could sort myself out. I also left one instruction that on no account should Toluwanimi's life, routine, education, be disrupted by anyone one else other than me."

Monisola heard her father take a deep breath and sighed, she smiled, it was just the beginning of numerous ones to come. She looked at her brother, her very own brother, from the same loins and womb; she got up, walked to him and embraced him. They both cried and laughed. "Toluwanimi."

"Egbon mi, inu mi dun lati ri yin layo ati alafia."

Monisola was shocked at the fluency and proper indigenous accent from him; even she could not speak with such ingenuity. She smiled; her mother had done a thorough job however she did it. She went to her mother and hugged her, her mother sobbed and cried, it was like releasing a dam that had been locked up for years. They both cried and laughed. She took her brother's hand and they went into the kitchen, it was time to leave the two alone. The problem at hand was before their time and it was only those at the genesis that could resolve their issues and differences, right now she was starving, she needed food.

———

Monisola returned to work on Wednesday and when she got to church on Sunday she found out how the surprise for Andrew had turned out.

"Sexy M you are one heck of a girl, how on earth did you pull all those strings and got me a house of my own."

"With GOD all things are possible, never underestimate the power of Jehovah."

"I don't. I just wonder why he choose you to carry out this one mission that seemed impossible to everyone else. Do you know how many times I've knocked the same doors you have knocked and received rejections? 'Sorry you don't qualify', 'Sorry we cannot accommodate you at the moment', how did you do it?"

"You only knocked, I pushed."

Andrew looked at her hard and long and then laughed.

"I knew you were special the minute I set my eyes on you, marry me."

She wasn't taken by surprise and wasn't offended because she knew he was saying it genuinely.

"I can't" she answered softly with tears in her eyes.

"Why?"

"I'm not into this marrying thing again, I've had enough" she blinked back the tears.

"One bitter experience ..."

"Please let's leave it at that, I don't want to talk about it. How is your new place?"

"Is it because I'm lame?" his lips quavered as he spoke.

"No and we both know it takes more for a marriage to survive than prowess in bed and I'm positive that you are not lacking in that area", she winked at him.

"Honestly I think I've fallen in love with you Monisola."

"Please don't", she begged him.

"I don't want your pity I want your love."

"I can't."

"Can you at least try?"

She moved away from him.

"At least give me a chance later or even ten years' time, I'll still wait."

She laughed; Andrew is willing to wait while Raymond couldn't wait. Life was just too complex.

"Even if you wait forever, it would never be, I can't."

"OK I'll stop calling you Sexy M, I'll even work hard to provide for you, I'll do anything to have your love Sexy M."

She laughed, "We both know you can but remember what you told me, be who I am and I don't want you to change either and all those compliments from a younger man is sure enough to make a woman's head swell with pride."

"I guess not yours and who told you I'm younger, how old do you think I am and if I may ask how old or how young are you?"

"I'm nearing my thirties."

"I turned thirty-two last year."

She took a double look at him he still did not look thirty. "How old is your brother?"

"I am four years older than Peter."

"I thought he was your older brother."

"It was Andrew Jesus called first and then Peter"

She laughed, "Honestly be serious."

"I am older." he insisted.

"But you don't look it."

"Taking a complement from a young beautiful lady like you should make any guy's head swell but I think mine is about to burst, marry me Monisola."

She shook her head.

"I'll like to know the brute's name and I'll shoot him for spoiling my chances with you."

"You never had a chance especially with that tongue of yours. No, I'm only joking, it's me I am not willing to go that road again."

"Are you insane, you do not want to get married?"

"I'm not even considering dating."

"I'll pray for you."

"Thank you, that's the nicest thing I've heard you say to me."

"Apart from you being sexy, curves in the right places, tormenting me in my dreams and making me wake up in the middle of the night sweating and ...."

"Oh, just shut up and let's go see this new place of yours", Monisola interrupted him before he said any more.

"Good, maybe you can help me, I have been having a fit trying to let my decorator know that I want a living room very masculine in features and design but the bedroom very feminine and attractive and she has a problem with that, which I don't understand. Who says a guy can't have his bedroom walls painted pink or purple, GOD did not state any colour is masculine or feminine, it's all human perception and discrimination that caused it in the first place, all I want is my room painted......"?

Monisola shook her head, this guy was one heck of trouble alright, pink or purple walls, even the thought made her shudder.

The house was being renovated but they had access to it and from what Andrew was telling her, he had a very good sense of design and he had also thought about everything that would make life easier for him without being dependent on anyone. He was trying to describe something to her when her phone rang. Her heart skipped a beat; she hoped her parents were okay.

"Hello" she answered the phone and at the same time trying to picture in her mind what Andrew was telling her.

"Monisola how are you, you left a message on my phone. Sorry I just flew in today and didn't get your message until now, how is your mother?"

"Daniel?"

"Yes, your royal highness."

"Hi, I thought you didn't want to pick my calls so I assumed ...."

"You did not want my calls so I backed off. Is your mother alright?"

"Can I call you when I get home? I'm with a client at the moment."

"Sure, but on this number this is my main line."

"Ok, I'll speak with you later, thank you for calling."

He ended the conversation and did not bother to say anything. Well it was her fault for sending that message to him.

"Are you alright?"

Andrew. She had forgotten about him.

"I'm sorry, I ...."

"Forgot where you were."

"Sorry, I'm here now."

"Is he the one ...."

"Please I don't want to talk about that."

They got talking, he told her what he wanted, she made some suggestions but he was still adamant.

"Do you know you are hard to please?"

"I'm not it's just people who are stereotyped and cannot think outside the box."

"Ok if you paint this area this shade and your girlfriend or wife does not like it what would you do?"

"I don't have a girlfriend and if I do have a wife whom I hope will be you, I'll change it."

"Andrew, please be serious."

"I am."

"I'm having a headache do you have pain killers or something I can take?"

"The bedroom is over there .... and I know a few tricks that can sort out the headache."

Monisola picked up her bag and was moving towards the door.

"Please don't go, I promise I will not open my lousy filthy mouth to say such things but at least I can enjoy my thoughts."

She opened the door.

"Okay! Okay! I will bring my mind under the subjection of the Holy Spirit and Christ."

She took another step to go out.

"Monisola for the love of GOD please don't go, just help me sort the finishing design and I still need a lift back home."

She went out and returned with a sticky tape, sealed his mouth and gave him a pencil and paper to communicate.

What did he write?

"Dear GOD,

Thank you for this divine platform to communicate with Monisola AKA Sexy M, I'm still in love with her but she won't just budge. Right now, I just want her to help me with my interior decoration and hopefully drop me at my brother's house otherwise I will have to crawl all the way home, which by the way is just a few streets from here.

Also, for the guy that ruined my chances with Sexy M please GOD sort him out if you haven't done so already.

The invitation to my bedroom is still open as I have some pain killers and snacks which she can eat before taking the pill so that I don't become responsible for the pregnancy she is nursing in her mind against me.

Monisola renew your mind, to the pure all things are pure."

She laughed and laughed and whacked the paper on his head. He shook his head, mumbled something and lifted up his hands as a plea to GOD. She slowly removed the sticky tape and kissed him on the cheek. "You are such a clown; I wished I had met you before ....."

"You would not have liked me then and anyway who said I would even give you a second glance after all there are lots of pretty chicks out there"

"Are you always this mouthy"

"I was worse, you are looking at the redefined me, saved by the blood and name of JESUS. Alleluia! Glory!"

Later on, when she got home she still had that headache and she wondered if she had let Andrew wore her out with his jokes and all, as he continued when she took him home and they had lunch with his brother and his fiancée. They were so much at home with each other, she wondered why he felt the need for the space but then it was better at least everyone had their space and peace of mind. She was getting into bed when she remembered she had not call Daniel, she wasn't in the mood so she slept.

She was half way through the week when she realised Daniel had not bothered to call her. Shouldn't he be concerned about her? Monisola hesitated and thought to herself, since when did she become his responsibility. Frankly she wasn't sure what tricks her mind was playing on her but she wanted it to stop and to do just that she made a phone call to Chichi.

"Hello Chic" she called as soon as her friend picked up her phone.

"Hi" her voice was low.

"Am I disturbing something going on?"

"I don't know what you mean but I'm fine."

"But you sound so low."

"I just woke up."

"Didn't you go to work today?"

"I did."

"So why are you sleeping at seven o'clock in the evening?"

"Good question. Have you ever heard of the word T.I.R.E.D before?"

"Don't use that tone with me young lady, I am not one of your class pupils, honestly I don't know why you are still teaching when you can make a better life for yourself."

"Who told you I want a better life for myself. This is the life I want to live and may I remind you, you suggested teaching."

"Yes, for one-year trial and you have been at it since."

"Look Monisola, we can't all be like you, princess royal, bank full of money and an exciting job that takes you round the world all year round..."

"To the most deprived areas and poverty-stricken places, may I remind you Miss Nwabueze."

"Yeah right and a fat cheque to show for it."

"Pick on something else I know you are in your funny mood; how is Mano, I hardly see him these days."

"Monisola I have to go."

"Chichi don't you dare drop the phone on me, I said where is Mano?"

"I believe you know where he lives."

"I'm sorry, what happened?"

"Who told you anything happened you talebearer, I said you know where he lives as I live in my house."

"But you said .... never mind I'll speak to you another time"

"Now you are going to drop the phone on me?"

"Chiamaka what exactly is the matter with you?"

"Nothing", she snapped.

"Fine! Bye" Monisola snapped back.

CHAPTER SIX

"Y"ou didn't call me."

"You said you were going to call."

"Anything might have happened to me and you wouldn't know."

"I'm sure nothing will happen to you or any member of your family in Jesus name."

"Amen. Why didn't you call?"

He kept quiet for a while, then asked her what had been on his mind.

"Monisola what do you want from me? I'm in your past and not in your future."

"Please don't say that, you know I didn't mean that."

"What you mean is clear from what you say, except you are not truthful to yourself."

"Daniel please let's talk about something else."

"What does your royal princess want to talk about to a commoner like me, this is indeed a privilege."

"I... I.."

"Admit it Monisola we are two poles apart and we don't have

anything in common."

"I don't agree, I'm comfortable speaking to you and ..."

"I'm sure you are quite comfortable talking to a complete stranger, don't make this too difficult I think we should stop ...."

"Daniel please don't."

"I don't understand you, what exactly do you want from me?"

"I don't know but I just need to know you are and will be there for me to talk with, that all I'm asking."

"What about what I want; does that matter?" Daniel asked curiously.

"What do you want?" Monisola asked cautiously

"I don't want to be someone you pick and drop at your whim; I'm not a toy, I'm human as well." Daniel stated firmly.

"I want to talk to you because I trust you and I have a connection with you through ..."

"Your past that you will like to forget."

"I can't forget, I can never forget Omoniyi, he was my brother." she began to sob.

He let her cry.

"What do you want from me?"

She cried and cried again.

"Monisola get off the phone, I'll call you tomorrow, get a good night sleep."

Monisola slept like a baby and even when her alarm rang she switched it off and turned in her bed. She got to work late for the first time and when Valerie raised her eyebrow she just smiled. She was having lunch when he called.

"How are you today Miss Adewunmi?"

She quickly swallowed her drink and smiled.

"I'm good, how are you?"

"I had a restless night."

"I slept like a baby." Monisola beamed.

"At my expense, I could hardly sleep thinking of you crying and alone."

"I wasn't alone."

Silence

"I have Jesus with me."

"Oh" was all Daniel said.

"What else were you thinking Mr Daniel, you should have a pure mind you know."

"Pure mind, what are you talking about? I thought maybe you had a friend or someone with you and you still felt the need to disturb me."

"Is that what you think I do?" Monisola asked slyly.

"It's something you are capable of doing, we both know how mischievous you can be."

"You are so mean", Monisola had a feeling this guy knew her well.

"Mean? Monisola if I decide to be mean with you, you won't want to be in the same city with me."

"Now why would I not want that, when being in the same town would afford me the opportunity to carry out my full mission?"

He laughed and laughed. "Good gracious Omoniyi did not mince his word about you."

"What were you expecting, some girly talk about red roses and chocolate? Please, I've had enough of that, I need some action, I'm bored."

He laughed again.

"What is so funny?"

"Monisola I don't believe it, I thought you've been redefined."

"Now I know." Monisola gasped.

"Excuse me."

"Now I know what I want from you."

He took a deep breath.

"I want you to be the one I can relate with and be myself without having to think what does he want? Am I annoying him? Can he take more of my sharp tongue? I just know you are that person that I can be myself with."

"Are you proposing to me because if you are, it's a no."

"Now why would I 'epo pupa', smooth red oil of the delta wants to mix with black charcoal like you."

Silence.

When she didn't hear anything from him, she quickly apologised.

"Why are you apologising 'epo pupa', I was just wearing my shield so that I would protect my heart from being hit and also set the rules of the game. Number one Monisola, I am not your brother so I would give it to you raw, rare and will not spare you. You will cry and I will not even blink or move to console you and I will not play fair, are you ready for this game your royal highness."

"I'm on my mark, I'm set and we are even."

"Good. I'll get back to you soon."

"Mr Daniel you don't know who you are dealing with."

"Neither do you Miss Adewunmi."

On Monday morning while at work she received a parcel from a courier company. She opened it and could not believe her eyes, plastic frog eyes and fake rabbit tails. She laughed and laughed; where did he get them from at such short notice.

She didn't have his address so she couldn't send anything to him. She knew she would soon be inspired so she turned to do her bit of work before anyone else came in.

Seven in the morning Chicago time, he received an email stating he had won a syndicate lotto and he should send a thousand dollars to receive the money he had won. He replied her and told her that was child's play and he wasn't into lotto. She smiled. By midday he wasn't smiling when a group of elderly people from a home within the district called at his office to thank him for the huge pledge he made towards renovation of their home. He also got a call from a nearby kindergarten school who wanted to thank him for volunteering to take part in their campaign for safer route for children by reducing the speed limit in the area.

At first he didn't get it but when he received a message from Monisola asking how the campaign went, then did he begin to think. No, it couldn't be, there is no way she could know where he worked or the needs in his area. He called her.

"You are not playing fair; I only sent some plastic toys now I have to pay some hundred dollars to some folks I don't even know."

"See it as good money going towards a good cause instead of buying fake toys and not the real thing. It won't have cost much to get the real things, only ...."

"Some broken bones, few cuts and bruises on my charcoal body just to satisfy your royal highness."

"If you put it that way, yes and I would be so pleased."

"I think I want to change the rules of the game."

"Go ahead you never can tell what I will be inspired to do."

"No third-party involvement it's just between you and I."

"So, I can't send anything to your address."

"You don't even know it and it's not online."

"I know, I've checked."

"Monisola!"

"Don't belittle my GOD given talents and brains Daniel."

"What have I roped myself in?"

"You are free to back out."

"Throw in the towel, Never!"

"See you at the finishing line."

"I'll be there waiting."

CHAPTER SEVEN

She was in the gym on Saturday when she saw Mano, at first, she thought he didn't see her so she walked towards him and when he saw her, he turned towards the door.

"Mano."

He did not answer her.

"Mano!" she used her authoritative voice. He stopped but did not turn.

"Hi" she walked up to him.

"What do you want?"

"A good morning to you too Mr Mano, I'm sure you woke up on the right side of bed that is why you are so cheerful this morning."

He shook his head and smiled. "What do you want Moni?"

"You haven't returned my greeting or should I kneel down?"

"We don't do that where I come from, a courtesy is enough but since it's you, I should be the one bowing to your royal highness."

"Can we talk?"

"What about?"

"You guys."

"As you can see I'm all alone, so I don't know what you mean by you guys."

"You and Chic better stop passing me like a basket each time I ask after the other, what is going on between the two of you?"

"Look I don't know what you are talking about, as far as I am concerned I don't have anything to do with Chiamaka, excuse me I have to go."

"That's not what you were saying a couple of years back. Mano what is going on?"

"Moni, I have to go, I'm hungry and I want to fix something to eat."

"You! Since when did you start to cook? I'm yet to see you lift a spoon in the kitchen."

"Why don't you come over to my place and I'll show you how good I can cook."

"Hmm! I have another place in mind; let me get my things, I'll lead the way and you follow."

"Why are you both here? I don't remember inviting anyone to my house this morning"

"Mano, you know where the kitchen is; I can't wait to see and taste what you are going to cook. Chichi we did some shopping, be a good girl and help unpack while I sit and put my feet up. Go! Go!"

She was sitting down looking through her emails on her laptop when Chichi returned.

"Monisola what exactly are you up to?" she folded her arms across her chest.

"Nothing, I'm going through my mails as well as waiting for Mano to fix my breakfast. I hope you don't mind that or would you rather we go back to his flat and have breakfast alone?" Monisola glanced from her laptop to look at her friend.

"What you both do is none of my business, I just want to be left alone, I need my rest."

"How far gone are you?"

Chichi's eyes popped open and so did her mouth. She quickly recovered, sat beside Monisola and was about to say something when Mano came in.

"Breakfast is ready, anyone joining me?"

"Please don't say anything to him, I'll handle this."

They were eating at the table, Monisola was trying to keep the conversation going when suddenly Chichi bolted out of the chair and ran to the bathroom.

Mano looked from Monisola to his girlfriend that just did a Bolt one hundred metres, right in the living room and wondered what was wrong.

"Is the food okay, did I put too much salt or what?"

Monisola turned to look at him and when he saw the expression on her face he couldn't understand what was going on. He got up and went after Chichi.

Hearing the footstep and assuming her friend came to see what was happening to her, without looking up Chichi said, "Monisola please I don't want Mano to know I'm pregnant."

She washed her face and was trying to get the towel when she felt a hand give her the towel. She slowly wiped her face realising that her assumption of the identity of the person who was with her in the bathroom was in error, now she knew she was in trouble.

Mano was dumbfounded, he was looking at her as if he could not believe what she just said. They both stood there for what seemed like an hour before Mano spoke.

"What did you just say?"

Silence.

"Chiamaka what did you just say?"

"I was talking to Monisola" she refused to look at him.

"What did you just say" Mano asked again dumbfounded.

"I was talking to Monisola."

He moved closer, she moved backward and almost tripped. He quickly held her and steadied her.

"Let's get out of here."

He took her hands and walked her to the room and sat her down.

"Chiamaka, please tell me the truth."

"I don't want to talk to you, I have nothing to say."

"It would be in your best interest if you speak now."

"If I don't what do you intend to do?"

"Please, I just want to know, are you ..."

"Monisola!!!" she screamed.

Monisola heard the scream and broke her friend's Bolt record when she ran up the flight of stairs in less than one minutes or so it seemed. She stopped when she saw Mano squatting besides Chichi with his hands over his ears.

"What is going on in here?"

"Gosh, your scream is deafening, my ears are turning deaf every time you do that."

"Monisola, please get yourself and the visitor you brought to my house out before I scream again."

"Please don't, especially for our baby's sake."

She went hysterical and started screaming again.

"Chichi, stop behaving like a child and shut up."

"Just get him out of here, I don't want to see him, I don't want to see him", Chichi went hysterical.

Mano went out of the room while Monisola held Chichi in her hands and tried to comfort her.

"Chichi please, please stop crying, for the baby's sake, please."

She cried more and eventually stopped.

"Are you satisfied now?" Chichi asked Monisola.

"Excuse me?" Monisola who had no clue what she meant, asked.

"Why did you bring him here? I was doing just fine on my own and you brought him here. Why can't you take a stand and stop playing the devil's advocate. First, I was a fornicator, now you are trying reconciliation. What do you want now that you know I am carrying his child?"

"I didn't know anything, you just confirmed yourself."

Chichi sat up and wiped her face, "What?"

"I only asked a question and the next thing I knew you were flying past the room; Mano comes up and you start screaming my name and you just told me you are pregnant."

Mano wasn't sure what to do when he saw Chichi and Monisola come into the living room, should he hide or what. Of course not! He was a man and it was high time he started taking his responsibility serious.

"Chichi please don't scream again."

She ignored him and sat down while Monisola got her a glass of water.

"Can I go now? I trust you two can sort out whatever is going on between yourselves" Monisola asked her two close friends since secondary school.

"No!" they both exclaimed.

"Why?"

"I need you here" Chichi cried.

"I also want you here" Mano stated.

"You guys did not need or want me when you did whatever you did so I beg to take my leave."

"Sit down", they both turned to her and commanded her.

She looked at both of them and sat down, mumbling under her breath.

"Why didn't you tell me?" Mano began the interrogation.

"Tell him what?" Chichi turned to Monisola who in turn looked at her.

"I'm still not talking to him" Chichi replied.

"Am I to act as a go between now when I wasn't there when you were doing your tango."

"Just shut up" Chichi ordered Monisola.

"Why are you not talking to him" Monisola asked her friend.

"He knows what he did."

"What did you do?" Monisola asked Mano, she was getting fed up and dizzy turning from one to the other.

"I said I was sorry, it's just that when it comes to seeing you with another man I go bonkers and can't stand it."

"And then you hit her" Monisola concluded.

"What?" Mano almost fell of his seat.

"I did not do such thing, what have you been telling Moni?"

"Moni I did not insinuate such, it was you that said I should leave him."

"What!" Mano was dazed for the third time.

"Chiamaka!" they both shouted at her.

"I've had enough of these; I want both of you to leave my house right now" Chichi screamed.

Monisola turned to go.

"She's not leaving and neither am I or have you forgotten I do have a share in this house as well as ..." he looked at her tummy. "Chiamaka put me out of this guessing game, are you pregnant!"

"Didn't I tell him in the bath?"

"Am I still acting as the go between even though you just lied against me?"

"I didn't, you said the earlier I leave him the better"

"If he was beating you" Monisola tried to explain the reason behind the advice she gave.

"Beat her!" Mano screamed; this was getting out of hand. Did they still think he was that teenager who had a crush on Chichi and would do anything for her? He turned to go but he came back and walked towards Chichi, gritting his teeth, "I have had enough of your bullying, threats, accusation and if not for our baby I would turn you over my knees and trash out that manipulating streaks in you which your mother should have done but instead gave in to you. Don't you dare bait those eyelids at me again you ... you... gosh you are driving me crazy Chiamaka, please I want to come back to you."

Oh! Oh! What is going on?

"I thought you said you will never come back."

"I know but each time I spend away from you drives me crazy, I start to think, is she with someone else, what is she doing? I don't want to live my life like that. I want a clean break from our mistake but it's difficult especially when I told you to let us wait and you didn't listen. I don't want our baby born out of wedlock and neither do I want us to rush into marriage, I'm going crazy right now because I should have been stronger and not give in to you but..... I'm in a mess"

Nobody said anything for a while.

"I think I should go....."

"I still want you here, as a friend and a mediator"

"I'm not mediating into something I do not ..."

"Monisola I would bite off your head if you say another stupid word. Mano, I think it's useless crying over spilt milk now, we've done it and it has happened. I take all the blame as I had forced you into something you did not want to do but nevertheless did and only GOD knows for how many times more. I have also been thinking, I don't have to get married because I'm pregnant, I am not rushing into something else I should have waited for when I should and then make more mistake. One is enough to last me a life time. I'll take full responsibility of my baby; you don't have to do anything; in fact, the baby does not have to bear your name. As for your share in the house, I'll pay you back as soon as I can, probably in instalment. And that reminds me, Monisola I need a job, one where I will earn thousands of pounds in less than six months. That's how far I have to go before delivery and for the life of me I should have taken that injection for contraception because that pill did not work, I did not plan for this but I'm not going to do anything stupid. As for GOD, I still have a lot to ask for forgiveness. Mano please take the rest of your belonging and good bye.

An hour later Monisola was still with Chichi.

"Chic I want you to come with me, just for tonight and you'll come back tomorrow or Monday night."

"I have to go to work."

"You'll go from my house, it's even nearer."

"Why are you doing this? You should be gloating by now and saying I told you so."

"I actually agree with Mano you need some spanking. Speaking of Mano, what are you going to do, you need him you know?"

"The only one I need now is GOD."

"You should have thought of that before you forced the guy to sleep with you."

"Monisola are you so dumb to believe that? Even, if I forced him the first time what about the second and the hundredth time!"

Monisola blushed.

"Sorry I forgot you are still a saint, don't worry when you get married we will see what your husband will do."

"No one will know", Monisola smiled awkwardly.

"I know you are such a very good girl; I am the evil one now; how our lives have changed."

"Chic I don't like you talking like that, GOD has forgiven you so forgive yourself."

"It's hard, Monic, it's hard. I can't just believe it's me that all these has happened to, if anyone told me, I would have doubted but now I know what the scripture means when it states 'he that thinks he stand let him take heed lest he fall'."

"But do you believe GOD has forgiven you, you must know that, His love and mercies endures forever and even when our sins are red and crimson, HE will wash as white as snow."

"Thank you Miss Righteousness but this is something I did on my own accord"

"Why?"

"I know Mano would never ask me to marry him but I love him and want to spend my life with him. He has so many dreams that he wants to achieve sometimes I don't think he makes room for me in them. I just wanted to show and tell him I love him and was willing to do anything for him. It was stupid of me but I just went along with seducing him and he hated me. Monisola you need to have seen his face, he felt like killing me and after that we broke up. Two days later I was talking to one of my students, he saw us and just went wild; honestly, I was terrified. He followed me home and you should have seen the drama he made and the things he said. I was a whore and a bitch who went after every other man and that was how I seduced him and he was not going to let that happen again. Monisola I was scared, you know how I used to make fun of him at school and Uni saying he was just a boy and wouldn't hurt a fly, no, he is a man alright and did he show me. I think I underestimated him because all the while he is ever so gentle and timid but Mano is not the Mano I knew then; he's changed and it's all my fault. I should have let sleeping dogs lie but no, Miss Chiamaka the trouble maker had to bite off his tail now he's going to bite off my head. What do I do?"

"Well you've told him to move out you can always tell him to move in again and you don't have to, he still has a share in the mortgage."

"Ask him to move in again, Monisola are you listening to what I've said at all?"

"Yes, do you have another option B that you had when you were planning to sleep with him?"

"You are such a dear friend."

"I know, what are you going to tell your mother?"

"My mother must never know."

"Never know that you are pregnant when she comes to see you, which might be couple of months or when you have the baby and she pays a visit?"

"Must you point everything out like that?"

"Yes, so that what Sister Teresa told you then will sink in now."

They both remembered their favourite teacher in their secondary school and echoed, "Young girls the seed you sow today will grow one day but you must think through the process, think, think before you plant your evil seed."

"Well I did think through only it did not work, honestly I don't know what happened with those pills Monisola, I should have taken the injection but you know how I hate needles"

"*Krankenschwester!*"

They both laughed as they recalled stories of Heidi and Monisola fears of anything to do with a nurse or injection.

They were still talking when Mano walked in.

"What do you want?" Chichi asked.

"I believe this is my house and I have as much right as you do."

"Mano please don't make this difficult for her", Monisola begged him.

"Difficult for her! What about me?"

"What do you want, is it your share of money that you want, I'll find a way to get it for you."

"How, by sleeping with another man?" it was out before he could stop it and he knew he had gone too far.

Chichi took her bag and motioned for Monisola to lead the way. He didn't stop them and they left.

The next day was Sunday, Monisola had to beg Chichi to come with her to church, hoping her spirit will be lifted through the worship, prayer, Word of GOD and also promised to treat her for lunch.

"Please keep your treats, I am already doubled and I don't want to triple my size."

After the church service, Chichi came to meet her in the overflow. "Monisola, I don't believe that you are actually an usher. Do you know how long I've been begging you to join the church workers, those who you would have started with are now pastors and you are just ushering."

"Thank you, do not despise the days of small beginning and you never can tell, I might become head usher after ten years."

"Head usher not even Pastor, girl you are not serious. At least I volunteered to sing but they wouldn't accept me"

"Why? But you have a good voice!" Monisola exclaimed.

"Yes, but when I did my interview and they asked me how many times I would be prepared to come for rehearsals and I said once they quickly let me go."

"Once a week?"

"Once in a year!"

Monisola laughed, "Chiamaka you are not serious, how do you expect them to take you as part of their team."

"I didn't because when I saw the number of times suggested for choir practise and my work load, I just told GOD to find another team for me and that I would be singing for Him and Him only in my bedroom. Imagine singing every Sunday service, meeting every Monday, Tuesday, Wednesday and Friday; the two days you have left you use it to practice sixty songs every week, please tell me how I'm supposed to do that, what if I had family?"

"Sexy M how are you?" a voice called from behind.

Chichi turned round to see who was calling her friend such a name, when she saw him she was taken aback. It couldn't be!

"Andrew?"

"Felicia?"

"What are you doing here?"

"Look who is talking, what are you doing here?" Andrew replied.

"I'm here with a friend."

"Well I'm here to seek GOD's face."

They both laughed.

"I see you haven't changed; you are still as funny as ever."

"You my dear are still as beautiful and s....."

"Hmm! Hmm!" Monisola coughed trying to get his attention.

"Ah! Yes, not as sexy as Monisola but still provokingly beautiful."

"You know Monisola?" Chichi asked curiously, wondering how her best friend with her upright and royal upbringing could put up with Andrew.

"I met her here in church, she is a GOD sent, I really thank GOD for her. So, what brings you here and where is that follower of yours, Mano, don't tell me he's finally left your side so I can have a chance to sweep you off your feet not that you would now....."

Chichi was already crying, which left Andrew wondering what he said. Monisola motioned for him to keep quiet while she took Chichi away from preying eyes.

"Are you going to cry each time someone mentions Mano or is it the lost chance with Andrew you are crying over?"

Chichi whacked her hands away, "Silly girl, who said anything about Andrew, I never liked him, he was so annoying and huh! I could run him under my car."

"Please don't, someone already did."

"Oh! I'm sorry I didn't mean…"

"I think you need to ask GOD to put a guard over your mouth, lately the things you say, make me wonder what has gotten over you."

"Foolishness and fornication" she cried in anguish.

"Are you sure it's not love?"

"Love waits, it does not rush, I rushed."

"Rushed or did not trust?"

"I beg your pardon?"

"Think about it Chic, if you love and trusted Mano, you would have waited. There was no need to rush but because you did not trust him and you even said something about him not putting you in his plans so you just went ahead and did the first stupid thing you could think of. You gave in just like Eve did to the suggestion of the serpent. What if Mano became rich and famous would he still remember me?"

Later that evening Chichi went back to her house and sure enough Mano was still there, he was still in the same spot she had left him when she walked out on him.

She moved near him and sat beside him; she used her finger to trace his lips and moved close to kiss him.

"Please stop it" he told her.

"I'm sorry" Chichi apologised

"Are you back or are you moving out?"

"No."

"You are moving out?"

"No."

"You are back?"

"Yes."

"You know I'm not moving out again."

"Yes."

"Good."

"Mano?"

"Yes."

"I'm sorry."

"For what?"

"For making you sleep with me when you didn't want to."

"Who told you I didn't want too, it was not just the right time, that was my problem."

"So, are you sorry?"

"Depends on what you mean."

"Are you sorry for sleeping with me when you didn't want to?"

"I regret that I slept with you, fornicated with you and I have asked GOD to forgive me. But I am sorry that after that I still went back and committed the sin so many times because I could not control myself even when you said no and now that you are pregnant I ..."

"You don't want the pregnancy" Chichi asked fearful that her world was beginning to crumble.

"I told you those pills won't work; you weren't taking them regularly. I don't want anything to happen to our baby, we both want our baby"

"So, after the baby you would move out?"

"Yes."

"Thank you."

"For what?" he sneered at her

"For being considerate."

"Actually, I think you would be a fool to think I would move out."

"But you said ….."

"Chiamaka why do you want me out of your life all of a sudden, we've been friends since our childhood, we know each other, we've lived with each other so why now?"

"Well those things you said are true but things have changed."

"The baby?"

"Yes, and not just that. You have changed, you are not the same person you used to be, you are different."

"In what way?"

"Well like Andrew said you don't follow me around anymore, you.. .. ouch, what are you doing"

He gently placed her on his knees and gave her a gentle whack on her bum.

"If not for our precious baby that you are carrying I would give you a good spank. What do you take me for, a thirteen-year-old boy? Chiamaka I am no longer that boy who used to follow you everywhere. I am a man, I am no more the boy you tease, make fun of, use, even abuse, I have feelings too, if not that I love you I would have walked out on you a long time ago"

Her eyes popped when she heard that.

"Yes, I was going to leave you at some point in time only....."

"You won't but you .... said you love me."

"Of course, I told you didn't I?"

"Mano you told me when we were in year eight, that was a long, long time ago."

"Yes, I said till my dying days didn't you hear that part?"

"Yes, but that was once, you never repeated the first part again which I did almost every day until I got tired of it."

"If I don't love you, why would I put up with all your nonsense and mild madness?"

"So now I am mad."

"If not why would you propose to me and help me seduce you?"

"What are you talking about?"

"Chiamaka you gave me the fright of my life when you asked me to marry you and then seduced me. I was mad at you and also worried that something had gone wrong somewhere."

"You are not making any sense."

"Ok, when you asked me to marry you what did I say?"

"Yes and No, you wanted to wait"

"Wait for what?" he asked her.

"To achieve your dreams, make more money than my family and then if you ever got round to doing it, ask me to marry you which I wasn't prepared to wait for."

"What about when you started the seduction business?"

"You... said it was a bad timing as you had to leave or something, how was I to remember?"

"Chiamaka on that day was our anniversary, the fifteenth year we've been dating since year eight in secondary school and I was going to give you this and ask you to marry me", he brought out a small red velvet box, opened it and inside it was an engagement ring. "It was bad timing because it was also the day I was going to take you to meet my parents and officially tell them of our engagement and intention to get married. I could not resist the temptation in front of me even though I wished I did neither could I take you to my parents after that, it was impossible."

Chichi left him and went to the toilet.

"Young girls the seed you sow today will grow one day but you must think through the process, think, think before you plant your evil seed." How she wished she had listened to that mentor GOD had brought her way, to prepare her not to make such a mistake she had made to ruin her life.

GOD please forgive me, please forgive me.

She came out of the bathroom and went straight to her room, she started to pack her things, only the ones she would need for this journey.

He was still sitting on the floor when he saw her struggling with the case, he did not make a move to help her; she left without saying goodbye and dropped the keys through the door letter box when she had locked the door.

CHAPTER EIGHT

"**D**aniel please pick up your phone, please."
He didn't so she left a message. Monisola was on
her way to the airport and she desperately wanted to
speak with him. She hated it when she called him and he didn't pick
his phone. Go easy girl, you don't have any ties on him so don't expect
him to be at your beck and call, an inner voice warned her. She didn't
agree, she wanted him at her beck and call, her personal aide who
she could call anytime but knew that was a lie. She smiled; she knew
Daniel would never be that even if she paid him. The guy did not
tolerate any nonsense, he wasn't like her brother or Raymond, he did
not spare her or indulge her. She wished he was more relaxed with
her but how could he when she had defined their relationship, she
couldn't call it that, it was more of friendship and even though she
wanted more, she was afraid what the more would be. She wanted a
breathing space after Raymond and definitely not a repeat experience,
no, not ever.
She was in the airport lounge waiting for her flight to be announced
when he returned her call.

"Yes, Princess Monisola, what do you want?"

"Daniel, hi, how are you?"

"I'm good, what do you want?"

"How have you been?"

"Get to the point."

"Daniel can't I call and ask after your wellbeing?"

"You've got two minutes left."

"Why didn't you call and why didn't you pick my call at the first ring?" she accused him.

"I've been busy and I don't remember signing any contract of employment with you that states when my boss Monisola calls, I must pick up at the first ring."

"What if I want to employ you?"

"I can assure you Princess Monisola I do not come cheap, moreover I am not interested in working for you."

"I need your help" she begged him.

"One minute more."

"Daniel please."

"What do you want?"

"I'm going home to Nigeria and I don't want to...., can you come with me?"

"It depends on my schedule, I'm free next year if that's okay with you."

She rolled her eyes and gritted her teeth, "I am already at the airport."

"I'll join you next year then."

"Daniel please be serious" she pleaded with him.

"What do you want me to do? Jump on the next available plane to meet you?"

"Why not? Can't you do it for a ....."

"A what? Am I your friend or someone you pick up the phone and call when you want or when you....? Monisola, each time I ask you what do you want, I'm asking what do you want for the two of us. How far do you want us to go and when will you stop defining how far we go with whatever this is because it's not friendship and if this is your idea of friendship I want more but I'm not going to rush you. You can take all the time in the world to make up your mind but when I'm ready to quit this game you keeping playing I sure do know where the exit is."

"Daniel you are not being fair."

Silence.

"Ok, I want us to be friends and you can call me whenever you want or ...."

Silence

"Daniel are you listening?"

"I can call you but ..., what is the but? I've got to go Monisola, I've got work to do."

"What type of work do you do?"

He laughed, "I was expecting this question to be asked in the next decade not so soon into our nine months restricted talk time relationship. I'm what you call a body guard, security agent, 'personal aide' or whatever the cliché is, I protect people like your royal highness from common people like myself who cannot deal with such affluence and often gets carried away."

"Before then?"

"Why do you want to know?"

"I want to."

He took a deep breath and said almost in a whisper, "Marine."

"As in?"

"US Marine."

She exhaled, "What!"

"Look I don't want to talk about it."

"Were you dismissed or ..."

"Monisola you ask too many questions, no, I called it quit."

"Why?"

"Monisola, go board your plane, safe journey."

"Why?"

"I wanted to, ok. I ...I... had an injury and as far as I was concerned there was no going back as half bodied ...." he groaned. "Monisola please talk about something else."

"Does it hurt?"

"No but I still go for therapy and all that stuff."

"I mean emotional and psychological; how do you cope and how do you relate with the loss of ..."

"Are we now in a counselling session? I don't have money to pay your fees your royal highness I only live on ....."

"Daniel my flight has just been called; can we talk when I get on the plane or after?"

"You make the rules Monisola, it's your choice."

"I'm not sure I'm ready for whatever my father is about to ask me."

His heart skipped a beat but when he spoke he was calm. "What is he asking you to do?"

"I'm not entirely sure but with my brother on the scene and all the circumstances surrounding the whole issue..."

"What brother?"

"Oh! I'm sorry, it's a long story, it happens that I have another brother, a likely candidate and heir apparent to the throne. I'm not sure what my father wants but he's insisted I come home; I don't know what to do."

"Why don't you find out what he has to say first before you start worrying about what you think he'll say or do?"

"You don't know my father."

"I don't him but I know his daughter and I know she can't be pushed into something she does not want to do; I can testify to that."

"You don't know my other side, I'm as soft as egg yolk and can change and yield to anything."

"Not if you've been boiled first and become as hard as rock, though I don't mind seeing your soft side."

She noticed his tone of voice had changed, time to stop this conversation.

"I've got to go."

"I knew you were going to say that."

"Say what?"

"Every time the conversation verges to an area outside your confined pattern you abruptly end it."

"I don't know what you mean."

He laughed, "Bon voyage Mademoiselle."

"You are the one saying goodbye, I was still talking."

"I have to go."

"Ok talk to me about anything you want I would do my best to answer."

"What does a man want in a woman?"

"I don't understand."

"Ok I'll leave you to think about it, take all the time you want and when you are ready, call me."

She was grateful that he ended that conversation because she definitely knew the answer to his question and there is no way she was going to tell him because they both knew what it was and it is a no-go area for her.

Daniel shook his head, Monisola was one lady he did not have a box to label her kind of person. He knew her alright but he wasn't sure what game she was playing. He would play by her rules for now but not for long. He was getting bored and was ready for the next level but he wasn't sure what that level was. With a girl like Monisola you have to tread carefully or she would just withdraw, she was hiding something but he wasn't sure what but he will soon find out.

He was still thinking about her when he was going through his next work schedule and he started laughing. He accused Monisola of hiding something but he knew he was hiding a lot from her as he had that nudging from his heart and he could not deny it. He needed to clear his mind so he went out of the room to embrace the cool crisp air outside and he began to separate his thoughts, the brooding ones, the funny ones and the serious ones and then began to pray, LORD I need your help.

CHAPTER NINE

It was good to be back home, she didn't know she had missed home so much and it was strange walking into the house and still expecting Omoniyi to pop behind her and call her name, she felt uneasy but yet calm. She went to her room and was glad for the peace and comfort it offered, she had a quick nap and later on went to see who was around.

Ayaba Adekemi was home, happy to see her and eager to hear all she had to say.

"Monisola, it's good to see you. Come, let's talk. What is the latest over there? Who is who and what is the latest fashion and colour?"

"Ayaba, you should know by now that I do not have the time for all that, I'm too busy to be popping my noise into anyone's business."

"Oh! So, who is he?" she asked her eyes glimmering with mischief.

"Who?" Monisola tried to keep her voice neutral from any form of excitement.

"The man that is keeping you preoccupied from even noticing what the world is saying or wearing."

"Man, which man?" Monisola asked casually.

"Are you asking me? Abi kilo se e? Ba mi soro jo. Sit down and let's talk. Even if you cannot tell Kabiyesi, at least you can tell Olori and I will also put my mouth in and of course before you know it, we will be planning the wedding and you will get married. Do you think your mother and I like it that you are not married? Look at your junior sisters they are married and they have children. Don't you want yours or is it Kabiyesi and the throne you want to stay loyal to? Monisola you are a beautiful woman but iwo' na ti dagba o. Please think about this very well" Ayaba gently clasped her own ear as a sign of the urgency and seriousness of the matter.

Monisola smiled as she recognised Ayaba Adekemi's gesture as one an elder would use to convey the seriousness of a matter to a younger person who trivialised an issue at hand. She gently replied, "Yes Ma."

"Don't be like your ... Omoniyi, I told him to settle down; if only he had listened to me at least I would have a grandson or granddaughter to hold unto in my old age."

"Omoniyi is my brother", Monisola could not bring herself to refer to Omoniyi in the past, but stated emphatically "As for a man, I'm not ready."

"Why? What else are planning to do, read more books? Ah! Monisola time is going oh!" Ayaba nodded her head and did the holding of the ear sign again. Monisola had to suppress her laughter so she won't appear rude to her stepmother.

"Ayaba, I'm not ready, let's leave it at that please."

"Oh! It's the throne you are ready for, Omoniyi is out of the way so the coast is clear."

Monisola thought she had gotten over this but the tears welling in her eyes proved her wrong.

"I knew it, I knew you had such a strong tie with your brother despite the years you spent apart. He was forever asking after you each time your sisters and I visited you. You have to get over him, he's gone but thank GOD we will meet at the feet of Jesus. Monisola you know your brother wouldn't want you to live like this so please take heart, so' gbo, pele, it is well."

"I should be the one comforting you", Monisola wiped the tears from her eyes.

"You've done well, you stayed with him when he ordered us out of the hospital room saying we were driving him to his grave earlier with our tears. You've also stood by me and gave my son a befitting burial, what more can I ask. Also, the break to America did me well, thank you for arranging it, I really thank GOD for you."

They were walking towards the living room when she turned to Monisola, "Monisola do you have someone you are dating?"

She shook her head; she was telling the truth as she was not dating anyone.

"Ok, I will find a man for you" Ayaba's eyes glittered with an idea.

Monisola laughed, "Ayaba what era do you think we are in, your days? Please don't say that to anyone. They will think you are from another century; you don't find husbands for young women like me; he will come to me."

"When? How? When you are working today in Sierra Leone and tomorrow Indonesia. I am going to open the discussion tonight at the dinner table; at least you will know I am serious and I know I will have supporters even though I might not get Kabiyesi's vote but majority rules."

They had dinner quite alright but no one mentioned anything about her, the full concentration was on Kabiyesi's pre - dinner meeting.

"I have called you here as family members of this royal house and ikan kan o gbo' do' sele' ka maso'. Thank you all for coming at such an impromptu time especially Monisola, I do apologise for taking you out of your work and various schedule but it was expedient that all attended. Kayode and Taiwo thank you for coming, you are part of the family and everything concerns you.

The house that stands united is difficult to break, unity and loyalty is of essence to one's house and we cannot afford any division. We are of the same flesh and blood and the mind of Christ reigns in us. We have the Greater One in us; the Holy Spirit of GOD and HE teaches us all things. We have the Word of GOD which is our precept and guiding light and we follow what the Spirit of GOD is saying and we have the blood of Jesus that speak of a better covenant for us all.

You all know that my coming to this position is not by the will of man but by GOD's divine order and purpose as he chose me from my mother's womb and brought me out in His time for the use of His glory.

I have been the under shepherd of this great people and GOD has not caused me to look back or sorrow. I say sorrow because the passing of my son, my first son Omoniyi was not in sorrow but GOD who knows all things allowed it. I know we will meet again at the feet of Jesus never to depart no more.

As much as I can be liberal in many things that some of you take for granted, I can be very obstinate; Monisola and Omoniyi can testify to that, you ask her. I will not see black and call it white; neither would I call what is a lie the truth and I thank GOD for the grace HE has given me."

As Kabiyesi continued talking, Monisola looked at the time she realised she had missed lunch and going by this meeting, dinner would take another two hours. She stood up to go to the ladies but one look from her father made her sit back. Goodness what was this old man up to now.

".... you all know that every time I visit Europe I always like to go and see the latest technological and scientific development going on there. I visited Frankfurt to attend some seminars as well as see what new ideas I could bring home. You know with this farming business; one has to keep abreast of everything. Nothing should stop a whole nation such as ours, great Nigeria, the giant of Africa from becoming a fully mechanised and commercial agricultural developing nation, nothing at all. We have the money; the brains and we can use our resources. I agree we can benchmark but for goodness sake let's stop all these imports and do away with hoes and cutlasses; machinery is the order of the day. This would reduce the labour input as per human effort, it will also increase job opportunities as we still need to employ human beings to operate the machines and it will most definitely quadruple the output, that we will soon be asking other nations to buy from us because we would have so much in abundance to feed ourselves and others.

I was on my way home from all these eye openers, reactivating my brain cells to be motivated and know how to implement the ideas and technology I saw at the trade fairs, when I decided to visit Zurich. Of course, I didn't need an invitation, there was no need for such as there was nothing to be suspicious of and nothing to hide. I boarded the plane and when I arrived there, I resisted the urge and excitement to see the familiar places and people but headed straight to the one place I have not visited for such a long time as it was deemed to be the place of solitude and rejuvenation for one so dearly loved that I tried over the years not to invade her privacy which was so precious to her. In fact, each step I took towards the gate and the door was weighty as I asked myself what excuse to give for the invasion and disruption of her quiet and solitary times. I had my keys, used it as there was no need for me to announce my arrival. To my uttermost shock, disappointment, unimaginable distraught, heart wrenching and near fatal heart failure I saw my Olori's arms wrapped over a man!"

The hundred thousand pins dropped but no one heard them because they were all in deep shock and the thought waves were creating a traffic of unspoken words:

What did Kabiyesi just say?

Is this a joke or what?

What did he just say? I missed that part. I switched off when he started talking about agriculture and stuff?

Se Kabiyesi ti mu oti yo ni? Abi isokuso wo' lon so'?

Monisola looked from one person to the other and tried to imagine what was going through each of their minds, she could give a thousand dollars just to know. She laughed, her father was a dramatist, what was all that talk about family loyalty, nation building, technology and all, then landing a bomb shell. Poor mother she wondered what was going through her mind, revenge number three, because with new insight about her mother, she was the one to watch out for not her father because she could sell him and his kingdom all at once and she would not even bait an eyelid.

Kabiyesi continued as he was sure the bomb shell he dropped had a ripple effect. "She is here, I have not said it behind her, let her tell it as it is. Why did she go to Zurich, what has she been doing there all these years and who is the man?"

Kayode cleared his throat, he thought as the first son-in-law he should make an effort to speak but a kick from his wife and his mother-in-law murderous look made him sit back. So much for being part of the family.

When no one else spoke, Kabiyesi pressed his bell and his aide came. He whispered to him and with a nod of head the guy disappeared.

"I see my beloved is not ready to speak, so be it. However, I do not want it to be a case of my word against hers or denial or evasion of answers so I brought the man here, Bruno has just gone to bring him."

Bruno came back with someone who had his face covered and hands behind him.

A swish of silence swept pass the room again. This time the silence was filled with unspoken words which sounded like the dropping of hundreds of coins in a large metal container. Monisola smiled inwards and continued to enjoy the unfolding drama.

"Olori Tinuola Olaniwura Adewunmi by the power vested in me as your husband and Oba to the people of Ifedolapo Kingdom, I command you to unfold this mystery standing before us your family."

Olori looked at her husband, stared at him for a while and then with head held high, went to the man, placed his hands from behind to the

sides and carefully took off the blindfold. Each time she unfolds the
blindfold she shed tears of relief, tears of unburdening her long secrets
and tears of what is to come.

"My goodness!"

"Oh my GOD!"

"Ah! It's a lie!"

"Oloriiiii!!!"

At the dining table, everyone was seated, dinner was served and apart
from Monisola no one else seemed to be interested in the meal. All
eyes were on Toluwanimi, the mother and then the father. Monisola
paused for a while to guess what their line of thoughts might be. She
looked from Toluwanimi to her mother, no resemblance whatsoever,
he couldn't be said to have come from her lineage let alone her womb.
Unlike her who in every way has her mother's physique, features and
skin colour. She looked from Toluwanimi to her father; it was as if the
man spat him out of his own loins. He took everything from his father,
from his eye balls, the shape of head, dark skin, to height, stature and
that nose which was a trade mark in the family, it was an exact replica!
Awesome GOD! Always at work to confound the wise.

After dinner everyone went to the living room and the grandchildren
were brought in and introduced to their new uncle. Children being
who they are began to ask question no adult present dared to ask.

"Are you our real uncle?"

"What is your name?"

"Where exactly have you been all these years?"

"Yes! Where have you been even before I was born?"

"Why do you look like Grandpa so much, is he your grandpa too?"

"Are you staying or going like Uncle Omoniyi, I miss him."

"Ejo' ti eyin omo yi bere ti poju, wo, Aduke wa ko' won losi bed" Ayaba ordered the nanny to take them to bed.

"Ejo'ma, e je ki wo fi ara numi, inu mi dun lati ri gbogbo ebi mi, o ti pe ti mo ti reti iru' ikan bayi" Toluwanimi asked that the children be allowed to stay past their bed time because for the first time in his life, he was in the midst of his own family, his own people.

Everyone was amazed at the fluency, accuracy and mastery of his mother tongue even though he had been born and bred in a foreign land. The children continued with their interrogation while the adults kept pondering in their minds the unfolded mystery of tonight's event. Eventually they started to take their leave in batches and left Kabiyesi, Olori, Ayaba, Toluwanimi and Monisola.

"Monisola you must be tired now, let me escort you to your room."

"Thank you Ayaba, I want to speak to Monisola please."

"Alright Kabiyesi" she walked to her Olori, bowed and gave her a hug. "My Olori, I bid you good night but I must say if all refuse to acknowledge it, I commend your bravery in keeping him for all these years, emi o' le se'. Most importantly you have saved the royal throne because we have our heir and no one can take what rightful belong to us, Kabiyesi e jo' e' fi pele' pele' se. You might be angry at my Olori but look at the turn of events, we can only thank GOD for everything. Monisola good night we will continue our talk tomorrow, don't forget."

"What talk is this?" her father asked her.

"Father, it is women's talk."

"The same talk that might have gotten your mother into trouble because I don't know how she managed to execute this plan and secrecy for so long, it just beats me."

Monisola smiled, she hoped her father knew there was a private storm brewing in his tea cup from his first wife as she had refused to say anything to anybody.

"Father I need to catch up with my beauty sleep and I'm sure Mother and Toluwanimi would like to do the same."

"Take your brother with you and he is not to be let out of your sight, we still have so many catching up to do but I want to be with Olori this night, I am entrusting my son to you Oluwamuiremiwa."

Monisola laughed at her father's use of her middle name as his warning code, she pulled her brother to her and they both walked out of the room.

Kabiyesi turned to his first wife, "Olori please lead the way to my inner chambers."

She led the way but once they got into the room she changed her mood and the look on her face.

Kabiyesi took off his dinner jacket and hung it in the wardrobe, he moved towards his wife to help him undo the cuff links off his shirt but she completely ignored him and moved away from him. So soon, he thought he still had five minutes grace before the war between them started. Well thank GOD he could do them himself, he changed to his shorts and t-shirt and sat on the bed.

"Olori please come and join me on the bed."

"I prefer to go to my room."

"I have requested that you join me" he insisted.

"I want to go to my room" Olori also persisted

"Tinuola come and sit here" Kabiyesi summoned with his hand.

"And if I don't" she turned her back to him.

He got off from the bed, walked up to her, his face placid.

"What do you want? Do you want me to prostrate for you in front of everybody, you know I would do it for you."

Olori looked at him surprised that he would say that.

"Of course, I will, I know I have wronged you Tinuola, it was my impatient and the fact that I was trying to help GOD that landed me into all these deep waters. I only wanted to drink from my own cistern but I gave in to the pressure around me. My mother warned me but I ignored her warnings. She said she knew you will give me a male child, that it was only a matter of time and that I should hold on to GOD and if I couldn't bear the wait I should train Monisola who was equal to the task. She did not mean to take Monisola from you during those times, it was at my insistence that she began to coach her and all. I am sorry", he knelt down before his beloved and began to cry.

Olori resisted, if he likes let him shed tears of blood, she was through with all this royal mess, she wanted out.

"Please stand up" she stated without any emotion.

He stood up but the look in her eyes told him she was not convinced.

"I have forgiven you long time ago so there is nothing to forgive again, I thank GOD for the mercy and favour HE bestowed on me and gave me a son to nurture. I just hope I still have time with Monisola, I still want to nurse her."

He looked at her with a squint, she smiled though it was a flicker of a smile, "I don't mean that kind of nurse, se' eni to' ti dagba' be'yen," she said shyly, "I want to be there for her, spend time with her, the time you took from me"

"I'm sorry" he pleaded with her again.

"Your sorry won't bring back the time, Zachariah, I have been loyal and faithful to you, by GOD's grace I have given you female and male children, please let me go."

At first, he did not understand but he was quick to tread her line of thinking, he grabbed her with both hands and turned her to face him.

"I am sorry for my being unfaithful and all that but let me tell you one thing, you are mine, no one can take you away from me, GOD will be the one to fight them and if you dare to make the mistake of leaving me, ah! I will find you. Yes, you now have male and female children, thank GOD but I want more. I want more children from you, you are my priceless jewel, you are the one that would give me more, that is why I have called you here."

Olori remained calm and refused to let anything create fear in her.

"I believe you have your equally priceless jewel Adekemi, you better quickly go into her because I am not available."

"Adekemi has told me right after giving birth to Morolake she was through with child bearing and frankly I do not blame her and moreover she is older than you"

"And there are younger ones you can pick from", Olori advised him.

"It is you I want and I did have my choices but none could give me the child I wanted or could keep up with my desire. Do you know that of all the women I have had, only you fills my desire? I keep coming to you and the more I dig the more you give. There's just something about you Tinuola that I have not found in any other woman, you are the one for me. I can take a thousand women but none can make me complete like you do. You are GOD's gift to me, I need you Tinuola even to my old age and grey hairs, please don't leave me."

Now she was completely shocked, for Zachariah to say all that after all these years. Hmm! Papa GOD you do wonders, You did it in bible times with Zachariah and Elizabeth and my name is not even Elizabeth or Sarah. She laughed and thanked GOD.

"Kilo pa lerin" her husband asked when he heard her laugh.

"OLUWA lo pamilerin, GOD has made me laugh."

"That will be the name of our next child."

She quickly snatched her hands from his and walked towards the door.

"Tinuola if you so much as touch the door handle or open that door, you will be here until you give birth."

She stopped and turned to look at him, his expression had changed and he was no longer Zachariah he was Oba Zachariah.

"I am having my ..."

"You lie."

"I have a headache"

"Another lie, add another one and you will not come out of this room for seven days."

She started grumbling.

He pulled her to him, "Why are you resisting, you should be glad that you have my full attention for the next seven days and also after our third and fourth born"

"Ah! I'm too old for all these o", Tinuola shrugged her shoulders.

"Have you passed Sarah's age? If you waste more time I'll add two more children."

She laughed. "Are you not ashamed?"

"Of what? Go to the bible and you will see how many more children

Abraham had after Isaac and I'm giving you the privilege to carry all the rest, at least eight more."

She wriggled out of his hands and moved away.

"Ten."

She backed away.

"Thank you, twelve" Kabiyesi continued.

She realised he was counting so she moved towards him, slowly at first.

"For that slow deliberate move, fourteen."

She stood in front of him.

"Sixteen, thank GOD. Kabiyesi olori aiye gbogbo, the KABIYESI of all Kabiyesis, the owner of the whole universe, honour, majesty, power, dominion belong to YOU and YOU alone, there is nothing too difficult for YOU to do. I ask in the name of your son JESUS, as I go in into my wife Tinuola, Father remove all barriers, let her take in and be fruitful, every nine months as from tonight let her put to bed more male and female children in Jesus name, children that YOU would use for your glory in these times in JESUS name I pray."

He carried his wife, entered and GOD did grant his request.

CHAPTER TEN

Monisola could not call Daniel because she decided he was someone she wanted for herself and keep for herself, she wasn't ready to share him with anyone else especially her family. She longed for him and was beginning to contemplate going back to England just to speak to him. However, her father did not give her permission to travel as he still wanted to talk to her but was busy and she rarely saw him. She had not seen her mother since the night of her arrival and she had only Ayaba and Toluwanimi to talk to as her sisters and their families had returned to their base.

She had promised her father she would not let Toluwanimi out of her sight. Not that he needed a baby sitter, he was old enough to take care of himself as he was out and about most of the time and all she did was tag along. She was delighted when her father told her he was taking him back to Zurich because he had to finish his course and since he was studying engineering like he did, no time was to be wasted. She asked after her mother and he said she was under house arrest and when she probed further he told her to mind her business.

As soon as her father and Toluwanimi left and Ayaba was visiting relatives she quickly called Daniel.

"Hi!"

"This had better be important, I can't live on what you don't pay me."

"Not even if all I want to say is that I miss you and wish you were here with me."

"Don't play games with me Monisola" he said with an irritated tone.

"I beg your pardon?"

"I don't want to play your games anymore."

"Who said I was playing? I missed you and the reason I haven't called is because I didn't want any interruption from my father or anyone and you are telling me not to play games. Ok forget what I said, goodbye."

"Please don't drop the phone on me", he quickly pleaded.

Daniel saying please, Monisola wasn't sure she heard him say that.

"Monisola?" he called when she didn't say anything.

"Yes."

"Do you mean it?"

"Are you deaf?"

"I said I'm not playing games."

"Oh, my goodness what is the matter with you, I'm telling you I miss you; I want you here and I'm even thinking of taking the next flight back and you still think I'm playing."

"Monisola if what you are saying is true, come straight to Chicago."

"I can't ..."

"I knew you were joking."

"The only reason I am not taking the next flight is that my father is out of town and he left strict instructions that I should not move an inch near the gate; so, I am keeping cool because things are a bit heated and I want to stay out of my father's fury. Why don't you come?" she begged him.

"I can't" Daniel replied with regret.

"Oh! I see."

"It's not what you think. I have therapy sessions booked up and I've been having some pains lately; I think I overdid things a bit and tore a ligament or something so I've been prescribed bed rest and like you I cannot move a centimetre, Monisola I miss you too."

"What do you miss about me?" she asked, she loved what she just heard him say.

"I can't say it over the phone I need to see you in person."

Her fears returned again, so she kept quiet.

"Monisola what are you afraid of? Each time you keep going back anytime we make a progress in this relationship, what in GOD's name is it?"

"Can you please calm down; I can't say it over the phone."

"What?" he shouted over the phone.

"I'm serious" she insisted.

Silence.

"Daniel, why don't you believe me?"

"Why do you keep shutting me out, I want to come in."

"Where exactly are you asking permission to come in?"

"Your wounded heart, your trust and your body."

She disregarded the last one, she just did not hear that.

"I want you Monisola, all of you" Daniel continued.

Trouble! Trouble! The alarms were going off in her head.

"I've got to go."

Silence.

"I'll call as soon as I can."

"I want all of you Monisola and I'll be waiting."

This cannot be true she thought to herself, GOD where are You?

"Oluwamuiremiwa are you listening?"

"Not exactly father, why are you asking me to do this?"

"Why are you being so difficult just like your mother, goodness no wonder you look so much like her."

"Father, I have to be back at work and I am not staying another month or whenever you choose, I do have my own life to live", Monisola's heart was already beating fast.

"I know, which is why I am asking you to do this for me, just this once."

"Why father? Why?" Monisola closed her eyes wishing she could be anywhere but right here in the palace.

"First I need to spend some time with your brother Toluwanimi, he has a lot to learn. Your mother did a good job but he still has to meet my standards so I have to personally train him. I would have asked your mother to stay and look after the palace but I need to keep an eye on her, you never know what she may plan, probably trade the kingdom! I'm joking, please do not say that to her. Monisola you are the only one I can rely on, just this once and I won't bother you again."

"How long are we talking about? A month, two?" she groaned.

"At least a year", her father said calmly.

Monisola almost fainted. She started to shake her head and was already crying. Her father was shocked to see her cry, something he had not seen since she was a girl.

"Monisola, are you crying?"

She turned away from him and tried to blink the tears away.

"Is there something I should know that you haven't told me about?"

She shook her head, not trusting her mouth not to blurt out the main reason.

"Monisola if what I am asking is something you can't do please let me know and I'll find an alternative."

"I'm alright father, I'll do it" Monisola accepted.

"Monisola I'm your father you don't have to hide anything from me."

"I'll do as you have requested sir."

He knew that was the end of story she was not willing to open up to him. "Monisola please talk to me."

She left the room without looking at her father and once she got to her room she started crying. Why GOD? Why do I have to be the one to step in for others. Am I not entitled to my own joy? Why?

She left for England the next day and when she told Mark she was ending her contract he refused to let her go.

"Monisola, I don't want you to leave, you can take leave for another month and then be back." He shook his head wondering why on earth she was taking this step now.

"I can't Mark, I have to go and I'm not sure when I'll be back, let someone else take my place."

"Even if you go, you can still work from Lagos or wherever you are based, you'll be paid in sterling. I know the money is not an issue but I just can't let you go; you've been working with us for less than two years and you are invaluable and I mean that."

She looked at him, why did he have to say that now. "I'm sorry Mark I wish I could stay."

"I know it's none of my business but why do you have to jump every time your family barks? Do excuse my expression."

She laughed, "I could sue you for that."

"I don't mind, at least you'll be forced to say it in court"

"Mark, you are so obstinate, I need to do this and even if I told you, you wouldn't understand, it's family and I have to do it."

"I do understand family but you can't drop everything each time they call you, you need to have your life you know, get a boyfriend or even get married."

"When did you start advocating marriage? I thought you were sworn to celibacy for life."

"Not after I met this very beautiful enchanting girl called Monisola, she's captivated my heart and ...."

"Mark!"

"Ok, just to let you know I would go to any length to make you stay."

She laughed and gave him a peck.

"I think I've fallen for you Monisola" he said in a bemused tone.

It was hard telling Andrew she was taking leave of absence.

"Why do you have to go? Why the indefinite period? If it's just a month or two, I'll understand but saying you are not sure how long, is not acceptable. Is it because of me?"

"Andrew my family needs me and I just have to go."

"Are you saying if we get married and your family ask you to come you will abandon me and go just like that!"

"Andrew be serious!"

"I am serious. I knew you were special the very first moment I saw you and the way you've helped me not just with my accommodation but you've given me hope, encouraged me and I'm going to say it now, Monisola marry me, please."

She knelt before him and took his hands, "Andrew I can't and it's nothing to do with you, I just can't."

"Even if I'm willing to wait?"

Monisola shook her head, Andrew is willing to wait for her but not Raymond. "You better not, otherwise you miss your GOD-intended, forget about me and get on with your life."

"How can I ever forget Sexy M, the most ..."

"I will throw you off this wheelchair if you start again."

"Start! I've never stopped. Oh! You think because you helped me get the house I will shut my mouth, you've got to be kidding, sexy, vivacious, head spinner ..... what happened to your miniskirts you don't wear them anymore?"

"I'm not going to wait for you to run me mad and do what I'm not supposed to do especially in the house of GOD ..."

"We can carry on in my house, you know it's not far and who knows, nine months from now I could be the proud owner of two brand new legs after you've thrown me out of a moving car."

She looked at him and gave him one of her sweetest smiles, "I'm going to miss you."

"I will not, the earlier you get out of my life the better, then I can refocus and start running I mean chasing after some girls, after all that is why I came to church."

Monisola shook her head, this guy was impossible.

"Congratulations, I heard you are now teaching in Sunday School."

"I don't know who told them to. I was just enjoying the exposition during one of the bible study groups when the teacher said something in error. I corrected him and also opened my big mouth on what the historical event was and how it relates to us today; Monisola if I have you by my side I would just be silent forever. I will not be too mouthy, the only place you will hear my voice is in the bedroom when ...."

"Andrew!"

He chuckled and continued, " ...... I say please pass me the bible and my glasses."

"You are just a joker"

"So are you Monisola, so are you Sexy M."

She was already crying when she called him.

"Ok, so when do you hope to be back?"

"I don't know."

"So, what is going to happen to us?"

Silence

"Monisola talk to me."

"Daniel, I told you before I boarded that plane I wasn't sure of this but you said I should go and find out what he wanted and now I can't tell him no."

"I know you can't say no but you can define how long you stay, it's up to you Monisola."

"I never wanted this, why do I have to be the one to always pick up the pieces, why can't they call on someone else?"

"It's your time now and you have to give it your best shot."

"I don't want to, I lost interest since Omoniyi came on the scene and my feelings still remain the same."

"Ok let's look at it this way, your father has trained you and believed you will one day take after him, even with Omoniyi he still held on to you as his last card. He now has a son who he wants to mould just like he did with you and Omoniyi and all he is asking is for six months say the least, then you can have your life back and he would never disturb you again. Tell me Monisola what is stopping you from taking such an offer? On the other hand, you'll put to good use, all you've learnt from him and your work experience."

She didn't see it that way but then that was not all.

"Did I ever tell you about Raymond?"

"No but I'm listening."

"All I asked from Raymond was just two weeks, two weeks for me to stay with my family after Omoniyi left and he didn't."

"I told you I will wait."

She inhaled and exhaled.

"I've not even asked you."

"I'm getting to know you Monisola and sometimes you speak in parables but I'm learning."

"What if I do this one big favour for my father and then I decide I like it and stay?"

"I'll wait for you Monisola, you have something I'm interested in and I don't let go easily" Daniel assured her.

"I've got to go."

Silence

"Aren't you going to make fun of me?"

"I've changed the rules of the game, I am no longer playing. Now I'm serious, tell your father you can only stay for six months."

"I can't tell him the length of time."

"Then I'll do it for you."

She knew he was serious.

"Daniel maybe I don't want to play your game anymore I want to ...."

"It's too late Monisola, we are deep into this together and there's no way out, six months. You wouldn't want me to come for you."

"I'll let you know when I'm ready."

"I call the shots from now on."

CHAPTER ELEVEN

She was back home and things were going to take a different turn.

She started with the house rules, some of them were outdated, so she discarded them. She began to put her father's estate and properties into good use. She also stepped over her boundary when she opened her father's workshop of inventions for schools to come in and learn a few things. When he called she was gearing herself for his fury but he thanked her for bringing his work to limelight since he couldn't blow his own trumpet.

For all the employees, she put in place an option of open employment and new contractual terms which meant they could end their contracts of employment provided they gave ample notice. She also introduced pensions especially for those who had been employed for over a long period or had taken over from their parent's jobs. She added other benefits which included ownership of their own homes and the provision of free education up to tertiary institutions for employees and their children.

She also introduced changes in the roles her mother and step mother played, so as to bring awareness to the importance of women rights, their wellbeing and contributions to their families and nation. Female employees were also entitled to certain benefits tailored towards the wellbeing of women and children.

She went to Omoniyi's study and began to look at all the proposals he had submitted to their father which had not been approved and after a few consultations with some professionals and team of experts, she gave approval for the work to commence. Her father called to let her know he heard what she was up to and she told him if he wasn't pleased all he had to do was come back home and relieve her of her duties.

She worked from dawn to dusk and when she was all alone she called him.

"I don't think I can take any more Daniel."

"Yes, you can and you will."

"You say that because you don't know how difficult it is."

"It better now than later."

"What do you mean?"

"After this we don't what any disturbance because I want you to myself."

"I've been working in Omoniyi's office and you need to see the diary he keeps but none of them mentions you."

"Have you ever known him to call people by their names or even remember some?" Daniel noticed she had changed the subject but played along.

She laughed, "You are right, he had so many names for me and eventually I had to open a book to write them in."

"What are you doing next week Friday?"

"I don't know, I'm not even sure what day of the week we are in."

"I would be in Lagos on Wednesday but I'll be leaving Saturday night, would you like to join me on Friday?"

"Daniel I can't."

"Ok" he agreed without an argument.

Tuesday evening, she couldn't concentrate, she wondered why she made life difficult for herself. He only asked her to join him on Friday not the whole week and maybe just seeing him would ease the pain and longing in her heart.

"Hi"

"Hi, what can I do for you Princess."

"I... I want to know what time you will be in Lagos on Friday."

"I won't be in Lagos this Friday."

"You said so last week."

"I'm entitled to change my mind, aren't I? I've cancelled the trip; it was for a wedding but I sent them money instead."

"You were coming for a wedding, not to see me."

"I wanted to see you; the wedding was just an excuse."

"I'm sorry, I didn't think."

"Opportunity only knocks once."

"Twice and for as long as we want it to knock."

"And until you actually take advantage of it, it will forever be an opportunity."

"Daniel please come on Friday, please."

"How are things going with your royal highness and her kingdom?"

Now was his turn to change the subject. "I hope you are keeping the subjects happy and your father is thrilled with all the new changes you are introducing. It's high time someone initiated these changes and I hope others will take a cue from you and your kingdom."

"It's not my kingdom, please Daniel I need to see you on Friday."

"I've got to go Princess; I'll speak to you another time."

Friday afternoon, she received a delivery of fresh flowers, baskets of fruits and vegetables. There was an envelope which had a card and all it said was 'I'm missing you.'

She was tempted to call her father and tell him she was quitting and wanted to go back home, but knowing her father he would probe and before she knew it she will be telling him things she was not ready to tell anyone, not even admit to herself. No, she wouldn't, she will do what she believes GOD was using her to do and then leave when it is time.

Six months down the line, their town had a brand new functional maternity ward, health centres in all districts with resident doctors and nurses and pharmacies. A new polytechnic for engineering and agricultural sciences were established and also a high school.

Her father called her to inform her he was coming home in two months' time and his first agenda would be to lecture in the polytechnic.

"What's the hurry father, I'm sure you have a lot to do with Toluwanimi and also mother to take care of."

"I know but I can't hold back the excitement with what is going on at home. Do you know how long your brother has been planning this, we've talked about it over and over but we just never got around doing it."

"Father I didn't do anything, everything I did was based on Omoniyi's ideas and plan, he had everything laid out and I guess he was just waiting for your approval."

"The last time we spoke about it he said we should leave it aside for a while that maybe it wasn't the time for it and we never spoke about it again."

On the inauguration of the polytechnic, maternity ward and memorial high school, everything was dedicated to GOD for the service of men and in memory of their dear Prince Omoniyi Phillip Adewunmi.

Two weeks later she was back in England and began to notice the changes around her.

Her friend Chichi had her baby boy, had gotten married and moved back with Mano.

Andrew had finally found the girl of his dreams and was getting married soon.

Most of her team mates in the workers-in-training classes at church had been posted to various department and some were even assisting the team leaders. Good for them but she wasn't going back to the ushering team, as she left before completing her 'training, she would rather start all over again. She informed Ifeanyi who laughed at her and told her she had two weeks to get settled as she was assisting him in the training department. She gave him all sort of excuses but he had already made up his mind and if she persisted he would send her back to the ushers' team; that kept her quiet.

She didn't want to go back to her old job so she did some research, made a few enquiries and was soon invited by some organisations for interviews. She received quite a number of job offers and in the end, had to make a choice. The organisation she selected was a small one compared to all the big names she had consulted at and worked for. The job was flexible though the money wasn't much but she just liked it and the new opportunities it offered. On the day she started work the CEO when welcoming her, asked why she chose to work for them as she was sure the pay wasn't great, she smiled and said she wanted a change and also to make changes.

CHAPTER TWELVE

"When are you coming over to Chicago?" Daniel asked when she finally called him after her return from Nigeria.

"I never said I was coming."

"I'm inviting you."

"I can't."

"What is your excuse this time?"

"Why don't you come over?"

He laughed, "At least we are not back to square one, we've graduated."

"Daniel are you coming or not"

"I can't, I've got to go, my father won't allow me, I have work to do, my kingdom is waiting for me", he mimicked her.

"Stop it."

"If I come are you ready?"

She shifted on her sofa, why did he have to go this way all the time.

"Ready for what?"

"For me, I'm taking what belongs to me, I've waited and I'm not waiting anymore."

"Time and place" she asked though she was quivering with fear.
"I'll let you know."

Every week she received a gift from Daniel.

He sent her poems, quotes and love notes.

She also received books especially those that were out of print, they were priceless. She squirmed with delight when she received them and sent emoji kisses to him.

"I want the real thing" was his reply.

For a week it was just flowers: single, bunch, bouquet.

Then chocolates, she groaned and told him if she gained any weight it was his fault. He replied stating he would be her personal trainer and trim her down. Then ordinary things, pens, hair clip, mug, scarf, perfume, bag, designer shirt and then it stopped.

For two weeks nothing came, she was disappointed but then thankful for the things she received and she sent her thanks. She was opening her door one evening after coming back from work, when she saw a slip which the postman had left saying she had a parcel to pick from their depot. She wondered what it was and put it in her bag and hoped she would remember. She was getting ready for work the next day when she opened her bag and saw the slip; she still had some spare time so she went to collect the parcel and then dump it in her car boot. She was having dinner at home when Daniel sent her a message asking if she received her parcel. She was surprised because all the gifts she received from him were sent to her work place and never at home, she wondered what the gift was. As she opened the parcel her heart skipped a beat and then her phone rang.

"Do you like them?"

She didn't know what to say as he had caught her off guard.

"I can't accept them."

"Why not, it's a gift."

"Yes, but not these."

"I see."

"Daniel you don't understand."

"I do understand you very well Monisola. You can let me into your life but only on your terms and condition, I can't accept that, I guess this is goodbye."

"What do you mean, I told you to come over and you said you will."

"You want me to come over and do what? Hold your hands? For crying out loud Monisola, I am a man not a boy, I need you and want you. I have waited and I am not waiting anymore and I can see you are not ready for me."

"I am" she whispered.

"If you can't accept that gift then you are not."

"Daniel I can't, I ..." She tried to plead with him as she feared what he was about to say.

"Good bye Monisola, have a nice life."

She was miserable throughout that week. She called him but he didn't answer his phone. She sent private messages via his social media network but still no reply. She didn't know what to do or who to talk to so she kept everything to herself but the pains wouldn't just go. This wasn't happening to her again, she knew she would go mad if she didn't speak to someone. She tried calling him again, it went to voicemail, she left several messages for him to please call her. He didn't.

Andrew was the only one that noticed something wasn't right so he invited her to lunch at his place but she declined, she wanted to go home.

"Ok if you won't come home with me at least we can talk here."

"I don't want to talk about it."

"Fine can we pray about it then?"

She shrugged her shoulders.

"Ok, Lord I'm praying on behalf of Monisola and whoever is causing her this grief that she is trying to hide and nobody but you see. LORD can you please sort it out and let her know she doesn't have to carry the burden alone. Thank You Lord for answers to our prayers in Jesus name. Amen.

Monisola forgot all about the prayer and just continued as normal throughout the week. She was on her way to work on Friday when Toluwanimi called to say he would like to spend Easter with her.

"Are you sure you want to spend your holiday with me instead of your girlfriend or Father?"

"I'll rather spend it with you, I think our parents want some time alone so father was quick to give me permission to come to you and honestly mother has been so cranky lately you would think it more than the pregnancy."

Monisola laughed, "Maybe if you were carrying one yourself you would tell us how it feels."

"No way, GOD did a great job giving that duty to women, I can testify to that. So, do you want me to come or not."

"I'll love to and you don't need my permission, you are my brother."

"So, you wouldn't mind if I bring some friends with me."

"Toluwanimi" her tone changed.

"Yes Monisola" her brother answered cautiously.

Monisola noticed it, laughed and said, "Don't push your luck."

"I'm favoured and everywhere I go, GOD's favour follows me, any way I was just kidding, I need some me time with my sister, see you Thursday."

"See you."

Toluwanimi came on Thursday alright but all he wanted to do was sleep and sleep, something he had not been able to do since their Father arrived from Nigeria. They were forever talking and going for one seminar or exhibition or the other and coupled with his studies he needed time to rest. She left him at home and told him all he had to do was make sure he ate as she had cooked and prepared different kinds of dishes for him.

She was having lunch with her colleagues when her phone rang.

"Hello"

"Monisola it's me Daniel, I need your help."

She felt the pain in her heart ease up and she tried to calm herself.

"Are you there?" Daniel asked when she didn't say anything.

"Yes."

"I need a place to stay and also some clothes."

Now she was getting scared.

"What happened? Are you okay?"

"No. I got into a fight with a dog."

She laughed and then quickly apologised.

"Daniel people don't get into fights with dogs."

"Are you going to help or not?"

"Sorry but how do you expect me to arrange a place for you in Chicago when I am here in London."

"I am here somewhere in Essex and I know my friend's partner set me up."

Okay this was getting serious. "Where exactly are you?"

"I don't know; where are you? I can come to you."

"I'm at work right now but I would be leaving in the next ten minutes, can we meet up at..."

"Monisola my pants are torn and I might be bleeding and I need to get to the hospital."

"Okay, get a cab to take you to my house and I'll meet you there."

"Do I have to wait outside till you get there?"

"No, my brother is there, I will let him know you are on your way."

As soon as she put her phone down she told her colleague she had an emergency and would see them after the Easter celebration and hoped they had a great time off.

On her way home, she went to the shopping mall bought Daniel some clothes and underwear and also arranged for a doctor to see him at home.

When she got home the doctor was just leaving; he told her everything was okay and that he had given him some injections. He prescribed bed rest but had no cure for his phobia of dogs.

When she saw him lying on the bed sleeping, she smiled, he was looking rough but still handsome.

She went to meet her brother who had finally woken up and was eating.

"Are you going to finish all that?"

"Yes, I might have more."

"But you are so skinny."

"Do you know what Father has been putting me through lately?"

"Well if I survived so can you."

"Have you been mountain climbing and surviving on canned meals?"

"Have you been in the forest and had to make food from what you caught?"

He shook his hand.

"Then don't complain about canned food."

"Gosh I don't think I want to be a prince anymore."

"You are a prince and the heir apparent and everything you are doing now is to prepare you for the future."

"I'm not sure of the future especially outside of Zurich."

"You might have been born there but your place and home is with your people and kingdom."

"Monisola, I'm scared."

"You don't have to be, you always have father to help you; I can also help but most of all you need GOD, that's if you believe in Him."

"Oh, but I do, that's one thing mother did not spare me with, she told me the meaning of my name, that I was GOD's personal property that no one could mess with, that GOD gave me to her when she had completely lost hope and that one day our family would see GOD at work."

"You should be thankful for mother raising you."

"Yes, I am and she used to talk so much about you. I sometimes think

I would never measure up to my big sister."

"You have nothing to fear from me, I am no competition."

"Even with Omoniyi gone?"

"Why do you all think I was competing with him? We were siblings and the rivalry between us was only natural and nothing to do with the throne. Omoniyi and I just have this competitive streak in us and we used it to get whatever we wanted from our parents and later we boasted about who had the most impressive and manipulative method of getting things from them. Honestly don't listen to anything anyone says about Omoniyi and I, people never understood us and the slightest game test of who was better than the other was misconstrued."

"You mean you didn't hate him?" Toluwanimi asked, surprised.

"For what? Being a brother and a companion in mischief and getting told off for what I did, no, I loved him."

"Wow! I think I'm beginning to see why Father said I should be careful about you."

"He said that?" Monisola asked with a raised eyebrow.

"Not directly but something to the tune of don't play games with Monisola, she always plays to win."

"Hmm! I see that old man has not forgotten."

The next day Monisola was in the kitchen preparing breakfast when she heard someone whistle.

"Sexy legs."

"I was enjoying the view but you just distracted my attention"

She ignored both her brother and Daniel, "If you guys don't have anything to do please come and make yourselves useful by helping me."

"What are you cooking?"

"Hot dogs" she replied and heard Daniel take a deep breath. "Just joking."

She felt him move closer and she turned to look at him. He was looking better, well rested and his smile was sending messages to her whole body.

He moved closer and wrapped his hands around her, "Good morning, how could I ever thank you for saving my life second time around", he kissed her lips and if not for her brother's whistling she knew he would have carried on.

"I have to finish cooking."

He released her, gave her a peck and went to the living room.

"Toluwanimi."

"Yes."

"Can you keep a secret?"

"I did it with mum, I can do it with anyone."

"Good. I don't want father to know about Daniel."

"Why?"

"You would not understand."

"Try me, I'm not as naive as I look."

"I know but this is just something between father and I. Trust me I know what I am saying."

"Why don't you just come out and tell him you've found someone you love, I'm sure he will be happy for you."

"Have you ever seen a leopard shed his spots before?"

He shook his head.

"Good, leave father to me."

He wasn't sure if his sister was making the right decision but perhaps she knew their father better so he raised his hand in surrender.

It was when they were having their breakfast that it all came back to Monisola. GOD had answered Andrew's prayer when he prayed on her behalf. How could she have doubted GOD and the fact that HE loved her and wanted the best for her? She smiled, not only was Daniel here in her house but with her brother and certainly he couldn't carry out his intended mission. The table had turned, he was the one seeking her help now and the game was hers to play. She quickly excused herself while they were still eating and went upstairs.

After breakfast Daniel and Toluwanimi decided to go for a walk and she decided to go to the shops to buy a few things. She was trying to decide what flavour of ice cream to buy when her phone rang.

"Monisola quit playing games with me", Daniel stated in an angry tone.

"I beg your pardon, what do you mean?" she feigned some innocence.

"You understand perfectly, why did you put that sexy lacy underwear I sent to you on my bed?"

"Your bed?"

"I mean the bed I am currently occupying in your house."

"Your bed in my house, surely that means I'm ready to play your game now that you've come back to me."

"I didn't come back to you I was desperate when Lynn set those dogs on me..."

"You can always go back to Lynn" she laughed.

"Monisola I feel like ..."

"In my own house and after all I've done to care for you and show you I'm ready."

"You know that's impossible, not when your brother is under the same roof with us."

"Why not? All I have to do is send him to his ......"

"Oh! Just shut up, you might have won this time but I will get you?"

"Chocolate or Vanilla."

"I prefer toffee, it goes with your skin colour."

"I was talking about ice cream."

"I was talking about my preference of women; you know you are winding me up" he stated when he heard her laughing.

"You know I'm just playing your game."

"I'll catch you."

"I'm waiting at the finishing line."

By the time she got home, both men were sleeping, which gave her time to herself and catch up with the rest of the world. She was watching TV when Mano called.

"Mr Mano, you finally remembered me today."

"You know you have a special place in my heart after my son and wife"

"Wife! Have you paid the bride price or brought a truck load of yam to greet us your in-laws?"

"You see, you should ask your friend, when I asked for a list of all her family, it was the names that she gave that I sent a trailer load of not only yams but rice, beans, corn, cows, even fish and lions too."

"Why the lions? Did we tell you we eat lions?"

"Oh, the lions are just to guard all the food stuff from the likes of people pretending to be family not that I am mentioning names."

"Ah! Don't worry when you need a baby sitter just let me know, it's either I charge you a thousand pounds per hour or I flatly refuse."

"A thousand pounds an hour, that's great! I'd like that, which means when we pick him up to go home, he should be able to feed himself, change his nappies, know all his alphabets and ....."

"Mano, Eman is not even one year old and you want him to do all that."

"Why not, what is the thousand pounds for if not to teach him all that?"

"Your oblong head"

"Princess Monisola, from your mouth, insulting your friend-in-law!"

"Did I, I do apologies, I was only thanking GOD Eman looks like his mother."

"Now I know you are looking for a fight because that is a no-go area, my son, I mean our son looks exactly like me, except nowadays when I look at him I keep seeing traits of Chichi in him."

Monisola laughed and booed him.

Just then Daniel came into the room and sat beside her, here comes trouble.

"What are you guys doing for Easter?" she continued her phone conversation, hoping to deter Daniel from any mischief.

"Your friend is the best person to speak to, nowadays she is so cranky?"

"Cranky? What is making her cranky?"

"The same question I keep asking her."

"Mano? What are you doing to my friend?"

"You mean what is she doing to me?"

Monisola felt Daniel's arm go round her and pull her to him. Now the trouble had landed.

"Chichi oginni?" she asked her dear friend wondering what her problem was.

"Biko don't pester me with questions, that is all I get from the people here."

"Eman is also asking questions, that's good, very commendable, he must take after his father not olodo like you."

Daniel's hands were going astray so she moved away and stood up.

"What are you guys doing for Easter?" she took a few steps from Daniel but he moved closer and began to poke her and trickle her, which made her laugh.

"Why are you laughing?" Chichi asked.

"I'm not" she moved from Daniel and wagged her finger for him to stop but he ignored her.

"Are you laughing at yourself?" Chichi asked.

"No. Stop it! Sorry Chic I'll call you later", talking to both Chichi and Daniel at the same time.

"Don't you put that phone down on me, who is there with you, is it Raymond?" Chichi demanded.

"Are you out of your mind? Of course not."

"Who is it then?"

"Mind your own business."

"Oh! Who or what are you hiding?"

"Chic I'll call you later." She ended the call and turned to Daniel, "Stop it, I was on the phone, that was rude."

"I didn't come here for you to ignore me and be talking to your friends on the phone."

"I don't remember inviting you."

"Ok I'll go pack my bags then."

She step aside for him to do just that but as soon as he got to her he grabbed her and tickled her again.

"Daniel, please stop it" she laughed.

"Beg me"

"I never beg"

He tickled her again which made her fall on the sofa, the very opportunity he had been waiting for. He wasted no time, he moved closer and just looking at her sensual lips made him want to lick it and without hesitation he began to. Her lips tasted like orange, mango and watermelon, it was juicy and he liked the taste of her. He wanted more. Monisola felt his lips and his tongue on her and she knew strange fires were burning in her. The way he kissed and licked her lips and mouth was as if he was sucking a juicy fruit and the noise he was making about it made her laugh.

A cough from the door made them stop.

"Are you sure you don't want to tell father how you feel?"

Monisola's finger on her lips made her brother stop.

"What do you mean?" Daniel asked Toluwanimi.

"Nothing?" Monisola quickly interrupted, moved out of Daniel's embrace and asked "What do you guys want for lunch?"

"Actually, I was thinking about taking you out tonight." Daniel stated, with his eyes sending signals to her.

"I don't want to eat out, not tonight."

"Monisola you just missed out on a big invitation most girls would run for."

"I'm not most girls, I just want to stay home, you guys can go if you want."

"Nope, I'll just make some sandwich and back to the land of nod", Toluwanimi yawned.

"Too much sleep is not good for you", Monisola advised him.

"At least when I sleep, I dream of Lisa."

"Lisa?"

"My South African lover, that girl drives me nuts; do you know how long I have been asking her to go out with me? I've practically chased her round the continent and back but all she says is wait, wait for what? Girl I need some action."

"I think Father still has lesson to teach you."

"We've been to that chapter and he says I can be free as a bird as I am a man."

"I don't believe you" she stated in disbelief, wondering if they were talking about the same person.

"Neither did I when he first said it. When I probed further he explained the ordeals he's had with women and the latest with mother. He concluded that it was safer and far better to weather all storms with your one true love than go from one argument, fight, war, battle and total wipe out with a dozen women."

Daniel laughed and laughed until she tugged him with her elbow.

"What is so funny" she asked with her eyes alight with fire which made him quickly shake his head and said nothing.

Monisola turned to Toluwanimi, "So where does Lisa come in?"

"I like Lisa, I think I'm in love with her but she is wearing me out with her determination to wait, how long do I have to wait?"

"What exactly are you waiting for, are you ready to marry her or what?"

"Marry! Monisola please! I'm still a very young man and marriage is not an island I want to perch on right now, I just want a taste of what is to come and then enjoy the glide when I finally decide to settle down."

"In that case you will wait forever" she snapped at him and walked towards the kitchen.

"Eh! Where are you going? We haven't finished this conversation, it's getting interesting, don't you think so?" Toluwanimi stated excitedly.

"I sure would like to know how long a guy needs to wait for before the girl says yes", Daniel asked, enjoying the line which the conversation was treading.

"Like I said forever? If you are waiting for a taste to just sample and go, forever and ever, Amen" Monisola stated in an angry and high-pitched tone and marched towards the door.

Both guys looked at each other.

"Hey! Wait a minute Monisola, let just imagine, no, let's consider my bruv here, Daniel and you. You are into each other, you are both in love, you can't take your eyes and hands off each other and my bruv wants a taste. Are you saying you are going to tell him to wait, you can't do that?"

"Why not?" she asked him; her eyes already spitting fire at him.

"Okay I guess I should back off now, my one and precious sister is about to have my head for dinner. I'll catch you guys later. Just let me know when lunch is ready and I'll be back" he ran out as quickly as his legs could carry him.

She was cooking when Daniel came into the kitchen, she didn't even bother to look at him.

He watched her cook and then moved closer. Each time he moved closer there was a magnet that seemed to pull them together and though right now she could have his head for lunch as he was sure she was angry but he just couldn't stop himself.

"Daniel please," she tried to push him off.

"Monisola please."

He began to kiss the back of her neck and was caressing her shoulders.

"Daniel please stop."

"I can't."

"You better if you don't want any part of your body to be cooked with this food."

He laughed and turned her to him. "I knew your hands were itching to cut off my head."

"I won't cut off your head, just a little piece as a reminder for next time."

"I did not start the conversation so why bite my head off, go talk to your brother."

"Honestly I wish I could train that boy myself, I will give him some good training"

"He is not a boy anymore and thank GOD he doesn't have to go through what Omoniyi went through in your hands."

She stepped on his toes but he did not bulge.

"It will take more than that for me to back off, how long do I have to wait Monisola, you are slowly driving me insane."

"How fast can I drive you into insanity."

He laughed again, "Stop playing games with me Monisola you

wouldn't like it."

"I would love it, who said I'm playing games, I'm ready."

He looked at her and when she did not bait an eye lid he knew something was amiss.

"Take me to your room."

She shook her head, "Right here now."

He began to kiss her and was already placing his hands where they were forbidden. She knew she had called for trouble and she would have to bear it.

The doorbell rang, he stopped, breathless and looked at her.

She moved towards the door but he stopped her.

"Leave it."

"I can't."

"Who are you expecting?"

"I don't know."

He was about to start again when they heard voices.

"Hi, you must be Toluwanimi, Monic told me about you."

"Monic?"

"Monisola, I'm Chichi, my boyfriend Mano and our son Eman."

"I'm her husband, not her boyfriend, please to meet you T."

"Hi, look who is here, it my baby Eman, gosh you've grown again. I'm sure I saw you last week and you weren't this big, what has your momma being feeding you with?" Monisola said as she rushed out of the kitchen.

"A month more like it, hello to you too". Chichi greeted her with her eyes already rolling.

"I've told you drama doesn't fit you, stick to your teaching. How are you my dear friend-in-law, I am still waiting for my tubers of yam."

"This is the sixth time I'm sending that trailer maybe I will try a bicycle this time."

"Bicycle, for a princess like myself, ok don't ask me to do anything for you because it is already a no."

"Even if it is to babysit Eman tonight?"

"Night gini? What do I feed him with?"

"The very thing your friend does every night" Mano winked at her.

They were still talking when Daniel walked in and immediately Chichi saw the reaction on Monisola's face.

There was silence at first but Mano soon broke it.

"Hi my name is Mano and you must be ..."

"Daniel."

"I'm pleased to meet you."

They shook hands and soon started a conversation.

"Don't I get an introduction?" Chichi demanded looking at Monisola with a glint of mischief.

Before she could say anything else Monisola quickly ran to the kitchen stating something was burning.

Lunch was served and everyone dived in.

As soon as Chichi tasted it, she sighed with relief, "This is food."

"And what about the one I've been cooking, what is it called" Mano asked his wife.

"Plastic food." she munched some more.

"At least I cook."

"I'm not even going to start another argument with you, I just want to enjoy this food and then I can get cranky again."

"What is all these talk about being cranky?" Monisola asked the couple.

"She's been ...."

"Hey, she asked me a question and when I am ready to answer her I will, that is after she tells me why she was laughing on the phone and hung up the phone on me."

"I didn't."

"You did."

"Did not."

"Here we go again, can you two just quit these childish games, I've endured them for too long" Mano begged the two ladies in the room.

"So, who put your mouth there", his wife replied.

"Endure some more", Monisola added reminding the three of their teenage years and pranks.

Mano turned to Daniel and Toluwanimi, "This is what I go through every time they argue, which is like every other day, imagine if I had married the two of them."

Daniel shot him an invisible but eye piercing dagger across the room which made Chichi laughed.

The chatting continued with subjects ranging from sports, international affairs, women, men and almost every other thing. When they finally finished their meal, Monisola asked for volunteers to do the washing up; Toluwanimi, Mano and Chichi declined and they moved to the living room leaving Monisola and Daniel to tidy up.

"Thank you all for eating, at least you did something."

"You are welcome", Mano replied.

"When is dinner going to be ready, maybe we should wait because I

am not eating plastic food tonight after all the delicacy I've just had"
Chichi added and winked at Monisola.

Daniel helped her stack all the dishes in the dish washer and also
tidied up.

"Anything else?" he asked

"No, thank you. I think you should also put your feet up."

"Only if you join me, it's your holiday remember and I don't want you
to overdo things."

"I'm not, from tomorrow you and Toluwanimi will do the cooking
while I ...."

"Hey! Did I tell you what a fantastic cook you are, your food is so
delicious I almost licked the plate; do me a favour, cook all the meals
tomorrow and after that we eat out."

"Why? Can't you cook", she asked in disbelief.

"Monisola, what century are you in, haven't you heard of the word
personal chef or cook before? I can cook but I don't cook, I don't just
have the time."

Her eyes began to glimmer.

"Monisola please do not attempt to play with my food. I do not joke
with two things after GOD, food and pleasure, you've been backing
out on one don't attempt the other, you won't like it."

"Is that a threat?"

"Monisola! Monisola! My Princess, Epo pupa, oil of the delta, don't
mess with me. I keep warning and you refuse to listen; my people say,
every day is for the thief, one day is for the owner, watch it or you are
going to slip into my net and I won't let go."

She moved closer, "I keep telling you, I like to play because in every game I never, ever lose."

She began to kiss him, making sure her hands were on his upper body, she wasn't going to play with fire again.

"I like this kind of dish washing and tidying up, I wish Mano did this type."

"Chichi, just shut up", Monisola turned away feeling embarrassed that she had forgotten her guest.

"Of course, I will, after I've said my own"

Chichi and her family finally left, Toluwanimi went straight to bed which left the two love birds.

"What did Toluwanimi mean when he said you should tell your father about us?"

"Nothing."

"What are you trying to hide from me?"

"Nothing" she quickly stated.

"Monisola ..."

"Daniel go to bed and leave me alone."

Her voice was so commanding that he almost obeyed her but something in him rebelled. He swung her round and forced her to look at him, "Don't you ever talk to me in that tone again."

"I'm sorry" she almost cried.

He didn't expect that so quickly, he dropped the guard, "I'm sorry too."

They both sat down and said nothing for a while.

"Please let me in."

"Daniel I can't."

"I mean your thoughts."

She sighed with relief.

"Am I putting pressure on you? I don't like doing that, I'll leave tomorrow"

She turned to him and shook her head and in a whisper said, "Please don't. I need you here."

"But you don't want me."

Okay maybe this was her last chance to tell this guy what the issues were but before she could say anything he was already kissing her. She responded, stopped and held on to him. There was no one to stop them and she couldn't. He knew she wasn't ready and he knew he couldn't do this to her so he stopped. "I'll leave tomorrow."

"It's not you, it's me."

"Let me in then, talk to me Muremiwa."

"It not you and I that should do the talking, it's between my father and I."

Her father again, the mention of her father, bothered him and he wanted it to stop. " What is it about your father?"

"I can't talk to you about it until I sort it out with him first."

"I see, you will rather talk to your father first than talk to me. It can't work that way. Monisola you come to me first, no GOD first as your Heavenly Father, then me."

"I don't see it that way. GOD first, followed by my father and then my friend."

He nodded, "I see."

"What do you see?"

"Whatever is between us can only go as far as friendship nothing more."

"For now, yes."

"What is stopping us from going a step further right now."

"I need to talk to my ..."

"Monisola please don't say that word again, I respect the authority of your father over you but not over me or us."

"You don't understand."

"Tell me, I can assure you I am no dunce, I do understand."

What was she supposed to tell him, that she needed her father's permission to sleep with him? Of course not and she wasn't going to sleep with him like that. Which only leaves one thing, if she told him why she needed her dad's permission he would suggest only one thing - marriage. That was one thing she wasn't ready to face with him because she knew they were both singing from different hymn books.

"Daniel if I ..., if we make love now what next, I mean what happens afterwards?"

"What do you mean what happens afterwards. The natural thing of course, we make love, all night if possible. Tomorrow I'll go back to Chicago and then as soon as you can, you come over spend some time with me, I'll come and thereafter we sort something out as to where we want to meet"

"Meet as in ..."

"Where to meet to make love, talk, make love and talk."

"Can't we do that here or in your place?"

"Sure, why not?"

"And that's all we do, make... ..make love.... and talk."

"Yes! What more do you want?"

"What if I don't want to ...urrrh.....do it all the time?"

"You will."

"How do you know?"

"Because once we start we can't and won't stop."

"Anything else to come with it?"

"Nothing you don't want."

She couldn't believe he was saying this to her.

He couldn't believe she was taking all these in.

"Good night Daniel."

"Are we not making love again?"

Her eyes told him what her mouth could not say. He started to laugh and his body was quivering from the laughter that she actually begged him to stop.

"What is so funny?"

"Monisola..." he tried to catch his breath and held on to his side. "Monisola in my entire life I have never ever met anyone like you, girl you are one of a kind."

She got up from the sofa while he was lying on the floor holding on to his side. What on earth was wrong with this man?

"To actually think that you believed all that rubbish and garbage I fed you with, girl you are dumb."

He made a mistake, no one ever called her dumb, not even her teachers, so she taught him a lesson, one he would never forget; she gave him a kick by the side he had been holding. He screamed and that yell was one that Monisola would never, ever forget in her life, it frightened her.

At first, she thought it was a joke but when he did not get up, she quickly knelt beside him and tried to move his hand away from his side but the grip was so tight it was as if he wanted to wrench his side inside out.

"Daniel please talk to me, please, I'm sorry, I was only playing ..."

"Go to the room.... urrrh... on the bedside table, there's a black bag, please bring it quickly"

She did as she was told and when she got back to the living room he wasn't there. A movement from the kitchen alerted her and she saw him with a glass of water. He beckoned for her to open the bag and as she did she saw some tablets and he snatched it from her and took four at a go.

"Isn't that too much?"

He waved her away and lay on the sofa.

She looked at the prescription, it wasn't something she was familiar with but the dosage was high. Why was he taking such a high dosage for just a little pain not that she kicked him hard? She moved closer to him and tried to move his hands but he still held tight.

"Don't! You might not like what you see."

She was even more determined, she moved his hands away and as she moved her hands under his shirt, what she felt made her stop. She looked at him and his face was completely blank. Slowly she pulled the shirt away and what she saw made her gasp and cover her mouth. She didn't know when she started crying.

"Monisola please go away and leave me alone"

She took off her slippers and joined him on the sofa, she lifted his shirt again, gripping it as she did and slowly pulled it. She started crying and this time loudly.

He wasn't sure what to do, leave her here or just push her away. He was in so much pain he couldn't think. He made room for her on the sofa and hugged her. She cried, wept and all he could think of was GOD help me with this girl.

"Monisola, the wound is healed and you are crying like this, what if you saw it when it just happened what would you do?" She held him tight and sobbed a bit more.

"It's okay, I'm alright now, the prescription is taking its toll but you are squeezing me."

She held him tighter.

"Ease up girl or you get it now."

She was past caring she just held him.

"Monisola I mean you are arousing me and I don't want to do anything now than just ease this pain, please move over."

She ignored him and begin to trace her hands on the scar, gasping in pain as she did.

"Who did this to you?"

"Do you want to fight them?"

"I want to rip their body apart" she answered in anger.

"Not these ones, they are military trained and the facts remains that no one has owned up to doing it so you are welcome to do the research because I've given up and left everything to GOD"

"I'll find them out."

One look at her told him she would. He groaned, GOD why this girl, the more bait I throw she catches them all, she is tough but then wasn't she the one who was crying just now. He laughed but then he obeyed the nudge in his heart.

"Monisola, I don't want you finding out who did what to who, leave everything to GOD and let HIM sort it out. All I want right now is to feel your body next to mine, I'm only going to hold you and lie beside you, that's all I want, please."

She turned over to him and could see the plea in his eyes. For now, she would let go.

"Promise me one thing."

He groaned, "What?"

"You will let me sort out the issue between my father and I and then you will come to me."

"No, you tell me what is between you and your father, then go to him and sort it out. Then you Monisola, my princess will come to me. How many times do I have to tell you I call the shots?"

"That's not fair, what about me?"

"Did I predestine you to come into the world as a woman? Thank GOD, He made you a woman. My GOD, as a man you would have been a tough contender. Just one kick and I have to take four co-codamol tablets to relieve the pain, tell me are you going to be this wild in bed?"

Her hands were already up but she remembered she had just sent him into some spasm of pain so she lowered her hand.

"Thank you. I wonder if my face would have recovered from that slap. She bit his shirt and groaned, "I am trying so hard not to hit you."

"Please do and you will tell my sister what I did to deserve such a beating."

"What about your parents?"

"I don't have parents; they died several years ago."

She started to cry again.

"Monisola please go to your room, you are irritating me with your tears, what past events do you want to cry for again?"

"What happened to them?"

"One died first and then the other, I don't want to talk about it please."

"Why not?" she asked, fearing that he had so much emotional baggage.

"I just don't want to" he snapped.

"And you accuse me of keeping secrets."

"I am not keeping secrets; I've told you they died and I wasn't even there when they did. I was in the Marine then, I only received the news some weeks after, they couldn't tell me because I was in ..... Monisola I beg you stop opening fresh wounds tonight or I'll make love to you."

She started to kiss him but he held her back, "We are not starting tonight, until you sort whatever it is and you don't have to if you don't want to."

"He made me promise not to sleep with anyone until I'm married that's all"

He looked at her, sure enough she had eaten the bait he threw and if that was the truth then only one thing was in perspective.

"Marry me Monisola."

It took her a second to realise what she had done; he had purposely set her up.

She moved away from him but he held her back.

"I still want you beside me, honestly your body against mine is the only treatment for the pain."

"Liar!"

"Believe it or not, it's the truth."

"You deliberately...."

"I did not force you to say what you did not want to say, I have asked a question please give me my answer."

"No."

"Why?"

"You only said it because I told you the prerequisite and anyway our views of marriage are different, all you want to do is find a venue to make love and reconvene again and again, no attachment, no strings, I wonder what kind of life you've been living. Meet, find a venue and reconvene" she said in utter disgust.

He was laughing uncontrollably and then he started coughing and was forced to sit up. She passed him the glass of water and after several sips he calmed down.

"Goodness gracious me; GOD see me see this girl. Monisola please either you go to your room or you lie beside me and just shut up because I can't take....." he began to laugh again.

She got up, left him in the living room and went upstairs. A few minutes later she went into his room.

"Monisola please leave me alone, I need some rest."

"I promised to stay with you."

"I don't need you anymore, go to your room."

She ignored him and lay on the bed. He couldn't resist so he joined her.

After a few hard breathing, they began to kiss each other, she was trying to unbutton his shirt when he stopped her, "This is the only night we are going to spend on a bed together and do nothing, the next time we do it will be as man and wife, so hurry up and sort out the issue with your father and then come to me as mine"

She smiled, closed her eyes and laid in his arms.

He could hear her breathing, the rhythm of it and how her breathing made her body heave up and then down. He liked this, in fact he loved it. GOD this is the one I have found by your help, please make her mine and help me to keep my sanity and not lose it before tomorrow morning. Soon he was fast asleep and both were breathing in rhythm to their heart beat.

This page has been left intentionally blank

CHAPTER THIRTEEN

L ater in the evening they were getting dressed to go for a concert, which was organised to raise funds for children in the worst deprived areas of the world. Lola Gospel, the lady organising the concert was from Monisola's church and they had talked about it for quite a while and she did not want to miss it. Initially Daniel declined her invitation; he preferred to stay at home.

"Why?"

"Why not?"

"I can't leave you here."

"I can assure you I won't sniff through your things."

"You know that's not what I mean; I want you to come, please."

"No! No!"

She moved closer and baited her eyelids at him.

"I bind that seducing spirit in JESUS name."

"It wasn't seduction when I kissed you last night."

"I kissed you and I'm not going."

"Oh! Please Dani baby."

"No Moni baby, go with your brother."

"He's coming but I also want you to come."

"Ok, I don't have anything to wear, I have been waiting for my friend Des to bring my things but I don't think he's coming again."

"I could lend you some of mine."

"Your dress or your miniskirts?" he asked looking at her intently.

"You could pass for a girl if I just ....." she used her hand to shape up his eyebrow and turned his head to see his features.

"Make no mistake I am a man and I'm about to show you how manly I can be, yesterday was just starter."

He began to kiss her and just as he was about to pull her closer the doorbell rang.

"What kind of a house is this, every time someone keeps interrupting one thing or the other; I can't take this anymore and you are coming to Chicago with me."

She smiled and quickly went to see who had come to save her. She laughed at herself; no one was going to save her but herself.

She looked through the keyhole and saw someone with his back to the door, he turned and looked at his wrist watch and pressed the bell again. She slowly opened the door, there was a suitcase beside him, he was looking at his watch again and also looking around; he turned, spotted her, paused, did a double take, smiled and smacked his lips with his tongue.

Huh!!! She hated it when guys did that.

"How can I help you?" she said in her near snobbish voice.

"D, is D here?"

"D?" she repeated for his benefit so he could know and say the proper name or apologise for knocking at the wrong door."

"My friend Daniel."

"Oh! Daniel. And you are ...."

"Des....Desmond!"

D, Des, Desmond, why can't people just use their full name.

"Good afternoon, please come in."

He came in and was looking around and eventually his eyes came back to her and he smiled in a sly way. Monisola readjusted her posture just in case someone tried to be silly. She sighed - this was one of the few times she wished she had a butler; she would just clap her hands and D, Des or whatever his name was, would be thrown out. She burst that bubble because it wasn't going to happen and just then she heard Daniel come in.

"Des! Des! How you dey now, na your twelve o'clock be dis, useless time keeper."

Monisola was shocked to her socks, well her slippers, did she just hear her man speak in pidgin English! Wonders!

"You self you be useless boy, I don tell you say make you no dey fear dog, you con dey run from ordinary dog pickin."

"You dey craze! Dog pickin abi a dozen puppies, how do you live in that house with all that mess?"

"How I no go live there, no be my house and the girl wey I wan marry, no worry, after wedding we go sort out what comes in and what goes out. I can assure you those dog pickins na dem go commot first, I no dey sleep with dog for bed, na my wife bodi I wan wrap for mi bodi no be puppy."

They both laughed and hugged each other.

Monisola could not believe her ears, birds of the same feathers did flock together and she wasn't sure which of the birds was corrupting the other.

She was still staring at them when they realised she was watching them.

Daniel coughed and tapped his friend.

"Des, I'll like to introduce you to Monisola, my .... friend."

"Girlfriend abi friend-friend?" Des asked curiously.

Daniel slapped his shoulders and said something through clenched teeth. He cleared his throat, "Monisola this is my friend Des, Desmond he brought my things."

Monisola smiled though her eyes were telling a different story.

"We've met, would you like a drink ..."

Daniel slapped his back and said something again.

"No, erm! I have to go, it's a pleasure meeting you Monisola I hope to see more of you", he did the lip licking again and Monisola was tempted to shove him out of her house.

"You weren't nice to my friend", Daniel stated when he returned from seeing Des off.

"Your friend wasn't very polite either."

"You can't judge a book by its cover."

"I don't even pick up just any book."

"Come down from your high horse Princess."

"Well I could give you a ride, commoner."

He looked at her and shook his head, "Me a commoner?"

"Aren't you, if I am a princess, who are you?"

"Don't worry, next time I will find somewhere else to stay and avoid your Buckingham palace."

"Like I said I did not invite you."

He took his suitcase and was moving towards the door when she quickly blocked his way.

"Where do you think you are going?"

"Sorry Princess, since I wasn't invited, how can a mere commoner like me come and stay in your royal palace in fact I should have been sleeping in the kitchen..."

"Oh, just shut up and take your suitcase upstairs and stop this Nollywood drama you are acting."

"Nollywood, na jardonwood I go show you now."

He grabbed her hand and pulled her to him, he was about to kiss her and then look towards the door, "If that bell rings again I will tear that door down."

The phone rang.

"Are we set?" Monisola came down the stairs hoping Toluwanimi and Daniel were ready. They were ready alright but stood still when they saw her.

Her brother whistled, "Lord have mercy on some brothers tonight, I'm just glad you are my sister and I don't have to be counting the ceiling tonight."

"Watch it! You look dazzling in that shirt; did Mother make it for you?"

"Yes!" he did a catwalk in his linen embroidery designer 'buba' and skinny fit jeans.

She turned to look at Daniel, he was wearing a white shirt, jeans and a cut to fit jacket and he was already making her head spin except the look on his face. What now?

He shook his head, "Please baby go and change."

"What?"

He smiled and moved closer, "Please go and change."

"Why?"

"I'll help you pick something suitable."

"Why is this not suitable?"

"Are you sure you want to go for that concert?"

"Daniel you are wasting my time."

"You are making my blood rush, goodness Monisola you can't wear this dress; it's too... too short and before the evening runs out I will definitely be thrown out of the hall because I will knock down anybody that dares looks at you."

"Daniel don't be silly; this is what I'm wearing and I'm not changing."

"Ok, Toluwanimi do you know how to fight."

"Not over my sister. I mean I will fight over Lisa but not over Monisola, you are on your own bruv."

"Lazy bone" Daniel sneered at him.

"Yes, let me be, I know it will be a hundred men against two, so what do you want me to do?"

"Can you please stop this and let's be on our way" Monisola begged as she didn't want to miss the concert.

"Who's driving?" Daniel asked

"I am."

Daniel threw the key past her; she didn't catch it and it fell.

Monisola stooped to pick it up and while she was rising up she saw

Daniel's eyes following her.

She stood up and walked up to him, "Mr Daniel did you see anything?"

He shook his head.

"Good! Let's be on our way then."

"Who is sitting at the back?" Toluwanimi asked as soon as he saw her car.

"My legs are longer than yours", Daniel quickly chipped in as he also saw the sport car.

"Why do you have a two-door car when people are getting four wheels drive, you are cramping my style though this car is bam!"

"Toluwanimi you can always take the train."

"From where to where?"

"In that case sit at the back and keep quiet. Mr Daniel are you sure you don't want to drive?"

"I'll rather watch you so I know whether to write to the DVLA to revoke your licence or you get a kiss."

"A kiss", she pouted and winked at him.

"Drive woman."

They were on the motorway and Monisola was driving carefully but at the same time increasing her speed and changing lanes.

"For a woman you do drive safely."

"Are you sure? I know you've been stepping on the imaginary brake from your side every now and then."

"You keep switching lanes and you drive fast"

"You don't expect me to be going on twenty; if I had my way at least a hundred."

"Monisola please I want to live to see Lisa", Toluwanimi cried from behind.

"Maybe a broken arm would help her decide quickly."

"Yeah! That she doesn't want me."

The concert was just about to start when they arrived at the hall, she picked up her tickets at the door and turned to the guys. "We have a slight problem here; I had already ordered two tickets before tonight and an extra one now but we can't all seat together. So, do you both want to sit together or one of you sit with me?"

"You are not moving away from me." Daniel stated firmly.

"Sexy M that dress is a killer" someone said from behind them.

Daniel groaned while Toluwanimi laughed.

"Hi Andrew, how are you, where is Laura?"

"She's inside but you and I can just steal away into the night and no one would notice."

Having Andrew in the same room with Daniel could prove to be a disaster as Monisola remembered Daniel's earlier comment about fighting anyone that looks at her, so she quickly introduced her companions to him and hoped Andrew would take a cue. He did not.

"Hi, are you her body guards, I can assure you she is safe with me, you guys go inside while Sexy M and I ..."

"Hmm! We are all going in, see you later", Monisola quickly interrupted.

"Actually, I need your help; I need to swap a ticket. Laura's sister decided to come at the last minute and the ticket at the door is different from the one I bought earlier and I wouldn't like to leave Ashley on her own, do you know anyone who would like to swap?"

"Andrew you are GOD sent, your name should also be Gabriel, bearer of good news" Monisola sighed with relief.

"Who is that guy?" Daniel asked as soon as they sat down.

"A friend."

"Are you sure, because if he calls you that name again, I would straighten him out."

"That would be good and his fiancée Laura would have you to thank for it."

Daniel sat with her while Toluwanimi sat with Ashley just a few seats away. The concert began and the audience were soon wrapped up in the atmosphere in the hall which was dimly lighted with various colours, with all the stage effects and the music luring their soul to the lyrics and the beat. The musicians ranged from Lola herself to some school choirs, to well-known artists from around the country and also as far as West Africa and Asia. Though she loved music and had been looking forward to this concert, Daniel's presence was purposely distracting her attention. Not that he did anything intentionally but her thoughts and her eyes were focused on him. Her mind went back to what happened from their first meeting to now. She felt she was in a web, which thanks to her father, even Omoniyi had net her in and she wanted to be free but she wasn't sure to what extent she wanted her freedom to be. What kind of conversation was she going to have with her father especially as she did not want him to know about Daniel? How did he ever find out about Raymond? Well knowing Raymond, it wouldn't surprise her if he had introduced himself to her father. Her mind came back to the concert, what a good performance she thought though she barely heard the song.

The concert ended with more donations received and she saw Daniel speak to one of the usherettes who gave him a card, she wondered what that was all about but soon forgot to ask him when Andrew, Laura, Ashley and her brother came to meet them.

This time she made sure a proper introduction was done and though Andrew suggested they all went to a restaurant for a meal, she declined, said their goodbyes and were soon on their way.

"Why did you refuse his invite to the restaurant?"

"I'm sorry I didn't know you were interested; you can still join them."

"How would I get back home?"

"Toluwanimi, I believe you are quite capable of finding your way and I deliberately said no because I thought I was saving you from Ashley as she seems to be smitten by you."

"Well I was just trying to get to know her but then you dashed the hope of ever meeting her again, Oh my Ashley where art thou?"

"I thought it was Lisa a few hours ago."

"Oh, leave Lisa out of this, she's not here and Ashley might as well win me over."

"I think Mother is the best cure for whatever ailment has befallen you, she would soon bring you back to your senses."

"If Ashley be the music of love, let her play on, play on."

Monisola laughed and tried to look at Daniel who had been quiet throughout the concert as well as in the car; she wondered what was going on in his mind.

She soon found out when they got out of the car as he held on to her while Toluwanimi went in.

He wrapped her hands round him and began to kiss her as well as stroke her arms and back, he was already moaning and his touch was already setting her body on fire, maybe she should have let him stay home and not dragged him to the concert.

"Daniel please stop", she tried to pull away from him but he had her back to the car and made sure there was no gap between them.

"Daniel please I want to go in."

He let go and she ran into the house while he stayed where he was.

As soon as she got in, one look from Toluwanimi told her he had seen what had happened.

"I think you should learn to mind your business."

"I am, you are my sister and I do not want to see you hurt again."

"What has father been saying about me?"

"Mother", Toluwanimi corrected her assumption.

Monisola looked at him and took a deep breath, was she ever going to live her life without a member of her family prying into her private life?

"Monisola I think you should let ....."

Daniel came in and the conversation stopped.

"Would anyone like to eat?" Monisola asked.

"It depends on what is on offer" Daniel asked with smouldering eyes that told her he still had something else on his mind.

Toluwanimi declined and said he was off to bed.

"Are you sure? You haven't eaten in the last four hours, which is unusual."

He laughed and said he was fine.

"I don't usually eat like that; your dishes were just too tempting to miss out on especially since I have been eating whatever father cooked and believe me he is not a very good cook."

"I don't think we've had any luck with the Adewunmi men in the kitchen, you can be an exception."

"No thank you, though I'm sure I can cook but why do it when there is a master chef in the house. Good night Monisola, don't forget what I said" he kissed her and gave Daniel a tug.

They stared at each other for a minute and then both simultaneous called each other's name.

"Monisola."

"Daniel."

"Ladies first"

"I ......I...."

"I want you and I don't think I can wait anymore."

There is fire on the mountain!

"I'm going to try as much as I can and GOD help me not to do anything while under this roof because we need our privacy, your brother being here and that bell or phone that keeps ringing."

She smiled and sent a million Halleluiah upwards.

"It's not funny anymore Monisola and I think you are playing with fire and you will get burnt. I want you to come to me and this time I am not playing games, we are going to sort out what we both want from whatever it is between us."

She looked at him and she knew he was serious; the question was how was she going to sort herself out before then.

"When do you want me to come?"

"When you are ready."

She looked at him and laughed, "I thought you were the one calling the shot from now on."

"I'm learning a great deal of lessons from you Monisola, one of which is not to push you to do what you don't want or you'll rebel."

She laughed, he knew her alright but how much did she know of him and was this an opportunity to get to know him?

"I'm making some sandwich, want some?"

"Allow me to show my skills in that area."

She looked at him wondering if he could even boil water let alone make a sandwich.

He saw her look. "What? I can make sandwiches, you'll love them."

She watched him as he prepared the ingredients for the sandwich, slicing the tomatoes, cucumber, iceberg lettuce as if each one was a delicate piece of work that had to be perfectly sliced. He did the same with the bread, ham, bacon, cheese, chicken and pickle. She wondered how long she was going to wait till he finished his master piece.

"How long do I have to wait for this to be ready?"

He told her to be quiet and not disturb him. Goodness, just over a sandwich! What if he was making Christmas lunch or preparing turkey for Thanksgiving, he would probably start a month before. She warmed some milk to make hot cocoa and put some marsh mellows in his. She took out a pack of tortilla crisps, poured it in a bowl, popped some corn in the microwave, sliced some Cantaloupe melon, pineapples, mangoes in a platter and added some Smarties, M&M and Snickers in some bowls.

"I wouldn't eat those melons if I were you ?"

"Why?"

"They are quite harmful if not treated before you eat them."

"These are melons and how do you know any way?"

"I...."

"I smell a feast, what's cooking, now I'm hungry" Toluwanimi came in, sniffing the aroma in the air.

"I thought you said you weren't hungry", his sister replied.

"Well I am now, wow! What a master piece!"

Monisola laughed, precisely her line of thought.

She set the 'feast' on the centre table, plumed up the cushions and sat to watch the TV.

"What are we watching?" Monisola asked.

Toluwanimi who was already engrossed in the programme replied, "I don't know, some kind of horror thriller."

"Can we please watch something else."

"Why? This is interesting."

"Not to me, please change the channel."

"You've not watched it, so how do you know it's not interesting?"

"I .... I...."

Wonder shall never cease. Princess Monisola was scared of horror movies. Well! Well! Well! Daniel smiled to himself, he would have to note that down and use it in future, actually now.

"Monisola" he plumped the cushion beside him and patted it for her to sit down, smiling, desperately praying that she would catch this bait like she did before. She sat down alright but placed a throw pillow between them. What was that for? Surely the reason why he wanted her to sit near him was to tap some body warmth, what kind of girl is this?

Monisola sat down quietly, gritting her teeth, why do guys watch such movies and not one of the comedies or even silly romantic films, why horror? She shifted in her seat, maybe if she protested once more they might just change the channel.

"I think we should ...."

"Shhhh! Monisola go to bed if you don't want to watch."

Monisola closed her mouth and turned to Daniel hoping he would say something in her defence.

Daniel smiled, stretched towards the table, took the bowl of M&M, popped two in her mouth, removed the pillow encroaching on his space, moved closer and draped his arms around her.

"If you don't like any scene just use me as your screen shield" he whispered in her ears.

Toluwanimi's eyes were glued to the television. He was so wrapped up in what he was watching that the sandwich hung between his hand and mouth, dangling, wondering if its life expectancy was nearing its end towards the mouth or prolonged while in the hand though the force at which it was held was smouldering life out of it.

Five minutes into the film, Monisola was already sitting on the edge of the sofa, asking herself why she was still seated watching such a nasty movie. She wanted to go up to her room but couldn't, she hated watching these films, it always had an effect on her. Not that she was scared, how could she be when she knew it was all make belief and the actors who played dead were already shooting other films in other roles. How could she be so silly and scared over a mere ..... The next scene made her dash for Daniel as she lurched towards him and grabbed his shirt. She hid her face in it and at the same time kicking her feet against him, mumbling how she hated watching these devilish images and wondered why people couldn't put their GOD given sense of imagination to good use instead of scaring people.

Daniel on the other hand was trying to release her tight hold on his shirt which was almost choking him and regretted his earlier suggestion to use him as her shield, as it was creating a minor thriller especially with her kicks. Goodness, this girl is strong, scared or no scared; if he ever was to engage her in a combat, GOD help him.

"I'm not watching this rubbish, Toluwanimi switch the channel now", Monisola barked her orders.

He didn't even answer her but finally took a bite of his sandwich.

She got up and went for the remote control and so did her brother at the same time and both were fighting over it.

"I got it first."

"So, it's my remote, TV and house."

"Well as your invited guest you should show some courtesy and let me watch what I want to watch."

"No, I don't like such movies and anyway they are demonic."

"No, they are not! They are just stupid dumb tricks that ....." Toluwanimi started shaking his head.

"What?" his sister asked him curiously.

He laughed, "Don't tell me you are scared of these silly movies, it's all acting, it's not real."

"Acting or no acting I don't like them, please change the channel or let's watch one of my favourite ones."

"No way, I've seen your collections and there is no way I am spending my Saturday night watching those silly childish movies you call love or romantic whatever, I'm a man not a teenager. Daniel what do you say?"

Daniel had been watching them, amused that sibling rivalry knew no bounds, no age, gender, or even dignitary, it was just plain old rivalry! "Monisola, I'll suggest you let him watch what he wants to watch after all you invited him and being the good hostess you are, you will allow him just this once, why don't we go upstairs ....." Two pairs of eyes narrowed down on him which made him laugh, "...... and talk, I'll be leaving soon and we still have some issues to resolve."

"What issues are we resolving Mr Benjamin?" Monisola asked once they got to the lounge upstairs.

"You and I."

"What issues?"

"Actually none, I just wanted to be alone with you."

"Daniel I don't think..."

"Don't think, I just want us to be together, there's no need to look like that I'm not about to eat you up and if you don't want me I'll leave you and continue with the movie."

"Please stay!" she quickly begged.

"Movie! Thriller! Horror! He's coming to get you."

"Stop it! I don't like it."

"Baby it's only a film."

"And I still don't like it; please let's talk about something else."

"What would you like to talk about?"

"You!"

"There is nothing to talk about."

She looked at him and for the first time realised she didn't know much about him and he hardly spoke about himself.

"I want to know more about you, tell me about yourself."

He didn't like this and was thinking of how to change the subject as he wasn't comfortable talking about himself. He moved forward to kiss her but she stopped him.

"We are talking."

"Kissing is also an act of communication."

"I'm sure I will understand your vocal cords and the words they form better than any other action your lips wants to take or make."

This wasn't going to be easy; Princess Monisola was in one of her moods and this time it was talking time. "Okay what do you want to know?"

"Everything."

"Everything?"

"Everything."

"Okay born in October, schooled, graduated, joined marine, out of marine and here I am now."

She patted the sofa beside her and smiled.

"Monisola I don't want to talk; I think I want to watch that film.

"I'll allow you put your head on my lap."

"And take all my power, no thank you."

"You don't have long hair.

"Who's talking about long hair, you start to stroke my chin, I get talking and before I know it you have all my secrets at your fingertips!"

"Your secrets are quite safe with me" she placed her hands over her chest.

"Monisola, you have started again, don't play with me."

"See me see trouble?"

"Monisola!"

"What now?"

"What now" he mimicked her. "I've told you be careful; every day is for the thief but one day ...."

"..... is for the owner, tell me about yourself is all I ask, what is so difficult in talking about yourself, were you not taught in school how to do presentations or pitch your ideas?"

Daniel stood watching her as she crossed her legs and began to tutor him like a child. Honestly this girl was calling for something tonight and he was going to be the one to teach her a lesson. Imagine! She wasn't born when he was wearing diapers to kindergarten. Okay, he would watch and enjoy the entertainment for tonight. He hoped she has not forgotten about church tomorrow and how early she has to get up because he would not rush to anywhere with her tomorrow.

"......my interest are basketball, rugby, I enjoy swimming, food...."

"sex, music" he purposely interrupted her.

She ignored what he said, "I am a GOD-fearing person, who loves the LORD with all my heart and soul...."

"...and still enjoy sex because GOD created it for man's pleasure."

"..... I am Holy Spirit filled and do not say rubbish with my mouth...."

"I am not saying rubbish; I am talking about sex..."

"I do not fornicate and I want to be holy and hear holy things around me."

"Sex is holy within the context of marriage as that is how GOD intended it."

"I wish someone would just shut their big mouth and let me continue with my presentation."

"It's just you and I; there is no one else here and remember I am the one telling you about myself and what my interest are and one major one right now is sex, sex as GOD intended."

She covered her ears and told him to stop.

"Why? I'm not doing anything wrong, am I? I'm just telling you about myself and also to let you know my interests, I love GOD because HE is my father, HE has always been good to me even when I thought I didn't need HIM, He saved my life, He's given me new beginnings and what more can I say! Ah! Yes, I love Him and I thank Him for sex. It's what I like and enjoy and it's better you know it now."

She wasn't going to listen to his razzmatazz about that thing so she got up.

"Monisola we haven't committed any sin; we are just talking about my interests."

"If your eyes cause you to sin..."

"You can pluck yours out because I am still talking and my mind hasn't gone anywhere except yours is already fantasising and that is a sin and we have to gouge out your eyes, though beautiful it is."

She walked out on him and went to her room; she wasn't in the mood for such jokes; they were too expensive for her liking. She could take it from Omoniyi or laugh about it with Andrew or even Raymond but with Daniel no!

He knocked on her door but she did not respond though he knew she was there and was not asleep.

"Monisola can I come in?"

Silence.

"Please."

She did not respond so he left, went to his room and began to pack his things. Maybe it was a mistake coming here after all, not that he wanted to but Lyn and her stupid brats had caused all these otherwise he would have been at home doing something useful instead of running after someone that wasn't interested in him or in a relationship with him. He wasn't even sure if she loved him, not that he could force her to but most girls professed their love after one or two dates and that usually put him off.

Monisola on the other hand was not professing any love; she was going to ask her father for permission. Permission for what? In this day and age! The girl should just grow up. He was tired of all her games, he wanted, he wanted? What exactly did he want? This girl is really messing up his mind, how can he not know what he wants, he wasn't a child anymore, he's passed that stage. The earlier he left Monisola alone the better. The trouble was that he couldn't leave her. He was so into this girl ever since her brother talked to him about her and even without seeing her he was so in love with her. Dumb! Dumb! How could he be in love with a person he had never met then and even now he wasn't sure what feelings he had for her. One minute she drove him crazy, the next he wanted to be far away from her as possible. He was leaving tomorrow no matter what.

Monisola was in church but her mind was at home. Please GOD let him still be there when I get back, please. They had an argument that morning and it was just emotions running high as far as she was concerned and it had nothing to do with yesterday's conversation. Fine sex is from GOD and all that but she didn't just want to hear it. This morning he had refused to talk to her. When she went to his room, his bags were already packed, which made her wonder if it had anything to do with yesterday. She apologised and told him he had ten minutes to get ready for church and he just flipped. He told her not to speak to him in such childish manner as he was fed up with her games as it seemed they were both chasing after the wind and he was calling it quit. At first she thought it was a joke until she heard him call his friend to come and pick him up and then he went into the bathroom. She quickly called Des back and told him not to bother as she would be taking him to the airport herself, she left for church hoping and desperately praying that he would still be there.

Her mind returned back to the service and thank GOD it was time for the Word of GOD and she hoped she could concentrate without any distraction.

The pastor began to preach.

"If Jesus did not rise up from the dead, we of all men would have been the most miserable. Turn to your neighbour and tell him or her, Jesus is alive! I testify this morning that Jesus died and rose again and He is seated at the right hand of GOD interceding for you and I. That is why we can call on His name in our time of troubles and He answers, call Him anytime and anywhere and He is there because He is alive. The purpose of our celebration every Easter is to remind ourselves what He did on the cross, that cross where He took all our sins, my sins, your sins and the sins of the world upon Himself. He died on our behalf so that we do not have to go through the sting of that horrible death of eternal separation from GOD but have the choice to eternal life, eternal life with Him.

Somebody join me this morning to celebrate the Resurrection Power and Life in Christ Jesus with the eternal hope of glory in Him."

As soon as the service was over she quickly searched for Toluwanimi but he was ready engaged and would be spending the afternoon with Ashley, Laura and Andrew. She hoped they had a good time and she drove home with speed.

She went in and as soon as she opened the door she saw his bags were where he had left them. "Thank you Jesus", she whispered. She ran up the stairs, straight into his room, he wasn't there neither was he anywhere in the house. She quickly called his phone but it went straight to voicemail.

She told herself not to panic; he is a big boy and wouldn't just wander off like that. Couldn't he? she thought to herself. She was lying down on the sofa in the lounge upstairs when she heard him come in; she stayed still and waited for him. He went to his room; she heard some movement and then silence. She waited, silence and then silence. She couldn't bear it anymore so she went to him. He was lying on the bed with both hands under his head and staring at the ceiling. She joined him on the bed and took the same position.

"I'm sorry."

"For which of your sins?"

"I didn't do anything."

"Lying to Desmond or locking me out of the house."

Of course, she forgot to leave the keys with him when she went to church and Toluwanimi still had his.

"Daniel, I totally forgot, I am so sorry about the keys" she turned to look at him.

"But not the lie."

"Well I was going to take you there."

"After I would have missed my flight."

"I told you not to go."

"Monisola I am not your toy; I do as I want; it's not for you to tell me what to do or not to do."

Oh! That was the reason for the outburst this morning, she smiled; Mr Benjamin you don't know who you are dealing with.

He saw the smile and wondered what was funny, he was about to throw another outburst when he decided to chill. He was dealing with Miss Smart here so he had to put on his thinking cap and he was tired of all her games.

"Monisola."

"Yes Daniel."

"I'd like you to drop me at the airport in the next forty-five minutes or at least call a cab for me."

"Ok."

She sat up looking at him, smiling.

Why was she smiling now? What did she have up her sleeves? She went out of the room, came back with the phone and gave it to him.

"Call the airline, cancel your flight for today and book another one for Tuesday."

He took a deep breath to calm himself down.

"Why should I do that?"

"Because I told you so", she saw him trying to get off the bed, she gently pushed him back and gave the phone back to him. He called and did as he had been told. What next?

"Are you hungry?"

His eyes threw invisible spears at her which made her laugh. She cuddled up to him and began to give him a peck.

"If this is a bribe for the lies you told, it is not accepted."

"Actually, I was compensating you for all the times we were interrupted as we have some hours to ourselves without any interruption."

"What about Toluwanimi?"

"With Ashley and ...."

He didn't let her finish her sentence as he began to kiss her and touch her. She laughed at the sound he was making again and at the same time trying to hold back the desire that was already tearing her apart. She tasted so juicy he could eat her up and he was enjoying the pleasure her body was causing him and the silly noise she was making until he heard what she said.

"Love me Daniel" it was a deep moan and it snapped him right out of the wave of pleasure that had engulfed him. He got up and walked towards the window. He was the one playing with fire not Monisola, he had started all these and he was the one to take the blame.

"Daniel what's wrong?"

"Nothing."

"Why are standing there?"

He laughed and at the same time groaned. "Monisola call the cab, I'll stay in an hotel till Tuesday."

"Why? I thought this was what you wanted?"

Exactly his point but no, this was way out of his hands.

"Monisola, please get up, we have to talk. Outside this room."

She ignored him and walked up to him and wrapped her arms round him.

"Monisola we are not playing games any more, we've got to talk."

"We tried that this morning."

"This won't help either. Monisola I want to make you mine; I want to marry you."

For the life of her she didn't know what to say.

"This is the second time I've asked, by now you should have an answer."

"We both know that is not what you want, it's not you Daniel so don't play games with me."

"Who said I'm playing, I'm serious."

She looked at him but was not convinced.

"What do you want me to do to show you I mean it?"

"Daniel please let's not go that far, we are not ...., let's just concentrate on us for now, go along with what you suggested, we convene and reconvene, it might just suit us fine, we are old enough, people do it and we just go along."

"Where does GOD or the fear of GOD comes in all these?"

"I don't know and I can't pretend I know. Let just do what we have to do."

"Why don't we get married?"

He was working on her nerves if he mentioned that word again.

"Marriage seems to be the only solution here."

"And then what next?" she shouted at him.

At first he was surprised by the outburst, something was eating this girl up.

"What is wrong with you? Why are you raising your voice? If you don't want marriage, that's fine, we go our separate ways. Why am I begging you, are you the only girl in the world, call my cab and let me get out of this house."

He walked past her and went out of the room.

She took three deep breaths and followed him.

He ran down the stairs and she followed.

"Monisola leave me alone."

"Daniel I was all alone and fine until you started this madness in me and now you want to dump me again"

"I'm not dumping you, when did I?"

"Does it matter? You keeping saying it's over and yet we come together again. Daniel, you are the one playing games with me and I'm not sure if I can keep up with you, I've met with my master in the game and I surrender, please Daniel come to me."

He held her as she started crying, this was not what he had planned but he was glad it had happened, he was now in control and he was free.

"Baby please don't cry, please."

He carried her upstairs and lay her on the sofa in the lounge.

"Monisola I want to marry you because I love you. I've loved you ever since Omoniyi told me about you. At first I thought it was infatuation but the feelings didn't go even when I had to go to Uni, join the marine and all that. Somehow you were always there. I use to talk to you every day, I had this picture of you I stole from Omoniyi and it went everywhere I went, even in the midst of the war, when I got shot, in the hospital, you were there. It was as if you were there with me. Seeing you at the funeral was too emotional for me, because I knew how much Omoniyi meant to you and I couldn't say what I felt and had carried all these years so I left. It was GOD's divine intervention that we met again or that Valerie was kind enough to let me see you. Monisola I want you in my life now and I want all of you, spirit, body and soul, I can't talk to some photos of you anymore, it's the real you I want, if I have to get married to keep you, have you, then so be it." Daniel was making things difficult for her and he knew it.

"I don't want to get married."

"Why not?"

"I just don't want to, ever since Raymond...., I'm just not interested and also you ..."

"What have I done?"

"Seriously you don't mean it, you just want me and I'm okay with that, I can live with that."

"Monisola I love you I want to marry you."

"I think I love you but I'm not marrying you."

"Do you need to talk to your father about us?"

"NO!" she shouted.

"Monisola, how are we supposed to have a healthy relationship when you don't tell me things."

"As if you do."

"Okay guilty as charged but I'm trying, at least you know I like sex which probably is the reason why you are frightened."

"I'm not."

"Okay if I say that word twenty times what would you do?"

"Slap your face."

"Monisola!"

"What else do you expect?"

"I need to tame you; you are getting out of hand."

She smiled, looked away and said "I was ready but you backed out on me?"

"You better thank GOD I did otherwise you would be a fornicator and if Jesus comes that is it."

"Oh! And what about you Mr Co-fornicator?"

"Have you ever heard of the man fornicating, no it is the woman, the same woman who ate the apple, was caught red handed and about to be stoned; so, you better be careful the blame is on you not me."

"GOD forgive you for that lie."

"Amen. The rapture one, none of us will escape if we are caught red handed but if not you are the one to be blamed, do not say I did not tell you."

"I still don't understand your stupid logic."

"Stupid! Girl, it's a man's world out here. I know they teach you equal opportunity and all that but sincerely look around you, who rules, who is in charge? Who are the punters and hustlers? Men! Who keeps a roof over your head and clothes on your body? Men! Even if we do it for more than one woman. Who plants the seeds and a baby evolves? Men! By the grace of GOD. Who are the ones in the majority in every institution, state of affairs, world affairs? Men!

So, baby girl your father might have trained you to be a leader over his kingdom and maybe one day you might take over but know one thing, a man would always rule over you, lord over you and you will be subject to one."

"Absolute crocodile ...... you know what! What planet are you from? You need to come out of your coma. Men! Men! Men! Okay fine you are the majority, the lead in the home, state, county, country and world affairs, good. Why don't you look closer? After you plant the seed, who waters it and carries it for good nine months and bring forth? Women with the help of GOD! Who stays with that child or the twenty something seeds you spread across the country and nurtures, raises, educates and cares for each child? Women by the grace of GOD! By the way I hope you don't take me literally and spread your seed around."

He gave her a poke and she screamed.

"Who stands by the bull dog at the realm of affairs catering for his every need when he comes home knocked out from his routine at work? Women!

Who wakes up at five in the morning, get the household ready, cooks, washes, feeds, bathes, make packed lunches and goes to work herself; comes back with all the headaches she gets from the men at work who without reasons complain about her incapability to hold things together? She continues with her main job when she gets home while the male counterpart walks in as usual, expects everything to be clean and sparkling, food to be ready and afterwards wants a galaxy ride before a good night rest. Who does all that? Women! Women! Women! By the help of GOD!

I'm not saying I won't submit to you as my husband but please don't take me for granted. Don't abuse me, don't underestimate my GOD given ability otherwise you are slowly falling into the trap set long ago and I was just waiting for the fall. So, Mr Men advocate I'll advise you thread that line carefully otherwise......"

Daniel scratched his head and smiled. "O GOD of Abraham, Isaac and Israel, deliver me and behold the threat of this wo-man."

"You started it Daniel."

"Ok! I'm sorry."

"Only accepted if you stay till Tuesday"

"Of course, I will, where else would I go? At Des place I was set up by a woman and her dogs. Here, I am faced with this one-woman band who made me miss my flight and also made me rebook it on the day she wanted. I better stay otherwise I don't know which one I will meet out there."

"Congratulations now you are thinking."

This girl was playing with fire, he chased her round the house, until they were both exhausted, panting and fell on the floor.

"I'm hungry Monisola, what's for lunch this Easter Sunday?"

"Me", she baited her eyes at him.

"No thank you, I prefer proper food that would refuel my brain cells and recharge them for another contest of words; whether you like it or not it's a man's world, take it or leave it"

"In that case you are cooking."

"Have I ever told you, your beauty is ever so captivating that anytime I see you my head spins and I start to say rubbish."

"Just like you are saying now."

"Monisola! Do you know you have no respect?"

"For who? You! Ha! My lord, the crown of my head, the girdle around my waist! What! Daniel just leave me alone, now I'm the one saying rubbish, girdle on my waist indeed."

"Actually, I prefer to be the beads around your waist line, what do you call it in your language?"

"Which language?"

"Yoruba."

"Aren't you one?"

"No!"

"What?"

"What do you mean, you think I'm Yoruba?"

"Yes! My GOD where are you from but you speak Yoruba don't you? At least you understand."

"Yes, but that doesn't make me one, I'm Tiv"

"What?"

"Tiv?"

"Which state is that?"

"Monisola you ought to be ashamed of yourself and you call yourself a Nigerian."

"I am but just in Diaspora."

"Please don't give me that excuse? You can read and you listen to the news ..."

"Okay, I'm sorry but Daniel, Tiv?"

"What? Are your parents tribalistic?"

"No but ....?"

"But what?" he shouted at her.

"As the first and heir ..."

"Monisola cut that crap, Toluwanimi is on the scene, you are free to do as you please."

"Tiv!"

"Do you take an exception to that?" he asked cautiously, his heart beating fast.

She shook her head and smiled. She couldn't believe it. With

Raymond she had interrogated and practically made him outline his family history and ancestry and she had been very cautious with him but with Daniel she just went with the flow. She didn't even care if he just dropped from the moon at least he was human and not an alien. GOD! She was in love with this guy and she never knew it. She did not suspect it would be this soon, for all she knew, it might have started from the time she met him and how she didn't want him to go. What was she going to do now?

"Monisola I'm not going to apologise for who I am and where I come from, if you are drawing a line because I'm a Tiv man ..."

"Just shut up and ....." she began to kiss him.

There was something about this kiss, it was gentle, soft and it was like she was surrendering and letting him take charge. She teased him with her tongue and bit him on the lips gently.

"Monisola, what's wrong?"

She shook her head; she was afraid to speak and the tears just flow.

"Monisola please don't make me leave you because of where I'm from, baby please"

"I love you Daniel, I love you" she whispered.

For a moment he starred into her eyes not believing what he just heard. She closed her eyes and smiled, silly guy, he still thought she was fighting over their ego and stubborn streak, she was his and no one else.

"Marry me."

This was a no-no. "No?"

"Why not, is it because I'm ..."

"Daniel shut up and just love me, it's nothing to do with you, it's me!"

"I'm still going to spank your bum; you are so rude."

"You are so bush."

"Is that why you don't want to marry me?"

"Yes! Beside you are too black, imagine if all our children take after you."

"Sixteen to one is not that bad."

"You dey craze! I be baby factory?"

"Baby incubator, you go just dey born pickin like fowl dey lay egg for dozen dozen. Monisola marry me, please."

"Please don't beg me, not on this one.

"What have I done?"

"Meet, convene, reconvene!"

He laughed and laughed. "Goodness, I was only joking."

"I was serious but your mouth decided to do some babbling and say the most profane words I've ever heard - meet, convene and reconvene."

"Okay I'm sorry" but he started laughing again

"How can I take you serious?"

"Why did you ever take me serious, you ought to know I was joking."

"Honestly I thought you had gone bananas."

"You are calling me a monkey now."

"No! Yes! Monkey."

He grabbed her and tickled her which made her laugh.

"Marry me Monisola, I'm not going to ask you again."

"When I decide I'll let you know"

He shrugged his shoulders, while she moved closer and began to toy with his buttons.

GOD what I'm about to say does not make sense especially the way

I'm feeling right now but I'm going to say it. He kissed her and was leading her on, he could hear the moan in her throat and as their bodies were so close the fire was already engulfing them, he had a second more, he held her tight as if he would never let go and all of a sudden let go.

"Monisola if you marry me I promise you our nights will be filled with wild passion and love making and I will even surrender to you but if you won't marry me, you'll be denying yourself and myself what is meant to be. I love you Oluwamuiremiwa and I badly need you now but I'm not going to let go until we are husband and wife, the decision lies in your hands."

She wrapped her hands round him and tried to lure him but he did not budge but gently moved out of her embrace and left the room.

By the time he left on Tuesday morning, Monisola knew Daniel meant business. He wasn't budging and he also told her not to come to Chicago if she wasn't ready, she wasn't sure if she would change her mind about marriage there but she was going, maybe just maybe she would break his will power. Not that she was testing him but she was going crazy and right now her hormones were playing funny business. She turned to GOD, Father I have sinned and I'm about to sin more if I don't stop thinking about Daniel. I'm in love with him and I'm lusting after him, as your child I should know better but I can't help it. I can if I try but I don't want to, I'm playing with fire and I can't say I won't get burnt but LORD because You are GOD, please help me. I know I am bursting the bubble of some serious born-again disciple and I know in your word it is sin and ......gosh why am I even saying this. She quickly chastised herself. Lord can you please understand I don't want to sin but I want to, not me but my flesh, you know what GOD forget all the jazz I've just said, wipe it out with the blood of JESUS and please forgive me. Daniel is not here so I will try and keep clam and try as much as possible not go near him or even go to Chicago, I don't know Lord, all I know is that I need your help, I am willing to be helped and please I need the strength of the Holy Spirit.

Wednesday night Chichi called her.

"I don't know why I've been thinking about you lately, everything alright?"

"Hmm Hmm!"

"Are you sure, how is Dani boy?"

"Gone back to the States"

"Oh, I thought he had moved in permanently with you."

"Very funny."

"Indeed, so why are we not laughing"

"I'm in a terrible mess; I don't know what to do?"

"What to do or what to do about what you've already done."

"Goodnight Chichi."

"Don't do it Monisola"

"What?"

"Don't do it."

"It may seem I got away with my sin and everything seems okay, GOD has forgiven me, Mano has forgiven me, Eman is fine and the baby is fine but...."

"What baby?"

"Oops that slipped."

"You don't have to say anything, I understand."

"It's okay. Mano is okay with the two of us being friends at least he says he trusts you but not our families, any way that's by the way. You know the cranky business and plastic food; well it turns out baby number two is on the way. GOD help us, Monisola I don't know what to do but one thing I know is that I am grateful to GOD for His mercies which I must never take for granted ever, ever again.

Now back to my point, everything is good but there's still that voice that comes once in a while that sneers at me; what if I had waited and allowed GOD's will to be done in His timing. That I can't stop because I'm guilty and I know my sins have been forgiven but what if? Monisola please don't do it, even if he pressurizes you, don't give in."

"It's not him it's me, I nearly seduced him the other day; it was so shameful after I thought about it."

"It will be more than shameful if you ever try it again, silly girl have you not learnt your lesson from me?"

"You know what they say, birds of the same feathers flock together."

"We are not of the same feathers; GOD expects a better and proper behaviour from you; you are His epistle to the young people you coach and mentor who still believe they have the right to say no to sex before marriage. Monisola I beg of you please don't let the light go out, please hold the baton. I failed big time, yes, GOD has restored me but we need you to carry the beacon of hope and good example for the next generation, please my dearest friend and sister."

"Chic, o di ka hard."

"Pele, put all that desires and emotion into your work. What am I saying?" Chichi's friendly tone changed into her firm, authoritarian teacher voice. "Put your body in check my friend, when did you meet him that all this nonsense started? Do you know how many years Mano and I have been dating and nothing happened, except for the stupid excuse I gave and decided not to wait before I asked him to marry me?"

"He's proposed about three times now" Monisola sighed.

"What? Three times and what did you say?"

"I'm not ready", Monisola replied.

"What? Are you mad or something? What's gotten over you?"

"After that Raymond experience I've just lost interest."

"Ray what? Monisola if you miss this good opportunity because of mad Raymond you are worse than a fool. Raymond is enjoying himself all over the continent and you are still drowning in your loss, I'm going to tell your mother."

"Please don't."

"I am", Chichi firmly stated.

"Seriously don't, she has so much on her now with the babies ..."

"What babies?"

"Ok! I'm not supposed to spread the word yet but she is expecting, well would soon by GOD's grace put to bed. Can you imagine at my age, I'm going to have baby sisters or brothers."

"Hey! You've had yours; these ones are for Toluwanimi! Your mother is strong and of course still young and your dad is something else. Ha! Ha! Ki lode! Na wa oh!"

"Don't worry my friend-in-law will do likewise."

"You better go and read your bible and stop thinking of fornicating."

"Yes Ma."

"On a more serious note Monisola I'm begging you, please don't do it; please at least for the sake of Eman and Emani."

"Emani?"

"Baby girl in the tummy."

"Wow! GOD is great! Girl! So, are you happy now?"

"Of course, especially since this is the last stop for us."

"In your dreams, with Mano you heading for a football team."

"Yours will be an Olympic team in Jesus name."

"Mind your mouth."

"You too."

"Got to go."

"Remember hold the beacon and wait till you pass the baton."

She decided she was going to Chicago after all but would be staying in an hotel. Daniel flipped when she told him.

"Why?"

"What do you mean why? Remember our last encounter. I don't want to lure you into sin so I will be staying in an hotel."

"Who told you I don't want to be lured?"

His voice suddenly changed. Monisola took a deep breath, LORD I've prayed! I'm holding the beacon; this man is luring me!

"Hold the beacon" she whispered to herself but he heard her.

"What?"

She told him about her conversation with Chichi.

"Well that's good for you, I don't think I can, right now I just want to sink in."

"You better hold on to your anchor and stay put my friend, old things have passed away and all is become new."

"Preach on preacher, I didn't know I have a preacher for a wife."

"I haven't made up my mind."

"If you like take a hundred years by then I would have a hundred grandchildren."

"So, you will marry someone else!" Monisola's heart nearly missed a beat.

"Someone else, why should I? Monisola I told you, you have what belongs to me and I'm going to get it, marriage or not because as far as I am concerned few months from now, I'll just go to your father, drop the dowry money, sheep, cow, carry you, make love to you.....and the rest will be history."

She kept quiet.

"No comment from your royal highness."

"I am pleading the blood of Jesus over that thought."

"Sex is not a sin."

"So why are we not doing it?"

"We are not married and ..."

"So please stop painting pictures in my mind, you are the one enticing me."

"Don't tell me you don't talk about some aspect of sex, well not too much details but ...."

"You are the one I love, crazy about and near intimate with so you can guess what you do to me anytime you freely open your big mouth and speak categorically."

"I'm sorry, I should have known better but it's just the thought of you in that sexy lacy underwear lying beside you drives me insane."

"You are a trouble maker."

"You are the mega trouble maker, if you agree to marry me now, in two weeks' time we will be going with the flow gently as a river and then when you are well settled like an avalanche."

"I bind that spirit of lust in you."

"I bind that anti-marriage spirit working against you in Jesus name."

"Amen."

"What did you say?"

"I said amen."

"Is that the problem area?"

"I don't know but I trust GOD is at work"

"So, should I be expecting a yes?"

"Daniel you know it's a yes but I'm not ready."

"Monisola let's not play games any more. What do you mean yes but you are not ready, what sort of a kill joy answer is that, look if you don't ...." she noticed his raised voice and equally matched it with hers?

"Daniel don't attempt any more breaking up or good bye forever, it's not going to work, we are into each other and soon, hopefully soon we'll be together so please don't drag the clock back."

"I will whack your bum the next time I see you, you don't respect your elders."

"It's not my fault, it's you a commoner who wants to marry a princess. Do you think it will be so easy like a fairy tale story, wake up man."

"Monisola, my baby, my sugar, I will show you pepper."

"You know me, I don't beg and I'm not afraid, so see you at the finishing line."

"You mean my bedroom."

"What date am I booking to come over to Chicago?" she quickly changed the subject.

"I might not be in Chicago."

"Where would you be?"

"I'll be at home."

"Home where?"

"Not to worry, you see when you get here."

"Which is the nearest hotel to you?"

"There are no hotels here, I live on a farm."

"What?"

"Yeah baby, I'm your American farmer."

CHAPTER FOURTEEN

Her mother gave birth to twins a week later, a girl and a boy. She had never seen her parents this happy before. As soon as her mother was discharged Monisola went to Zurich to spend time with her.

"GOD is so great, I was looking forward to doing this for my grandchildren, I never thought I would be doing this again for mine", her mother looked at her as she was bathing her sister.

Monisola smiled, her sister, thank GOD!

"I think you should read Sarah and Elizabeth's personal diaries and I'm sure they would have had the same thoughts written down."

"Very funny! Actually, the bible states that Sarah said, ... 'who will have thought Sarah would nurse a son for Abraham...' and here am I, nursing twins for your father after my Toluwanimi."

"Olori your Toluwanimi is a man not a boy, so leave him alone and concentrate on these little ones."

"O! Wait till you have yours then you know what it means to be a mother, no matter the age; you always see that child as your child, you just wait."

Monisola kept quiet, did that mean Olori did not see her as her child as she did not bring her up herself. She took her baby sister from her and quickly wrapped her in towel and wiped her.

"You know what? I've been looking at Oluwatosin and Oluwatoyin, they don't look like me in facial features or complexion, they and Toluwanimi take after your father, which only leaves you my dear daughter as mine. So, you see even with all their nurturing and king making business, GOD gave me victory over them, just look at you Omolabake Omo to' rewa, you keep glowing every day. When are you going to get married and give me grandchildren?"

"Mother you can't be serious! You've just had twins and you are thinking of grandchildren!"

"Eh eh! So! Does that disturb you from getting married, I hope you are not using that as an excuse because if you are, I will shout it out and the whole world would know what you are hiding."

"Olori I am not hiding anything", Monisola quickly stated before their conversation leads them to the door of her secret.

"But you are hiding someone! You can't tell me you don't have anyone looking at you or asking you to marry him. Or is it a case of you don't know who to choose? Let me know and we will put heads together and decide."

"We? As in father, Ayaba, my sisters, aunties and the latest seems to be Toluwanimi. Olori I don't want to be a topic of discussion in your family gatherings and talks."

"Topic of discussion? So, we can't say what our eyes are seeing? Ok! Anyway, please leave your father out of the list, we all know you are his favourite and GOD help that man that would come to ask for your hand in marriage, you better tell him to prepare well well."

"I don't understand"

"Close your eyes and be walking with your head looking at the ground, you will soon know."

"Soon know what?" her father interrupted their conversation.

"Nothing, father."

"Nothing? So, what we have been discussing is nothing? Monisola mo so fun e`, ja ra' re' gba, deliver and redeem yourself."

"From what and whom?" her father asked, wondering who or what was holding his precious daughter captive.

"I have said my own and you will soon hear from me."

"Don't let your mother bully you into anything you don't want to do, lately she has been flapping some wings and I would soon cut them to size. I am just enjoying this new fatherhood business after such a long period but I can assure you I would be watching her closely."

Her mother ignored both of them and continued to bath for her baby brother while Monisola dressed her sister who was looking so cute and adorable.

"Iya Ibeji let me bathe Joseph while you go lie down and rest."

"I'm fine, Monisola is here to help me."

"Father can you bath a baby, I mean are you allowed?"

"What do you mean am I allowed? Am I not their father and anyway I did bath your sisters so why not these ones?"

She was the one missing out again even from her father's care, Monisola thought to herself.

"I'm sure your father changed your nappy once or twice" her mother tried to reassure her, hoping Monisola did not feel left out.

Very reassuring she thought to herself, once or twice out of twelve months or more. She concentrated on dressing Josephine also called Oluwatoyin by their mother; she wondered why both parents could not decide on what names the twins were to be called.

She was washing the feeding bottles when her father came to the kitchen; she assumed her mother wanted something so she asked. "She's sleeping as the babies have been fed and are also sleeping, it's you I came to talk to."

Another family discussion, GOD help her today.

"Oluwamuiremiwa I know that recent events have brought to light things from the past that might have not been handled well and I am so sorry that I did not have the wisdom then to have corrected a lot of things. Then I felt my hands were tied but looking back now I should have done better. I wasn't there for you or your mother in the early years after your birth and I could blame it on the circumstances around then but that was no excuse. With your two sisters I tried to be there for Adekemi in fact I had no choice but to because she did have difficult times. With Toluwanimi, I had no choice in the matter but with Joseph and his sister, I have a choice I have to be there for Tinuola, the twins, Toluwanimi and you"

"Father I'm sure I can take care of myself; I am a big girl now."

"I know you are a woman now but the fact still remains, I am still your father and you will always be my daughter."

"Father I think it's a bit too late for regrets now, what you should do is channel your attention to Josephine and Joseph and let me be, I can take care of myself and in fact I have since I was twelve, so please let me be."

"I know you are angry and you have every right to be."

"You are wrong father. I am not angry I might have regrets but not anger, I have far better things to do than that."

"Such as?" her father asked curiously.

She wished her parents would stop probing into her life. If they are feeling guilty because of their past mistake that was their headache, she prayed she would avoid their pitfalls and if she falls into new ones, GOD help her.

"Oluwamuiremiwa I am talking to you", her father ordered.

The use of that code was not going to break her; she had made up her mind. No more meddling into her life by her parents or family she's had enough of them.

"Kabiyesi please leave me alone, I am just fine."

"Your mother doesn't think so and for once I think I agree with her."

Well that's your business not mine. "Father seriously you should reserve your energy for your new born babies and leave big girls like me to fend for myself."

"That's why I don't regret all those times with you and then Omoniyi, I am glad that I did what I did then ..."

Despite the fact that majority of what you taught me might be some of the areas that is affecting me now.

"...however, I sometimes think I handled some things a bit more mature for you and looking back now I can see my pitfalls, you are too independent and stubborn, a combination of your mother and ...."

Monisola laughed, yes, you father, very strong characters.

AS SOON AS she got back to England she called Daniel.

"How did it go?"

"You should have seen the twins they are so cute I can't wait ....."

"Hey slow down, no rush, we will take our time and spread them evenly, as we might want some when we are old and grey."

"Daniel renew your mind I can't wait to see them again was what I meant."

"Oh, I see."

"Hmm! Your mind seems to be so preoccupied lately, what's up?"

"We are nearing our harvest time; also, shipment and courier businesses are at their peak and that means my workload is piling high and so are my travelling commitments from state to state. I beginning to grow white hair again."

"What do you usually do before, don't you have back up plans and help? Since when did you start growing white hair?"

"I have all the back up and everything in place, it's just that anything can happen and you have me running like a mad man all over town. As for the white hair you are the cause of it, Monisola you are putting me under undue stress."

"Wait a minute did I ask you to do a million things all together? Haven't you heard of taking life easy and taking things in their strides. Today Chicago, tomorrow farm, not to mention body guard, which you should start again so that I know I would be a lonely house wife with my husband travelling all over the globe."

"First thank you for accepting my offer of marriage but that answer was so unromantic, no flowers, no champagne, no kisses? Haven't you heard of multiple income before especially for some of us without royalty and wealth like yourself? What do you expect me to tell your father when he asks me what I do for a living and I just open my big mouth and say farmer sir."

"Well he married a farmer's daughter so I don't see that as a problem."

"He did! Who?"

"My mother of course, silly"

"She doesn't look like a farmer's daughter to me, especially from the pictures you sent."

"That's what royalty does, it separates the commoner from you."

"Like marrying me a farmer would separate the royalty in you and make you a commoner like myself."

Monisola could not help but laugh. Daniel was so funny and knew how to bring her down from her high horse.

"Ok Mr Commoner I accept, at least I would know how it feels to be a commoner."

"No baby, in my arms you will know what it feels like to be queen of my castle, the rose in my bed bush, the nectar in my flower and I would suck ....."

"Hey! Hold it! Just hold it! I've heard, thank you I want to sleep tonight not turning and tossing on my bed."

"Oh! So, you have caught the bug."

"What bug?"

He started singing "Can't sleep without you by my side, can't eat without you, can't live without you in my life."

"I don't know about that but I Monisola can and will live without ...."

"If you say any rubbish there, I will deal with you when I see you."

"You can't do me nothing, with Jesus in my life you can't do me nothing" she started her own song also.

"Oh! so it's singing competition we are into now, okay let me introduce you to MC Dani, the man in the house; check this guy out, he's the man about town, looking for a lover, found Monisola, the babe with a eight figure, talkin bout the body not the money, cos that girl drives me crazy, I'm always thinkin bout her and I can't live without her....."

"Daniel I think you are in the wrong business, stop all that farm business and go start your record label."

"Thank you, not only record but CD and DVD and you see me posing with a car, fine chicks by my side and bling bling chains and earring. Please go get a life. Ain't my style."

"You know what I'm saying Mr lover man"

"Oh, just shut up Monisola."

"You started it."

"Did not and don't you dare repeat ..."

"Did two, did three, did four."

"You are too childish; I can't stand that."

"You are too manly and I ....."

"Hm? Say it! Can't stand what?"

"Daniel leave me alone."

"And if I don't?"

"I'll tell my mother and father for you."

"At least you have one."

"I'm sorry I didn't mean to ..."

"It's not your fault. When are you coming over Monisola I need to see you?"

"Why don't you come over?"

"That wasn't the deal. We both convene and reconvene", he started laughing.

"Black goat."

"Yellow pawpaw."

"You can take some 'epo pupa' and rob on yourself, maybe you will tone up a bit"

"I tell you say I wan bleach! You dey bleach oh you dey bleach, yellow fever, yeye thing."

"So, you are a Fela Anikulapo fan!"

"Don't tell me you listen to Fela, holy sister!"

"It's not just a matter of holiness, some of the things he sang about were politically eye openers for some of our people then, if not the whole world."

"Bang on that baby girl, that's why I still listen to some of his songs though I don't approve of his lifestyle."

"Hm! So, I'm not to be wife number one or twenty."

"If there were fifty-six of you in the USA and thirty-six of you in Naija I will marry you all, but since there is and can only be one Monisola my GOD ordained, I am yours and yours only for life, no sharing and same goes for you."

"So, if there were one of you in each of the two hundred and fifty something countries of the world you think I will only choose you, no! Variety is the spice of life o jare`."

"I bind that spirit and cast it out of you in JESUS name."

"Oh, so you are spiritual now."

"Say amen."

"Why should I?"

"Monisola say amen otherwise I will give it to you tonight.

"From where Chicago or wherever you are."

"I'm boarding the next available flight."

"Good that means I don't have to come to you."

"Don't even try that, you are coming, I'm sending my calendar to you now so you work around it and choose the dates...." she heard some ruffling of papers, ".... preferably May or you could come now and also in May but not June."

"Why not?"

"I will be too busy to have the time for you ......" oh no he realised his mistake; he was giving her the perfect excuse to come later than sooner.

She laughed when he didn't say anything but took a deep breath, "Thank you Mr Daniel, see you in June, and amen to your prayer."

"Monisola please don't do this I am already longing for you."

"The more reason I will be coming in June, see you."

"One day is for ..."

"...the owner, until then let me enjoy"

CHAPTER FIFTEEN

Though she had planned to be with him in May, circumstances beyond her control prevented her from travelling.

"Don't tell me your father wants you to come home."

"No."

"Your mother wants you to help out with the babies?"

"No!"

"So, what is it this time Monisola? I just knew you were going to cook up some story since I told you about May being my free time. What I don't understand is how are we supposed to be in a relationship when we don't have time for each other and if I say anything you'll be the one to tell me I am drawing lines, tell me which one are you drawing now?"

"It's not like that. I am trying to explain but...."

"But what? What is so important than you being with me?"

"I want to come but ....."

"I'm listening."

"There are no rooms available for May as the hotels are fully booked and I could only book three days in June."

Daniel kept quiet as he wasn't sure where Monisola was coming from.

"Daniel"

"Go on."

"I could only book hotel reservations for three days but the rest of the week I'm not sure where I would stay."

"Is that all?"

"Yes."

"Okay, cancel your hotel reservation, I'm sure you can get a flight for tomorrow and be on your way here."

"Where would I stay?"

"In the barn if you want but I do have a roof over my head with rooms, even though they might not meet your royal standard."

"Daniel I can't stay with you."

"I see."

"It's...... it's not that I don't want to but I don't trust us."

He laughed because he was sure she meant him. "What stops me from coming to your hotel room then?"

She had not thought of that. "Daniel I don't want to, not that I don't want to but I think I should after all if I don't then it's ok or is it not?"

"Monisola I do not have a clue of what you are talking about. If you are not coming now, that's fine and when you do come you will be spending time with me in my house so don't waste your time making any hotel reservation because I am not prepared to drive some miles just to see you when we can be under the same roof, that's even if I get to see you with the tight schedule I have. Just let me know when and I'll arrange everything."

Three weeks later she was on her way to O'Hare International airport and as she looked at the itinerary Daniel had outlined for her she laughed; the guy knew how to get to her. He didn't argue with her hotel reservation, he even paid for it and all other expenses and after that all he said was, he'll be waiting for her.

As soon as she got to her hotel she had a lie in, went for a body massage, slept and then went downstairs for dinner. She sat alone and ate alone but her mind was on one thing. What was she going to do after her three days here at the hotel? She wasn't sure but she knew what she wanted to do while she was here so she went to bed early and prayed for a good day.

The next day she spent her day going to Macy's which initially was just to look around but she ended up doing a little shopping especially for Oluwatosin and Oluwatoyin. She also bought something for her host and smiled knowing he would not find it funny. She had lunch, went for a walk and back to the hotel hoping she would have an early night. She was just walking into the lobby when she saw him, he had his back to her but she knew it was him and smiled.

"Good evening Mr Daniel."

He turned and saw her, "Good evening Miss Adewunmi."

"Do we have an appointment or are you waiting for someone else?"

"I have been waiting for your royal highness; I felt it was rude of me as I was not here to welcome you to our state on this royal visit. Where have you been?"

"Daniel I need to drop these bags and I have a swimming session booked so if you'll excuse me."

"I hope you don't mind me joining you?"

"Not at all that is if you have your swimming gear."

"See you by the pool."

They had a swim, ate dinner and went to her room.

"Are you going back home tonight?"

"Are you coming home with me?"

She went into her suite and he followed.

She offered him coffee he declined but sat on the sofa looking at her.

"Daniel"

He was looking at her and thinking of all he had to do and had forgone just to be with her.

"Daniel?"

"Yes Monisola, I'm tired, I have to go back tonight though I wish I could still be with you but I can't."

"What do you have to do?"

"A lot and a thousand more; I came here when I should be back at work. I won't be able to see you tomorrow and I just want to apologise for my absence tomorrow and probably the day after. I wish I could play the perfect host but I can't, I've got so much to do, I had hoped you'll come in May but ...never mind you are here now and it's good to see you."

Monisola felt bad, if only she had come in May as he had suggested but she let her egocentric thoughts get the better of her. She moved closer and gave him a kiss. He hugged her and then walked to the door and was gone.

The next day she went to Lincoln Park, visited the museum, had lunch and did some shopping. She hoped she wasn't going to exceed her luggage limit, as she struggled to get into her room. She dropped the bags on the floor and slumped on the sofa, she just wanted to sleep and sleep she did.

The phone woke her up and she drowsily answered it.

"Monisola where are you?"

"In my room."

"I've been calling you for the last four hours."

"Four hours! I just had a nap.....gosh! Is that the time?"

"Gosh is that the time" he mimicked her.

"Hmm!"

"Hmm all you want, you have less than twelve hours to check out of that room, sorry I couldn't extend the stay but it fully booked till August."

"Where would I be staying?"

"You could try under the bridge or the park."

"Thank you for your generosity."

"Genevieve will be picking you up at twelve noon, so get ready, she doesn't like being kept waiting."

"Who is Genevieve?"

"Now that's a good question because she has so many roles she plays; let's see, she works on the farm as in accounts, she's also the strategic manager for the logistics business, she's also an ex-marine and she does one or two things for me once in a while."

"Such as?"

"She is an expert cook and a body masseuse."

"I see."

"It's not what you think."

"And what was I thinking about?"

"I know you; you are already putting two and seven together."

"I do not have the time or mind for such vanities, anyway where is she taking me, to the airport?"

"No to visit the president, you are coming home."

"I'm sorry I can't."

"Why not?"

"Daniel I have already explained to you, we are not sleeping under the same roof."

"Ok you can sleep outside in the garden."

"What about you?"

"Well by the time I get home my bed will be waiting for me."

"Where are you now?"

"At the port?"

"Which?"

"NY."

"Why?"

"Work."

"When are you coming back home?"

"I like that, home."

"Dani...."

"Yes, Moni baby."

"I'm serious."

"I want to play, hey amigo! Monisola I've got to go, I'll call you tomorrow, don't keep Genevieve waiting pleaseeee, love you."

Monisola laughed as she got up from the bed, she heard him speaking in Spanish and wondered how many languages the guy spoke. She changed into her night wear and checked the fridge for anything she could munch as she had skipped dinner; there was nothing except some biscuit and chocolates, she ate and slept again.

He woke her up the next day.

"Are you ready?"

"For what?"

"Genevieve is coming to pick you in an hour's time."

"I'm not ready, I'll get a taxi."

"To where?"

"Your apartment or wherever you live."

"Monisola go pour cold water on your face, you need to wake up."

"I'm awake, you woke me up."

"If Genevieve gets there and you are not ready you will find your way home."

"Sure, I'll get a cab and go straight to the airport."

There was a bit of silence between them. Daniel finally broke it with the way he exhaled.

"GOD help me with Monisola, I am not in the mood for this and I still have a lot to do."

Monisola decided to have a change of heart, "Okay, I'll get ready."

"Thank you."

Genevieve did come to pick her precisely an hour later and contrary to the impression Daniel gave, she seemed to be a sweet lady with a beautiful smile. However, by the time she was driving especially once they got on the highway, Monisola held on to her seat and was praying and pleading for journey mercies.

She was shocked when they finally arrived at the farm. It was not what she had expected. Once again Daniel gave her a wrong impression, she expected to see a small piece of land and a rundown shackle for a home but she was shocked with what she saw.

The expanse of land from the time Genevieve announced they were at the 'farm' till they drove to a beautiful Spanish styled villa was more than a small piece of land, it was more like ten Olympic stadiums pulled together. She was speechless, she thought she was hiding things from Daniel, he was the one keeping secrets.

"Are you alright girl? You look like you've just stepped on the moon?"

"Daniel didn't tell me how ...."

"He doesn't know how to blow his own trumpet and you are not the first he's done it to and I'm sure won't be the last. He is just an easy-going regular guy."

Monisola muttered to herself, easy going indeed.

Genevieve showed her round the villa and all she could do was just smile and nod her head; she was eagerly waiting for his arrival then she would talk.

"Would Daniel be back soon."

"I'm not sure darling but I know he won't keep you waiting for too long."

Monisola ignored the comment and once she got to the room where she would be staying she lay on the bed trying to take everything in. What game was Daniel playing with her? She thought he was just a regular guy and was okay with it. There are many girls who marry guys they were richer than but hers was like the reverse. Even her earnings and savings combined with her father's kingdom will not match Daniel's acquired wealth. She didn't like that, she is used to being in control, calling the shots but that would prove to be difficult with Daniel. Daniel! Daniel! Daniel! Why did she fall in love with him and was she better off without him? She couldn't truly answer that question because she knew her heart was already entwine with his. GOD I need help here, mega one.

She spent the night alone and in a way she liked it as everything was peaceful. She could hear sounds that were similar to the ones she heard back home when she went hunting with her father when she was young. Omoniyi had taught her how to be quiet and listen to the various sounds of crickets, owls and differentiate them. She missed her brother; she wondered what he would have said about Daniel and why he never mentioned him to her. She eventually drifted to sleep as the sounds of nature lured her with their lullabies.

Daniel came in early the next morning; he was so tired and knew he would fall asleep while standing if he didn't go straight to bed but he could not resist the urge to check on Monisola. He quietly went in and saw a figure on the bed, well it could be anyone so he tiptoed and when he saw her he felt better. Yes, she was here and he loved the smile on her face. He went back to his room and fell asleep as soon as his head hit the pillow while his legs were hanging from the bed onto the floor.

"This little light of mine,
I'm gonna let it shine
This little light of mine

I'm gonna let it shine...."

Why couldn't she just take her loud voice, little light and shine elsewhere, he wanted some sleep, uninterrupted sleep. He hated it when she did this to either annoy him or get him up. He draped the bed cover over his head but that didn't drown her voice nor the laughter that accompanied it. One of these days, just one of these days he was going to let her know what he thought of her singing he couldn't stand it anymore.

He was soon drifting back to sleep where he heard her laugh again, who was she talking to?

"Chris are you coming out or not, breakfast is ready and remember Mo is here."

Mo? Who is Mo?

"I don't want to disturb him especially if he is tired and needs the rest."

Daniel jumped out of his bed. Of course, Monisola was here, how did he ever forget.

".... of course, I can cook, all I need are the....."

Monisola was talking with Genevieve when she nudged towards the door; standing there was no one other than Mr Daniel looking as if he hadn't slept a wink and the shorts he wore showed his sexy skinny legs.

"Good morning ladies."

"Good morning" both ladies chorused.

"Did you sleep well?"

"Nope!"

"Why?"

"Gennie you know why, I hate it when you sing."

"Well as long as I live I'm gonna sing for my Lord and Saviour and nothing and no one is ever going to stop me, not even you Chris. What do you want for breakfast?"

"I'm going back to bed."

"Come now boy, are you going to ignore our guest after you left her all alone yesterday?"

"It's all her fault she should have come when I told her to, I'm so tired I need more time to sleep."

"That's alright I can still catch that flight."

"Mo I'll drive and after that I'll take a long vacation."

Daniel ignored them, all he said was 'see you at lunch' and left the two women on their own and went back to bed.

Lunch was sumptuous and Monisola ate until she could eat no more.

"I'm stuffed."

"I'm well fed and grateful."

"Thank you Lord for this food, all I need now is to go home and sleep"

"Where is home?"

"Where my heart is and always will be with that old boy."

"Old boy?"

"The boy who tried to get into my pants when I was twelve."

The shock on Monisola's face made Genevieve laugh. "Now don't go all naive with me, what do you think most men want from a girl, love, companionship? No that's most girls' dream; a man just wants what he wants. Your Chris is no exception, so give him what he wants and I can rest and retire. He's really getting on my nerves lately and I don't want to do something that will spoil our long-term relationship between our families but seriously he is driving me crazy"

"Are you suggesting I ...."

"I'm not suggesting anything, all I'm saying is ..."

"You said I should give him what he wants!"

"Yes, give him what he wants from you, I don't know what he wants but it's not so hard to figure it out. Chris is not the kind of guy that fools around; he's that kind of person that knows what he wants and goes after it. I don't know what he wants but please just give him, your heart, love even your body on the condition of marriage of course."

"Have I been the topic of your discussion?"

"Not at all but I've known Chris for a long time and even George agrees with me on this one, something is eating him up. Now that you are here it's easy to see why, please Mo, I'm not asking you to do what is against your principles but give Chris a chance, I just want him to be happy, he's been through a lot and it seems you make him happy and mad somehow which is a good sign."

"Where does my feelings and what I want come in?"

"I don't know, you will be a good judge of that but Chris is my main priority and I want my life back, I'm sick and tired of all the travelling, work and pressures he puts us all through, I quit!"

"Alleluia thank you LORD for answering my prayers."

They both turned to see Daniel thanking GOD, smiling and all dressed up.

"You're thinking of firing me?"

"No, you quit and that would be easier for me."

"Well then I quit"

"Thank you."

Monisola looked at both of them, were they serious or joking. Daniel was smiling and Genevieve looked like she was about to burst into tears.

"I think you should apologies Daniel, you've hurt her feelings."

He was about to say something but thought best to shut up. "Look Genevieve it's not that I don't want you to do what you enjoy doing but really you need a break once in a while like every one of us. You should take a vacation, go to the island, I'll even sponsor you."

"It's not the same without George."

"Take him with you."

"But you always have a project or the other to deal with."

"So what! There would always be projects otherwise they would be no income but that does not mean we put aside every other thing. When I get married I'll be taking vacations and taking time off to spend with my family, I'm not going to let some business run and dictate my life. When the children are older, I'll be taking my wife for a vacation not a business trip. You know what, you book where you want to go and once George agrees just go, the rest of the team will sort themselves out."

"And you won't bite off their heads?"

"Why should I when I have Monisola here with me."

"I thought you were too busy to have time for me."

He laughed, kissed the top of her forehead and brought out some fruits to make juice.

The rest of the day Daniel did whatever he had to do via his laptop and phone and when he had concluded all his work he gave her his undivided attention.

"Your royal highness I'm all yours, your wish is my command."

"Wish! I don't wish, I command."

"Well my order is at your command."

"Good, take me home."

He laughed, "You know that is impossible, you are here for a purpose and you haven't fulfilled it."

"Daniel what do you want?"

"You."

She moved away from him.

"You can't run away babe, I have you just where I want you to be" he held her and the look in his eyes told her to run but her legs refused to obey the command.

"Daniel, I ... we shouldn't.

"Why not? You are here and I am here so what's stopping us?"

"Daniel for the love of GOD I don't want to sleep with you."

"Marry me then?"

"No."

"Then you leave me no choice" he was kissing and touching and she knew there was no escape.

"Dan please let's talk."

"I'm done with talking girl, I want you and I want you now."

He carried her to his room and continued with his love making, he was already ignited with fire and there was no stopping him, probably he'll regret not waiting but he couldn't care less.

"Daniel, I don't want you please stop."

He ignored her and continued.

His touch was sending signals her body had never received before and while her body was trying to tune in and adjust itself to the new heights of passion her mind was sending red alerts and the speed was at almost zero level. She pushed him away and ran as far as she could. When her body regained its composure and her mind took over she went into the house. It was all dark but the door was opened, she went into her room and packed her things, she should never have come, that she regretted but more so she was going to break up with Daniel.

The next day she was sitting in the kitchen having breakfast when she heard his car drive in. The minute he came in she knew she had spent the night alone in the house as he looked as if he had a rough night. No words were spoken and neither did she feel like talking to him so she got up, washed her mug and went into her room. By night time she decided it was best she broke the silence between them.

"Daniel, can we please talk?"

He refused to answer her.

"Daniel I did not come here with the intention to... to sleep with you, I came so that I ...I promised I would and now that I have I would like to go home."

"When?"

"Tomorrow or day after."

"You might as well go now."

"It's night time."

"I drive you to the nearest motel and you can get a cab and catch your plane."

"Is that what you want?"

"Would you give me what I want?"

"I'm not going to sleep with you."

"And you won't marry me, what exactly do you want from me? What exactly are you trying to prove Miss Ice queen! That you are tough, over- righteous or what? You don't want me to make love to you now, that's fine. I offer marriage but you refuse, so what do you want, tell me Monisola because I'm missing whatever message you are trying to pass across here."

"I'm not trying to send any coded message; I have told you I don't think you want to marry me you just want me for .... for ..."

"Sex" he finished her sentence for her.

"Yes."

"What's wrong with that? You want sex in the context of marriage and I have offered you that and you refused, so what do you want?"

"You don't love me and you just want my body."

He laughed and laughed. "You know what? You are so in tune with your fairy tale princess world that you don't know what is real or not. I told you I want you and I want to marry you if you can't accept that then you have no place in my world because I am not going to say something to comply with your fairy tale movie script and live happily ever after. Do what you want Monisola I don't give a damn anymore."

WHEN SHE GOT back to England she concentrated on her work and when her contract with her employer ended she did not renew it as she wanted time for herself. She spoke to her family every now and then but did not tell anyone what she was going through. Even when Toluwanimi pried she refused to let him in.

She was going through another phase in her life and it was worse than the time Omoniyi left or when she lost Raymond. She was beginning to think she had sunk lower than lower and no one but GOD could save her. She did not even want to think about him, each time she did she felt a pain that kept cutting at her heart again and again. She had to do something otherwise she knew she would go crazy. She had lost weight and the lack of sleep and the bags on her eyes were beginning to tell tales.

"Monisola, I don't like the way you are looking what is wrong?"

"Chichi I've told you a dozen times, I am fine."

"You don't sound fine and the last time I saw you, you weren't looking fine."

"That was some weeks ago, I am fine now."

"That wasn't what Esther said when she saw you."

"Esther, which Esther?"

"Esther my cousin now, the one we went for her wedding last year."

"Oh! That Esther but I didn't see her."

"Precisely her point, you were looking straight ahead and miles away from planet earth that you wouldn't even realise if a naked man walked past you."

Monisola laughed, a naked man indeed.

"Maybe I was deep in thought."

"Has he called?"

"I don't want to talk about it."

"It or him."

"Both! Whatever."

"Ok! I know I am no longer your best friend but you can't let what has happened affect your life, you've got to take charge and get going."

"Believe me I've tried, this one hurts, even more than Raymond."

"I've told you not to worry yourself about Raymond even though he is my cousin he is a ....."

"Chichi you have children in your house, don't say any nasty word and don't spell it either as that's easier for them to grasp."

"Okay I will say it in Igbo then."

"You will have to interpret."

They both laughed.

"What next then?"

"I don't know, maybe I'll get a job or something."

"You mean you've not been working and I have been looking for a baby sitter."

"I said job not work and you know babysitting demands your full attention and right now I can't concentrate."

"Why don't you call him or go and see him?"

"Are you mad?"

"Monisola!"

"I'm sorry Chic, I'm sorry"

"Forgive him."

"For what? He hasn't done anything. I'm the one who is guilty and stupid for allowing a man into my heart."

"Which is natural, Monic I think you really love this guy but I don't know why ..."

"Chic I have to go, speak to you later."

She quickly hung up the phone before her friend could say anything again.

The phone rang, she was reluctant to pick it but she did.

"Chic I'm sorry."

"Well I'm not chic but apology accepted."

It took her a while before she recognised the voice on the line.

"Mark?"

"Yes Moni, how are you?"

"I'm fine, how are you?"

"I need your help."

"Mark ....."

"Moni I wouldn't call you at this hour or at all if I did not need you, I desperately and urgently need to see you."

"Okay where are you?"

"I'm in the office and before you come you must promise me you will grant my request otherwise don't bother."

"Okay what is it?"

MONISOLA COULD NOT believe it. She was back in Nigeria not in her own state but Benue state working for her former employer in a capacity she had never dreamt of and with so many benefits. She had a duplex to herself with her own staff, driver and heading a project with over a hundred people working in her team in different operations. The programme known as E.A.C.H was designed to promote better qualitative Education, Agriculture, Communication and Health Care. The areas were so diverse and they were starting from grass roots levels reaching out to indigenes especially women and youth. Monisola experience of working with different NGO all over the world and her knowledge, skills, techniques and work ethics proved to be very useful. Coupled with her determination and passion she soon had a good rapport with her team and her ability to work with everyone even doing the most mundane tasks earned her a good reputation and genuine love from the people.

She worked tirelessly from dawn to dusk, Monday to Saturday and Sunday was her only rest day. She visited several of the local government areas from Makurdi, Vandeika, Oturkpo, Gboko, Oju, Katsina-Ala, Konshisha and several other towns and villages. What she enjoyed most was the warmth and reception of the people, they were open to her and her team and worked with them. She had her interpreter with her who was well versed in speaking the major languages Tiv, Idoma and Igede languages and when she had any difficulty she readily helped her.

Since her arrival she had been so busy she hardly ever had time to socialise and each time the opportunity or invitation came she politely declined, she just wanted to be alone. Her mother complained of being in the same country with her and not seeing her; Chichi murmured that while in the same country they talked at least every now and then but in different continents she hardly communicated with her.

Mark who was supposed to head the operation but declined at the last minute and put her name forward, complained that he only got to speak to her once a week. She laughed and told him he should be glad she spoke to him at all. She asked after his new found love and wife and all he said was that the decision to get married and decline to take up the prestigious job offer abroad was the best decision he had made and he did not regret it one bit.

"Not even the offer of a fat bank account?"

"Moni even all the money in the world can never give me this love I've found. I love her so much and just being by her side is enough for me and I count my blessings every day."

"I never thought I would ever hear that from you Mark Burton."

"The pleasures I derive from Mrs Burton not just physical but emotional are all I need to make me happy. All I want is to be happy. Moni if you find happiness don't ever let go, cling to it until it clings to you."

Sunday came, she was happy she had the day to herself as she sent most of her staff home by Friday night and only if occasion demands did they stay till Saturday. This Sunday she attended the first service though it was in the local dialect, she still stayed and enjoyed the peace and presence of GOD when the choir sang or the minister prayed.

She was on her way home walking up her street towards her house when she saw a boy and a man afar off, there was nothing suspicious about them so she continued to enjoy her walk. However, she saw them turn towards her house, the gateman opened the gate and the man probably the father went in and came out again with a ball and passed it to the boy. She smiled and thought to herself boys would always be boys. She was almost walking up to her house when suddenly she noticed the boy dash into the street and as he kicked his ball, it went flying in the air, almost hit her in the face but she quickly dodged the ball and all of a sudden the smile, peace and tranquillity of the Sunday afternoon left her.

"You should be careful of where you play that ball especially on the street, a car could go by any time and GOD forbid if....."

The remaining of the sentence left her lips when she saw the man who she thought was the boy's father.

"I told you to stop running like that ....."

He stopped and was transfixed to the ground, his mouth wide open and his eyes blinked several times, he could not believe his eyes.

"Monisola!"

She took a deep breath and turned to go into her house.

"Monisola wait."

"I ...."

"Monisola, what are you doing here, I can't believe my eyes."

"Uncle do you know her?"

"Know her, yes, yes I do, Tertseagh take the ball and go home I'll be ...."

"Not so fast. You are not going anywhere and I'm seizing that ball, I don't like the way you ran on the street with that ball, you can play in the field or somewhere..."

Tertseagh suddenly burst into tears which made Monisola stop and take a closer look at him. She thought he was about ten years old but with the tears and taking a good look at him he could be six or seven.

"How old are you Tertseagh?"

"Six" he sniffled.

"Okay, I'm still going to keep your ball until you learn how to play safely, I'm sure your parents would not like it if you get hurt and as for your uncle ...." she decided to let that pass. "Do you like cupcakes?"

He nodded.

"Good I baked some before going to church this morning and I'm sure they would have cooled off by now, do you want some?"

He nodded, turned, looked at his uncle and then shook his head.

"Don't worry we won't tell your mum", Daniel seemed to know the reason for his reluctance.

"You will tell your mum and in fact take some for her."

"Really! Can I take some for my dad and sisters?"

"Well, that depends on if they like them."

"Oh! We all like cupcakes, don't we uncle?"

Daniel was still looking at Monisola wondering what she was doing in this part of his neighbourhood and why she was here of all the places on earth.

The three went inside the house, Monisola excused herself and told her young guest to go wash his hands while she ignored Daniel.

She locked the door as soon as she got into her room and took a deep breath. What was he doing here and what was she going to do now? She took her bath, quickly changed and went downstairs.

Her young guest was sitting comfortably watching the television while the intruder as she preferred to call him was filling their glasses with cold drinks. At least he was being useful.

"Do you want to choose your cake now?"

The boy nodded but his face was glued to the TV. Monisola smiled as she remembered that her nephews and nieces did the same thing. She went to the kitchen and started to select some of the cakes for him and his family. As soon as Daniel came in she was tensed and felt unease.

"Monisola."

She ignored him and put the cupcakes into the box.

"I still don't believe my eyes, what are you doing here?"

She packed another box and marked it with Tertseagh's name.

"Monisola talk to me."

"I've packed his cakes and for his family, please leave."

"Tertseagh!"

"Uncle."

"Come over and say thank you to aunty."

Tertseagh walked into the kitchen and seeing the different cupcakes on the kitchen table smacked his lips with his tongue which made them laugh.

"Are you going to eat all these?" he asked with amazement.

"No, I'm taking them to a school I'll be visiting tomorrow and I still have a lot more to bake and cream so I have to start baking as quickly as I can."

"Tertseagh say thank you for the cupcakes and we'll be on our way."

He obeyed his uncle and also gave her a hug which made her eyes watery.

"You're welcome and maybe soon I'll play football with you."

"That would be great and we'll team up to score more goals against my uncle; he's always wining all the time."

She laughed at the innocent comment but knowing the truth behind it.

She was still mixing the dough and preparing her utensils when he came in. What now?

He came over to where she was and touched her as if confirming it was really her. She moved away from him and continued with her baking.

"I don't know what to say."

"Please leave me alone."

"Of all the places on planet earth, I never imagined I would ever see you again especially not here in my homeland and backyard."

Oh! So, he had planned not to see her again, well she equally and precisely now he was just a fragment of her imagination. However, he chose that moment to move closer and hug her, as if to reassure himself he wasn't dreaming. He held her so tight that she could feel his heart beat.

"Now that you've verified that it's me can you let go, I've got work to do."

He ignored her and began to tread on dangerous ground, she quickly pushed him away and opened the kitchen door for him to leave, he did and she was glad.

She had just removed the last tray from the oven, longing for a shower and a cold drink when he came back again. She was annoyed that the gatemen let him in again and thought of what to tell him about letting strangers in.

"Monisola we need to talk."

"I don't want to talk and we have nothing to say to each other."

"It's been almost a year since ..."

"Daniel, get out!"

He took a step towards her and she took three back.

"Daniel for the sake of peace, please leave me alone, I don't want to have anything to do with you whatsoever, please leave."

Monisola begging him? That was strange, very strange indeed.

"What are you doing here?"

"I can assure you it's got nothing to do with you, I haven't tracked you down or anything, the job opportunity came and I took it to help a friend please leave me alone."

"I can't. Not now or ever"

She left him in the kitchen and went up to her room hoping by the time she had a shower he would have gone. He was still there.

She poured some fruit juice in a glass and went to sit in the living room.

"How are your parents?"

"Good."

"Toluwanimi?"

"Good."

"Chichi and her family?"

"Good."

"You?"

She kept quiet.

"Monisola I still want you."

She threw the glass at him and when it landed safely on the carpet she thanked GOD, she hated having to vacuum over and over again for bits of glasses.

"I still want to marry you."

If he was hoping for another tantrum she wasn't going to give him one, she picked up the glass, took it to the kitchen, switched off the lights in the living room and went upstairs to her room.

The visit to the school the next day took all the energy she had left; coupled with the fact that she did not sleep all through the night as her eyes were wide opened. She came home exhausted and was hoping to have a good night rest when she saw him at the gate.

"Usman how are you?"

"Fine Madam, Oga has been waiting for you since and I told him you will be back at four."

Surely this man had no sense of what was called privilege information and privacy, and who was he referring to as her Oga?

"Monisola we need to talk."

She led him into the house and into her study.

"What do you want from me Daniel?"

"I meant what I said yesterday and I would like you to think ...."

"The answer is no, never."

"Monisola do you want me to beg you?"

"Look here Mr Daniel I can see you've got nothing else to do, I've had a long day and I need to rest."

She left him in the study and went up to her room. She was having her shower when she heard someone come in, none of her staff came into her room and she wondered which of them it was.

"Who is there?"

There was no answer. She quickly stepped out of the shower and put on her robe.

"Is anyone ...." she almost fainted when she saw Daniel standing in her room.

"Please leave me alone."

He moved towards her and before she could move she was already in his arms and he was kissing her. She wanted to push him away but he had secured her hands in such position that she could not move so she stayed still, thinking if she should call one of her staff or shout for help.

"I want you now Monisola, I was a fool to let you go."

Mr Fool, well said. "Daniel I'd like to get dressed can you please leave my room?"

He laughed and shook his head.

"I'm no longer a fool, you can dress while I'm here, I'll be watching or rather still....."

"Daniel I don't like this and I've asked you to leave me alone like a thousand times what do you want from me?"

He began to show her with his hands and lips and when she could no longer resist him she let go. He sensed her willingness and he began to smile.

"Marry me Princess Monisola, I've been having nightmares that you've left me and married someone else and I can't bear that, I'd rather ...."

She put her finger on his lips to stop him from saying the last word. "Please go downstairs I'll be down in a minute."

Monisola took her time in dressing, thinking what conversation she was going to have with Daniel and what decision she was going to make. Well she wasn't going to make one or decide anything, she was just going to enjoy her evening and if he persists with his stupid talk she would have him thrown out.

They talked about everything except themselves, she smiled whenever he made a funny comment but his eyes never left her. After their meal Monisola decided she wanted to go for a walk which she did whenever she had the time.

"I hope you don't mind; I'll like to introduce you to my sister."

"I'm not in the mood to socialise; I'm very tired and I just want some peace and quiet."

He shrugged his shoulders and led the way out. As they were walking he held her hand and showed her the neighbourhood.

"How long have you been in Nigeria?"

"A couple of months."

"When do you intend leaving?"

She wondered who told him she was leaving. "When my contract ends."

"When is that?"

"As soon as I complete my job."

"Which is ..."

She ignored him.

"I want us to get married"

Silence.

"I'm heading back home in a week or two but before then I want us to set our wedding date and I'll like to see your father."

She laughed, that would be the day.

"Have you ever told him about us?"

"No!"

"Your mother?"

"Daniel I don't want to get married, just leave me alone."

"Monisola I love you and can't live without you."

"You have for the past one year and you will."

"I've not been the same this past one year."

"But you survived and so did I, so let just be."

"I'm going to see your father."

"If you wish but the road won't be easy and I am not going to help you when you come back crying."

"Big man like me cry, wetin you think say I be, I beg no be America we dey, I no dey take no shit from anybody na Naija we dey so."

Monisola shook her hand and laughed.

"Any tips before I go and see your father?"

"GOD will go with you.

"Is that all?"

"What else do you need, if GOD be for you who can be against you?"

"It's your father we are talking about."

"Is he not a human being?"

"He is but what if he says no?"

"Then you've heard from both of us because I am not saying yes."

"You know you can't marry anyone else?"

"Says who?"

"It's you I love."

"I don't ......"

For him that was an assurance that he still had a chance with her, the ball was in his court now and he had to play it well.

CHAPTER SIXTEEN

"Chris, are you sure of what you are saying?"

"I'm very positive."

"You are asking a hard thing."

"I know but you are the only one that can help me."

"Me! No! If it was anything else you could count on me but this...."

"Kunle you know I would never ask you for anything that I know you cannot do but please this is very important, it's my life we are talking about, my future! I would do the same for you if you come to me."

"Eh! My father-in-law is not a kabiyesi and more so not Kabiyesi Adewunmi. Do you know how tough that guy is, in fact before talking to him sometimes, I would have fasted and prayed days ahead before I go and see him."

"Come on, he is only a man, he is not GOD."

"Eh! So, go to him, you don't need me."

"I do. You know I am an orphan; I am not a Yoruba man and besides...."

"You should have thought about this before deciding to marry his daughter."

"Oh! You mean you considered all such factors before marrying your wife?"

"Well .... no, I just fell in love..."

"Exactly! I fell in love; I am in love with Monisola and I can't bear to leave her again."

"Eh! Wait a minute! What do you mean by that? I hope you are not doing playboy here because I will not go and disgrace myself before that man, please I have my good name, reputation and status to maintain."

"Not even for an old friend?"

"Not even for you."

"See life! Even though I followed you to your own in-laws and begged on your behalf."

"My own wasn't complicated; I just wanted them to know that I have Tiv connection and a good and respectable friend."

"Would you not reciprocate the same gesture towards me and speak on my behalf?"

"No! I mean I would follow you, introduce you and you do the talking, no be me wan marry now, I did my years ago."

"Ok, call me for anything relating to your farm again and see me running to help you."

"If you like crawl or even drag your feet, all I know is that you are a man of your words, you do not go back on your word and as you said years and years ago you will always be a friend in need, so I know you will come when I call."

"You are a joker; you are on your own."

"You know you are a long-time friend and I would do anything to help you but..."

"You are going with me."

"Why me?"

"You are one of the few, good and trustworthy friends I have and know that can help."

"I wish Niyi was still here."

"Even if it is his father we are talking about?"

"How did you even get to know her? Through Niyi?"

"It's a long story."

"So, tell me."

"It would take days and more so I need to see her father this week, in fact tomorrow if possible."

"Eh! Wait a minute, so soon! I thought maybe in a month's time or so."

"Month! Do you want to kill me? I want to set the ball rolling so we can get married as soon as possible."

"Chris, I trust you have fasted, prayed well and I hope you are not just going to open your mouth and say mere words with no power from Almighty GOD backing you up!"

"Leave that one between GOD and I, you just come with me tomorrow."

"GOD what kind of wahala am I putting myself in, Chris I hope you are serious."

"Trust GOD, all is well"

The next day while sitting before Kabiyesi Adewunmi, Kunle wished he had refused to help his friend as his tried to articulate the words he had rehearsed overnight. He said a quick prayer, cleared his throat and began his first line of words which he hoped will grant him favourable audience before the king.

"Good afternoon Kabiyesi, I'm very grateful that you could see me at such short notice, I am very grateful sir, thank you sir. Ki ade pe lori, ki batá pe le se', long will be your reign in our land, filled with Almighty GOD's peace, vigour, strength, abundance and unity among the people, thank you sir, GOD bless you."

"Senator how can I say no to your honourable self, like begets like, it's a privilege to have you in my humble presence, you are the brain behind the powers that be, please sit down."

"Thank you Kabiyesi, I am so grateful."

"Yonga, please see to the entertainment of the Senator and his friend."

"Thank you sir but we are alright sir, thank you."

"Are you sure?"

"A ko le gba wa ju ile oba ka ma ko ba. It is totally ill-mannered and lack of respect if we pass by the king and not observe protocol."

Kabiyesi laughed, "Beni, beni."

Daniel looked at Kunle and nodded.

Kunle cleared his throat, "Kabiyesi I would like to introduce a very good friend of mine, I have known him for a very long time and if there is someone that I can call a friend or stand surety for, he would be one of the very few ones."

Kabiyesi looked at the man that came with the senator, he could not recollect if he had seen him before and he did not know where the conversation was leading to so he listened carefully to what the senator was saying.

"..... he is currently based in America but comes into town every now and then, as he has several businesses here and there and he is the one that helped me to start my farm business. In fact, he took care of every single thing and he did not take a single kobo for all the work he put in, he owns a farm here and one in the US....."

Now this was getting more interesting, a farmer, farms here and America, he hoped he wasn't referring to a back-yard farm as he wasn't interested in that.

"...... the last time I visited his farm here we drove miles and miles over a huge expanse of farm land, well cultivated with the use of machinery and all, in fact I was dazed. Sir, you should see the technology used and storage facilities, it is A class."

Daniel saw the twinkle in Kabiyesi's eyes and he sent a million thanks to GOD; he was grateful for an effectual door that had been opened to him.

Kabiyesi did not waste much time as he began to question Daniel himself and since it was familiar grounds, Daniel answered all his questions to the best of his knowledge giving current and expert advice as well as offering to visit Kabiyesi's farm that very day.

After the impromptu farm visit and inspection, Kabiyesi was so thrilled. Never had he met a man with so much knowledge, sound counsel and advice, in fact he wished the young man could stay for dinner but he politely refused and promised to be back as soon as possible but he had no idea when that would be.

Later that evening Senator Kunle received a call, as soon as he saw Kabiyesi's number his heart skipped a beat. What did Chris do? He had left them because he had an important meeting to attend and he hoped everything had gone well otherwise...

"E Kale sir"

"Senator, the youngest, most brilliant and power shaker of our time, okurin meta, the one GOD is using in our times to shape and sharpen our land, GOD bless you, ikan nla ma lo se fun mi loni. You have been used by GOD to bless me today."

Senator Kunle's ears tingled and his eyes twitched as he heard what Kabiyesi was saying. Did Chris make his intention know so soon, that boy must be a fast runner, how did he do it or what exactly did he say?

"Thank you sir but I didn't do anything, I merely introduced my friend..."

"Merely? Please that is an understatement. GOD used you to part my red sea and you say mere introduction. That young man is a genius, how come I never met him before? Anyway, he promised to come as soon as possible but I hope his soon is very soon."

"Sir one thing I know Chris for is that he is a man of his word."

"Chris? I thought his name is Daniel."

"Chris Daniel Benjamin is his name sir but I call him by his first name."

"Oh! Ok, it was GOD speaking through him and I really appreciate you for introducing him. I am very grateful. I have almost given up regarding taking the farm estate to the next level but with this young man on the horizon I am full of hope. Once again I thank you and please do not hesitate to ask for anything that I can do for you, goodnight, my kind regards to your family."

Kunle began to dance as he called another number on his phone.

"Hello! My man how you dey, you don score."

"Hello! Kunle, how you dey?"

"I dey dance."

"Dance! What's the celebration?"

"I am celebrating a long-term friendship with you that I pray will last a lifetime."

"Amen!"

"You must come over to my house tomorrow and let's celebrate."

"Celebrate! I wish I could but I'm back home and will be coming down to your side again tomorrow."

"Why did you leave so soon, I thought your meeting with Kabiyesi went well?"

"I hope so."

"What do you mean you hope so? Are you not interested in his daughter again?"

"Dem swear for you?"

"No e'bi like say na you. Kabiyesi just called to thank me for introducing you and you are saying hope, the man likes you in fact he said anything I want I should ask."

"Don't just ask for his daughter's hand."

"Of course not, the one I have here is enough and I love my wife."

"Good."

"Did you ask him?"

"Not yet."

"You are doing slow coach."

"I am tendering and watering my grounds before I plant my seeds."

"Okay Mr tender and watering, see me tomorrow when you get back to town."

"I might not see you; I am going straight to see Kabiyesi, come back home again and back to him the next day."

"Chris."

"Yes."

"I beg take am easy."

"Just pray I get the answer I need to hear."

"I am on your side."

"Were you not before?"

"No! You were on your own?"

"With friends like you, who needs an enemy?"

"You know I am not your enemy; I am your pal."

"For mouth only."

"See you tomorrow."

"See you when I see you."

Kabiyesi sat in his study and was ruminating on the last three days' event. How was he not sensitive to what was going on? Did he miss any signs? Was he so mesmerised with the whole thing that he could not detect the intentions of the young man? The last three days had no bearing, gave no indication to tonight's request. Where did he miss it? After the first meeting, the young man came the next day and he was shocked by what he came with. A trailer load of cows! He, Zachariah had to blink twice and almost four times because he could not believe his eyes. The next day it was another trailer of crops and by the third day it was fruits, vegetables and poultry. It was then he started to think deeply and began to make series of enquiries about the young man but each feedback gave him no clue and he had no choice but to ask him himself.

The reply startled him, confused him and then he felt like kicking his own shin. How could he not have guessed or have the slightest inclination? Then the thought came to him that he was not GOD and for GOD not to reveal this to him weighed his heart because it meant only one thing and he was not ready for that.

When will you be ready my son?

Father, please not yet.

In my time or yours?

Zachariah bowed to the KABIYESI of all Kabiyesis and began to cry.

"Monisola."

"Father! E ka le sir."

"I want to see you."

"Father I am in the middle of ..."

"Who is Chris Daniel Benjamin to you?"

Monisola took a deep breath, "I'll be home tomorrow Father."

After speaking to her, Kabiyesi called Daniel and asked him to come to see him.

"Daniel what did you say to my father?"

"Good evening Princess Monisola, how was your day?"

"It was going perfectly well until my father called and asked me about you."

"And what did your princess royal tell his royal highness?"

"I told him I never met anyone by that name."

"Liar, all lies Monisola!"

"How do you know it's a lie?"

"Your father just asked me to come and see him tomorrow and if I guess right I will be seeing you there!"

"Daniel I don't want any wahala, please."

"Neither do I, I just want to marry you.

CHAPTER SEVENTEEN

On her way home Monisola thought of what to say to her father when he started his interrogations about Daniel. She had never mentioned him because she wanted to keep her love life away from the prying eyes of her family. She knew they meant well but she did not want to be the topic of discussion at every family gathering or conversation and after all the drama with Omoniyi's death, Raymond's rejection and the fact that her father knew about Raymond without her telling him had bothered her a lot hence her decision to keep Daniel away from everyone. Everyone except Toluwanimi and thank GOD he had not misplaced her trust in keeping Daniel a secret from her father.

The question now was what was she going to tell Kabiyesi? What were her feelings right now about the whole issue? Deep within her she had almost given up on her love for Daniel, she thought she would never see him again and even if she did, it would be too late as he would have married someone else. Her state of mind was confused, did she still love him, what if something happened and just like Raymond he left her? Did she really want to spend the rest of her life with Daniel?

Was there someone else out there for her? She knew the last thought was negative and did not really ponder on that which left her with one thought, was she ready to get married?

Her mother was pleased to see her and she was delighted to see her siblings who were now toddlers and were all over the place keeping everyone on their toes.

"Olori how do you cope with such bursting energies; they are quite a handful."

"I can't complain, I just thank GOD for them every time, imagine life without these bundles of joy."

They were still talking when she was summoned by Kabiyesi, her heart began to thud and she quickly asked the Holy Spirit to help her and give her the right words to say.

"Good evening father."

Kabiyesi did not respond at first, he took a good look at his daughter, his first born, the little baby he carried in his arms yesterday; the toddler with wide inquisitive eyes staring at him and he often wondered what her thoughts were and right now he hoped he could get answers to the matter at hand because over the years she had turned from a sweet girl to a rebellious teenager and then an elusive young woman, what a wonder GOD had bestowed on him.

He took a long good look at his daughter and he had to hold back his tears, was she going to leave him so soon.

Monisola moved closer to her father as he stretched his hands towards her. She was shocked when her father hugged and gently rocked her. The last time he did this was when they reconciled after Omoniyi's death and before then probably when she was ten or younger. What was going on?

"How are you Monisola?"

"I'm fine thank you sir and you?"

"I'm ......" Kabiyesi's voice trailed into silence.

Monisola wasn't sure what this was all about as it seems it was more than Daniel.

"Father why did you ask me to come, is there something that you are not telling me?"

He shook his head and hugged her again, then Kabiyesi comported himself.

"Monisola ever since I carried you in my arms the very day you were born, I have been thankful to GOD for giving you to me. You are everything a father wants in a daughter. I used to wish you were a boy but you are worth more than ten sons. You are a woman of substance and calibre, highly esteemed and honourable."

Did he really see her that way or was he just teasing her?

"You know I don't blow people's trumpet if there is no tune to it. I am blowing yours today because you are worthy of it. Monisola, wa da gba, wa se' omo re' kale fun emi baba re ati iya re, wa se egbon fun awon aburo re', wa serere ninu ebi, ijoye, ara, ore', ilu, ijo' ati ka kiri gbogbo agbaye. Wa se aya rere fun oko re, wa bi mo le mo, wa' bi okunrin, wa' bi obirin, wa bi ibeji, wa bi ibefa, wa' se orire ninu ile' oko re, ese ire lo ma gbe ni gbogbo igba, Emi Mimo Olorun yio ma dari re si rere. You will be delightful and favoured by all, all who see you will see GOD's grace, mercy and favour upon you and will have no choice but to reckon with you. While your peers are taking one step towards good things you will be taking gigantic steps towards great things and you will get there and get it. Monisola, I love you and I really thank GOD for you."

Monisola was overwhelmed by the words from her father and she was soaking in the power of the words, receiving them, declaring affirmative with her Amen in JESUS name and thanking GOD for everything. She got up from kneeling down to receive all the blessings her father bestowed on her and sat down.

"Monisola, what I'm about to say is with mixed feeling but I still have to say it because, one, it is a father's pride and joy and secondly I wish I still had more time with you.

I had the privilege of meeting a young man a few days ago and ever since I have been thanking GOD for him. What I have been praying for, searching and toiling for, this young man within three days was used by GOD to bring solution to my troubles and now what he has asked for I cannot refuse him, Monisola I need your help."

"Father I don't understand, what has that got to do with me?"

"Everything my daughter, absolutely everything."

"How?"

"I know that since your brother, then that Igbo boy, you have not mentioned anyone so I assumed you were taking your time and though I have been meaning to ask but I was burdened with the matter of your mother, your brother and then the twins. It seems I have neglected you but you have always been on my mind.

Daniel Benjamin has asked for your hands in marriage and I would like to hear what you have to say."

Monisola took a deep breath, what was she expected to say? That she loved Daniel and wanted to marry him? Or that she still wanted time?

"Father I don't know what to say?"

"What do you mean?"

"I...., I...."

"How long have you known him? Do you not love him? Did he do anything to hurt you?"

"No!"

"What is it then?"

"I don't know"

"Oluwamuiremiwa we are talking about your life and future; what do you mean you don't know?"

Monisola made up her mind she was not going into too much details about Daniel. "Father, Daniel and I met after Omoniyi's burial and we've been friends."

"Only friends?"

"Yes, we lost contact over a year now and recently met again."

"He has now proposed so what next?"

"I ... I don't want to marry ...."

Her father did not let her complete her sentence, "I want you to think about this very seriously, whatever your reason before, I want you to reconsider before you give your answer."

"Father I have made up my mind."

"Oluwamuiremiwa please, reconsider again for my sake."

She was in no mood to argue with her father so she politely took her leave and went up to her room.

A few minutes later there was a knock on her door. She didn't want any more discussion before dinner so she refused to answer. Her mother came in and sat beside her.

"Monisola Oluwamuiremiwa Oluwafiadekemi Omolabake

Adewunmi, e' melo ni mo pe o?"

"Once mother."

"Listen and listen well, abo' oro' lan wi fun omo lu abi to' ba de inu re' a di o din din, o kin se omode' mo. You are not a child anymore, you have grown into a beautiful, desirable woman and you are a jewel waiting to be adorned by her fine, handsome man. It is your turn Monisola. Now is your turn to be married, there is no time to think over anything, you have had more than enough time to think, you are getting married and I am well prepared."

Monisola didn't bother to look at her mother but closed her eyes and wished she was back in England or somewhere far from everyone especially Daniel. Why did she bump into him? Why? Why?

"Monisola, I don't know what happened between you and Daniel but I think you should give him a chance, when he came looking for you after the burial ...."

"What?" Monisola turned over to look at her mother, surely she was mistaken.

"Remember the reception we had after Omoniyi's burial, he came and asked for you. At first I thought he was a friend of yours but he said you had never met but knew about you through Omoniyi and he just wanted to pass his condolences. I don't know what has happened but please be willing to forgive; no man is perfect even your father is far from perfect. If I had my way ......, anyway that is not what I came here for. I want you to pray about Daniel, ask GOD who knows and sees all to reveal the love of your life to you and also help you to forgive, you can't hold on to past mistake forever."

"Mother I'm still hurting and I don't want to give him another chance to do that to me again."

"Then you want to marry an angel because as long as you and him are human beings you will one way or the other step on each other's toes. The best thing to do is learn to talk about it, forgive each other and move on. Life is too short to hold on to grievances and hurts, one will just send oneself to an early grave and the one you hold something against will live on, so my dear daughter, forgive him, please, for my sake and the sake of my grandchildren to come."

"Mami, Daniel is not the only man on earth; I can always choose any one."

"Ori mi ko, o ni gbe' egu ele' gun'. You will not carry another woman's bone; you will carry your own bone in Jesus name. Daniel is the bone from which GOD hewed you."

"Mami!" Monisola laughed for the first time, "How do you know Daniel is the one for me, remember you just said I should pray and I have not even closed my eyes and you already have the answer."

"My dear, one knows these things, one knows as GOD reveals to the waiting eyes, I have prayed for you Monisola and I know this is your time and Daniel is the one."

"Mother I am the one Daniel wants to marry and not you so until I am convinced I am not moving an inch."

"Monisola, do you want me to deal with you like I did your father because I am not in the mood for all these, you are getting married and that is final."

"I will get married when I am ready and that is the conclusion."

"In this house?"

"Mother, I am in my father's house and no one can chase me, did your father chase you out of his house?"

"No, my mother and your father did, they made it hot for me to stay."

"Thank GOD for air cooling units, I'm sure the atmosphere will be conducive and bearable."

"Monisola, don't play games with me; I am not your father."

"Mother I will get married when I am ready."

At dinner time, Monisola precisely came in late and sat far away from Daniel. While the conversation was going on, ranging from farming to business and politics, she made sure her eyes were glued to her food and her ears to the ground. If anyone should mention anything to do with her and Daniel, she will leave the table, her peace of mind has been disturbed since she arrived and she wasn't going to give anyone the opportunity to prolong it.

As soon as dinner was over, she was making her way out to the garden when Daniel came over to join her.

"You were very quiet during dinner, are you alright?"

"I'm ok."

"Can we talk?"

She was about to lead him out to the garden when her father requested for both of them to join him in his study. All eyes turned to her and she wondered what was going through their minds. She had deliberately excluded herself from the conversations around the dinner table, knowing Daniel's presence would cause a stir if there was the slightest chance of anyone linking both of them and thank GOD the discussion around the table had been general and until now everyone apart from her parents thought Daniel was Kabiyesi's guest and she only made an appearance. Goodness gracious!

Her father was smiling and looked relaxed and so was Daniel, well she hoped after this meeting both would still be smiling.

"Mr Benjamin, I am very grateful and indebted to you for all you have done these past few days and only GOD the owner of the heavens and earth will surely reward you bountifully in return, in JESUS name."

"Kabiyesi please call me Daniel, you are just like a father to me and I have only done what GOD has asked me to do."

Kabiyesi smiled, he liked this young man and was reaching the point of calling him a friend but now he is like a son which now brings him to the point of discussion, Monisola. GOD please touch this girl's heart for me, please GOD.

"I am sure I need not go into any story about why we are here, Daniel has made his intention to marry you known and Monisola I would like to hear from you before I say anything. I would also like you Oluwamuiremiwa to please use your endowed gift of wisdom from GOD to give a favourable reply."

The last statement shook her off balance and it was deliberate. What was she going to say now as her prepared speech has been altered, she quickly prayed.

"Father, I'll ...." both eyes were focused on her, steadily watching every move she made with her mouth and their eyes narrowing to decode and dissect each word, it was now or never.

"I don't want to ...." Her father coughed; Daniel shifted on his seat. Goodness! What was all the fuss for, it was now or never.

"Daniel is not that ...... but I have made up my ....."

Another cough from her father made her turn to him, his eyes were issuing silent warning signal as he had now raised an eye brow and his lips were crunching together.

She took a deep breath, opened her mouth when Daniel suddenly interrupted her.

"Monisola I just want you to know that I love you and would never ever hurt you or let go, ever again."

This was tough.

"Kabiyesi can you please give me time ...."

"Two minutes" her father quickly replied.

Monisola got up and left the room.

As she made her way to the garden she had to go through the first reception to get to the main door and her family were all seated and turned to her as she came in.

Ayaba Adekemi was the first to speak.

"Monisola, oreke lewa larin awon omoge, this is your time you cannot escape this, I have waited long enough and you need to put your mother's mind at rest."

"Sister mi, I agree with our mothers, it is time, after all you are the first born and ...."

Morolake quickly interrupted her elder sister, "My dear sister though I agree it's your time but I believe GOD will help you make the right choice."

She smiled and without another word went into the garden.

Everything stood still and she relished the peace and serenity more than the dinner she had. She was not going to think about anything, let them say whatever they want.

Twenty minutes later she was still in the garden and was not surprised when Daniel came to join her.

He sat beside her and held her hands.

"I like the calmness of this place and I'm sorry to disturb you but Monisola I need to know your answer."

"I told you before Daniel, I am not marrying you."

"Why?"

"No reason."

"Is it because I left you?"

"I left because you said I should."

"Monisola I'm sorry please forgive me."

"There is nothing to forgive, you or I left because we wanted to: Omoniyi left, Raymond did the same so why not you?"

"You can't compare me with them."

"Why not?" she sneered.

"You know Monisola, you know. You know no one can love you like I do and you did not love them the way you love me."

"Daniel please leave me alone."

"As long as we live I will never leave you and until you marry me I will give you no rest."

She left him in the garden and went up to her room.

She was back at work and the long hours, travelling from one local government to the other, meeting people, setting up centres coupled with other issues helped her focus, kept her on her toes and allowed her to stop thinking about Daniel. However, true to her words her mother was making things unbearable for her and this time it was getting to her because for the first time her father who usually was on her side decided to aid and abet her mother and so did the rest of the family. Daniel also did not make things easy. He introduced her to his sister who at first was not friendly but after, decided to join forces with the plan to get her to say yes to Daniel.

Daniel had come to her house and practically dragged her to his sister's place and introduced her to the sister, her husband and friend. Francis her husband was pleased to meet her but his wife Justina and her friend Hembadon were cold which to her was even better and would prove to Daniel that he was wasting his time.

After they left for her house, she was the first to let him know. "Your sister does not like me and that should tell you something."

"Yes it tells me to never give up on you and tell my sister to mind her own business."

"You are her business, she's the only relative you have."

"I do have other relatives."

"She's your closest and I think you should listen to her."

"Monisola can I ask one thing, why are you so adamant not to marry me?"

She laughed, "The same way you are to marry me, I refuse to be bullied or coerced into anything"

They were in her house and she flung herself on the sofa, she was getting irritated, angry and tired.

"Monisola please don't push me out."

She kept quiet.

He left and she did not hear from him for a week which was good, as she had her peace of mind, well at work but not when she got home.

Her phone rang and as she answered it, she groaned once the caller spoke.

"Good evening Mother"

"Good evening Monisola, have you given Daniel your answer?"

This was getting unbearable. "Mother why are you being so difficult, is it by force?"

"Eh! E ma gba mi lowo Monisola O! E'wo mi niran ni? Difficult? I am asking you to make the best decision you can ever make and you are saying difficult, Monisola I am given you the last chance, by the time Daniel returns from the US, if you do not give him your answer, I will personally bundle you and dash you to him, no bride price!"

This was exactly what she had been thinking, "Mother since you know the in and out of Daniel more than I do, why don't you personally bundle him and make him your husband, it seems you are getting closer to him than I."

Her mother kept quiet and silently prayed that she would not rant over the phone to her daughter as that was her intention, she signed heavily and ended the call.

With her mother not saying a word, that should have made Monisola think twice but she didn't and as she was very tired she slept off.

Two days later she regretted her action.

She was at work when an entourage of cars arrived unannounced. Monisola was expecting the local chairman or another VIP; she was shocked when the governor's wife and her mother stepped out of the vehicle. Monisola held her head and shook it several times; she had indeed stepped on her mother's toes.

As the entourage went round the centre, observing the work they were doing and asking about the challenges faced, Monisola tried to catch the attention of her mother but she gave no clue as to what was on mind but only smiled.

At the end of the tour she was invited to join the first lady for dinner later that evening and the entourage left as they had arrived.

She was having a shower and was going over the day's event. Monisola you have landed yourself in Olori's trouble, Kai! Why didn't she allow her mother's silence at the end of their telephone conversation last one minute instead of two days. Two days! Only GOD knows what the woman had done to get the attention of the governor's wife and then to come down with her and then have dinner. Who told her she wanted dinner, she wanted to run to the Korean praying caves and pray until her mouth was hurting and her mother pacified. GOD why won't this woman leave me alone, na by force?

What is the joy of every mother?

Monisola heartbeat skipped a beat as her inner man spoke to her.

"Holy Spirit but she did not have to go into such length."

What is a mother's joy?

Monisola had dressed with care and as her driver dropped her off at the governor's private residence she was praying for her nerves to calm down.

She was welcomed by the staff and escorted to a reception which was the family living room. There were photographs of the family at the mantel piece as well as those of friends.

"Princess Adewunmi, it is so lovely to see you again and I am glad you could make it at such short notice." The first lady of the state welcomed her.

Short notice? Who born monkey banana make e no come, she thought to herself.

"Your excellence it's a pleasure and honour Ma."

The governor's wife smiled thinking only if she knew.

"Actually, we've been waiting for you, we started dinner a bit earlier."

The way she said we and the emphasised placed on it made Monisola raise an eyebrow, we?

Her Excellency smiled and led the way.

Monisola thought at least her mother and a few other women were the invited guest but when she saw her own mother, Justina and husband, the governor himself, a few other people and Daniel, she took a deep breath, GOD I'm in your hands.

The conversation flowed freely; everyone was relaxed and were enjoying themselves apart from her. At a point in time the children came to join them and as if pre-planned, each nuclear family sat together, even her mother had the twins with her and it was just her and Daniel sitting alone. Then she saw the bigger picture especially as the governor himself began to narrate how he met his wife, the role his family played and the finally acceptance by his bride and how GOD has helped them thus far even in the rough times. He made jokes about his encounters during his courtship which made others almost crack their ribs from laughter but for Monisola the message was clear as crystal.

The next day Monisola went to work early, left instructions for her team and by twelve noon took the day off. She had spoken to her mother earlier in the morning so she knew she was on her way to the airport and she called to thank her once again.

"Monisola, I don't want any thank you, just get married to Daniel and give me grandchildren."

"Mo ti gbo Ma."

"So' ti gba?"

"Mother I will speak to you soon."

"How soon is your soon Monisola?"

"Very soon."

She called Daniel and asked him to meet her at her place.

"Why?"

"I'll like us to talk."

"I'm done with talking Monisola, you know what I want?"

"Daniel, please."

"What time would you be home?"

"I'm home already."

"Didn't you go to work?"

"Daniel I'm waiting."

He met her at the house an hour later, he kept her waiting on purpose so she would know how it feels, he smiled and thought to himself, naughty girl, almost driving him crazy.

"Your royal highness, I'm here as you called."

"You kept me waiting for an hour."

He looked at his watch and shrugged his shoulders.

"Daniel I am trying to make peace here the least you can do is show some empathy."

"Are we at war?"

"Daniel!"

"Monisola!"

She looked at him and she knew he was deliberately being difficult. Ok she will take this bull by the horn.

"Daniel, after yesterday's dinner, looking at the individual family setting and all, especially his Excellency's speech which I believe was indirectly aimed at me, I now see the bigger picture which everyone has been trying to paint especially my mother and I've come to the realisation that yes, no man is an island. No matter how successful or rich, poor, young, old or whoever you are, you still need a family. Your family will be there for you in bad times, good times, rough times; you can rely on them, they can rely on you, give you their shoulders to cry on and you also do likewise in return. I also thought about the other side of family, they can be very ambitious for you, driving you insane, wanting to live your life for you all in the name of being your family and also if you allow them they can ruin your life for good as in ......, Daniel what I am trying to say is that, you and I have come a long way and it hasn't been so smooth and sometimes I ...I... anyway what I would like to say is that I am willing to give you another chance, that is to be your friend."

Daniel took a good long look at her, this girl is either insane or wants to drive him insane, friend?

"Friend?" he repeated.

"Yes friend" she nodded and added, "just like old times"

He got up and moved closer to her, "Miss Monisola Adewunmi, daughter of Kabiyesi Adewunmi, you mean after all your travels around the world, meeting and interacting with people of low and high esteem, learning their socio-cultural behaviours and patterns, history and all you can come up with is friendship! Friendship between a hot-blooded male like me and an alluring female like you! Tell me Monisola, are you planning to drive me insane or what? I don't want to be just your friend because all you did was play some pranks or used me as your therapist, I'm over and done with that, I want you and all of you!" he shouted at the top of his voice.

"So, what is stopping you?" she gently and quietly replied.

His boiling point reached a height and simmered down. GOD help me! GOD help me! GOD help me!

He went on both knees and with both hands raised to heaven, shouted at the top of his voice, "GOD please I am about to ask this girl one more time, just one more time. Monisola Oluwamuiremiwa Oluwafiadekemi Omolabake Adewunmi will you please, I beg you, please marry me?"

"Hm! I'll think about it, ask me in the next millennium."

Daniel got up and was walking towards the door.

It was now or never.

"I'll marry you."

He stopped, turned and saw her smiling. He took one step towards her, she took two; he took one again and she another, until she was in his arms.

"Monisola, Monisola, you drive a hard bargain."

"Daniel, Daniel, you underestimated me."

"Me? Never! I knew what you are capable of doing, trust me I know."

"So, what happens next?"

"I'm taking you into my house and giving it to you."

"Daniel we are not married yet."

"We would if you were not playing hard to get."

"Trust me Daniel I wasn't, that is not my kind of game in fact I do not play."

"Monisola, Monisola, I will show you!"

"Show me what?"

"Say khaki no be leather, na different material."

"That's your cup of tea."

"Gosh! You almost drove me insane you this babe, I give it to you and I applaud you. However just know that this regime we are going to enter is a military one and I would not take any ....."

She stepped on his toes.

"Ouch! What was that for?"

"Oh, sorry I was only testing what you can take and by the way that is just child's play."

"Monisola did I tell you that I have a black belt in taekwondo?"

"And I'm sure you are familiar with all the rules that you only use force when you are being attacked and since this is a friendly fire you will take it as it is."

He laughed and laughed. "Monisola you are quite a girl; I can't wait to make you mine."

"When do you want to ....?"

"Any time just speak to your parents and I'm all yours."

"Will ten ..."

"Monisola don't try me."

"I was going to say ten months but as that is so soon maybe ten ..."

"I am warning you."

"Ten hundred and ..."

"Which school did you go to? There is no such thing as ten hundred."

"Ten hundred and ..."

"Olodo."

"Agbaya"

CHAPTER EIGHTEEN

The meeting in her father's study went very well; it went so well that both her parents were filled with joy.

"Monisola, you do not know how much this means to me" her father stated.

"So much you don't want to return the cows and food."

"That is so easily replaceable but no one can replace or match the kind of spirit that dwells in this young man, it is an excellent spirit, the very Spirit of GOD. That is what I don't want you to miss Monisola, that is what I have always wanted and prayed for, for years. For your information so many have asked for your hand in marriage but I refused because what I see in you, what GOD has deposited in you, I do not see it in any of them and I cannot allow just any man to contaminate what GOD has designed for you and generations to come. I am not talking about royalty, no, I mean the excellent Spirit of GOD, spirit of wisdom, understanding, knowledge and most importantly the fear of GOD. Most of those young men did not possess it even the older vultures that dared to come but when I met Daniel, with his humility and ingenuity, I liked him and when he asked for your hands in marriage though at first I resisted but GOD in His mercies opened my eyes to see the answer to my prayers. Thank GOD for all your mother's scheme and all, it did pay off but if you had resisted that one, I myself would have dealt with you and trust me you have no choice in the matter. My son, you are welcome home."

Daniel prostrated again and thank his highness and Olori.

Olori gave Monisola one of her looks and she quickly knelt down, thanking her father and mother. She was about to get up when her father coughed. What now? She looked at him and he turned his eyes towards Daniel. Goodness gracious, thank GOD she wasn't marrying a prince or she will forever be kneeling. She got up and knelt beside Daniel, who smiled, laughed and pulled her to him and planted a kiss on her lips. Father and mother applauded and together they joined hands to pray.

"Our Father and our GOD, we want to thank you. You are great and plenteous in mercies and rich in glory, indeed there is no one like you, we are forever grateful, we thank You, adore, praise and magnify Your holy name, OLUWA awon oluwa, Oga Ogo, ajuba re, Alade Ogo, Eleruniyin, Olugbala, Olupese, Eseun, Adupe, A yin yin logo."

Monisola was in her office rounding up her last assignment on the project and she couldn't help but give GOD all the praise for all HE has done. Not only was she rounding up her project which has been so successful, giving all the glory to GOD but she was getting married, that was unbelievable. When she set out to come to Nigeria for this project the only thing on her mind was just go, work and be used by GOD. However, GOD had gone far beyond her wildest expectation and she was forever, eternally grateful to GOD, to GOD be all the glory.

Her phone rang and when she saw the caller id she smiled.

"Yes Mr Benjamin, what can I do for you?"

"Mrs Benjamin ..."

"Not until two weeks' time."

"Na you sabi; would it be chocolate, pink or red?"

She laughed, "What are you talking about?"

"I'm in this lingerie department store and there are some serious looking underwear that is a must have for you."

"I'll rather have the black ....."

"Black! That is boring."

"Actually, I was saying before I was rudely interrupted, I'd rather have your black velvet shinny skin next to me than any other material but ..."

"Monisola just keep that thought till our wedding night! GOD I love this girl, thank you for her."

Contrary to all she had heard before and even seen from being some of her friends' maids of honour or even part of the party planner for weddings, hers was without stress. Looking back now it wasn't just a matter of the money being available but she had made her mind and thoughts very clear to her parents, that she did not want a society wedding or a gigantic, mega celebration.

She wanted a small and beautiful one with her family and Daniel's family and friends. There were various arguments and when they did not concede she told Daniel to meet her in England when he was ready and they would get married in the registry or church. Daniel then started his own palaver questioning why everything had to be in England and not America. She tried to reason with him but he refused to budge, Nigeria was a neutral ground and moreover all their families were here, eventually she gave in.

Olori did not even bother her with the plans, all she wanted to know were the details; where did she want her wedding dress to be made, how many traditional attires she wanted including Daniel's native ones, her accessories and bridal train.

"Mother have you forgotten I said we are not inviting too many people?"

"Leave that to us to worry about, just tell me what you want."

"Olori you already have a lot on your hands and the wedding is six months away."

"Five months and twenty-three days to be exact."

"Alright, I want the church venue to be one the family attends ...."

"Tele nko? Were we planning on going to the one in London before?"

"Actually, I was hoping that you could persuade...."

"Forget it, church venue has already been settled, reception is still being debated..."

"I want the palace grounds"

"Nope, not enough space"

"For the kind of crowd, I want yes but not the whole of Nigeria you want to invite."

"Monisola, reason with us, you are not an ordinary girl, you are a princess, so your wedding must be...."

"As I want it, not what you or father or the ijoye or ilu' wants. Mother, honestly if you and father refuse to listen you'll be sorry for ignoring me and what I want."

Her mother took a deep breath, in her heart of heart she wanted what Monisola wanted but then her mind was screaming Royalty! Show them! Kabiyesi's first born! Princess royal! Ikoko baba isasun! Eh! Ah!

"Monisola I want what you want but you know how people would talk, they did for the others, why not her?"

"Mother I don't care what people say, if you are bothered about what they say and go along with them, the same people will start to wag their tongues about the millions that was spent just because she is a princess. Mother we could do with that money."

"Your father is not complaining and neither is Daniel, so what is your problem?"

"They might not be complaining but I am. Mother what joy will I have if the dress or all my costumes which I may never wear again, cost a fortunate but the man living just down the road is struggling to feed his family and yet we throw parties and waste money on things that won't last."

"Monisola so you want us to spend the money for your wedding on just one man down the road? Ok I will inform your father."

Monisola knew her mother understood what she was saying and rather than argue over it she changed the subject and within a minute wrapped up the conversation.

Her people had a saying, 'abo oro lan so' fun omo lu abi to' ba de inu re a do dindin' so she left the wise to follow their heart desire.

As her project was nearing its completion she had to go to the head office to hand in reports, analysis, feedback as well as discuss reviews and recommendations; a six-month supervision and final hand over which she wasn't keen on taking on board. Mark asked her to come to England and hand in the report as well as present to the board all she had done.

"Mark I don't understand. This is your project so why should I be the one to face the panel, you want me to speak to the patrons, trustees, chair.... are you sure you are willing to sabotage your own project and loose the integrity of your name?"

"Moni if that is your way of telling me that you are afraid of facing the board of panel and you need my help; I will be more than happy to guide you but what I won't do is take credit for the wonderful job you have done. You deserve this, you've gone far beyond my expectation. I would never have accomplished a third of what you did and I'm not saying this because it's your home base but I know if the project was in the Kalahari Desert you will equally succeed."

There was silence.

"Moni don't go quiet on me now and moreover I have precisely two minutes to spare."

"Sorry I didn't realise you were on your way out ....."

"I'm not but I've been doing a study of my two weeks old daughter and I'm not kidding she has her exact and precise time when she flexes all her lungs just to let us know she's awake."

"Oooo, I can't wait to see her."

"Sorry you will not be able to do that?"

"Why?"

"You have a lot to accomplish, I have drawn your itinerary and apart from dropping your bags at home and picking a few things you will not have the time for any social visit. You will be sitting on three panels, review your strategies and making recommendation to carry something similar in three other African countries, two in Asia ...."

On the plane when she saw the reports and her schedule she knew Mark had not been joking. Usually when she finished her projects she handed the summary and all to him to make recommendation but now she had to do everything as well as draw plans to take to five other countries, she silently prayed that she would able to deliver as expected.

She wasn't even praying to surpass, if she got a pass mark she was more than satisfied as this was far beyond her level. As much as she liked Mark she would personally be giving him a piece of her mind when she eventually see him as it seemed like he had pushed her over a cliff and left her hanging on a fragile branch and telling her go and conquer, yeah right, conquer indeed.

I will help you.

She was getting to know that still and peaceful voice so she quickly held on to GOD's promise to her.

The next day she was sitting with the third panel at four o'clock and was more relaxed than the other two she had previously sat before. Mark was sitting with this panel and he was the first to ask how the first panel went? At first she wanted to tell him to go jump off the cliff but she took a deep breath, put her professional cap on and in her cool, calm voice said she hoped it went well as she did her uttermost best but it was nerve racking.

The panel laughed and told her to be at ease as this was the last one and it wouldn't take much time. When she finished three hours later she was relieved she was still alive and breathing. Gosh! She needed fresh air so she quickly walked towards the next available lift and exited. She was still inhaling the not so fresh but clearer air free of anything to do with the smell of the plush carpet, wooden walls and air-conditioned office when her phone vibrated in her bag.

"Moni, where are you, the whole panel is sitting in the next five minutes."

She took another heap of air and slowly but steadily walked back into the building.

"I will go before thee and make the crooked places straight, I will break in pieces the gates of brass and cut in sunder the bars of iron."

The scripture which she had memorized and recited times without number every time she went for her exams in school or universities and even some tough job interviews kept ringing in her mind and for a moment with eyes tightly shut she thanked GOD for His unfailing promises and offered unreserved thanks.

The entire panel were indeed sitting and she was facing fifteen of them including Mark who being the initial project lead had to defend and accept the recommendation by the board. Well if heads should roll let them have his first, hers was small in the matter as she only helped in carrying out his project.

The first panel gave their review and recommendation on the initial stage of the project which had more to do with Mark. Their view was that the project lead should have considered the diversity of the country chosen and earmarked three to four centres across the country to reflect the main tribal groups so that their research, project, observation, integration would be a true reflection on the nation as a whole but on hindsight it was still a very good project and they recommended its continuation. Voila!

Monisola heard Mark let out a big sigh of relief; probably the execution was for her especially when the panel members whispered among each other. GOD I'm still hanging on to your promises, she quickly prayed in her heart.

The spokesperson for the second panel, a woman cleared her throat and as she was about to speak, Monisola's heart beat twice. A woman! Why a woman! To empathise with her or deliver her sentence mildly with a softer tone?

"Overall, I believe my colleagues will agree with me that indeed this project out of all the five we have selected for review, is the most thoroughly well planned, perfectly executed and properly implemented. Initially when I was told the lead project wasn't even part of the exercise I had my doubts, coupled with the fact that the project leader was also an indigene. I wasn't so sure as there could have been malpractices or short cuts taken. However, I've been proved wrong and I have gone over these reports five times, watched the video clips and all I can say is, an excellent job has been carried out. If I were to rate this I would rate it one hundred percent – it's been perfectly and excellently done. Moreover, being a woman, I would be a bit biased and rate it as one hundred percent, with top grade A."

Monisola did not know when the tears started flowing and when she was offered a tissue by the same female panel member; she smiled and thanked her.

"No, I should be the one to thank you; you've upheld the feminine flag here today and on behalf of all other women and womanhood, I say thank you."

The person from the third panel that spoke, more or less reiterated what his other colleagues had said and in his recommendation he was of the opinion that the present project leader should be involved in at least one of the future projects and once again congratulated her and thanked her.

When she left the room, she knelt down in the corridor and thanked GOD not caring who saw her or what they thought. She went into the ladies and began to cry; she was so overwhelmed by GOD's faithfulness to her and thanked Him from the bottom of her heart. Her phone vibrated again and she wondered who it was. It was her alarm reminding her of her appointment with the dressmaker. Dressmaker! Goodness she forgot all about her appointment with the dressmaker who was going to make her wedding dress. How could she! It had taken her days to get an appointment with the lady and also assured her she will be in for her first fitting today. She recalled what the woman said, that once she missed an appointment she would not get another until six months' time and Monisola knew she did not have that six months. She looked at the time she had precisely five minutes to run to the station and catch the train, she hurriedly ran along the corridor towards the lift when she heard Mark called her, not now.

"Moni, I've been looking for you."

"Mark I really have to leave now."

"Please this would only take a few minutes."

On her way from the dressmaker's studio she should have known when Mark asked for a few minutes he really meant half an hour. They had gone to his office where he presented her with a gift which was crystal frame with a picture of Annabel his daughter and at the back, the words read, "Thank you for the time you gave up for us to start a family we pray GOD brings countless gifts of love and joy your way. Love Mark, Christine & Annabel"

The words made her cry because while she had taken the job offer she had no idea GOD was using it to make a way for her own miracle as meeting Daniel wasn't something she had envisaged but she thanked GOD.

When she got to the dress maker, she was ten minutes late and was offered another appointment in seven months' time. She thanked the receptionist and refused the offer which only left her with one option.

"Hi babe, missing me already?"

"No, actually I'm upset."

"What or who is upsetting you, tell me?"

"You."

Daniel laughed, "You missed the appointment."

"It's all your fault, you didn't want me to get my wedding dress from England."

"You can get your gown from anywhere even Abakaliki market but with that schedule you had, there was no way you could have made that appointment and you are the one not following your preaching."

"I beg your pardon."

"You are the one advocating that everything about the wedding should be low key to the barest minimum, I'm sure you would have suggested two people eat from the same plate; just joking but seriously the amount of money you want to spend on that dress is too much and you know I hate that style."

"The more reason why I wanted it."

"Mrs Benjamin you are to do things to please me not annoy me."

"Until we are pronounced man and wife, I'm free to do anything to drive you ....."

"I'm immune to all your devises to drive me insane Monisola, GOD has given me victory, thank you JESUS!"

Monisola laughed, "Honestly I was looking forward to wear that dress."

"I can say no when the pastor asks if I do."

"You know you can't."

"Yes, but I will still protest about the dress."

"It's the latest vogue."

"Vogue my foot, I've seen people wear more daring things for a wedding dress but that one is just drab, shapeless, as if you were dumped inside the gown or sack."

"Daniel you are so old fashioned."

"No with that dress you are old fashioned, it looks like something from the eighteen century, I hope you don't think once we are married you will be dressing anyhow, no way, capital NO."

"Does that mean I am allowed to wear micro minis, figure hugging, cleavage open ....."

"Monisola, don't even go there, you dare not reveal my private properties to the entire world, no way."

"I thought you didn't want me to be old fashioned?"

"Babe dressing well and covering yourself is not old fashioned it is compulsory and expedient."

"So was the dress."

"Oh please, you can always get one from America."

"Why does everything have to come from America?"

"Where else can you get the best?"

"Look who is being unpatriotic now, what about your homeland?"

"True, it's up to you, provided it's what you want and you look ravishing."

"Ravishing? I thought you are on the decency side."

"I am! Moni baby, do what you want, just make sure you look, look......
decent, lovely, beautiful, sexy, ravi........"

"Mr Benjamin, which side are you on, the Lord's side or the devil?"

"I am for the Lord! But I want my bride to be a head spinner."

"See you tomorrow."

"I'm in Chicago I ....."

"Daniel!"

"I know baby I'll be back in two- or three-days' time."

Later as she lay on her sofa in her house she picked up the phone and called her mother.

"Ekale Ma."

"Ekale iyawo, se dada le wa?"

"Adupe Ma, Mami, I'm ...."

"Kilo de?"

"It's nothing Olori, I missed the appointment to see the dress maker."

"Oh! Book another one and you will change your flight date."

"The earliest I can get is seven months' time."

"By then you will be married and with twins."

"Amin to the first one."

"The second one nko?"

"Mother do you know any good dressmaker that can make my wedding gown?" she asked ignoring her mother's question.

"I know the best."

Monisola sighed with relief.

"Mother I don't know what I would have done without you and I don't think I can measure up to you."

"You will be greater and better than me, that is the joy of any good parents. Monisola you will make an excellent wife and a loving mother. That I am very sure of, GOD has given you the grace and ability."

"Amen."

"When is your flight?"

"Tonight, which reminds me, I better get ready, Mano will soon be here to pick me up."

"Have you sorted out your house?"

"Mami I really want to keep the house."

"Why?"

"I want a place where I can come to and be myself."

"Your husband's house is where you belong, don't hold on to that house; for now, let go, you don't want another Toluwanimi in the making."

They both laughed.

"Mami!"

"It's true, your home is in your husband's bosom not your spinster hideout."

As soon as she got back to Nigeria she went to see her parents before leaving for Makurdi, just to see how her wedding preparation was going. Everything was still the same as the last time she left it and she wondered if she had gone overboard with her emphasis on low key wedding, maybe next time, well there wouldn't be a next time.

"How was your trip Iyawo? I heard you missed the dressmaker's appointment, don't mind those oyinbo they don't know anything about business; they've just lost the opportunity to show case their business where dignitaries and people from all over the world will be attending."

"Ayaba, I'm not asking for the whole world to be at my wedding, just family and few friends."

"You are still adamant about this your low key. Ha! O jeri eni toni. If I were Olori I would take the wedding to another level and it would be the talk of town for quite a while."

Monisola deep in her heart, quickly thanked GOD that Ayaba was not her mother.

"Anyway, thank GOD your mother has connections with all these top fashion designers, you should see the one we went to yesterday, in fact I felt like having a wedding dress myself."

"Ayaba!"

"I'm still of marriageable age?"

"You are already married and if Kabiyesi should hear you talk like this, he might just carry out your intention", which made her step mother laughed.

She went with her mother to the two dressmakers selected by her and after the second visit even Monisola was undecided.

"Mother, honestly I cannot decide; both designers, their styles, expertise and collections are so beautiful, they are better than the one in England, I ...."

"I told you I couldn't make up my mind as well."

"Maybe I should ask Daniel?"

"Oti o! Leave him out of this, he only gets to see you at the altar so that when he sees you, his head will be turning and spinning."

"Mami!"

"I hope you would not allow yourself once you get married to dress anyhow. My dear that is when you dress to letter T so that your husband will be proud to take you anywhere. Don't do the one that most women are leaving out their breasts anyhow and show casing it to the whole world all in the name of madness not fashion because any fashion that states you should display your nudity when you should be covering it is madness, ori won ti yi."

Eventually she decided on one of the designers to make her wedding gown and dinner wear whilst the other would make all her traditional outfits which seemed to be increasing in number and she decided not to argue with her mother anymore.

"Are you not going to say anything about the new attire I've added to your collection?"

"Mother why should we continue to argue over outfits and attire all the time, I've got better things to do with my time."

"Does that mean I can add more?"

"Mother if it pleases you, add more to mine, yours, Kabiyesi's, even get all the women to wear the same or change ten times I have told you my mind."

"By GOD's grace I will be there when you will be preparing for your daughter's wedding and I will see what you will do."

"Mother, right from day one as soon as she is handed over to me by the midwife we will start discussing very important issues."

"Eh! Such as?"

"Not giving me any aggro that I did not give my parents, to always agree with me or we both compromise on certain issues but some issues such as wedding planning is a fifty-fifty not less."

"I'm sorry for you, wishful and silly thinking because that child will take genetic traits from you her parents and we the grandparents and GOD help you if she is given the combination of your character, Daniel's, Kabiyesi's and a tint of mine, it would be such a wonderful household drama every day."

"Mother it's not going to happen like that, GOD loves me so much not to over bless me with such."

They both laughed as they imagined the possibilities of clashes of individual character traits.

When it was time for her to finally round up her project she did not want to leave. She wished she had more time but it was not possible as GOD had graciously given her the twelve months to execute plans which before seemed only practical on paper but the final outcome proved otherwise.

She was overwhelmed by the final ceremony at the office site which was attended by dignitaries including the Governor and his wife, the state commissioners for health, agriculture, education and information & technology; she was also shocked to see Mark who had arrived unknown to her the night before and very pleased to see her fiancé.

In her closing remark she thanked GOD for giving her this divine opportunity and a second chance, she laughed when Daniel winked at her, thanked Mark also for believing that she could execute the plans he initiated, for supporting her and not just throwing her in the deep end.

To her various teams she was so grateful and proud of them, she wished she could have them all on board wherever her next assignment would be. She thanked the governor, commissioners and other parastatals for their immerse support and also the people for taking on board the project's vision and making it a reality for their own development. She also encouraged and emphasised that this was not the end but the continuation of the project which should be taken to other parts of the country, empowering women, youths and children.

Later that evening at her soon to-be sister-in-law's house, she was having dinner with some of the family members and friends.

Justina came over to her, "How many more days left before you gain your MRS degree?"

"MRS?"

"Mrs Benjamin, what are you thinking about?"

"Honestly I just want to go to bed and rest, I am exhausted."

"You can sneak out I'll tell Daniel...."

"And he would come looking for me and I don't want him to start worrying, I'll be fine. How are you, are you ready for the travelling and ceremonies ahead?"

"Of course, we are flying over to Lagos in two days' time to get some few things, and before you know it we will be in your home town. We'll be fine, it's you I'm worried about."

"I'll be fine, I just need some days of rest and to be away from all the preparations at home; honestly I don't see what the fuss is all about."

"I do, we are coming to take our Amariya all the way from Benue State and not just any bride but a princess; please we have to do more than fuss. I only wish my parents were here, they would have been proud."

Monisola gave her a hug and tissue to wipe her tears.

"I was wrong about you the first time we met I hope you've forgiven me."

"Come on, we barely knew each other then."

"But you did not prejudge or assume the worst of me, you were so polite and all, it took my husband's warning to see the clearer picture."

"What picture?"

"That you were Daniel's choice and I either love and accept you or hate you and loose the closest family I have."

"I wouldn't dream of coming between you and your brother."

"Well I was! However not now or ever, I accept you and love you as my own sister."

Monisola was so overwhelmed she started to cry. "Honestly the rate I easily get to tears I'm beginning to wonder if I am strong at all."

"It's called pre-wedding jitters, I cried for weeks before the wedding and weeks after."

"How did you stop or who helped you?"

"No one, in fact my husband warned me if he saw me cry again he would return me to my family and collect his bride price back, of course he later told me he was joking but the look on his face then didn't give me that impression."

Monisola laughed and yawned again at the same time.

"You seriously need some rest, why not go upstairs and lie down, when you've rested a bit you can come and join us."

"If I should lie down now, it would be difficult to get up, you will have to drag me to my house."

"Daniel will carry you then."

They both laughed.

Daniel came over and asked them to share their joke.

"I just told your sister that if I should lie down now I won't get up and someone will have to drag me and she said you'll carry me."

"Of course, straight to my room and we...."

Monisola quickly stopped him, "Please I still have two weeks to go"

"Two weeks! Monisola! It's less than a week! What calendar have you been looking at? Girl I hope you are ready; I won't tolerate any lateness or delay."

"Justina did I tell you I was going to Dubai tomorrow and from there Switzerland and then ......"

Justina looked at her brother's bewildered face and the sudden heavy breathing and inability to coherently put into words what was going on in his mind at that very moment. To make matter worse Monisola added, "I think I might miss the connecting flight from Zurich to London so most likely I will be arriving on Saturday morning of the wedding..."

Both women burst in to laughter when Daniel's eyes seemed to pop out of its socket.

"I....I hope you are joking."

"Daniel I'm sorry I just have to make the trip it is so important ..."

"Monisola please don't make me pass out on you now, what kind of stupid trip are you making this ninety ninth hour for the love of GOD!"

"Daniel but you just returned from America not so long ago so why can't I ..."

"It was a business trip"

"So...."

"Monisola please don't give my brother a cardiac arrest, I just hope you won't make any attempt to travel otherwise you are coming with us when we leave in two days' time."

"I thought you were going to Lagos together?"

"No, she wants to be on her own until Friday before the wedding."

Daniel did not bother to say anything; he took his phone and was soon speaking to Monisola's mother.

After the dinner she was still talking with some of her soon to be in-laws when Daniel suggested it was time for her to leave.

"I was enjoying the conversation before you interrupted."

"Your eyes were drooping and you were half way from falling off your chair."

"I was laughing at the funny conversations going on."

"I hope you will not turn out to be one of them when we get married, narrating everything between you and I to the whole world."

She stopped walking and took a deep breath, "Daniel what is the matter?"

"Let's go in."

He pulled her towards the gates to her house, her house for the next two weeks and thereafter she will no more be a landlord or house owner but living with her husband wherever he chooses for them to live.

"Daniel where are we going to be living when we get married?"

"I was thinking your room in your father's house."

"Daniel be serious."

"I'm serious, whenever we go there that is where we will stay, here in my sister's place, the farm in America and ..."

"What about when we are in England?"

"If we go to England we'll stay in an hotel."

"Why can't I keep the house?"

"It is no longer yours; my house becomes your house."

"Logically my house belongs to you."

"Not according to my ways."

"Even in the old days Tiv women used to do everything ..."

"We are in the new era, you are not a Tiv woman, I am your husband with different nationalities and awareness, what I say goes and by the special grace of GOD I am the bread, butter and jam winner of the house. Understood!"

She grumbled and went to her room. She was tired and was glad she was back in her house and looking forward to the time she will spend alone once all the wedding preparation began.

A knock on the door reminded her she was far from being alone.

"I'll join you soon."

"Madam, Oga wants to let you know he is going."

"Hannah, please tell him I'll soon join him downstairs."

She smiled, Daniel was observing all protocol and keeping very calm, well not for long, she would soon burst that bubble of calmness he was surrounding himself with because she knew he was very anxious.

He was staring at the walls but stood up when he saw her coming. Mr Daniel was hiding something.

"Would you like a drink?"

"No thanks I'm fine."

"Fruits?"

"Monisola I'm fine we just had dinner."

"Okay I'll get you some..."

"Monisola I'm fine."

They sat down quietly for a while each one trying to read the other's mind.

"Daniel what's the matter?"

"Nothing."

"You don't seem fine to me."

"I can assure you I am."

"Why are you nervous then?"

"I'm not."

"Are you sure?"

"Monisola quit pestering me; let's find something else to talk about. I said I am fine."

"Daniel I ..."

"I've got to go."

He kissed her hands and rushed out of the house before she could say anything else.

The next day as she was not going to work or anywhere urgently she decided to use the time to pray. She began to commit her soon-to-be-husband into GOD's hands, to guide, guard, lead and direct, she prayed for his spiritual, physical, financial, social, marital life as well as his business and life. She was still praying when she remembered what happened yesterday and she asked GOD to please help her to get to the bottom of what was making him agitated. She read her bible, prayed for the rest of her family and the big day and went downstairs to see what was going on in her domain. Her house assistant greeted her and asked what she would like for breakfast.

"Hannah do you know you are spoiling me?"

"How Madam?"

"Asking me what I want to eat, cooking and everything, while I was in England I did everything by myself and soon I will be married and I'm thinking do I want to go back to doing it all by myself?"

Hannah laughed, "Madam you are so funny, of course you can always get a house assistant to help."

"I don't think I want to, I'll rather it's just me and my husband."

"Yes, for a while but when the children come, you will need help."

"I do know of many people in England who don't have house assistants, drivers or even nannies but they cope."

"Madam, but for how long? Even our mothers in their time needed help and did not hesitate to ask relatives to help."

"That was then, this is now, things are not like they use to be, now every man is for himself."

"True Madam, true, but you just have to pray and ask GOD for help."

"I agree, I do agree on that. So, what are you going to do after this?"

"When my contract finishes, I go back home."

"Home as in your ....."

"My parents' house and to my children."

"Children! I didn't even know you are married, I'm sorry I just assumed...."

"It's okay Madam, I was married but I left my husband....."

"I'm sorry, you don't have to tell me anything you don't want to"

"It's not a secret, we just went our separate ways and thank GOD I have my children with me."

"How do you cope? How old are they? I'm sorry if I'm asking too many questions."

"It's okay Madam. Two boys, nine and eight, I guess we rushed things too soon and I don't know we just....."

"What about their education and wellbeing?"

"It's challenging especially now that I have to stop school for the second time."

"I don't understand."

By the time they were making lunch, Hannah was still trying to come to terms with what had happened. Monisola had arranged for her fees and that of her sons to be taken care of as well as their welfare.

"Madam, I'm not sure but I think I'm dreaming."

"Just take everything in your strides and don't rush, just make sure you go back to school and finish your education this time around, no matter what."

"I will, I will, by GOD's special grace I will, I won't allow anything or anyone to stop me."

"Even if your husband comes back to beg you."

Hannah blushed and shook her head.

Monisola smiled and hoped that was not the truth and while she would love for her to get back with her husband her education was also important as it will pave way for a better job or business to make a good living for herself and family.

Evening came and she did not hear from Daniel, she didn't want to get into the habit of worry and panicking so she prayed but still felt she should call him. She called him but the call was diverted to the voicemail and she left a brief message.

"Hi Daniel, it's me, just to say hi and hope everything is well with you, love you, M"

Since she still had a week and few days to go she decided to book a flight to London and go home to sort out a few things as she hardly had time to do anything the last time she went. She was lucky to get a flight for the next day, she quickly prepared to get to Lagos the next morning and from there to London. Since she didn't hear from Daniel and did not want to bother her parents who were busy with the wedding preparation, she decided to go straight from one airport to the next.

At the airport she used her time to check emails, send replies, check her social networks as well as read up on what was going on around the globe. She searched for jobs but as she was unsure of her permanent place of abode for the first few months of marriage she searched worldwide, some seemed interesting and others she wished were two years or a year ago as she would have applied but it was too late.

She remembered what her mother and Daniel thought about her house in England but she didn't agree with them. She was not going to put it up for sale, at least not yet, until she was sure of how this location logistic was going to work. If Daniel was going to be working around the clock and globe she couldn't see herself accompanying him like a handbag everywhere he went. She would love to settle down in a house and making a home would be her primary assignment, somewhere they could both call a home and eventually raise their children. From all angles it was England as she had grown up there, schooled there, worked there; her friends live there and where else would she fit in like this?

You are being subjective.

She laughed and knew the Spirit of GOD in her had searched her out. Okay she was being subjective but even Daniel if asked the same question would be also.

He is your head – you both make and he takes the decision.

Monisola knew she still had egos that GOD needs to deal with and she prayed she'll let go and let HIM.

Wednesday morning, she was in her house in Hertfordshire enjoying a bit of British Summer, going through her wardrobe and thinking of what to do with all the clothes she had acquired and might need to change probably due to weather and climate wherever she'll be staying especially if it is Nigeria. She was still in the middle of going through her wardrobe when her phone rang. It was his Lordship, Daniel Benjamin.

"Hello"

"Hi"

"How are you?"

"I'm fine thank you and you?"

"I'm tired."

Silence.

"Monisola I ...."

"What is it Daniel?"

"I'm very tired."

"Is that all?"

"Yes, what do you mean?"

"I don't know what is going on but you've been edgy, moody and distant, I don't know what to make of it."

"Make nothing of it except that I am exhausted and I want to get this wedding over with and relax."

"We don't have to if you don't want to."

"Monisola I am marrying you next Saturday come what may, by the special grace of GOD."

"Are you sure?"

"Nothing will stop me."

"Even if I'm in England and you are in only GOD knows where?"

"Monisola where are you?"

"At home going through my stuff and sorting things out."

"It's good you are doing that but please don't travel without letting me know, I thought you were in Lagos with Justina."

She laughed; this guy doesn't know me.

"Daniel where are we going to live?"

"In my house where else?"

"As in Justina's house or the farm in Illinois or Chicago?"

"Or your apartment in your father's house or the farm in Kon....."

"Which farm again?"

"Mine, ours, where I live?"

"I thought you lived with your sister when you are in Nigeria."

"No, I only go there to see them when I can and the last time I went apart from when I saw you was about a year ago, I rarely have the time."

She was getting more concerned about this globetrotting and she wasn't so sure how to address it.

"Daniel I don't think I want to be changing address and location every six months or a year, I need somewhere I can call my home, space, do what I want to do, when I want to and not running and trotting with you across the globe. I'm a woman, I need stability and order and I don't think we can do that with all these travels."

"Monisola I've been thinking about it and I think we should make our home here in America."

"I thought you were in Lagos!"

"I had to see to some things here."

"You didn't tell me."

"Neither did you."

There was silence from both of them.

"I think we should give each other time to think and then agree on what we want."

"I don't agree to anything, come Saturday you will be Mrs Benjamin and if you want to make your home between London and Chicago or wherever, that my darling is your palaver. GOD help you when the children come."

"How soon do you want ...."

"Nine months exact by GOD's grace"

"What if .....?"

"There is no if ..."

"I still have projects to carry out."

"I believe you've heard of maternity leave and career breaks before."

"Daniel I'm serious."

"So am I Monisola. When are you leaving London, I want you to be home by Sunday at the latest."

"I'm coming Friday."

"Monisola don't play games with me."

"Daniel I'm not, there's a lot to do and I'd rather be alone than get in people's way"

"It's our wedding we are talking about here."

"I know but I'm not about to start a family feud just because of a ceremony. If my parent wants, let them invite the whole world, all I'm going to do is just smile and after the ceremony, it will be good bye."

"You are very stubborn."

"I'm not; I just like things done my way."

"You can't always have your way Monisola, you have to be accommodating."

"Daniel you should know by now that I am but sometimes I have to be determined and not let people push me about."

"Okay! Okay! Just hurry up with whatever you are doing and meet me in Lagos for Friday."

"You said Sunday."

"Did I? Ok I'll be in first thing Monday morning and I'm all yours."

"Are we going to spend time together."

"No!" he shouted.

"Daniel is there something wrong?"

"It's nothing, I'll see you on Monday, have a safe journey."

This page has been left intentionally blank

CHAPTER NINETEEN

Monisola returned Sunday night and her mother placed a restriction on her movements.

"Mami I am not a child anymore I don't have to take permission from you before I go anywhere."

"You are still my child and you will do as I say, until the wedding you are not to step out of your room without asking or informing me."

"Mami you said town now you've changed it to my room so I can't even go downstairs for dinner."

Her mother eyed her and then smiled. "Well since you've put it that way I will go the traditional way with you; until your husband's people come to take you, you are confined to your quarters only."

"Mami!"

"See it as a way of cutting cost with all these travelling here and there for the wedding; after all it was your idea."

Monisola moaned inwardly, trust her mother to outwit her in her own words but that won't stop her.

"I think you are just overreacting; nothing is going to happen."

"It is because we don't want anything to happen, that is why you are not to step outside your room."

"Mother I am not going ....."

"You will do exactly as I have said. I almost collapsed when Daniel told me you were in London, when I thought you were with Justina or still in your quarters in Makurdi. How can you leave the country without letting anyone know? I trust the man you are marrying, he will not take any nonsense from you, and I sincerely hope you will not be lording over him when you are married? Anyway, I trust him by the time he starts with you, you will know that ile oko ile eko ni."

"What exactly are you referring too?"

"Refer! I am telling you that Daniel as your husband will be your lord and master and no Kabiyesi to report to or run to for rescue, you are on your own."

"Mother you make it sound as if Daniel is going to subject me to some kind of torture or something."

"Of course not, he will not do that. What I am letting you know is that before you get married starting bombarding heaven with your cry for mercy and for GOD to take away all that stubbornness and headstrong attitude of always wanting to have your way."

"I'm not going to even bother."

"What! Monisola! Lenu re!"

"Mother see it this way, I know of a certain woman who allowed everyone to push her around and walk over her but given a second chance, she became stubborn, very decisive and her determination even saved the family."

"Eh! Who was that and where did you hear that from? I hope you are not using someone else as your case study and you might not even know the full details."

"I am one hundred percent sure of this case study and facts because the person happens to be my mother and since I have her genes in me it's most likely that I have inherited her strong personality traits and I am not going to let anyone including Daniel walk over me."

"He is not going to walk over you as such but you know two lions cannot rule a pride, as you and your father cannot rule at the same time, one will have to step down or step aside and cool down for the sake of peace."

"I can assure you Daniel will soon learn to play it cool with me and not lord everything over me"

"Monisola drop your princess's crown and take up the hat of humility."

"Mami, dignity also comes with humility and it is not because of my heritage that I insist on having my way, it's genetics from Kabiyesi and yourself. Anyway, this is the twenty first century, things have changed from your time."

"It is not a matter of genetics or DNA, it is a matter of the heart and orientation of the mind, ask GOD to purge you from some of the nonsense you have been brought up with, discarding them and taking up the fruit of the Holy Spirit which is love, meekness, gentleness, perseverance, humility."

"Mami invariably you are saying Kabiyesi is a bad teacher and all he taught me is wrong."

"Don't twist my words, you and I know that your father tutored you to take over the throne and not to live as a woman who will one day have a man over her. Is that why you broke up with that Igbo man."

Monisola took a deep breath thanking GOD she had gotten over

Raymond otherwise her mother would be opening fresh wounds. "Mami Raymond is history."

"I believe you know you can learn a bit from history. Anyway, Daniel is your GOD – ordained so you have to be prepared, focused and ensure you meet his every need."

"Mami you are so old fashioned, what about my own needs, am I not entitled to some pleasures of my own?"

"Ple- what? My dear, all your pleasures are derived from your husband and husband alone no other."

Monisola laughed, "I mean things that make me happy and fulfilled, such as travelling to different countries, helping people."

"Have you made arrangement to sell that house?"

Monisola wondered how her mother's mind works as she had zoomed in on one of the things she considered her personal properties and did not want any intrusion.

"No, I'm not going to sell it, I want to keep it."

"Why? Is your husband's house not adequate?"

"Mami, why do you keep the house in Zurich?"

"It was a gift and I was already married, I hope you will not use that place as a hideout. I wonder why you hold on to it so much, take it out of your system - it is only a structure."

"Mami I'm tired I want to rest."

"You can give any excuse you want but I hope it will not extend to your husband every night."

Okay so she was getting her first sex education lesson from her mother.

"Should I be ever ready just so that he can fulfil his pleasure?"

"Why did he marry you in the first place?"

"Mother! Sex is not the only reason why we are getting married; I do have a million things to do after the wedding and in my life time."

"I am not saying sex is everything but you must always make allowance to give him what he wants otherwise someone will give it to him."

"Is that what happened between you and father?"

"Ayi ni suru lo se baba re, he was not patient."

"Are things better now?"

"What has happened, has happened, I've learnt to live with it but I don't want you to go through that, please Monisola do everything to please your husband."

"And if ..."

"Leave no room or opportunity to allow anything to come between you especially when sleeping together."

"So, when we are sleeping together no pillow should come between us?"

Her mother shook her head, "E' kan' se e'"

"But you said...."

"You know what I'm trying to say."

"I don't Mother; I want to hear you say it."

"Say what?"

"What happens when a man and woman sleep together?"

"You will have that tutorial and practical in your husband's room."

"Mami, I will tell my daughter what happens."

"It's not that I don't want to."

"Then why not?"

"I find it difficult; my mother didn't tell me much and your father taught me most of the things I know and the rest my intuition, but with you, I feel inadequate, I feel I can't, I don't trust myself or I may not meet their standards."

"Whose standards?"

"Your father, Iya Oba and all those who were there when you were born. I was just a young first-time mother and anything I did; I didn't do quite well for the little princess. Even breast feeding you became something I couldn't even do and had it been left to them, they would have found someone else to do it. Monisola most of the time I cried and prayed that I will not drop you or do anything that will make them talk. I wanted to be the best mother that could ever be, for my daughter, my beautiful daughter but I was not given the chance. I've never been close to you as a mother should and it is my fault I should never have allowed it, now I am paying the price for it."

Monisola draped her hands over her mother and they both cried.

"Mami promise me you'll be there for Josephine."

"I still want to be there for you, Oluwatoyin's time will come and by GOD's grace I will be there for her but it is you I am worried about. Monisola I want you to go to your husband's house well prepared not to be a novice in some aspect. I want to let you know some of the things I have come across as well as what other women have experienced and with the help of the Holy Spirit in you, you will make better decisions, avoid some pitfalls, gain new experiences that you can pass on to the young and old generation. I know you are a woman full of GOD's wisdom and you have the ability to effect positive changes especially with women, so please my dear daughter ro' ra' se', fi suru ati ero se ohun gbogbo, patience and wisdom are tools a woman needs in marriage."

"Mo ti gbo Mami. I've been praying and asking GOD to remove every ego in me."

"Oti o! You need it, GOD did not create you to be a dunce. So you want a man to be walking over you all the time? What on earth did your father teach you all these years?"

"Ah Mami! You just said he was a bad teacher, I should always give in to my husband, giving him pleasure twenty-four seven and still in the same breath you said I should maintain my ego, stubbornness and pride."

"Yes, pride in who GOD created you to be, not a door mat for everyone. As far as ego is concerned, everyone has one and as for the bedroom I can tell you a few tricks that even your father is still racking his brains about."

"In other words, the student has now become the tutor."

"Ori e pe', emi lo jo."

"Mother, I can't believe the things you do and say. I see you as this scattered wit person and you prove times without fail that you are intelligent, smart, witty, beautiful, I ...."

"Shh! Baby girl you are more and better than I am and your children will be greater in JESUS name."

"Amen."

Monisola looked at her mother and smiled, maybe this pre- wedding tutorial should continue as she was learning and also felt some emotional barriers were being broken between her and her mother.

"Mami, Daniel wants us to start having children straight away."

"What do you want?"

"I don't mind but it's just I want a home first; I don't want to be travelling and living all round the world."

"Ise' to gba ni. A woman's world is not so easy but GOD has built us with the capacity to survive no matter the circumstances and with His help there is no limit to what we can achieve and I know you have what it takes to make Daniel happy."

"Mami, Daniel is not so easy as he looks, I sometimes hit a brick wall when it comes to him."

"Men are not easy, they have so many things to deal with and everything is on their head: work, business, women, children, dependent, friends and you wonder why they fall into temptation, give up or just burn out. That is why GOD said it is not good for man to be alone; he needs a helper, the softer side, the soothing side from all the worries and madness of this world.

Monisola Oluwafiadekemi you are that person for Daniel, he needs you to be there for him when the world is against him, when his world is upside down, when life seems not to have any meaning in the midst of chaos and all. He will be selfish in his needs for you but understand that he does it because that is where he can find himself, be himself. Do what will soothe, ease and release his pent up emotions and my dear that is where you submit to him, glue to him as if you will never let go and let him know that while others are saying 'no, you can't make it, you are not good enough' you are saying yes, you are the best, you can make it, you have what it takes to make it."

"Mami are you sure this theory of yours will work, what is the success rate?"

"Which man in his right senses would not want a wife that treats him like a king?"

"Mami there are many mad and crazy guys out there."

"And I thank GOD He hasn't given you olori buruku, Daniel is a good man, I really thank GOD for him, he is GOD's choice for you, forget anyone else."

"Are you sure you are not in love with him?"

"He reminds me of your father when he was young, the times we were courting, the things he said....."

"Olori are you alright?"

"I'm fine" she wiped a tear away.

"I'm sorry if I ...."

"I'm okay, just ask GOD to help you, now let me tell you the secrets your grandmother taught me."

Monisola knew that chapter was closed and she hoped she would find out what happened between her parents, but that would be for another day.

"My grandmother! I thought you never liked each other."

"Never... I loved that woman, she was the easiest person to live with, all the things I learnt about life and marriage were from her, things that even my own mother did not tell me. It was just that after you were born the attention switched to you and looking back now I understand because you were like the daughter she never had."

"Gosh, I must have received more than my own share of attention and you wonder why I am strong minded."

"That's a habit you picked from your father's side not mine, my family are humble people and hardworking."

"Do you miss them?"

"My parents and siblings? Not really, after the wedding, I rarely saw them and I guess life went on but I miss my baby brother, your uncle, Seye, the last born of the family. I practically brought him up that is why I was so confused when your people here said I could not take care of a child. That statement left me psychologically traumatised and for years I thought I was a bad mother. When I had Toluwanimi I was so scared, I used to cry but my midwife told me I was just doing fine and if I had any doubt I could ask or call her. I use to call her in the middle of the night, that the baby was sleeping too much or hasn't eaten after four hours and she will calmly tell me what to do or that I worry too much which is a sign of being a mother."

"Baby sleeping too much! Chichi would love that as she complains Emani rarely sleeps."

"How is she, you are going to miss her, is that why you want to stay in England?"

Monisola nodded.

"It's time to let go, she's a big girl now."

"I've known her almost all my life, I've been there for her and she has been there for me, I feel like I'm leaving my daughter behind."

"Hmm! Mother hen, the daughter you are talking about is older than you and is married and already has two children."

"Don't rub it in mother! She's only thirteen weeks older than me."

"Three months and a week is not a joke, Oluwatoyin can testify to that, the few minutes between her and her brother is a big deal; the little princess is already exercising her rights as senior. Just last week when I came in from the Aso Oke centre …. that reminds me, I have selected another colour of Aso Oke again, the one I saw that day was too sweet to miss, don't worry it's just the gele, iborun and fila for

Daniel, anyway....." her mother looked at her waiting for a respond. "Are you not going to say anything? That we are going overboard with all our spending?"

"What did Oluwatoyin do?" Monisola completely ignored her mother's remark about another addition to her wedding wardrobe, which made her laugh and continued her earlier conversation.

"Abi o jare' I came in and I heard your father telling her off for whatever she did and the next thing I heard, 'Even though you look like me you have your mother's strong character as well as your sister Monisola, why? Eh! Why their traits and character? I now have to go through all I went with Monisola and your mother combined in one, wo' I think I better start planning boarding house, university and marriage all at one go."

"Mami that is not funny, she's only a child." Monisola scolded.

"You refuse to see the humour in it because of what you went through but the circumstances have changed. Of course, Kabiyesi is not going to send her or her brother to anywhere I am not, he was only thinking of the tough times he went through raising you and probably doubts his own ability and skills unlike before where he would climb trees, go camping and all that, I guess he is getting old."

"And you believe that?"

"I don't.... I'm not too sure."

"I mean the getting old bit."

"Old! That one! He seems to be getting younger and when I want to ......"

"What?"

"Don't worry, just pray Daniel will still be strong and agile even till your old age."

"I don't believe you and father are still doing......" Monisola covered her face with the pillow and shook her head.

"Doing? Wo' you better get ready, that young man is going to ride you like a bull."

"I don't want to hear that."

"Take cotton wool or ear plug and block your ears, come Saturday you will know."

"I don't want to know."

"How I wish your grandmother was still alive, she would arrange all the traditional rites...."

"Olori that is a no-go area, I don't want any traditional rites."

"I am not talking about any fetish thing. It is just the way the chosen maidens will escort you to your husband's house, prepare the bed and wait till they bring out the stained cloth."

"Mother!" Monisola screamed and was horrified.

"What? Have you done it and you are not telling? O je je wo? You better not disgrace your father."

"I haven't done anything."

"I trust Daniel with the warning your father gave him...."

"What warning?"

"No show before wedding night."

Monisola laughed and laughed. "Now I know why he has been avoiding me. Hmm! I might just test ..."

"Please leave the boy alone, the pressure from your father is enough don't add to it otherwise ti o ba ki e mole!"

"Good evening Mr Benjamin, how are you today?"

"Who is this?"

"Who is this? You mean you don't know your ...."

"Monisola! Why are you talking like that?"

"Talking like what? I ain't no Moni... whatever, I'm Sandy your girl from Vegas."

"Monisola I have passed that level find another game plan."

"Oh! You are such a spoil sport."

"What is the matter?"

"I'm bored."

"With all that is going on around you, please find something to do or someone to help I'm sure mother will need some."

"I've been told not to lift a finger and for once I am going to obey. Anyway, when did you start calling Olori mother?"

"Since the day I became her son-in law."

"Seventy-two more hours to go."

"Less than fifty hours left."

"Na you sabi. Daniel why don't you come over?"

"To do what?"

"Just come over nooow, I'm bored."

"I've told you what to do, find something to do to occupy your time."

"Okay I'll meet you in your room at the hotel."

"Monisola if you dare step out of your quarters I will..."

"What are you daring me with because I'm game and I need something to keep me active."

"Monisola don't play with me."

"Danny boy you know I love your games they thrill me and stimulate my brain cells to do some proactive works."

"Monisola! I'm going to call Olori and report you."

"And so?"

"You this girl, you are not even afraid?"

"Of you, mother or father who placed the embargo on you, how could you fall for that Daniel? You should have shown him you are a man of the times and all that 'no go area' is archaic and old fashioned."

"Thank you Miss counsellor and have him take you away for good and I never see you again or carry out my revenge plan on you."

"What revenge plans are we talking about here?"

"Oh! Monisola my Monisola! You have no idea what plans, I your husband have in store for you."

"Plans to do me good and not to harm me, vengeance is mine says the LORD," Monisola quickly pleaded as she remembered her mother's earlier advise.

"Oh! So, you are afraid now, I can see you shaking", he laughed and seemed to relax.

"In your dreams, I am equal to the task ahead Mr Benjamin."

"I would like to be referred to, by you, as 'My lord'; after all, to be a husband to a princess like you is no joke and is hard work. I really thank GOD for His mercies and blessings."

"You better ask for more mercy, you will need it."

"Monisola! I am warning you; every day is for the ...."

"I myself will catch the thief don't worry."

CHAPTER TWENTY

TRADITIONAL ENGAGEMENT DAY

'Emi la oni yosi
'Emi la oni yosi
Bi ati bere kori
Beni JESU ba wa se ju be lo

The beats from the talking drum made the women and the damsels bringing the bride to meet her groom ki'ijo mole', twisting and shaking their waist to the beats. Soon everyone at the traditional engagement wedding began to dance as they welcomed the bride to the ceremony which had been ongoing for a few hours.

The marquee was decorated in white and gold trimmings and the colour code of the day was white and gold accessories. The royal family of Adewunmi from Oba Zachariah to his wives, children and grandchildren were all dressed in their native attires of white agbada for men, iro and buba for women and gold accessories were worn to accentuate the purity and brilliance of the white. The groom's family also wore white but used sky blue colour to reflect the beauty and majesty of GOD, the creator of heaven and earth. Depending on whose side they were invited from, the guest also had their variation of white and accessories of gold, sky blue and similar colours.

Olori Tinuola's attire distinguished her as the mother of the bride, she was looking so radiate that Kabiyesi himself could not but steal a few glances her way, as she could easily pass for the bride herself.

Ayaba Adekemi and her daughters and their family all wore white with the same shade of gold, design and accessories.

Toluwanimi wasn't too keen on the idea of uniformity but at the insistence of Kabiyesi he wore something similar to his dad. It was nothing like the 'old school' design but was trendy that also marked him out as a young eligible bachelor and the eyes of the single ladies were constantly baiting at him.

Daniel wore a sky blue and white complete set of Aso Oke; sokoto', buba and agbada with a gold fila while Monisola wore white buba made from shimmering Aso Oke, sky blue Aso Oke for her iro and gold gele.

A transparent white veil was used to cover her upper body and as she came in she was led by her personal escorts and handed over to the Alaga ijoko. The Alaga Ijoko the spokeswoman for the Adewunmi's family welcomed Monisola and led her to Kabiyesi and her mother to be prayed for as well as Daniel's family. She eventually led Monisola to Daniel where she knelt down and he also prayed for her.

The family exchanged gifts; there were traditional dances from the Yoruba and Tiv cultural dance troupes which kept the guest entertained. There were lots of food and drinks, the invited guests and villagers ate to their hearts' content. By six o'clock in the evening the whole ceremony was over and everyone on their way home.

Daniel escorted Monisola to her quarters and stayed in the living room.

"Tell me, how does it feel to be Mrs Benjamin?"

"I don't know, I'll have to wait till Saturday roughly around two in the afternoon before I know".

"You are already Mrs Benjamin, I just paid your bride price and you have my ring on your finger, in fact I have full claim and rights over you."

Monisola smiled, Daniel was pushing her to well-known waters and GOD help him if he didn't swim.

"Well if that be the case why don't we just take few steps towards the bedroom and you can claim your full rights." She walked seductively towards him.

"Why do you always like to play with fire?" he asked moving a few steps from her.

"You were the one claiming rights and I'm only helping you to fuel it well well."

"Well well indeed. I've patiently waited this long; another forty-eight hours of waiting won't kill me."

"Are you sure Danny boy?" she winked at him and was moving closer.

"Hey! Don't you start that. I'll scream if you come any closer."

Monisola took more steps towards him, with her defiant 'dare me' expression.

"Monisola I'm warning you, keep your distance from me and stop looking at me with that kind of eyes you naughty girl. I'll shout o!"

"Daniel I am in my room in my father's house and you were the one claiming right."

"Kai! Just thank GOD for your father if not ....."

"What would happen?"

The knock on the door interrupted them.

"Who is it?"

"It's me Joke, Olori wants to know if you are alright princess."

"Please come in, I'm fine, Mr Benjamin and I were just talking."

Monisola retreated but gave Daniel a wink and pouted.

"Good evening sir, congratulations sir."

"Thank you Miss Joke."

There was an awkward silence between the three.

"You can tell Olori that I'm fine, Mr Benjamin was just leaving."

"Ma, Olori said I should stay with you ma and she would soon join you."

Daniel sigh with relief while Monisola smiled.

"In that case can you please help me to take off my accessories and clothes?"

Daniel's head jerked towards her as if he did not just hear what she said clearly and on second thought he jumped up, muttered something about going to see her father and briskly walked out of the room.

Monisola laughed, shook her head and laughed more when she saw Joke's puzzled look.

Friday morning met Monisola feeling a bit restless. She was tired of staying in her room and wanted some fresh air and space to free the brooding on her mind. Why was she feeling restless? She sneaked out of her room and walked towards the garden. There were more trailers and people working on the palace grounds which made her wonder what they were still doing after yesterday's ceremony. She was pacing the ground when she ran into one of the guards.

"Good morning Princess."

"Good morning Kola."

"Do you need anything Ma?"

"No.....yes, is there any car available that I can drive?"

"Em! I will have to check your highness; it is not that there is no car but it's a matter of finding a driver and maid to accompany you Ma as everyone is preparing for tomorrow."

"I can drive, all I need is a car." Monisola spoke softly.

"I'm sorry your highness, but there are ..... I have to check first Ma, please do not be angry with me Ma."

"Of course I'm not angry I just ... never mind, I'll sort myself out."

She walked back into the house and as she was going in she heard her mother's voice.

"What do you mean you don't know where she is? Did I not leave instructions you were to be with her at all times? Joke' ma ma' pi' mi lemi."

"I'm sorry ma, ejo e ma binu Ma" the girl apologised profusely.

Monisola made her appearance and almost immediately her mother started shouting.

"Olori you are getting yourself worked up for nothing. Why all this chaperone at this my age and ninety-ninth hour, are you afraid I would run away or what?"

"Run to where? Your husband's house! With all pleasure and blessings but that will be after the church wedding ceremony. Until then you will do as you are told, do I make myself clear?"

"Explicit."

"Good."

"I'm going out to ... Can I ..."

"Monisola I am two breaths away from calling the guards to bundle you and keep you under lock and key until tomorrow."

"Mother this is unfair! I'm tired of staying in my room forever."

"Not forever, so' gbo. By GOD's grace, this time tomorrow you will be on your way to church and your husband's home."

"Mother you seem in a hurry to get rid of me."

"Who is trying to get rid of my darling daughter?" her father asked as he came in.

"Mother"

Olori shook her head and gave a sign to Joke, who quickly disappeared.

"What is all this about? Get rid of your daughter who is about to be married! Why, what is going on?"

"Kabiyesi ....."

"Father, Olori has promised to set the guards on me if I dare venture out of my room."

"Moni ...."

"Kilo de'. Ki lo le' to' yen? What is the meaning of all this house arrest in her own home? This is her home, her birth place and she is forever welcome to it."

"Kabiyesi it is not like that; I want her monitored so that she doesn't go anywhere without supervision and moreover tomorrow is Saturday."

"I am sure everyone is aware that tomorrow is Saturday but that should not restrict her, if she decides to go to China ....."

"Mo ko' ni oruko JESU! I forbid it"

"Amin". Kabiyesi quickly responded knowing that his daughter might just take up that challenge.

"It is for her good she has been disturbing Mr Daniel since......"

"Which Mr Daniel?" Turning to his favourite child, he asked again, "Which Mr Daniel is your mother talking about?"

Monisola masked her facial expression and gentle shrugged her shoulders.

Olori watched both father and daughter, knowing that today will establish her quest for an answer as to who was wiser and smarter between father and daughter and who was fooling who because they certainly weren't fooling her.

"Kabiyesi Monisola has to be careful, Saturday is already knocking at the door and by GOD's grace she will be handed over to her husband intact. I don't want any wahala o!"

"I am sure she will but are we talking about the same Daniel or another one?"

GOD help me with this man today. What has come over him that his senses are not so sharp to his daughter's prank? Is he really getting old?

"Monisola yo' oko re lenu Kabiyesi. E ranti ikan ti e' so' fun Daniel. She should observe protocol."

Monisola had been watching her parents trying to play on each other wits and hoping one of them will decide to give in to her request; hopefully her father as she had plans for tonight.

"Monisola, you are not to leave your room until further notice."

What? Surely her father was joking, which century did he think they were in, okay, change of plans ......not change of tactics then.

Later on, she had the same difficulty convincing Daniel when she complained she was bored during their telephone conversation.

"Daniel you don't understand, I refuse to be kept under guard and key, I'm a woman and this is the twenty first century for crying out loud."

"Monisola the bible says you should obey your ......"

Bang! The telephone line resumed its tone.

"Hello! Hello! Monisola."

Daniel shook his head; the girl was a tough cookie he thought to himself. Anyway, as she is under her parents' roof there was no cause for alarm, he could have a good nap before meeting up with his friends later.

The party was in full swing and everyone was enjoying themselves, eating, drinking and some of the guest were dancing. It was suggested that the Karaoke began and some of the ladies eagerly got up with placards which displayed their numbers from one to ten. Contestant number one opened the floor and half way through people were really trying not to cover their ears or burst out laughing and when she finally finished her song, people eagerly clapped their hands glad that their trauma was over while contestant number one thought she had nailed it.

Contestant number two was no different from one except that she stopped in the middle of the song and decided to sing another one which made some of the audience growl.

Three and four were better and the audience whistled, cheered and applauded them. The ladies who sang on the fifth to seventh rounds were good but not quite as good as the duet sang by contestants eight and nine who decided at last minute to sing together. It was Justina and one of her friends.

"Good Evening ladies, I'm sure we are all enjoying ourselves tonight especially one beautiful, gorgeous lady, who is about to bid farewell to singlehood and join the elite double club kwashe Uhe (new wife) as she ties the knot with no one other than my handsome brother. When I first met her, I wasn't particularly keen on her, not that she wasn't beautiful as you can all see she is a stunning lady but I didn't know her and my fear was that she was going to take my only sibling away from me. However, as I got to know her, I began to like her personality, she is kind, loving, fun to be with and yes she is definitely the best out of all for my dear brother. I really thank GOD for her and I pray GOD will keep them together forever. This song is for you, Monisola, trusting that GOD will perfect all that concerns you in JESUS name. Both ladies sang and the applause rang quite a while after they finished.

The last but not the least introduced herself.

"Hi everyone. My name is Monisola, I'm .....gosh! I don't know what to say. I'd like to thank GOD for today and yes tomorrow. I'm happy to be here and not sitting alone and letting my nerves get the best of me ahead of tomorrow. I'd also like to thank everyone for coming and also the people who organised this, I didn't even think of it ....."

"We know, you were thinking of Daniel" someone shouted from the party of friends which made everyone laugh.

"Yeah right. This song is a song I've known for a while now and from the first time I heard it I just fell in love with it. It talks about love falling like dew from heaven, love telling its lover to be sincere, speak and deal with her with integrity and not to leave but cling to their love forever.

I've been through some disappointments and for a while thought I would never find true love. GOD proved me wrong when HE brought Daniel into my life, in actual fact I fell in love with him without even knowing. What I'm trying to say is that when you find true love, hold on, don't let go, be sincere with love, open minded, don't take it for granted. For those of you still searching, don't give up, love is out there and when you find it don't be afraid to embrace it."

Monisola sat down on the stool that had been provided and took a deep breath, yes she was ready.

" Ba mi se otito

Mo fe' o' to' to

Ba mi se' ododo

Mofe o pelu ododo….."

She sang a remix of Ife Eji Owuro by Sola Allyson Obaniyi and sang it with all her heart to the point that tears were streaming down from her face and some of her audience. She opened her eyes after singing and sat still when she saw who was right in front of her. He had tears in his eyes and unashamed and unreserved he let it flow and moved to kiss her lips.

Later, outside in the car park of the hotel, Daniel escorted her to the waiting car and driver.

"Monisola I just want you to know that no matter what, I would never ever leave you."

"Don't make promises Daniel; let's just take one step at a time. I ......
I need to go before Olori sends out the whole entourage to look for me."

"She won't."

"How do you know?"

"She is aware of this party and kindly played along when you gave the excuse of coming to see Justina. Are you ready for tomorrow?"

"Are you?"

"Ever since the first time I set eyes on you, I've been ready."

"Even though you sent me out of your house and life for a year?"

"Please let the past be in the past, we are getting married and that's all that matters not when I was behaving like a goat."

Monisola smiled, moved closer to him, Daniel who was still aware of the less than thirty-six hours embargo of 'touch not' stepped back but close enough to hear what she said.

"I love you Daniel."

Embargo or no embargo he now moved closer, was about to land on her lips when one of her guards coughed. Okay still under restriction but not for long.

"I'll see you in church tomorrow."

"Actually, I was planning to ......"

"Monisola please don't, I beg you."

She laughed and went inside the waiting car.

This page has been left intentionally blank

CHAPTER TWENTY - ONE

THE WEDDING

"For this purpose, shall a man leave his father and mother and cleave to his wife and the two shall become one. Christopher Daniel Benjamin, are you willing, ready, to leave your father and mother and family and cleave to Monisola Adewunmi as your wife for GOD to make you both one?"

"Yes I am."

The church seats were filled to capacity as well as the overflow of the church hall. Despite the restriction on admitting only invited guest, the orderlies were constantly on their feet making last minute alterations to seating arrangements.

"Monisola Oluwamuiremiwa Oluwafiadekemi Omolabake Adewunmi are you willing, ready, to leave your father and mother and family and cleave to Christopher Daniel Benjamin as your husband for GOD to make you both one?"

"Yes I am."

Turning to the bride's father, the Minister asked, "Zachariah Omoloba Adeyemi Adewunmi, do you whole heartedly and without holding back, give your daughter Monisola Oluwamuiremiwa Oluwafiadekemi Omolabake Adewunmi as wife to Christopher Daniel Benjamin so the two shall live as one according to GOD's Holy Word?"

A brief pause and in one breathe, he gave his word, "I Zachariah Omoloba Adeyemi Adewunmi, give you my daughter Monisola Oluwamuiremiwa Oluwafiadekemi Omolabake Adewunmi as wife to Christopher Daniel Benjamin to fulfil GOD's Word and commandment, to live as one, cleave as one."

Everyone clapped, Olori heaved with relief and smiled. The Minister of GOD, continued,

"In light of this I now remind both of you that the vows you are about to make are to be made sincerely, with all of your heart, soul and body, as you stand in GOD's holy presence and before the congregation of His people. The vows are binding in heaven as we call the three witnesses in heaven, GOD the Father, GOD the Son - JESUS and GOD the Holy Spirit as witnesses. Your vows as you make them are also binding here on earth and we call on the three witnesses here on earth; the Word of GOD, the Blood of JESUS and the Holy Spirit as witnesses, that you are entering into a new covenant relationship based on the Word of GOD, the Blood of JESUS that was shed on the cross of Calvary for the forgiveness of your sins, your lineage and also for a godly foundation in this journey of life by the power in the name of JESUS.

That you will adhere to GOD's word at all times by asking the Holy Spirit to abide, dwell and reign in your hearts, souls, bodies and lives. That you will forsake all others and cleave as one, giving your bodies to each other, taking care of each other, seeing to the wellbeing of each other and loving whole heartedly.

I ask you again to remember that the vows you take now are binding for life and there shall be no separation or divorce for as the bible states, whatsoever the Lord doeth, HE doeth good and what GOD has joined together let no man put asunder. The only thing that can ever severe you from this vow is physical death. In times and seasons of life, whether it be plenty, few, healthy, ill -health, prosperous or poverty, sanity or insanity, challenges or victories, you shall continue to be together to mend and prevail over the storms of life, through prayers, trusting and holding on to the Word of GOD, as our LORD JESUS stated, 'In the world ye shall have tribulations: but be of good cheer, I have overcome the world.'

You both will overcome because you have the Greater One in you, the Holy Spirit who will lead, guide, guard, protect and direct you as you allow HIM into your lives, home and bringing up your children in the knowledge and fear of GOD.

As the book of Ecclesiastes states in the third chapter, to everything there is a season and a time for every matter or purpose under heaven. There will be time to weep and laugh but we pray that times of laughter will never cease in your home, more to dance than to mourn, more to build up than to break down, whatever situations you find yourselves, GOD will glorify Himself in your lives in JESUS mighty name."

"Amen" was echoed throughout the church.

"Are you both ready to take your vows?"

"Yes, we are" both Daniel and Monisola answered.

"Christopher please repeat after me, I Christopher......"

The Church service ended, the photograph sessions was wrapped up under thirty minutes and the wedding entourage went to the reception hall which was a different venue with a mega massive marquee.

While the reception was getting into full swing, the couple were still in their limousine and the driver had to step out because of what was happening inside.

"Daniel plea....."

He continued and would not let go.

A knock on the window caught their attention, it was her sister Morenike.

"I hope you guys have not started the honeymoon here already? The guests are waiting and Kabiyesi has been..."

At the mention of Kabiyesi, Daniel moved his hands from Monisola and mumbled under his breath.

"We'll be in soon."

Monisola turned to look at her fiancé, actually her husband and wondered what came over him a few minutes ago.

"Do we have to go in, we could make our excuses and ..."

"Daniel what's come over you?"

"Over me? Oh! You think there's something wrong with me. Let me tell you something my darling wife, nothing, absolutely nothing is wrong with me. In fact, I am one hundred per cent fine, I'm over the moon and I feel like I'm floating on air."

"Daniel are you drunk?"

"Drunk? I am very sober; I can drive this vehicle to Makurdi or Katsina-Ala now. The wine that is intoxicating me is you, my sweetheart, my epo pupa of the delta, my one and true love, I love you Monisola, I want to spend the rest of my life loving and caring for you."

This time it was Monisola who initiated the kiss and Daniel had to stop her.

"I would love to go on but the mere thought of your father knocking on the window is not one I want to see, we'll continue later."

Monisola was stunned when she had a glance into the hall, it was just perfect. The arrangement of the hall, settings, decoration was just perfect. The marquee had a white background, with a shade of blue akin to ocean blue as accessories to accentuate the sheer brilliance of the white background. The accessories were in form of fabrics in ocean blue colour draped vertically across the hall.

The oval shaped tables were covered with white damask, surrounded by chairs also covered in white overall caped with blue satin with bows tied at the back. The tables had a bouquet of red roses at the centre and the silver cutleries were displayed in uniformity on each table. The setting was just perfect and she hoped to see the lady that was in charge to thank her.

As she and Daniel moved nearer the entrance of the hall, she glanced at the seating arrangement for her and Daniel and this time her heart beat with excitement and delight. It was spectacular and she loved it. The seating arrangement was set on a stage with waterfall background, the love seat was carved in ivory with a matching side table set with fruits, it was just beautiful.

They danced into the hall surrounded by their bridal train and thereafter went through all the ceremony of the wedding reception; prayers, praise & worship, speech by chairman, cutting of cake, eating, dancing, groom's speech, more cultural dance and display, couple's dance, bride dancing with father and all. The couple finally went back to the palace where there was also a mini celebration going on and were greeted by those who attended. The couple were ushered to Monisola's room and left alone.

"I...." Monisola started to talk but was unsure of what to say.

"We are not staying here for the night."

"I....why?"

"It's still your parents' house and I have my own house."

"Daniel there's no way we'll get to Chicago or Illinois tonight."

"I'm not talking about Chicago; I mean my house in ....."

He was interrupted by a phone call which he answered immediately.

"Hello, yes! Ok, same place, we'll be there in the next ten minutes."

Monisola was looking at him wondering what was going on.

"Are your bags packed?"

"Yes, but where are we going?"

"I'm taking you home."

"Daniel I don't want to go anywhere too far; can't we stay in your hotel room or somewhere?"

"Hotel room when our castle is waiting for us, show me where your things are."

They were escorted by the guards and two of Monisola's personal maid but when they got to the air strip Daniel refused to have any of the escorts and took his wife in the small aircraft awaiting them.

Monisola was a bit apprehensive of the journey at first but Daniel guessing her anxiety, held her hand and kissed it to assure her they will be fine.

She wasn't sure where they were but they landed somewhere and there was a driver waiting for them in a car which she couldn't make out in the dark.

"U pande ver?" The driver greeted them.

"U pande nena?" Daniel asked

"M pande dedo" the driver replied

"Good, good, I hope everything is ready?" Daniel asked.

"En" turning to Monisola, the driver said, "Congratulations Madam."

She smiled and responded in his language.

Surprised he asked, "U fa zwa Tiv kpa?"

"En, m lamen zwativ chuku chuku tsegh."

Both the driver and Daniel laughed.

"Your husband will teach you and soon you will speak well."

Though she couldn't clearly see the surrounding of the house as it was dark but once they got in she could only describe it as grand. Daniel caught her unawares again but then she shouldn't be after the farm in Illinois. She took a deep breath and asked GOD to guide and guard her in this marriage business.

There were three other people in the house whom he introduced as his staff and they all welcomed Madam and congratulated them.

Alone in their room upstairs Monisola held her breathe for a second as it was too much for her to take in. How in the world did Daniel get to decorate his houses so elegant and beautiful in such remote places? She was tired and wanted some rest and was too glad when he showed her the bathroom and other things she needed.

She had a shower, dressed in her night wear and sat on the bed.

This is marriage now, no more wedding. The wedding was just for a day or how long it lasted but marriage is now and forever. She removed her dressing gown and slipped under the duvet, praying Daniel would take all the time he wanted.

She was just about closing her eyes when she heard him come into the room, he was on the phone. Take your time Honey, she thought to herself.

"Thank you very much Mother, I'll pass the message on."

He moved nearer to her, checked if she was already sleeping.

"Monisola."

"Yes, Daniel."

"I hope you don't think we are sleeping tonight."

She turned to him, he was already undressing; seriously this guy should know she was tired with the wedding and all. He moved closer and she quickly asked him if he wanted to have a shower first. He smiled and left her alone.

The shower only lasted ten minutes or less.

"Monisola, get up."

She wanted to protest but she didn't. She got up and stood in front of him. Happy now?

He held her by the hands and began to thank GOD, for everything, everyone, all the years he had known Monisola but had not met her, Omoniyi who told him so much about her, their first meeting, the meeting in London, the stay over, the visit to Illinois, the fight, their second chance and now marriage. He was grateful, so grateful to GOD. He also committed their lives, homes, family, children, grandchildren and great grandchildren into GOD's hands. They said the LORD'S prayer, the twenty-third psalms and the grace.

Monisola smiled and gave him a peck and turned to get into bed.

"If you think that is what will keep me all through the night, you my girl must be having a laugh, I'm ready for the business of tonight."

Monisola took a deep breath and wished she was in her mother's apartment. When Daniel's hand held her firmly she knew he was ready alright.

By Tuesday morning Monisola decided she wanted to go out for fresh air.

"Make sure you are back on time for the next groove."

She practically ran out of the front door and almost collided with Grace, one of the staff.

"Are you alright madam?"

"Yes, I'm fine, thank you" she was about to walk away when she called her back.

"Grace, are you very busy at the moment?"

The girl wasn't sure on how to respond, so she hesitated.

"I mean if you are on an errand or something it's okay but I'd like you to walk around with me, in case I get lost", she quickly added.

Grace did not ask for any explanation but her facial expression showed she was curious or unsure of the request.

They walked for about twenty minutes with Grace showing her what she knew of the vast estate of orchard, farm land, grazing, spring water and when Monisola remembered she had not eaten breakfast she asked if they could go back to the house.

She was in the kitchen asking Aunty Veronica for something to eat when her husband came in. She got a bit nervous and stumbled at her attempt to ask her request in Tiv language.

"She does understand English you know, so you might as well speak to her in English."

"I know but I won't master the language if all I do is speak in English. I want to learn."

Aunty Veronica smiled but Daniel only shrugged his shoulders and decided to go for a walk.

After her meal she went upstairs, had another shower and hoped she could get a few minutes' sleep before Daniel came back. She didn't get to sleep as her phone rang and she quickly picked it up.

"Chiamaka, you are already missing me."

"No way! I just couldn't stand the long wait any more, I am groaning with suspense."

"With Mano and the children, you still have time to be calling me on my honeymoon; don't you have work to do?"

"No, my mother is here and the children are with her and ..."

"Oh! I want to speak with her, it's a long time I spoke to her, please pass the phone to her", Monisola said with excitement.

"Are you okay? Who do you want me to tell wants to speak to her?"

"Me of course?"

"Mrs Daniels, I mean Mrs Benjamin, you are on your honeymoon, I am not supposed to call but the suspense is 'not' killing me because I am bent on speaking positively to myself as Mano has been telling me not to kill myself with suspense and that I must NOT call and now you want me to give the phone to my mother. Oginni?"

"Okay tell I asked after her."

"Monisola I ask again are you okay?"

"Yes."

"I'm not sure, tell her you asked after her, from where? The honey moon suite or under your husband?"

Monisola spoke a few insulting words she had learnt in Igbo and Chiamaka laughed.

"Hmm! I can see Mr Daniel is unleashing the real woman in you Monisola."

"Another word from you Chic and I will tell your mother and Mano."

"I will even give you the taxi fare only if your husband will allow you and not keep you under lock and key and is giving it to you twenty-four seven."

"You are crazy."

"I might be but I speak the truth. Monisola you have found your match, the perfect one for you and I can't wait to tell Mano... I've got to go, Mother is calling me, say hi to your lover man, ciao."

Monisola threw the phone on the bed and wished she could go out and drive, just drive.

"Are you alright Monisola?" Daniel asked as he came into the room.

"Daniel, can I please have a car, I'll like to go out for a drive."

"The driver can take you but where exactly do you want to go?"

"Out."

"Out where?"

"Anywhere, greet the neighbours or visit some of my staff from the project."

"During our honeymoon?" he stated emphatically.

"We've been in doors for three days; I just want to go out."

"Are you bored?"

Bored of course she wasn't bored, she just wanted to go out.

"I'm not.... I don't mean ....., I just ....."

He waited for her to finish her sentence but she didn't.

"Monisola is there something you are not telling me; this is our honeymoon and all you want to do is go out; I thought we are meant to spend time together."

What have they been doing since they got here, she thought to herself?

"Monisola, speak them out, I am not in your head and right now I can't read your mind."

"You are driving me crazy Daniel."

He moved closer and looked at her. "What do you mean?"

"We've.......we've...."

He looked at her closely, what in heaven's name was she trying to say now.

"It's..... we've...... here...... there..... I.. don't even get to sleep."

"I really don't understand what you are trying to say."

"I mean we've been doing it since we got here, aren't you tired or had enough?"

Daniel had been moving closer to her to reassure her everything would be fine, but on hearing Monisola's explanation roared into laughter. He laughed so much and remembering what happened the last time he laughed at her in her house, he quickly rolled off the bed, fell on to the floor still laughing.

What did she say that was so funny?

Daniel really tried to comport himself but he was far from it and anytime he wanted to pull himself together but caught a glimpse of

Monisola's face or her words earlier on rang in his ears, he started off his burst of laughter again. GOD help him.

Monisola sat down calmly and watched her dear husband make fun of her.

Eventually he got up and came around her to hug her but she refused.

"I'm sorry, I am. I didn't mean to make fun of you but ...."

The giggle and his trembling body started the laughter bouts again.

What was wrong with the man?

He leaned forward and began to kiss her, she tried to resist him but her body couldn't and like a new addiction she gave in to him.

Later on, still entwined with each other, Daniel asked if she was alright.

"I'm fine."

"If I'm rushing you please do let me know."

"Rushing me after how many days and times?"

"Monisola, please don't make me laugh again."

"I am now a clown."

"No, you are my sweet, sweet, delicious, savoury, beautiful wife that makes me want more and more, honestly I really, really want to stop but I can't."

"You mean we are still on the marathon?"

Daniel was about to start laughing again but controlled himself and started kissing her.

"Daniel, I'm getting tired."

"Don't you enjoy what we are doing?"

Enjoy wasn't the exact word she had for it but for now she just wanted to rest.

"Daniel I'm having a headache from lack of sleep and also anxiety during the wedding, can't we just relax?"

"What is wrong with you, I thought this is what we both wanted?"

She didn't like the way the conversation was going or the rising of tone.

"Daniel, all I am saying is that I want to rest and not make love, I've not had up to six hours sleep since we got here. Please I just need to rest."

"Rest from what? What exactly have you been doing that you need to rest from?"

She got up and went to the bathroom, Daniel wasn't making this easy for her, she looked into the mirror and sure enough her eyes were a bit sore and had a bit of dark circles. She washed her face and went into the room. Daniel wasn't there and she did not bother to find out where he was but crawled into the bed and slept.

When Daniel came back an hour later she was still sleeping, he had a shower, lay beside her, closed his eyes and he was fast asleep.

CHAPTER TWENTY - TWO

Daniel woke up around ten in the morning and could not believe the time. He could not remember the last time he woke up any time after four in the morning let alone ten, he turned to his wife who was still sleeping, he cuddled her and slept again.

Monisola woke up to find herself entwined with Daniel; he was so wrapped around her and it seemed like he didn't want her to go anywhere. Well she wasn't. She looked at him properly for the first time since their wedding and yes her husband was quite handsome. His eyes so narrowed and closed together like two lines, first parallel and then twined at both ends and when closed his eyelashes were thicker. His nose was like a hill slanting down, uphill and down again.

His lips were thick, wide and very sensual when he kissed her. She couldn't resist any more, she kissed him gently, slowly and was lathering with her tongue when he caught it and pulled into his mouth, flickering through her teeth, tongue and almost her throat. She tickled him and he laughed and released her tongue, only for a while as he looked at her.

"Do you know you are so beautiful, my smooth, red oil of the delta?"

She smiled and whispered into his ears, "You have the sexiest eyes and kissable lips I have ever seen and you turn me on each time I look into your eyes."

He looked into her eyes and without much ado she was already drowning, he caught her, saved her and lead her the only way.

"So, are you still tired?"

"Nope."

"How come?"

"I slept."

"But that is what you have been doing since we got here."

"No! You have been sleeping while I have been trying to sleep and you have kept me awake all the time."

"You know I can't do it while you are sleeping, I need your full attention, like I have since morning. Girl you get e' horse power, it was none stop and all that talk of been tired you weren't. The way you were screaming after the second ...."

She wacked him with one of the clothes lying around and he gasped when one of the buttons or something hit him in the eyes and he covered his face with his hands.

"I'm sorry babe, I didn't mean to, please let me see."

He removed his hands, half closed one of his eyes and quickly grabbed her and squeezed her. She screamed, he laughed and they were at it again.

At the dinner table they had some guest but both of them could not keep their eyes off each other.

Daniel was not interested in what his dinner companions were saying and was fully concentrating on her. As soon as desert was served, he excused himself from the table and pulled his wife along. His wife, his very own wife.

He had tried to relax all through that dinner but he couldn't as he was on fire and longed for his wife. As soon as they got into the room he started kissing her gently but when he realised that his wife's tempo was even faster than his own he changed and before they knew it they were tearing at each other's clothes and it was when skin met skin and the bucket lowered to fetch the water from the well, were they temporary relieved and did not stop until the night broke into another day.

"What is wrong with the reception around here, I have been calling but my calls won't go through."

"Who are you calling?"

"Olori....I just want to thank her and ....."

"Tell her all that I have been doing to you."

"I just want to speak with my mother."

"I just want to speak with my mother" he mimicked her. "Soon you would be running to her. When did you become a cry baby Monisola?" She pulled her lips in and tried to keep any word from coming out of her mouth, she was really trying to be a good wife and not give him an answer.

"Don't tell me the cat got ya tongue Moni, Monisola babe."

He really was pressing the wrong button this afternoon.

"Can we please go out; I need some fresh air."

"If you move about three hundred yards toward the window or glass panel and open both you might actually get some fresh air."

Monisola did as she was told, came back and repeated her earlier request.

"Actually, if you ..."

Her eyes signalled she wasn't in the mood for his silly talks.

"Okay! Okay! I have planned something and I'm only waiting for the driver to let me know when he is ready."

Monisola sighed with relief which made Daniel ask a probing question.

"Are you finding this marriage thing boring or ..."

"Daniel, I am not bored I just want to go out, honeymoon is not just for ...."

"Lovemaking!"

"I....Yes, no! Daniel just leave me alone, please."

LATER WHEN THEY got to their destination after a gruesome bumpy ride Monisola could not believe her eyes and the excitement glowed.

"Where are we?"

"It called the Gurgul Fall, it's a natural waterfall, it has some aquatic flowers and birds, we would have been here earlier but the driver was unexpectedly delayed."

"It's so beautiful, where exactly are we?"

"Actually, we are not far from Cameroonian borders, would you like to go there and say hi?"

All the while she had been complaining, he had been making plans to visit this breath-taking nature's beauty, she moved closer and gave him her lips. He quickly took it, groaned and whispered, "later in our privacy"

They walked, toured, did a bit of boat riding, took photos, ate and were heading back home as the sun began to set.

"I wished we could stay here."

"Actually, I did arrange for somewhere to stay but had a last-minute change of plans but we can visit another time."

She smiled, this was her kind of thing, sightseeing...... but she was on her honeymoon. Well no one said honeymoon should be restricted to the bedroom, they had all night for that.

Daniel wondered what was going on in Monisola's mind especially with that smile. He wished things could have gone according to his initial plans but then GOD knows best and he was still hopeful.

When they got home the first thing Monisola did was have a shower, then she crept into the bed and slept off. Daniel smiled, she had pestered him to take her out for fresh air and he had only taken her out to just one of the various scheduled places he had planned and on day one she was already tired, he laughed and went to the bathroom. He loved the games he played with Monisola and he was even happier that they were now married because he could step up his game plan. He cautioned himself, this was Monisola he was talking about and he had better be prepared, in fact well prepared.

Monisola woke up early the next morning to find herself all alone in the room. Where was Daniel? She wasn't sure if she had spent the night alone as she had gone straight to bed after they got back last night. She thanked GOD for a new day, had her bath and went downstairs for breakfast, she smiled as she walked down the stairs as she was enjoying the luxury of been treated like a queen, Daniel's queen.

She went to the kitchen where Aunty Veronica greeted her and asked what she wanted for breakfast. Monisola smiled and said something light would be fine.

"You didn't have dinner last night, so I have prepared something not too light but would last while on your outing later."

Outing? She did not know of any journey scheduled for the day but she smiled and went in search of Daniel.

He was in his study and on the phone; she went in and as soon as he saw her, motioned for her to come in. She walked in and looked round, the room was impressive as it had solid mahogany wood furniture, natural lights and a view of the landscape of the estate. She gave him a peck and was going out of the room when he pulled her back and his hands were going astray, she shook her head and wagged her finger at him and ran out to the dining room where Aunty Veronica was setting the table for her.

"Thank you Aunty, I like akpukpa u alev and byer" which made Aunty Veronica smile.

Monisola ate a small portion of the meal as it was a combination of heavy food that would soon send her to sleep. She had eaten akpukpa before while on her project, it was similar to moi-moi but thicker in texture and at first she did not like it because of the smell. However, after her first taste she could live with it but byer was her love. She just loved it; it reminded her of Weetabix but is definitely more tasty, nutritious and filling. She drank most of it and soon her tummy was signalling 'enough' to her brain but she couldn't resist not scooping the last of the river of byer on her bowl. She hardly ate the akpukpa and was starting to clear her plates away when Grace came in and told her not to.

"Please let me take it to the kitchen, I've eaten too much and I can hardly walk."

Grace smiled and told her Aunty Veronica would scold her if she did but made an offer to take her on another tour of the estate or the village. Monisola accepted but set the date for another day, she went upstairs, lay on the bed and slept.

Daniel hurriedly ended the call and hoped he had not been rude to his potential client but he wasn't in the mood for business, he was on his honeymoon and his wife was waiting for him. He went to the dining room expecting to see her there but she wasn't. He went in search of her in the kitchen but was told she had finished her meal and probably gone out or upstairs. Breakfast without him? How could she eat without him, they were on their honeymoon and are supposed to spend time together and everything. He ran up the stairs and sure enough his beauty was sleeping, there was only one way to wake her up, he gave her a peck but she murmured something and turned to the other side. He tapped her gently and told her to wake up, she slept more.

"Monisola you have to get up, the driver would soon be here and we still have a long way before we get to Calabar and the ranch."

At the mention of ranch, she turned to him with a puzzled look.

"It's all being planned, please get up and pack a few things, we'll be staying there for a few days."

Throughout the journey Monisola wondered how much further they had to go because she was tired and had enough of the jerking, jolting and swaying of heads against the other passengers in the vehicle or against the window as she sat next to the door.

They were travelling in a fifteen-seater luxury bus, with Steven as the main driver and two other men: Sunday, Bem; Aunty Veronica who she now found out was Steven's wife, another female Rebecca, Daniel and herself. The last seats were packed with their luggage, water, food and utensils. She was tired of the seemingly unending journey and the loud music blasting from the speakers that she was about screaming her head off when she saw the welcome to Calabar sign. Thank GOD for that as she wasn't sure she could take any more of their journey. They lodged at a guest house where everything had been prepared for them, the guys brought in all the luggage while the two women started cooking. Though she was so tired, she offered to help but they refused and she happily went to the room set up for her and Daniel.

Daniel later joined her and asked if she was fine and when she did not reply he came nearer.

"I'm sorry babe for the long ride but I promise it would be worth your while."

"With a headache, stiff back and droning my ear drum with that blast of noise."

He laughed and joined her on the bed.

"It's all part of the honeymoon dear; it can't be all rosy and no adventure."

His eyes were gleaming with mischief and when his hands started moving, Monisola threatened," If you touch me I will scream and bring this place down and besides you need to have a shower."

"So, do you", but when he saw the pouting of her lips he added, "what do you expect from almost seven hours' journey in this heat and Nigerian weather - Boss, Calvin Klein or Polo? This is natural manly perfume from heaven so you better get used to it, in fact I refuse to have a bath for the next two days."

"You can't be serious."

"Do you want to dare me?"

On a different note she would but not this one. "Daniel if you do not get into that shower in the next five minutes, this would only be a tour and sight scene; any other aspect would be suspended till further notice."

He looked at her and she gave him a 'dare me' look. He attempted to get up but then again he couldn't resist the stubborn streak in him, he rolled over her, tickled, kissed, licked and got her to the point of no resistance and then made love to her.

The next day they started another journey with just Steven, Aunty Veronica, herself and Daniel. The others remained in the house and bid them safe journey. It was another long journey, Monisola wished she could have a massage as she was having some cramps and couldn't wait to lie in bed all day. On second thought that would mean Daniel joining her and going by the events of last evening and night, she decided to pass. She would rather endure the ride, after all she had gone on longer journeys and walks during the course of her travels while on assignment from her work schedules and also holiday. She decided to relax and enjoy this as well; she smiled and closed her eyes.

Someone tapped her and when she opened her eyes she saw a sign welcoming them to Obudu town. Eventually they got to Obudu Mountain Resort. It was another breath-taking feature of nature in her homeland and she was fascinated by the beauty and it compensated for all the troubles of the journey earlier on. The ride from the 'bottom hill' to the top of the hill was quite an experience that made her hold on to her seat and wished Daniel was sitting closer and she could hold him.

"Do you like what you see?" Daniel asked, hoping she was not tired after all the journey.

"Of course, it's beautiful."

"And you don't mind spending a couple of days here?"

"Not at all, we could even live here."

He looked at her doubtful of the truth of that statement.

Steven and Veronica dropped them at their chalet and wished them a lovely honeymoon and when she asked Daniel why they were not joining them he glared at her and asked for what?

Their suite was comfortable but the scene from their bedroom window was breath taking, this time she held Daniel and hugged him tightly. He laughed and told her the perfume from her was so sweet that he would be suspending all other activities until further notice.

Their four nights stay on the ranch was exquisite that Monisola was begging Daniel to let them stay there forever. It was a haven from all their busy schedules and lifestyle and a time to enjoy, reflect and gaze at such heavenly beauty and peace here on earth. They went on the cable car which took them on a tour of the vast nature's endowed beauty and Monisola wished a thousand times she could stay there forever.

There were lots to see, do and when they came back each evening she was so relaxed and full of excitement and trust Daniel to seal the night with more passionate lovemaking. She took so many photos that Daniel warned her the memory card would soon be full. She enjoyed the mountain ride, the temperature at the peak of the mountains which was covered in lustrous green, the ranch, canopy walk and the water falls. On their last day at the resort, Monisola asked Daniel if they could come back soon, he laughed and said in hundred years' time when they were old and grey and all they would do is just sit and watch GOD's beauty here on earth.

Steven and Aunty Veronica picked them up and she realised they had also stayed at the ranch but more of a relaxation than tours. Monisola wondered why one would ever visit such a place and not do a tour; everything about it was relaxing even going on the canopy walk!

This time she sat next to Daniel on the bus, cuddled to him and slept. When they got to Calabar, Bem and Rebecca were happy to see them; they suggested that they toured the town before they left and started planning what to do, where to see and what to eat. Daniel and Monisola looked at each other, shook their head, got up and went straight to their room. Daniel started to say something about having a shower, she couldn't care less as she crawled on the bed and was soon fast asleep.

The next day they all went out to see the town and sight scenes, they ate and were stuffed with the food they bought from different well-known eateries. Monisola begged Daniel to carry her as she could hardly walk and he reminded her she still had more work to do in the bedroom so the exercise would be good for her. The others laughed while she blushed and walked away briskly at first but when the others started laughing again she slowed her pace and gave Daniel one of her looks and mouthed 'until further notice'. He laughed, pulled her and gave her a kiss and whispered 'you dare not'.

On their way back to Vadeika the next day, all Monisola did was sleep despite the fact that the road was bumpy and the music was loud; she rested her head on Daniel's shoulder and slept off.

She was glad to be back home and her routine of sleeping and lazing around continued while Daniel started work almost immediately. She took up Grace's offer of a tour of the estate and they went to most part of the estate as well as the village she came from. Monisola was delighted to see the village and people and she promised to link them up with the team from her former project for further development. They gave her the traditional A'nger materials woven in black and white yarn which at first she wanted to refuse because she thought she should be the one giving gifts but Grace informed her it was a way of accepting her into the Tiv culture. She thanked them and gave some of them money.

Since the period of honeymoon was officially over she decided she wasn't going to be a stay at home wife only and started mapping out projects for herself. She immediately linked up Grace's village with the new E.A.C.H project lead and hoped a new initiative will develop. She also planned to visit the state's first family and thank them for their participation during the wedding. She called home to find out about everyone and everyone was fine except Toluwanimi who was complaining about their father's heavy hand on him. She laughed and told him that he was being treated with his mild hand and warned him not to do anything that will make him change to being heavy handed. Chichi and her family were fine and she couldn't wait to see Eman and Emmanuella and hear about all the things they got up to.

"Honestly Monisola I wish I could send them over to you, to bring up children is not easy o. Chia! It makes me love and appreciate my mother every day, that woman tried."

"Good but I hope Emmanuella shows you as you showed that woman."

"I wish the same for you."

After her long conversation with Chichi, Monisola thanked GOD that all was well with everyone, which she was grateful for but there was just one thing left. She was bored. Daniel was away for a few days, something to do with his business which she did not mind as it was work but she was getting fed up just sitting at home doing nothing. She made her next move and booked a flight to Lagos with a connecting one to London; hopefully before Daniel thought of her, she would be back. She wanted to go to her parents first before leaving the country but she didn't as she knew her mother would ask questions and if she answered truthfully Daniel would be alerted to her next move. Of course, she wanted to speak the truth at all times but on this occasion she wasn't sure she would, especially under her mother's watchful eyes so she went straight to London.

She wasn't sure if she had her keys but knew Chichi had a spare so she dropped by her house to pick it up and that took hours. It was their first time of meeting after the wedding and there was a lot to gist about. Monisola carefully avoided telling her everything as she had decided her marriage was her business and though Chichi was her closest and dearest friend, marriage on the other hand was her life and intimacy with one person only, Daniel. Chichi also forgot where she kept the keys and thanks to the children they spent quite a while looking for them.

"Chichi you need to be more careful where you put things and especially out of their reach."

"Yes Mrs Benjamin, I'll remind you of that when you have your hands full of children, a house to keep tidy and a husband to take care of."

"Mano does not need taking care of he is an adult so leave him out of the equation."

Chichi kept quiet and attended to her daughter who wanted help with her toy and at the same time Eman was running round the house with a toy car making some noise akin to driving a fast car.

"Chic are you okay?" Monisola asked out of concern as she noticed the strain on her friend.

"I'm fine."

"Are you sure?"

"Of course, I'm sure."

"Chic you know you can talk to me, it's me Monisola."

"Oh! I didn't know, I thought it was Mrs Benjamin."

"What do you mean?"

"Well since you are now Mrs Benjamin, your status has changed, I am me and you are Mrs Benjamin."

"I don't understand."

"Monisola please stop asking questions, the ones I get from these children are enough to last me a life time, use your common sense."

Monisola did not like her tone and maybe they were both tired so she decided to leave but a sudden cry from Emmanuella made her stop. While Chichi was trying to pacify her, Eman also wanted her attention and their mother in the meantime, was trying to get herself together. Monisola carried Eman and told him it was time for a fruity treat which made him squeal in delight and ran to the kitchen. They made a bowl of fruits for everyone and by the time they took it to the living room Chichi was sleeping whilst Emmanuella was playing at her feet. Monisola left her to sleep while she fed the children and also tidied the place up a bit.

Mano came home later, happy to see her and asked after Daniel. She noticed he and his wife hardly talked except the welcome kiss, scooping the children in his arms, playing with them and he later disappeared upstairs.

She wanted to go home but she wasn't sure if she wanted to be all alone so she asked if she could pass the night there and leave tomorrow. Chichi shrugged her shoulders and said nothing.

She was going to break her rules, privacy or no privacy, this was her friend. After dinner and having spent half an hour getting the children ready for bed, she went to speak to her.

"Okay I know it's none of my business but what is going on with you two?"

Chichi ignored her or so she thought but realised she was deep in her thoughts.

"Mrs Dumisani!"

Chichi snapped out of her thought and looked at her absent minded.

"What is going on between you and your husband?"

"Nothing."

"Are you sure, you guys hardly said anything to each other all evening."

A shout from one of the children made her tense and when they heard footsteps and Mano's voice she relaxed.

"Mano problem or children rearing, which one be your wahala?"

Chichi looked at her and after a while burst into laughter and tears at the same time.

Monisola hugged her and rocked her gently.

"I don't think I can cope Monisola, I'm not built for this. I want more."

"More children?"

They both laughed this time and sat on the floor.

"You can talk to me you know."

"Like you've been talking to me since you got married?"

"That is different."

"How?"

"I'm married and I want .... my privacy and intimacy with my husband to be kept private."

"Ewo! So, it is me that wants to tell you how Mano and I do it everywhere in the house and sometimes...."

"Hey! Chiamaka I beg you, enough! Gosh! I'm still fresh and getting used to all this."

"After how many times, once you do it the first time that is the end of shyness, you are both naked, no more hiding."

"Please! I am still me and he is still himself."

"Eh! I thought I needed help. You, my dear girl is the one who needs mega help. What is all these 'me' stuff? Please tell me what is your name?"

Monisola rolled her eyes and kissed her teeth.

"Okay you've forgotten, well, let me remind you. Your name is Mrs Christopher Daniel Benjamin, wife of Christopher Daniel Benjamin, lover of Christopher Daniel Benjamin, mother to the children of Christopher Daniel Benjamin, tailor, housekeeper, chef, body masseuse, dry cleaner of Christopher Daniel Benjamin. In your case as princess you might not be the house keeper but the others most definitely fit and soon you forget your name and all you bear now is wife, darling, mum, momma. Got that!"

Monisola looked at Chichi, marriage and motherhood had changed her but does that mean she no longer has her personal identity.

"What happened to Chichi, Chic my friend since boarding school, university and now?"

"I don't know, I don't think I remember her anymore."

They both sat in silence for a while until Mano called her and she got up to go but first giving Monisola a hands up sign.

The next day back in her house, she wished she had not made the trip at all as her conversation with Chichi was still fresh in her mind. A call from Daniel also seemed to prove Chichi's point of losing her identity to marriage but she shook her head, no she still had her identity even though her status had changed.

He called again.

"Are you at the airport?"

"No."

"Why not, what is the delay?"

"I'm staying till Sunday night; I'll like to see my friends in church."

"Monisola I did not give you the permission to travel and you are telling me you are not coming until Tuesday."

"I'm sorry Daniel, I was bored and I needed to do some things over here."

"Your sorry is not good enough."

"I'm very sorry."

"What are you doing there?"

"I....I..."

"Monisola Benjamin, if you are not here by Tuesday morning don't even bother coming just stay there okay."

"Yes Daniel."

"What?"

"Yes Sir"

"Yes, to what and when did you start calling me sir?"

"Yes, I will try leaving and get there for Tuesday morning and if anything, happen due to unforeseen circumstances, I will come back to this house, sir, your lordship."

Daniel breathed heavily, muttered something in his native language, said goodbye and slammed the phone on her.

She went to Mano's office and gave him a surprise visit.

"Oh, my goodness, you've suddenly realised it's me you love and you've come to me."

"Not even in your dreams Mano, how are you, you seem to be growing a pot belly nowadays, are you pregnant?"

He burst out laughing and asked if she had time for a coffee.

"Coffee no but a chat yes"

They went to a cafe where they had a chat, Monisola told him about her conversation with Chichi, her fear and concerns. He allayed her fears and said Chichi was fine and yes she was losing her identity as a wife and Monisola would soon join the boat. He burst into laughter when he saw the look on her face but he reassured her he would talk to his wife.

"You guys hardly talk again."

"Yes, we do, we say good morning, thank GOD for the day, talk with the children, welcome and of course bedroom language."

Monisola blushed at the last words. Mano laughed again and called her fresh. Looking at his time he promised to talk with his wife and sort out things. When she asked what he meant by sorting, he reassured her again that he hoped to talk and put in action his promise of being a good husband and father to their children. She smiled and thanked him.

"I should be the one thanking you, you've always been a good friend to both Chichi and I, a very good one."

She smiled and gave him a hug.

"So how is Mr Benjamin?"

"Threatening and giving me ultimatum to be back home by Tuesday."

"Hmm! I wouldn't do that if I were him."

She laughed and didn't bother to ask what he meant.

"I plead on his behalf that you deal with him leniently as he is fresh to the new partnership and I sincerely believe a few lessons from your ladyship will re-orientate his mind and thinking."

She laughed, waved and blew him a kiss.

Tuesday morning, she was back home as she had come in the previous night very late and tired and had gone straight to bed. At breakfast, neither of them said anything but only looked at each other with Daniel glaring at her and she returning it with a smile.

Before he left for work, he asked what her plans were and replied 'nothing'.

"Nothing? What do you mean nothing? I thought you said you were bored; I would prefer if you let me know your schedule and if you don't have any I'll plan one or two things."

"I haven't got anything planned."

"Are you sure? So, if I leave you for just two days I would come back to find you exactly where I left you?"

Monisola got up from the dining table and began to clear the dishes.

"Leave that, someone else can do that. Do you promise me that you'll let me know of your every move so that I'll know where you are at all times?"

Monisola looked at him but did not say a word.

"Monisola I am talking to you."

"What do you want me to say?"

"I want to know every move you make or want to take."

Monisola got up and moved towards the door.

"Monisola I am taking to you."

She turned round and faced him.

"I said..."

"I don't have any plans."

"But you will, the minute I step outside that door."

You bet I would but she kept quiet.

"Monisola all I am asking is that you please tell me when you want to go out of town so that I don't start racking my brain wondering where you are or what to say when your mother calls. I won't even bother if it was your father because I wouldn't know what to say. Please Monisola I am now your husband, I am responsible for you, accountable for you and I have to go out to make a living otherwise I would love to stay with you twenty-four seven."

Okay he was making sense now, but then there was no way she was staying here or telling him of her every move because she didn't know, yet.

She moved closer and gave him a peck, "I'm not promising but I'll try."

"Please baby, please."

"No."

Since she had linked Grace's village with the E.A.C.H coordinator and the programme had a good kick start and was well received by the villagers, she would have loved to go and see how they were doing but again she did not want to intrude as she was no longer the project lead and did not want to undermine the present team leader there. She decided to go home and visit her parents.

Her family were happy to see her, especially her father who quickly invited her to take a walk with him as he was just going to the farm. Daniel had just introduced new mechanised equipment and they were doing a test run. She declined and went in search of her mother. She had expected a wide arm's greetings but one look from her mother made her halt in her stride. Maybe she was tired with looking after the twins or did she and Kabiyesi have one of their arguments again? She quickly greeted her and was on her way out when she asked where she was going.

"To my room Ma."

"Which room?"

"My apartment."

"Your apartment is in your husband's house and should you want to spend some days here you will give ample notice and we would prepare one of the spare rooms for you."

Monisola did a double take on her mother, was she really okay? In her own father's house? Spare room? She turned to go but her mother's next statement made her halt.

"Daniel did not mention that you were coming the last time we spoke; I hope you informed him and you are not just going on a frolic of your own?"

Monisola wanted to give an outburst but no, she remembered she was still 'princess cucumber' according to Omoniyi so she turned, smiled, held her head up, kept a straight back and walked in an elegant stride to her room. She laughed when she saw her room was still intact as she left it a few month ago, spare room indeed.

The next few days she worked with her father on some of the proposals he had for the village especially as the annual general meeting he held with his cabinet and local government was approaching. They talked about outstanding issues, projects that had been delayed for lack of commitment and support from the local government and the need to source funds from other areas. They were still discussing when Ayaba came in.

"Monisola Aya Daniel ba wo ni, se gbogbo e dun?"

"Tele nko ki lo fe je ko sele" Kabiyesi abruptly replied.

Monisola sensed the two were at it again or was it just one sided as Ayaba cut her eye at Kabiyesi, turned to Monisola and smiled. Hmm woman palava!

"Monisola Aya Daniel bawo ni jere, oko re nko, se e' bubble, I trust Daniel is taking good care of you because I know you are. With all the training you've received from us all, you are showing good works and care."

Monisola smiled, thanked her and said all was well.

"I just said I should come and see you especially as I will be going over to Morolake's place. She wants me to help with her twins, you know she is expecting soon and with all that her work, she needs all the help she can get. I might be gone for a month."

Monisola noticed the last statement was not directed at her as Ayaba had looked passed her and turned her eyes at Kabiyesi, baited it and cut her eyes at Kabiyesi again. She wasn't in the least interested in what was going on between the two of them so she made her excuse.

"Monisola ma yi lo o. It is even because of you that I came otherwise what would I be doing here. When are you going back so that we can gist more before you leave? I thought you were on holiday so why are they making you work again. Don't join them o! There is a time to rest and a time to work. Obirin ni e' don't follow your brother's footstep and be working round the clock. Some people should retire but ...hmm ... I have said my own."

Kabiyesi all the while had been looking at the papers in front of him and when Ayaba mentioned the word 'retire', he looked at her with a squint which was going steadily with a flaring of his nostrils. Ayaba quickly retreated and moved towards the door.

"Ah! I forgot again. Monisola there is a key to a safe your brother gave me while he was at the hospital, it had been with me since and I don't know what to do with it. I have not opened it. I trust you to deal with it."

Ayaba Adekemi gave the envelope to her.

Monisola took a deep breath and the tears were welling up.

"Ah! You still have tears stored up for your brother? O je nu ojure. Even I don't cry anymore so why should you. I'm sorry; I keep forgetting how close you two were. I didn't know you know, otherwise I would not have insisted that Kabiyesi......."

A cough from Kabiyesi brought her back to the present and she quickly left the room.

"Father what did she mean by..."

"Monisola some things are better left in the past and then we are able to move forward. The safe she is talking about is in Omo...... I mean Toluwanimi's office, you can go and have a look if you want to."

She didn't go to Toluwanimi's office until the next day. As she stepped in she remembered the day she had been there with Omoniyi after her home coming, how time flies. Her phone rang and even before she looked at it she knew who it was.

"You are not at home?"

"No."

"Where are you?"

"Toluwanimi's office."

"Zurich! Mother said you were at the palace."

That statement made a recall in her head but she calmed down.

"What are you doing in Zurich?"

Silence.

"Hello! I said what are you doing in Zurich?"

"On my way to Australia."

She heard him take a quick and sharp deep breath.

"Monisola how many times have I told you...."

"Save your breath, I'm at the palace, in Omoniyi's ..... I mean Toluwanimi's office."

"I see."

Silence

"When are you coming home?"

Silence

"Monisola .... I"

"Daniel I am trying my best to be a very loving and obedient wife to you. I need to keep myself active and not go insane with having nothing to do; I'm not built that way. If you want me to stay at home then give me something to do."

"I'm in Brazil now otherwise...."

"Brazil! And you are ranting because I said Australia, you know maybe I might just take that up."

"I'll be home in a week's time, please Monisola I want you home when I get there."

"I won't be there."

Daniel quickly loosen his tie and pressed the receiver tightly to his ear.

"What did you say? I didn't hear you."

She knew he heard but was not sure what she meant.

"I'm leaving......"

Daniel quickly muttered the only name he knew "JESUS"

There was a short silence between them.

"Monisola please ....."

"I'm leaving for London next week, I ... don't, I haven't been feeling well."

He quickly thanked GOD and with renewed confidence asked, "Are there no doctors in Nigeria that can attend to you, why must everything be England?"

He didn't even ask what the matter was and he was starting his silly argument about England versus America. Gosh!

"I am sure there are good hospitals in Lagos, Ibadan, Abuja or anywhere in Nigeria; so why do you have to rush to London and for what?"

This guy was surely about to press the wrong button, it's just a pity he wasn't nearby.

"Daniel, what is the name of your doctor and where is she or he based?"

"I live in the States so practically my doctor is there especially when I need prescriptions."

"Good. Naturally I live in London so..."

"I believe lived is the word as you don't live there anymore."

"Daniel I would move back to London this very minute if you hala me again."

"Hala? Girl what language are you speaking? Come back to the states baby girl, I don't want my baby speaking such language."

"You no dey serious."

"Monisola please do NOT attempt to speak pidgin English, it's not your style and moreover you are a princess, remember."

"So? I dem speak am with Chichi."

"Monisola my ear drums are already reacting and you and Chichi just coined words, none of you can speak so don't even go there. Moving on, come to Chicago and we'll arrange for you to see a doctor."

"Thank you but no thanks, I already have a doctor."

"Monisola as your husband you will listen to me...."

She took quick breath and muttered something under her breath; she sat down and put the phone down on the table.

Daniel was still mumbling on when he realised that he did not hear anything from the other end. He said hello a few times, he shouted and when he did not hear a response he called her mother.

"You really should be taking more care of yourself; you do need to rest and less of travelling all-round the globe. I won't prescribe anything but rest, complete bed rest for at least two days and you can carry on with your normal routine except from travelling within a week. What do you do for a living?"

Monisola smiled, what did she really do for a living these days. The lady doctor noticed her hesitation and had a quizzical look on her face.

"For now, let's just say I am a housewife."

"And a soon to be mother so I'll say take things easy for a while, normal routine but nothing out of the ordinary but I'm not sure what your ordinary schedule will be."

Monisola smiled again, she liked this doctor; she was young, female and she could relate with her.

"About the travelling.... I need to see my doctor in England and then meet my husband in America..."

"Hmm! What about going over to your husband in America and seeing a doctor there and moreover the doctor will see both of you together and be able to advice you both as new parents."

New parents! Monisola smiled, she liked that. She also liked the doctor's advice, if only...

"You won't by any chance be leaving for the States to further your career...."

She was already shaking her head, "No I love my country Nigeria and I believe there are also great opportunities here and GOD willing we will get there one day just as these other nations did at the initial stage, Rome wasn't built in a day you know."

Back at the palace Monisola decided to make her final move to the States. She had more of an opportunity of settling down with Daniel to start their family there as that was his main base. She packed her things and this time informed him and his lady detective - her mother that she was moving for good to the States. Her mother breathed a sigh of relief and Daniel said he couldn't wait to welcome her home.

This time coming to Chicago felt like coming home and the apartment was cosy, just what she and Daniel needed. A place that was theirs, where there was no one else but just the two of them and the growing baby. She put her hand over her tummy again and Daniel kissed her hand and her tummy.

"From now on, you will stay at home, I will try as much as possible to be here with you but please no more travelling or visiting or ...."

"Daniel, please stop all these do's and don'ts, from now on I will take care of myself as I have the baby to think of."

"Oh! So, with the baby you will stay at home otherwise you will be going from Japan to Chile and then..."

"Daniel, just keep quiet."

"What did you just say?"

"I said shut up!"

"Monisola Benjamin, who do you think you are talking to?"

"My husband, Mr Benjamin."

"And you told him, I mean me to shut up?"

"Actually no, yes! Do you know what Daniel, you are the reason I keep travelling from one place to the other? I am not that can of person that just laze around doing nothing; I need something to keep me going. I can't afford to sit around and waste my GOD given talents and skills; I will have to give an account to GOD you know."

"I am not asking you to laze around, I just want you to be at home or know your whereabouts when you decide to perch somewhere."

"Perch? What do you mean perch? Am I a bird with no home ....?"

"That is what it looks like! Today you are in London, tomorrow Togo, yesterday Bejing, you have a home, actually you have homes so just sit at home."

Monisola ignored him, got up but felt a sharp pain as she moved suddenly.

"Ah" she groaned.

"What is it? Monisola, what is it? Please tell me, how are you feeling? Should I call the doctor?"

"I'm fine, I just felt a sharp pain, probably because I moved so quickly."

"How do you feel now, do you want me to call the doctor or ...."

"Daniel I'm fine, I just need to adjust to new developments..."

"... and growth and not travelling all over the world."

"Are we still arguing about this?"

"Not at all, just to let you know you have a responsibility towards our son and he is of utmost priority in our lives."

"I do understand Daniel and I wasn't travelling all over the world. I was just looking for something to do and not just sit around......"

"You were not just sitting at home, you are supposed to keep the house and wait for me to come home, attend to me, feed me and play with me."

She kissed her teeth and moved out of his embrace. She decided maybe, just maybe she should plan one more trip to England. The movement in her womb made her think twice, she smiled moved towards Daniel, kissed his lips and whispered, "My darling husband, I will take care of you and our child and once we have him or her, be rest assured we will travel the world together."

Daniel laughed, shook his head and said, "I think we should start planning baby number two now at least both of them will keep you active and deter you from your travels."

"Dear, there are such things as nannies, that can travel with us everywhere we go so two or even ten children can't stop me."

"Are we setting the number to ten because that's fine by me, remember you are the one that will carry the ten."

"Won't you help me carry at least one."

"I am a man not a womb -man, so you will carry all the ten, you might do nine at a go after this one or space them out."

"Seriously Daniel what if that happens, nine at a go!"

"I will take a vacation and go to the moon, by the time I get back they will be teenagers and I'll take over from there."

Monisola laughed, "You're joking, you won't even set foot in a spaceship not to mention the moon."

"Believe me, the sight of nine babies, nappies, cries, waking up in the night to feed till dawn will make me take a very big bold step of faith and jump into the space ship."

"Channel your faith towards taking care of the children instead."

"Of course, I can do all things through JESUS, Oh! Oooooo! Yes!"

He starts to speak in 'tongues', dancing and moving round the room.

"Glory Hallelujah somebody, shout the name of JESUS, I receive faith to get nine at a go, come on Monisola say Amen, Hallelujah to that."

When he didn't hear a respond, he opened his eyes and saw he was alone. Where was she? He went out of the room and heard some movement from the kitchen. He crept towards the door, opened it quietly and caught his wife gorging down mint ice cream. He hated mint and mint ice cream was the height of it.

"Monisola!"

She dropped the spoon as she was caught unaware.

"The baby wanted ice cream" she said guiltily.

"The baby?"

"Hmm" she nodded.

"Seriously you are going to get so fat you won't be able to fit into your clothes anymore."

At first she showed some remorse and after two seconds, she shrugged her shoulders, got another spoon, scooped a mouthful, relished it and then offered her husband some.

He glanced at her with an irritated look and got some chocolate ice cream instead. The sight and smell of it made his wife dash out of the kitchen and head straight for the bathroom. So much for a kitchen raid.

Their son was born on a cold winter morning weighing eight pounds and looking every inch like his dad including his black velvet skin. Daniel could not help but cry for joy for the blessing GOD had bestowed on him. He thanked GOD for giving him Monisola, who though tired and exhausted from the delivery was smiling at them both. Daniel handed his son back to the nurse, gave his wife a kiss and promised to be back in a second.

He called his father in-law, congratulated him on the arrival of his grand-son and asked for his blessing on the child and mother. Of course, Kabiyesi not only spent time in blessing his first child and the grand son from her but also his favourite son-in-law.

Olori Tinuola was the next person he called and she was already in the spirit praying, she waited for Daniel to speak and when given the news of her first grandchild, she rolled and rolled on the floor thanking GOD for safe delivery. She congratulated Daniel, sent her love to mother and son and also to let him know she was on the next flight to meet them.

Daniel called his sister who though was about to start teaching in her class, quickly excused herself and shouted for joy.

Daniel went back to see his wife and son and was filled with joy when he saw Monisola cuddling their son and breast feeding him. He thanked GOD for another mouth to feed.

THE END

PS: Monisola had another baby, a beautiful baby girl who looked every inch like her mother especially her grandmother.

While Toluwanimi was going through the files kept in Omoniyi's safe, he found a document addressed to CDB regarding his son that was in Sierra Leone. Toluwanimi passed it to Monisola and she realised that CDB was no other than her own CDB - Christopher Daniel Benjamin, Omoniyi's very loyal friend. She discussed it with her husband and with Kabiyesi's permission Omoniyi's son was brought from Sierra Leone to live with his paternal grandmother Ayaba Adekemi Adewunmi.

No matter what you going through in life, you reach a point where you look back and know if it had not been GOD on your side.......

Thank you for reading this story to the very last pages. The story may continue in your minds or at the tip of my pen but please do let me know your thoughts on the book.

Thank you GOD Bless

Adesolape Oyeusi